PRAISE FOR SIMON GERVAIS

The Elias Enigma

"Gervais deftly shuffles his large cast of characters like pieces on a chessboard, with well-timed 'surprises' and many chapters ending in cliff-hangers. An adrenaline-fueled spy romp . . ."

—*Kirkus Reviews*

"With the publication of his action-packed yet intricately plotted thriller of a novel, *The Elias Enigma*, author Simon Gervais again demonstrates originality and a genuine flair for the kind of narrative-driven storytelling style that fully engages the reader's rapt attention from start to finish."

—Midwest Book Review

The Elias Network

"Secrets, lies, and wall-to-wall action! *The Elias Network* is a master class in globe-trotting international intrigue. Simon Gervais brings his A game and then takes it to an entirely new level. Absolutely riveting!"

—Brad Thor, #1 *New York Times* bestselling author of *Shadow of Doubt*

"Simon Gervais is a true master of action and intrigue—NOBODY does it better!"

—Mark Greaney, #1 *New York Times* bestselling author of *The Gray Man* and *The Chaos Agent*

The Last Protector

"Gervais has already cemented himself as one of the supreme writers in the genre, and this newest novel only adds to it. This is a book that thriller fans won't want to miss."

—Stuart Ashenbrenner, Best Thriller Books

The Last Sentinel

"The numerous action scenes are depicted with precision and authority, including technical details of armaments and vehicles. Gervais's action-packed odyssey of a righteous American Everyman continues in fine fashion."

—*Kirkus Reviews*

The Last Guardian

"[Clayton] White's third thrill ride spans the globe, unfolding in Monaco and Switzerland as well as China and Washington and benefiting as much from its numerous surprises as from its expertly choreographed action scenes. A brisk globe-trotting thriller with abundant tension and a timely premise."

—*Kirkus Reviews*

"Simon Gervais is back with another Clayton White thriller that'll blow you away and have you flipping pages well into the night."

—The Real Book Spy

"*The Last Guardian* has no shortage of head-popping action, and it's rife with gritty moments that give pause to readers in the middle of the explosive fast-paced narrative. Simon Gervais just doesn't miss."

—Kashif Hussain, Best Thriller Books

"Simon Gervais delivers another pulse-pounding, blood-rushing, race-against-the-clock thriller that will keep you in suspense and leave you winded. Electric and absorbing, *The Last Guardian* is another must read from the venerable Simon Gervais."

—Steve Netter, Best Thriller Books

Time to Hunt

"An action-packed thrill ride with plot twists around nearly every curve."

—*Kirkus Reviews*

"Gervais consistently entertains."

—*Publishers Weekly*

"Gervais weaves both villainous storylines together with action, intrigue, and suspense."

—*Mystery & Suspense Magazine*

Hunt Them Down

"In *Hunt Them Down*, Gervais has crafted an intelligent and thoughtful thriller that mixes family dynamics with explosive action . . . The possibilities are endless in this new series, and this will easily find an enthusiastic audience craving Hunt's next adventures."

—Associated Press

"[An] action-packed series launch from Gervais."

—*Publishers Weekly*

"Nonstop action meets relentless suspense . . . The blood flows knee deep in this one as Gervais uses his background as a drug investigator for the Royal Canadian Mounted Police to bring a gritty authenticity to his latest thriller."

—The Real Book Spy

"Gervais dishes out lavish suspense to keep a reader glued."

—Authorlink

"Superbly crafted and deceptively complex . . . This is thriller writing at its level best by a new voice not afraid to push the envelope beyond traditional storytelling norms."

—*Providence Journal*

"Another simply riveting read from author Simon Gervais, *Hunt Them Down* showcases his mastery of narrative-driven storytelling and his flair for embedding his novels with more twists and turns than a Coney Island roller coaster."

—Midwest Book Review

"From the first page, *Hunt Them Down* is a stick of dynamite that Simon Gervais hands you, masterfully lights, and then dares you to put down before it explodes. Don't. It's worth a few fingers to read to the end."

—Matthew FitzSimmons, bestselling author of *The Short Drop*

"Your hunt for the next great adventure novel is over. If Jack Reacher started writing thrillers, he'd be Simon Gervais."

—Lee Goldberg, #1 *New York Times* bestselling author of *True Fiction*

"A huge thriller with intense action and emotion. *Hunt Them Down* had me squirming in my seat until the last masterfully crafted page!"

—Andrew Peterson, bestselling author of the Nathan McBride series

THE ELIAS CONSPIRACY

ALSO BY SIMON GERVAIS

Robert Ludlum's The Blackbriar Genesis

CHASE BURKE SERIES (with coauthor Ryan Steck)

The Second Son

CASPIAN ANDERSON SERIES

The Elias Enigma
The Elias Network

CLAYTON WHITE SERIES

The Last Protector
The Last Sentinel
The Last Guardian

PIERCE HUNT SERIES

Hunt Them Down
Trained to Hunt
Time to Hunt

MIKE WALTON SERIES

The Thin Black Line
A Long Gray Line
A Red Dotted Line
A Thick Crimson Line

THE ELIAS CONSPIRACY

A CASPIAN ANDERSON THRILLER

SIMON GERVAIS

THOMAS & MERCER

Published by Thomas & Mercer, Seattle

www.apub.com

Amazon, the Amazon logo, and Thomas & Mercer are trademarks of Amazon.com, Inc., or its affiliates.

EU product safety contact:
Amazon Media EU S. à r.l.
38, avenue John F. Kennedy, L-1855 Luxembourg
amazonpublishing-gpsr@amazon.com

ISBN-13: 9781662533778 (paperback)
ISBN-13: 9781662533761 (digital)

Cover design by Damon Freeman
Cover image: © natalia_maroz / Shutterstock; © Collaboration JS / ArcAngel Images; © Hayden Verry / ArcAngel Images

Printed in the United States of America

THE ELIAS CONSPIRACY

PROLOGUE

Two Decades Ago
Ten Miles off the Coast of Venezuela
Aboard MY Cristo

Everett Westcott stood barefoot on the upper deck of his Viking 74, his two hands resting on the railing. Below, one of his deckhands was rinsing off the last of the blood and scales left behind by the fish they'd caught earlier.

Westcott thought he spotted a school of skipjack tuna a hundred yards off, but by the time he brought the binoculars to his eyes, it had disappeared. But that was fine, because the day had already rewarded him handsomely. Two massive tarpons had given him a fight that had left his arms aching in the best way, and a trio of yellowfin tuna now chilled in the icebox below, destined for the chef's grill that evening.

Behind Westcott, the yacht's polished wake stretched out in a gentle V before dissolving into countless ripples. Off to starboard, the low green ridges of the Venezuelan coastline blurred with the ocean, their peaks catching the dying light. Westcott turned to look at his wife, Nailah, who was seated in the shaded cockpit lounge, a novel on her lap. She was half wrapped in a soft linen shawl, her eyes on the horizon more than on her book, with the sea breeze tugging at her braids.

God, she's beautiful.

Nailah made eye contact with him and beamed before returning her attention to her book. That his wife was still able to smile like that despite the ache that had settled over them these past few years amazed him. They had tried everything, but nothing had brought them closer to having the children they both desperately wanted.

Westcott, who had made his fortune through a salvage start-up that recovered and processed plastic waste from the ocean and refined it into industrial resin for American and European automakers, hadn't hesitated to spend a considerable amount of money on fertility treatments. But even that had yielded nothing. It was obvious to him that all the tests, the consultations with the specialists, and the never-ending talk of possible alternatives had worn him down more than they had her.

Nailah had always been stronger than him.

He was about to join her when something off to port snagged his eye. He brought up his binoculars.

There. Something was in the water about a mile off.

"Ease to port, John," he shouted to his captain. "Bring us about. Something's in the water."

The Viking adjusted course, and as they closed in, the scene sharpened into something Westcott hadn't expected. A small boat had capsized, and a child was desperately clinging to it as it rolled with each swell. Westcott's heart seized.

"God," Nailah whispered behind him. "That's a little girl."

In a commanding voice, Westcott told his captain how he wanted the yacht to be positioned and then began to issue orders to his two deckhands. The moment the Viking's powerful engines went to idle, Westcott raced down the stairs to the main deck, then vaulted over the transom.

The water hit him like ice, shocking the breath out of his lungs, but he powered through. He fought to the surface, took a few short breaths, and oriented himself. The capsized boat was less than thirty feet away, but the current was stronger than he had anticipated. Still, he was an excellent swimmer, and with the adrenaline rushing through his veins, he'd reach the boat in seconds. Between strokes, he looked at the boat, and for a heartbeat, his eyes met the little girl's.

She couldn't have been older than eight or nine, and he could tell she was terrified. Her lips were blue, and her hair was slicked across her face. She was doing her best to climb atop a piece of the hull, but it kept sliding out from under her. He had almost reached the girl when her grip failed. Westcott watched in horror as she slipped under the surface without a sound, or even a splash.

He didn't think; he dove.

He kicked down, struggling against the strong current and the salt stinging his eyes. He could barely see, and with his lungs already spent, he knew he had only seconds left before instinct took over and he'd suck in a mouthful of water.

He kicked harder and frantically swept his hands in front of him.

Nothing. Only drifting strands of seaweed and dark bubbles rising past his face.

Panic jabbed through him as he turned in a slow circle, scanning, his lungs burning so hot he thought his chest was going to explode. He didn't want to give up, but he couldn't keep going either.

There. A flicker. A swirl of pale fabric drifting a few feet below him. And then he saw her, a small limp shape sinking into the gloom.

He dove deeper, pulling with desperate strokes. He could feel the pressure building in his skull. He was about to turn around when his fingers closed around the girl's frail wrist.

He pulled the child toward him, then pushed upward, kicking with everything he had. His vision began to narrow, and an instant later, his mouth opened against his will and salt water spilled past his lips. He gagged.

He was about to die. He was sure of it. He wasn't going to make it. The surface was too far away, and the urge to suck in more salt water was overpowering, almost primal.

A voice in his head screamed at him to let go, to breathe, to give up.

No. Not yet. One more stroke.

The water broke around him, and Westcott's mouth tore open in a ragged gasp. The girl didn't move. Her head lolled, her mouth slack.

Strong hands from above seized them both, hauling them onto the yacht's swim platform. Westcott collapsed, exhausted. His entire body was shaking.

He turned his head, only to see that Nailah was already by the girl's side, checking the child's pulse. And then, without hesitation, she locked her hands and began chest compressions.

"One, two, three, four—" Nailah counted under her breath.

On the fifth compression, the girl jolted, and a gush of seawater poured from her mouth. She coughed violently, choking and sobbing. His wife pushed damp hair from the child's face and looked directly at him. Something had changed in Nailah's expression, a softness he hadn't seen in months. His wife pulled the girl into her arms, murmuring soft Spanish into her ear as the girl's small hands found Nailah's linen shawl and clung to it.

Westcott rolled to his stomach, then rose unsteadily, his heart still hammering in his chest.

He had done it.

By sheer force of will, he had stolen the girl back from the ocean. And in that act, he saw a glimpse of something larger. The world was a cold, indifferent sea that swallowed the weak without remorse. But he, Everett Westcott, could be the hand that reached into water and chose who survived, and who thrived. Perhaps it was arrogance, or maybe a calling; he couldn't tell yet.

But as he stood there, dripping and trembling, he felt something settle inside him. Something that felt dangerously close to clarity. Or could it be destiny?

Fate was just another current, wasn't it? Blind and cruel, for sure, but hadn't he just defied it and won?

Yes. I did.

And this girl, this silent, shivering child in his wife's arms, was proof. She had been plucked from nothingness by his resolve alone. Without him, she wouldn't have made it, and that truth burned bright and absolute in his mind. He had chosen her. Saved her. He had redirected the course of her life.

And if I can do that for one girl, then why not more? Why not millions?

Someday soon, Westcott was sure of it now, it wouldn't just be one frightened little girl rising from the sea off the Venezuelan coast. No, it would be entire nations that would rise or fall by his hand.

No . . . by our hands, he thought, looking at his wife.

Hadn't they just proved that shaping fate was possible? That salvation wasn't random?

It can be engineered. Just like resin.

One only needed vision. And the stomach for it.

And the girl they'd just saved, she would play a role. He knew that too. She didn't know it yet, but her life had been claimed, just like his.

CHAPTER ONE

Palm Beach, Aruba

From the swim platform of the thirty-six-foot dive boat docked in front of the Marriott's Aruba Surf Club, the asset had a great view of Palm Beach in all its manufactured glory. From the powder-white sand freshly groomed by tractors to the palm trees swaying like props on a set and the wall of hotels rising behind them, she scanned it all with contempt.

To her, it felt fake. All of it.

No charm, she thought. *Nothing like Exuma.*

Palm Beach was like a resort rendering brought to life, a place where influencers staged bikini photo shoots, where tourists drank watered-down cocktails with pastel-colored paper umbrellas, and where, today, two of the most corrupt men in the Democratic Republic of the Congo had come to play with their families.

"Welcome aboard, messieurs," she said in French, helping the two men.

Her associate, Henry, stood at the helm, saying nothing. He wore sunglasses and a faded T-shirt, playing his part as just another quiet local helping the tourists burn through their money.

The first guest to step aboard, Destin Mpanga, was a former high-ranking officer with the Congolese National Police who'd become a powerful warlord within the Congo River Alliance, a rebel coalition whose main objective was to overthrow the DRC government. Mpanga was in his fifties, bulky with muscles gone soft, and his gut pressed against the zipper of his half-donned wet suit. The man was responsible for the deaths of at least a hundred civilians last year alone, and he had been accused of several war crimes, including enlisting child soldiers.

Behind him, Dr. Hervé Tchangana, a career politician and the current minister of land management of the Democratic Republic of the Congo, was the second—and final—guest to board. Tchangana was a parasite feeding on Mpanga's chaos, bleeding his own people dry in the process. Just like Mpanga and his family had done, Tchangana, his wife, and four children had traveled out of the DRC under assumed identities.

The asset watched as the wives and children of the two men boarded a second vessel moored nearby, a white catamaran flying a tour company's flag. The asset gave them a polite wave as the catamaran's crew arranged towels and fruit baskets on the upper deck. A minute later, the catamaran headed north for a three-hour snorkeling trip.

"Good morning, gentleman," she continued in French. "Perfect weather for today's dive."

"Better be," Mpanga said. "We're paying five-star prices for this private excursion."

The asset smiled politely, making sure to keep her disdain for the man out of her eyes.

For these two pricks, it was five-star everything. She'd kept an eye on them and their families for the last three days. They were staying in the most luxurious suites, eating at the most ridiculously expensive restaurants in town, and only ordering the most expensive Burgundy wines on the menu. Nothing was ever too much or too expensive for them.

And all of it, of course, was paid for with government funds and money siphoned from foreign aid.

And while they do this, their countrymen drink river water laced with diesel runoff, she thought. *Pigs.*

"We'll be diving the *Star Gerren* today," she said, as Henry gunned the twin outboards and pointed the boat away from the beach.

"Star what?" Mpanga asked.

"The *Star Gerren*," she replied over the roar of the engines. "A sunken cargo ship. It sank in August 2000. It's not as popular as the Antilla shipwreck, but the upside is that very few dive tours go out there. And it's perfectly safe. Trust me."

"Private dive. Private wreck. I like it," Tchangana said.

She had hacked into the diving platform app they'd used to book their trip three days ago. The men were convinced they'd booked a private excursion with the best-rated PADI-certified dive operator in Palm Beach.

Ten minutes later, they arrived at the dive site, and Henry put the outboards at idle speed. The asset opened the storage locker and pulled out the diving gear. She helped the two men don their equipment, adjusted their weighted belts, briefed them about the dive, then ran a final check on her own kit.

A minute later, they rolled backward into the sea.

——

Below the surface, the world changed. But today, the water was absurdly clear. The asset estimated the visibility at about eighty feet. She could see all the way to the bottom, where the 245-foot cargo ship had gone down, its bulk looming like a carcass on the seafloor sixty feet below.

She equalized her ears several times as she got deeper, then led the two other divers toward the shipwreck. As they got closer, she could see that the barnacled hull of the *Star Gerren* was split along the port side, which created a ragged entryway into the submerged corridors of the ship. She swam through the opening first, kicking lazily ahead with her fins.

Inside, weak beams of sunlight filtered through the rust-eaten portholes, and she saw a school of fish swim by in a silver blur.

She smiled. She was enjoying herself.

Behind her, the warlord and the politician paused to glance into the wheelhouse like curious children. She signaled to keep going. She had a schedule to keep.

They swam deeper into the wreck, past a collapsed stairwell and into what had once been the cargo hold of the ship. The visibility narrowed and the walls felt closer here. She turned on her dive lamp and directed the beam toward the two divers. She signaled for them to get closer to her.

Once both men were within three feet, she adjusted the beam to its highest setting, then directed the light into their eyes, blinding them. She switched off the light, plunging the cargo hold into total darkness, and pulled her dive knife from the sheath on her right thigh.

Then she struck.

She grabbed the back of the warlord's head and shoved the knife into his neck. The man's scream was all bubbles and terror.

Thirteen.

Because it was pitch black, she knew the politician had no idea what had just happened. Ultimately, she didn't even need to worry about his whereabouts, because he touched her arm, as if seeking reassurance.

She stabbed him between the ribs, twice, but then he pushed her away and tried to swim upward before she could stab him a third time. But he didn't get far. She caught his ankle, yanked him down, and plunged her knife into his side. She pulled the regulator out of his mouth and stabbed him one last time in the neck.

Fourteen.

Inside the cargo area, it would be hours, days maybe, before the two men were found. But by then, the fish would have done their work. She finned out of the hold and back through the hull breach. After her safety stop, she surfaced. Henry was crouched near the stern, busy peeling off the SeaBeach Excursions decals from the fiberglass.

She grabbed the ladder and hauled herself aboard, then stripped off her wet suit and toweled herself dry. She changed into a bikini and sat beside Henry, who was now in the process of starting the engines. She stretched her legs, slid on the pair of sunglasses Henry handed her, then closed her eyes, tilting her head toward the sun, enjoying the moment.

As Henry opened up the throttles, she didn't look back. Her job wasn't to dwell on what she'd done. Her job was to clear the path for the greater good. And she was very, very good at it.

"Operations reached out while you were underwater," Henry said over the roar of the outboards.

"Yeah? What's up?" she asked, keeping her eyes closed.

"I need to get you to the airport ASAP," he said. "You're needed somewhere else."

CHAPTER TWO

Port de Sóller
Mallorca, Spain

Caspian Anderson powered up the steep incline, his focus locked on the treacherous coastal trail ahead. The path hugged the edge of a sheer drop, and although it offered breathtaking views to anyone foolish enough to glance sideways, it was narrow, uneven, and in Caspian's opinion, designed by someone with a personal vendetta against joggers.

The Mediterranean sun blazed overhead, turning Caspian's morning run into a full-fledged endurance test. Sweat soaked through his shirt, plastering it to his back like an unwelcome second skin. He grimaced, regretting—just slightly—that he hadn't listened to Liesel and brought a hat. Sure, he would have looked ridiculous, but at least his forehead wouldn't be slow roasting like it was now and the back of his neck wouldn't feel like it had personally offended the sun.

Caspian usually preferred to run earlier in the morning when the air was cooler, but today, he and Liesel had stayed in bed a little longer. While the memory of Liesel's fingers and lips on his skin made him smile, Caspian was now paying for his tardiness. Though it was only midmorning, the heat was relentless, and the unforgiving sun was turning his eight-mile run into a real challenge. His legs felt heavy, and his hard, uneven breathing was a clear indication that his lungs were working overtime as he fought against the thick, humid air.

His Garmin watch vibrated with a gentle reminder that he should hydrate. Caspian slowed to a stop, wiped his forearm across his brow, then dropped down into a push-up position, his palms pressing into the dirt as he steadied himself for the next burn.

Fifty push-ups. Let's go!

He powered through them, the muscles in his arms and chest straining, the intense heat pressing down on him as if he had added a one-hundred-pound dumbbell to his backpack. When he was done, he stayed on the ground for a few more seconds to catch his breath. He had two more miles to go before reaching the hotel and the pool he knew was waiting for him. The thought of plunging into the pool's cool water was enough motivation to force him back to his feet. He stretched his legs and, as he did so, allowed himself a moment to take in the breathtaking scenery.

Caspian had heard about the Balearic Islands' exceptional beauty, but Port de Sóller, a picturesque coastal town nestled at the foot of the Serra de Tramuntana, was even more charming than he had imagined. A thirty-minute drive from Palma, Port de Sóller was located in a small, idyllic horseshoe bay on Mallorca's northwest coast. From his vantage point along the hiking trail, Caspian had an unobstructed view of the town and its bustling marina, where a mix of fishing boats and sleek, modern yachts swayed gently on the water. Beyond the harbor, a traditional wooden tram with four carriages rumbled along the tracks that ran parallel to the beach, shuttling tourists and locals between the port and the inland town of Sóller. A lively stretch of hotels, restaurants, and bars lined the waterfront promenade, their terraces offering a perfect view of the bay's turquoise waters.

The previous night, he and Liesel had feasted on sharpsnout sea bream—the day's fresh catch—and local grilled vegetables. Following the recommendation of the in-house sommelier, they had paired it with an excellent bottle of albariño. The fish, succulent, had arrived perfectly cooked, and they had savored each bite as they watched the sun dip below the horizon from the patio of a restaurant that had been praised by the concierge at their four-star hotel.

They had spent the last six days scuba diving, sunbathing, and yachting around the island. It had been perfect. While he and Liesel enjoyed their work with the Strategic Support Unit, or SSU—a small division within the DIA's Defense Clandestine Service that specialized in delicate intelligence operations and was the DIA's answer to the FBI Fly Team—after their last assignment in Bordeaux, the secluded seaside town offered the kind of peace they had both been craving. Knowing they had ten more days like these ahead of them made Caspian as happy as he'd ever been.

He reached for his water bottle, took a quick sip, then started on the last two miles of his run, wondering if Liesel was still in bed or if she had decided to hit the hotel's small gym.

He suspected the latter.

Liesel had always been disciplined when it came to training, but recently, her routine had become restless. Even here, while on vacation, he had caught her slipping out of bed before sunrise more than once, only to return about an hour later with her shirt damp with sweat and her skin flushed from exertion. Since Caspian lived in a world where any weakness could get him killed, he understood better than most the need to stay sharp. But sometimes, watching Liesel push herself so hard, he wondered if she was overcompensating, if this was her way to prove to herself, to him, to everyone really, that she was fine.

Caspian wasn't sure she was.

During a sanctioned operation against a North Korean sleeper cell in France—one that had been attempting to steal high-end satellite technology from an American aerospace firm—Liesel had been shot twice in Bordeaux. Once in the abdomen, and another bullet had grazed her right arm. For a while, she'd been touch and go. She'd pulled through, thanks to the brilliant French surgeon who had worked on her for hours, but Liesel had brushed off every attempt Caspian had made to talk about it. For some reason, she was acting like none of it had happened, as if she could erase the trauma by sheer force of will.

Caspian knew better than to press the matter.

She'll talk when she's ready.

Maybe he'd find her in the gym, maybe not. Either way, he knew one thing: Liesel Bergmann wasn't one to let anyone, not even him, see her struggle.

———

As Caspian rounded a bend, something caught his eye. A large yacht was anchored in a small cove just beyond the cliffs. Even from a distance, he recognized the specific design of an Azimut.

Holy shit! That's the S8 model, he thought, admiring the yacht.

Then he frowned. It was an odd place to drop anchor for such a large boat.

It's way too close to the rocks. What's the captain thinking?

Caspian had never seen a boat anchored there before. That was when it hit him. He didn't recognize this part of the trail.

I took a wrong turn.

Somehow, he must have missed a junction and ended up on a different path. He pulled his phone from the pocket of his running shorts and tapped the screen. The signal indicator was blank. There was no service.

He rubbed the back of his neck as he studied the vessel more closely. In his opinion, the Azimut S8 was a masterpiece of modern yacht design. Its sharp, aggressive lines gave it an unmistakable presence on the water. The yacht's hull, painted a crisp silver, had dark-tinted windows running along its length. Twin staircases led down to the swim platform, where a Jet Ski was fastened in place. If he had the money to buy a yacht, the S8 would be Caspian's first choice. But at a price of four million euros, chances were that it would remain a dream.

The distant hum of an outboard motor made Caspian shift his gaze. A dinghy was approaching the yacht, cutting through the water at high speed. Caspian noted there were three men aboard the dinghy as it neared the Azimut. The driver, a thickset man wearing sunglasses and a gray windbreaker, kept one hand on the throttle while scanning the water ahead. Another man, also wearing a gray windbreaker, was seated at the front, a baseball cap pulled low over his eyes. The third man, at first glance, seemed like just another passenger. He sat in the middle of the boat, his body slightly slouched, as if he was tired from the bumpy ride.

Caspian was about to jog to the previous junction, hoping to get back to his regular trail, when the yacht's sliding doors opened, and a woman stepped out onto the teak deck. She was tall and dressed casually in a flowing, floral-patterned dress. Her long black hair was tied in a ponytail. In her right hand she held a large glass filled with a green liquid.

Caspian watched her as she took a sip, her gaze drifting out over the water toward the approaching dinghy.

When the dinghy was about a hundred feet from the Azimut, all hell broke loose.

The man in the middle exploded into action, kicking the driver in the face with brutal force. The driver's head snapped back, and the boat lurched sideways. Before the man seated at the front could react, the kicker launched himself overboard in a desperate, almost suicidal dive.

And that's when Caspian saw it. The kicker's hands were tied behind his back.

What the hell?

The man at the front of the dinghy pulled a pistol from inside his jacket, but the driver, who was still reeling from the kick, shouted something. A brief argument ensued before the armed man dropped the gun onto the boat. Then, in a move Caspian hadn't expected, he dove into the water after the prisoner.

Caspian watched as the two figures broke the surface moments later. The rescuer, breathing hard, hooked an arm under the prisoner's shoulder and dragged him toward the dinghy. The driver, who had picked up his colleague's gun, leaned over the side, grabbed a fistful of the prisoner's shirt, and yanked him up. The combined force of the driver and the rescuer was enough to haul the prisoner over the gunwale and onto the deck of the boat.

A savage punch cracked across the prisoner's face as soon as he tried to push himself upright. The driver barked something at the prisoner that Caspian couldn't quite make out, then restarted the outboard engine. Caspian could see the restrained man struggling to sit up, but a second punch, this one delivered by his rescuer, sent him sprawling sideways. He teetered at the edge of the gunwale, nearly plunging overboard again. At the last second, the rescuer caught him by the collar and shoved him back onto the dinghy's deck. And that's when Caspian got his first good look at the prisoner's face.

His gut clenched.

Like millions of others, Caspian knew who the man was.

Paul Hobb.

A journalist. And a damn good one. The kind who dug into things people wanted to stay buried. The kind who made enemies. While Caspian didn't personally know the reporter, someone he trusted—and loved very much—did.

Florence Aldrich, the nineteen-year-old he had saved—or doomed, some people could claim—in Zermatt the year before.

Caspian had a complicated relationship with Florence, but he had kept an eye on her since she had moved back to New York. He knew she had befriended Paul Hobb after the reporter had taken an interest in her story and what had happened to her and her family in Switzerland.

The odds of this being related to Florence have to be low, right? Hobb's a shit disturber. There are plenty of people who hate him.

Despite the heat, a chill ran down Caspian's spine.

But what if it is related to her? What if Florence is in danger?

After what had transpired in Zermatt, he'd made a solemn promise to himself to always look after Florence, even if she'd been crystal clear that she didn't want to ever see him again.

He didn't blame her. After what he had done to her family, how could he?

Whatever Florence thinks of me, it doesn't change anything. I need to find out who these people are.

Caspian tracked the dinghy as it covered the last fifty feet to the Azimut. The rescuer stepped on the bow, coiled a docking line in his hand, then tossed it toward the yacht's stern. The black-haired woman caught it, looped it around a cleat, and pulled it tight. The dinghy's driver eased off the throttle and let the watercraft drift the last few feet until it bumped gently against the Azimut's swim platform. The rescuer leaned down and grabbed Hobb's arm. The journalist shifted his weight, using what little balance he had left to stand. He let himself be guided off the dinghy and onto the swim platform. Caspian could tell Hobb's legs were wobbly, but the journalist managed to stay upright.

Caspian was still processing what he had just witnessed when he heard something behind him.

He froze, listening. More sounds were coming his way.

He wasn't alone.

CHAPTER THREE

Port de Sóller
Mallorca, Spain

Caspian jumped off the hiking trail without hesitation, tucking his body low and letting gravity take him down the slope. He stopped his roll twenty feet down, his body flat against the uneven terrain. He winced as the sting of fresh scratches burned where some thorny underbrush had raked against him. His sweat made the dirt cling to his exposed skin, and a fine dust coated his clammy forearms, legs, and neck as he lay immobile. With his ears tuned to his surroundings, he pushed away the discomfort and focused on controlling his breathing.

Voices.

Not loud, but not hushed either.

A man.

And a woman.

They were coming his way. Caspian eased forward, just enough to peer through a gap in the foliage. He spotted two people moving along the pathway where he'd been seconds ago. From a distance, they could have passed for a couple out on a leisurely hike. They weren't trying to be covert. If anything, they seemed comfortable.

But the way they walked—not quite side by side, but staggered, maintaining just enough distance for maneuverability—felt off to Caspian. The man was tall and solidly built, mid- to late thirties, with blond hair and a short, trimmed beard. He wore loose cargo shorts and a gray windbreaker, which was identical to the one the driver of the dinghy had been wearing. The woman, slender but toned, had long, tanned legs beneath a pair of black athletic shorts. She wore a gray fitted tank top that showed off her lean shoulders. Slung across her back was a black waterproof pack.

Caspian's gut told him they weren't just tourists, but if the two of them had any suspicion they were being watched, they weren't showing it.

This means they haven't seen me.

Then, without warning, they veered off the trail.

The man led the way, cutting directly into the brush, stepping over rocks and ducking under low branches. Caspian wondered where they were going, because there was no path there. No obvious reason to leave the trail.

He tensed. *Or maybe they did see me. And I'm about to get flanked.*

But no, they continued down, not even looking in his direction. Earlier in the week, Caspian had briefly studied the map, and while he hadn't memorized it, he remembered that there was another path lower down, closer to the shoreline, that led to a small beach. If the man and the woman knew the area well enough, it was possible they were cutting through to reach it.

Or maybe they just don't want to be followed.

Caspian adjusted his position, wanting to keep an eye on them. He moved carefully, slowly, not to draw attention. He waited until they had both disappeared behind the thick brush before getting into a crouch. He checked his phone. Still no signal.

Shit.

He wished he could contact Liesel, the local authorities, or even Samantha Ranger—his boss at the Strategic Support Unit—to report what he had seen. But if he was to leave now and move closer to town to get a signal, he feared that by the time he got the message out, by the time someone responded, the Azimut would be gone, and with that, his chance of figuring out if whoever was on the Azimut represented a threat to Florence. And of course, there was also the journalist, who might not be alive by then.

The authorities would eventually intercept the yacht, of that Caspian had no doubt, but what if the kidnappers disposed of Hobb before anyone boarded the vessel?

Caspian didn't have the luxury of time. He had to act.

You know how to do this.

This wasn't the first time he found himself in such a situation. For ten years, he had been Elias, the cryptic assassin persona he had taken on as an Onyx operative—a black program buried deep within the Department of Homeland Security's Investigations Division. During his decade with Onyx, he had completed what he thought at the time were thirty-four sanctioned targeted killings. His very last one being Leonard Aldrich, Florence's father.

Keeping his distance, Caspian moved after the duo. The terrain was unforgiving, the slope steeper here than it had been earlier. Dry soil and loose rocks made footing treacherous, making him wish he was wearing hiking boots instead of his running shoes. He crouched lower, using the natural cover of the brush to stay hidden as he carefully picked his way down, watchful not to send an avalanche of dirt and stone downward, something that would surely betray his presence.

The man and the woman, who weren't worried about the noise they made, moved steadily downhill, weaving between rocks and patches of thick undergrowth much faster than Caspian could. Still, he shadowed them, making sure to pause when they did, and pressing himself against the hillside whenever they turned. Though he knew they were talking to each other, he was too far away to hear what they were saying.

They were still one hundred or so feet above the sea when the path Caspian had seen on the map emerged from the vegetation. The man took it, and the woman followed a few steps behind. When Caspian reached it, too, he paused for a beat to scan his surroundings. Once he was sure his targets weren't doubling back, he stepped on the trail. A few minutes later, the vegetation began to thin, revealing the small rocky beach he'd seen on the map.

Caspian picked a hiding spot with a clear vantage of the beach. A Jet Ski, identical to the one he'd seen strapped to the Azimut's swim platform, sat at the water's edge, half on the beach, half in the shallows. A weathered rope extended from the Jet Ski's front cleat and ran across the beach. The other end of the rope was securely tied to the base of a tree just beyond the rocks. The man unfastened the rope and threw it to the woman, who was waiting next to the Jet Ski.

"I need to take a leak," the man shouted to her. "Gimme a minute."

The woman barely acknowledged him, focused on whatever was in her waterproof pack.

The man veered off toward a natural alcove. The alcove, which was partially shielded from view by an outcrop of jagged rocks, was about fifty feet from Caspian's position.

With the woman facing away from him, Caspian slipped from his hiding spot and started making his way toward the man.

Then he stopped.

Between him and the rocks was an open stretch of beach. Thirty feet of exposed terrain. No cover. No foliage. The woman, who was only sixty steps away, was still distracted by the pack, but if she happened to glance back at the wrong moment, she'd see him.

The waves in the small bay were much smaller than the ones crashing against the rocks farther out, but they gently surged against the shore in steady intervals, and the sound they made as they washed ashore was loud enough to cover the softer sounds of movement. Like the scuff of Caspian's running shoes against the pebbles.

Caspian waited for the next wave, then he moved, each step calculated. The exposed beach felt endless, but he knew that rushing would get him caught.

Twenty feet.

The man was bracing one hand against the rock as he unzipped his pants.

Fifteen feet.

The woman angled her body to the right and pulled something out of her waterproof pack.

A pistol? Shiiit.

It was too late for Caspian to double back now. He was committed.

Ten feet.

Caspian adjusted his trajectory, angling his approach so that he could take advantage of the rocks to shield himself from the woman's view sooner. But that also meant it would take him an extra five or six seconds to reach the man, who was now looking up as he relieved himself.

Five feet.

Then the man stiffened. It was a subtle, brief hesitation, like a deer sensing a wolf behind it. But he was too late.

Caspian rushed forward and drove a sharp punch into the man's lower back, just above his right kidney. The man let out a choked grunt as his body arched back. Keeping his stance low, Caspian snaked an arm around the man's thick neck, then locked his elbow under the man's jaw. He tightened his grip, his biceps pressing hard against the man's carotid artery to cut off the blood flow to his brain. The man thrashed, trying to claw at Caspian's arm, but his strength faded fast, and within seconds, his muscles slackened.

But Caspian didn't let go. Not yet.

When the man's knees buckled, Caspian twisted sharply, slamming the unconscious man's head against the rock. Not hard enough to kill him but hard enough that he wouldn't wake up for at least a few minutes.

Moving fast, Caspian searched the man, who had a pistol—a Glock 19—holstered inside his waistband. Caspian yanked the gun free and ejected its magazine.

Full.

He then pulled the slide.

One round in the chamber. Good.

Craning his neck, Caspian chanced a quick glance toward the woman. She was still near the Jet Ski, but an instant later, she turned her head.

Caspian ducked, his heart hammering in his chest.

Had she seen him? He didn't think so, but he held still, listening, glad he had a gun in his hand.

Move, Caspian!

He patted down the man's cargo shorts. One pocket held a pair of flex-cuffs. In the other was a wallet that contained two fifty-euro notes and two credit cards with the names Oscar Turner written on them. There was also a laminated ID under the same name.

Caspian raised an eyebrow, then swore under his breath. The ID was a license to carry. The man he had just knocked out was legit.

Or at least this card says he is.

Caspian's stomach tightened. Had he made a mistake? Had he misread the entire situation? Was it really Paul Hobb he had seen with his hands secured behind his back?

I saw what I saw.

He had seen the renowned investigative reporter. He was sure of it.

Caspian quickly removed the unconscious man's shoes and socks, then shoved one sock deep into the man's mouth. He stripped the man of his gray jacket and used the flex-cuffs to secure his hands behind his back. With that done, Caspian pulled the jacket over his own shoulders, zipping it up halfway. It wasn't a good fit, but it would have to do. If he kept his head down, he hoped he could close the distance before the woman realized he wasn't her colleague.

Slowly, he dared another look toward the Jet Ski. His breath caught in his throat.

The woman was nowhere to be seen. She was gone.

"Looking for me?" came a voice behind him and slightly to his left.

Caspian froze, aware that he was holding a gun in his hand, his pulse roaring in his ears. He slowly turned his head toward the voice.

Ten feet away, the woman stood, her feet planted, her arms steady. She held a pistol in a two-hand grip.

And it was pointed straight at Caspian's head.

CHAPTER FOUR

Port de Sóller
Mallorca, Spain

Liesel Bergmann's stomach growled as she twisted the cap off a bottle of water. She poured the contents into the Nespresso's reservoir, then set the bottle aside. She grabbed one of the complimentary coffee pods—a dark roast—and slipped it into place before powering on the machine.

While the machine warmed up, she glanced at her phone, checking the tracking app. A large, imprecise circle covered the map, showing only a general area of where Caspian might be.

He probably has no signal.

She wasn't surprised. Mallorca's rugged terrain and patchy cell service had given her the same issue on her hikes. But Caspian had been gone for a while now, and she expected him back soon. She wasn't worried, though. Caspian was the last person who needed looking after.

They'd met by chance in a Krav Maga class he taught for fun. At the time, she'd thought he was a mid-level translator working at the United Nations headquarters. Truth is, she'd almost left him. Because apart from being good in bed—*well, better than good*—she'd found him to be a tad boring. But then she'd learned that Caspian Anderson wasn't just a UN translator who drove an old Toyota Camry; he was one of the most accomplished killers in the world. A top-level assassin known only as Elias.

This discovery, and the fact that he'd found out she was a German spy, had almost broken them up. But it hadn't. And since then, her life had been an exciting series of dangerous events.

Events that had nearly killed her.

Liesel opened a cabinet, found a small ceramic cup, and placed it under the dispenser. She pressed the flashing white button, and the machine hummed to life. Moments later, the scent of fresh coffee filled the air as a steady stream of dark espresso poured from the machine. The aroma was rich, deep, and exactly what she needed to shake off the last remnants of sleep. Because after their rather enthusiastic wake-up call, she had fallen into a deep sleep, a rarity for her.

At least since Bordeaux, she thought.

She had to admit that six days of sun, relaxation, scuba diving, and a whole lot of Caspian Anderson had worked wonders on her body and mind. She hadn't realized just how much she had needed this break until she'd arrived on the island.

Liesel took the first sip of her coffee, then crossed the room to the full-length mirror. Standing naked in front of it, she studied her reflection. She was attractive. She knew it. She was aware of the looks men gave her, the lingering glances, the furtive double takes. She was fine with that. Her excellent metabolism helped—there was no denying that—but the truth was, she worked damn hard for the body she had.

But it wasn't for vanity. It wasn't to look good in a bikini or to impress anyone. She trained hard because she had to be ready. Because the next time she had to fight for her life, she wanted to win. The French surgeon who had removed the bullet fragments from her abdomen had told her she had survived because she was in peak physical condition. The words the doctor had spoken to her still lingered in her mind.

You survived because you are strong and healthy. Your body did most of the work. I only removed what wasn't supposed to be there.

Liesel's gaze dropped to the faint scar just below her ribs. She traced it with her fingers. The skin was firm, but the pain was gone.

The memories . . . not so much.

She still had nightmares. Not every night, but often enough. Once or twice a week, she'd wake up, heart pounding, drenched in sweat, reliving the moment of her ambush and the impact as she hit the ground after flying off the motorcycle. Some nights, her dreams were so vivid that she felt the bullet impacting her skin again, and the searing pain that came with it.

She took a few deep breaths, then finished her coffee. She put the cup down on the counter, then went into the bathroom to brush her teeth. She then stepped into the shower and let the hot water stream over her shoulders as she let her thoughts drift.

Sofie.

Her sister. Her only sibling. A woman she had believed to be dead.

Nicklas Drescher, her handler at the BND—the German intelligence service—had shared with her his suspicions that she was still alive. Liesel had refused to believe him. Her sister had died in Afghanistan, serving as a logistics officer with the Bundeswehr. Liesel couldn't wrap her head around Sofie being alive. She had read the reports. She had attended the funeral.

I mourned her, for God's sake!

But when Liesel had learned that Caspian might have caught a glimpse of Sofie during an unsanctioned operation in Kenya . . . well, she had to reconsider everything she knew about her sister.

Could Sofie really be alive?

And if she was, then why hadn't she tried to contact her?

Maybe she did try, Liesel told herself, not for the first time. *Maybe she doesn't know how.*

The fact Liesel had been in the United States serving as a clandestine officer for the BND might have complicated things further. Liesel leaned against the shower wall, closing her eyes. A part of her hoped that Sofie would reach out while she was in Europe.

A long shot, she knew, but hope was a stubborn thing.

And a girl can dream, right?

She stayed in the shower longer than necessary, waiting, half expecting Caspian to walk in and join her. But he didn't. *His loss.*

After a few more minutes, she sighed and shut off the water. She grabbed a towel as she stepped out.

She checked her phone again. There were no new messages or updates.

Then a knock at the door.

Finally. Liesel smiled. *He has probably forgotten his key card. Again.*

She walked to the door and checked the peephole. No one was there. She cracked the door open and peered into the hallway. It was empty. But at her feet sat a small box. She picked it up, recognizing it immediately as coming from the café she and Caspian had visited three times this past week.

Her smile returned. Caspian must have sent it for her.

She carried the box to the table and opened it. Inside, nestled in white parchment paper, was an ensaïmada—a soft, spiral-shaped Mallorcan pastry dusted with powdered sugar. Her favorite.

But there was something else beneath it. A white envelope.

She pulled it carefully, her fingers steady even as her pulse quickened. She slid her thumb under the flap and lifted it open.

Inside was a Polaroid. She and Caspian sitting on the terrace of the café, smiling at each other and completely unaware that someone had been watching them.

A cold wave of adrenaline surged through her.

She flipped the Polaroid over. There was a handwritten note in German.

Liesel's lungs seized as she stared at the words.

I need your help, big sis. You're the only one I can trust. Meet me tonight at Ses Oliveres. 7pm. Come alone. S—

CHAPTER FIVE

Port de Sóller
Mallorca, Spain

Caspian's eyes locked onto the woman aiming a pistol at his head. The wind tugged at her dark hair, whipping loose strands around her face, but she didn't seem the least bit distracted by it. Her grip remained steady and her stance balanced.

This isn't the first time she's held someone at gunpoint.

"Drop the gun," she said, taking two steps in his direction.

Caspian noted that she had her finger on the trigger, and though he couldn't be sure, he believed she had already taken up the slack on her trigger.

"All right," he said. "I'm putting it down."

Since the man he had neutralized lay unconscious behind him, with his hands flex-cuffed and a dirty white sock stuffed deep in his mouth, there was no point in Caspian claiming this was a misunderstanding. The woman knew exactly what had happened.

At least her finger is no longer on the trigger but on the trigger guard.

Caspian quickly assessed his options. The woman was eight feet away from him. Dropping low and rushing her gave him at best a fifty-fifty chance of getting to her before she pulled the trigger. He'd taken worse odds before, but he couldn't afford a gunshot as the sound would carry over the water and alert whoever was on board. Not a good thing since his objective was to reach the Azimut undetected.

"Who the hell are you?" the woman asked, keeping her eyes on him while she pulled a phone out of her shorts pocket.

Caspian didn't think she'd get a signal, but in case she did, he couldn't risk her warning anyone of his presence, so he slowly raised his hands and took a step toward her.

It did the trick. She dropped her phone back into her pocket and returned to a two-hand grip on the pistol.

"Take one more step, and I swear it will be your last," she said, her finger returning to the actual trigger.

Caspian had been in dicey situations before, and he knew he had to take control. But violence wasn't the play here. At least not yet.

"You know the only reason you're still standing is because I haven't given the order, right?" Caspian asked, his voice calm, deliberate, as if he had all the time in the world.

The woman's expression didn't change, but he saw the faintest flicker of doubt in her eyes. "Nice bluff," she said.

"You sure?" Caspian's lips curled slightly. "I've got a colleague with a rifle trained on you right now. The second you squeeze that trigger, he'll put one through the base of your skull."

She didn't flinch, but her grip tightened on the gun. "If that was true, I'd already be dead."

Caspian made the decision to go all in.

"You've got this all wrong, lady," he said, forcing a smile. "You're just a cog in a big machine. The only reason you aren't dead is because I haven't authorized anyone to die yet. You see, I have more than one friend. There's another team inbound as we speak. Once they reach the yacht, they're extracting Paul Hobb, and they'll kill every soul aboard whose name isn't Hobb."

The woman swallowed hard.

"You can stop this from getting worse, but that window's closing fast," Caspian continued.

"A team? You expect me to believe that?"

"You don't have to believe anything," Caspian replied. "But you should ask yourself, why am I still talking? If I was alone, don't you think I would have rushed you already? Instead, I'm standing here, waiting. I'm giving you a chance to make a decision that won't get you killed."

The woman's nostrils flared slightly, and he knew her mind was working through the possibility that he was telling the truth.

That's good. Doubt's creeping in. And doubt leads to hesitation. I just need a little more.

"Again, ask yourself why I didn't kill your partner," he said.

She didn't answer.

"I'll make it simple," Caspian continued. "You shoot me, and you die a heartbeat later. My colleague will drop you before my body has even hit the ground. One squeeze of your trigger, and it's the end of your story. You prepared for that?"

Her shoulders stiffened ever so slightly. Her confidence was slipping.

Caspian shrugged.

"Maybe you are," he said, letting his tone shift, as if he was conceding a point. "Maybe you're ready to die."

He made a show of looking over her shoulder, as if someone was standing a few steps behind her. Then her grip faltered. It was minor, so small that an untrained eye might have missed it. But Caspian caught it. And then he saw the opening he had been waiting for.

The woman's eyes flicked away from him. Not for long, just the briefest glance over her shoulder, as if she needed to confirm she wasn't in someone's crosshairs.

But for a trained assassin like *Elias*, it was enough.

In a sudden burst of motion, Caspian closed the gap. His left hand deflected the pistol, guiding it away from him, while his right hand chopped sharply at the woman's right wrist with the rigid edge of his palm. The woman screamed as Caspian, who now had his two hands on the gun, easily twisted it out of her grasp. Before she could react, Caspian's right leg sliced out in a savage sweep that caught her ankles and ripped her legs from beneath her. She fell hard, her spine connecting against the edge of a pointy rock. The impact jolted her body, but Caspian didn't give her time to recover. He spun her onto her stomach, then twisted her arms behind her back before he straddled her, keeping her arms bent in place with his legs.

"Why did you abduct Hobb? What do you want with him?" he growled, pressing the tip of the pistol against her left cheek.

"Who the fuck's Hobb?"

Caspian had no time for this, so he whipped the pistol against the back of the woman's head, knocking her out.

Caspian checked the pistol had a round in the chamber, then tucked it into his waistband.

"You were right, I was bluffing," he said, though he knew she didn't hear a word. "Next time, trust your gut."

CHAPTER SIX

Aboard MY Veloce
Port de Sóller
Mallorca, Spain

Verena Kaine tipped back the last of her broccoli and spinach smoothie, swallowing the thick, bitter concoction without so much as a grimace. The taste didn't bother her, but the drink's temperature annoyed her.

Damn it!

Hadn't she asked the chef to make it ice cold?

If I had wanted it cold, I wouldn't have specified it needed to be ice cold, would I?

First-world problem for sure, but still infuriating.

Setting the glass down, she tensed. There was a condensation ring on the polished wood where she had previously set the glass on the small desk. She stood, her irritation spiking. The master cabin of *Veloce* was full beam, a blend of modern minimalism and high-end Italian craftsmanship, and like everything else in her life, Verena wanted it pristine. Large windows on either side bathed the cabin in natural light, which accentuated every perfect detail—the clean lines, the sleek finishes, and the immaculate order. And now, a water ring was marring it.

Unacceptable.

She strode into the luxurious en suite bathroom, pulled a facecloth from the neatly folded stack, and returned to the cabin to wipe the surface clean. She looked at her work, studying it from different angles. Only once she was sure the desk was perfectly dry did she return to the en suite to place the cloth back *exactly* as it had been.

Satisfied, she sat in front of her laptop, entered her ten-digit password, and brought up the live feed of two of her men working over Paul Hobb in the engine room. The feed came from the two cameras mounted in the engine room, one positioned high in the corner near the access hatch and the other set lower, angled toward the twin generators. Between them, she had a clear, unbroken view of the beating.

The journalist, who was on his knees beside the generators, had his wrists and ankles bound together. Verena heard Hobb groan, and she quickly lowered the volume. While the cameras' built-in miniature microphones weren't the best, the confined space of the engine room helped to amplify the wet sounds of her men's fists meeting Hobb's flesh, something she found . . . repulsive.

She tilted her head, scrutinizing the reporter. She had to admit, he had more grit than she'd given him credit for. Few people would have thrown themselves from a speeding dinghy while bound. Hobb must have known that whatever awaited him aboard the yacht would be as merciless as the sea itself.

Still, he jumped. And that took balls.

She respected people who had real courage.

But even the bravest break. They all do eventually.

Hobb had so far refused to talk. But as she watched his head snap violently to the left from the force of the latest punch, she knew it would be soon. After all, the reporter was not a trained operator, just a nosy journalist who had stumbled too close to something that needed to remain buried.

The vibration of a phone against the lacquered wood of the bedside table drew her attention. She looked back at the three devices lined up next to each other. One of them—black and untraceable—was the one that mattered the most. There was only one person who had this number.

Her employer. Blackstone Security's sole client.

She picked up the black device and placed it against her ear.

"I was just about to call with an update," she said.

"Then don't waste my time. You found him?"

"I did."

"And? Any complications?"

"None," she replied.

"So far," the man said.

"Yes. So far."

"Is he talking?"

"He will. I should know who his source is within the hour."

"Once you do, take care of whoever is fucking with me, and toss the asshole reporter to the fishes."

"Of course," she replied, but the line was already dead.

Her employer didn't do pleasantries, and that suited Verena just fine. She set the phone down and was about to return her attention to the live feed, but something felt off. Her fingers twitched as she glanced at the three phones. The one she had just used wasn't perfectly aligned with the others. Half a centimeter too far to the left. It threw off the symmetry and the vibe of the entire cabin, didn't it? She reached out and nudged it back into place. Then again, this time just a hair to the right. Still not quite perfect. She adjusted all three, lining them up precisely along the edge of the table.

There. Finally.

No. The spacing's all wrong.

She leaned in again, shifting the middle phone just a fraction of a centimeter.

Better.

Another nudge. Then another.

Enough!

She took a long, deep breath and forced herself to pull her hand back. She exhaled slowly.

There. Done.

Verena sighed, then swore out loud. She needed help, and she knew it. Her employer would kill her if he knew how much time she wasted on stupid things like that. He didn't trust people who had weaknesses, especially the ones who he had admitted into his close circle.

Blackstone Security had been an unexpected turn in her life. Five years ago, she'd been a rising-star detective in the LAPD's Narcotics Division, only months away from being promoted to lieutenant. Her career had derailed after a judge had deemed that emptying her entire magazine into the two men who had shot and killed her partner was *excessive force*.

She'd disagreed with the judge. Strongly. The two lowlifes had deserved every single bullet she'd fired at them. Still, facing termination and a possible civil lawsuit, she'd resigned. And, just as it had happened to many disgraced cops before her, the job market chewed her up and spit her out.

Unable to find a job that paid close to her detective III salary, she was about to default on her mortgage when her benefactor had called to offer her a job. She knew the man and had met him three or four times when she'd been a teenager, but she hadn't talked to him since her dad, who had served alongside him during the first Gulf War, had perished in the cockpit of an experimental aircraft fifteen years ago.

"I apologize for not keeping in touch with you, Verena, but I've kept an eye out for you," her benefactor had said. "I admire your resolve, and I watched the video several times, you know?"

She didn't need to ask which video he was talking about. She knew which one. Though the footage taken by her bodycam wasn't in high definition, it had captured the entire firefight.

"There's a poetic ruthlessness about you. One that can't be taught. I'd like you to run a private security firm I'm invested in."

That was the moment she'd realized she'd been given a second chance.

A sharp knock on her cabin door pulled her out of her thoughts.

Justin Burton, *Veloce*'s captain and a former lieutenant with the US Navy, stepped inside before she could tell him to come in.

"Ma'am, we have a problem," he said.

"You'll need to be a bit more specific than that, Justin."

"Something's going on at the beach. I think you should see for yourself."

She nodded. She picked up two of the three phones, including the black one, then followed Burton to the main deck. He handed her a pair of binoculars.

"Check the rocky alcove at your one o'clock," he said.

She raised the binoculars and scanned the alcove near the end of the small beach. Pam, one of the four operators she had sent to snatch Hobb, was moving in a combat crouch toward the alcove, her pistol drawn. Pam didn't spook easy. Burton had spoken the truth.

Something's wrong.

A moment later, Pam disappeared behind the rocks.

"Where's Oscar?" Verena asked.

"Can't say for sure, ma'am. I watched him untie the Jet Ski, then I went back inside to get the binocs 'cause I thought I saw someone else."

"Someone else?" she asked, lowering the binocs so she could look at *Veloce*'s captain.

"Again, I can't say for sure. That's why I went inside to grab these," Burton said, nodding at the binoculars. "Next thing I know, Pam has her gun out."

She brought the binocs up again. Through a gap in the rocks, she caught glimpses of movement. A struggle between two people. A man.

And he's fighting Pam. Shit!

A sudden realization settled over her. Oscar wasn't missing. Oscar had been taken out. And if someone was good enough to neutralize the former pro boxer, then whoever that someone was, he was a problem.

A big problem.

Verena's first instinct was to send backup. She was about to order Burton and the two men interrogating Hobb to take the dinghy, but she hesitated. It wasn't tactically sound. She had no idea what—or who—she was dealing with. Was it just one man? A team? Were they after *her*, or was Paul Hobb their target? Even armed, her men would be sitting ducks on the open water, vulnerable to enemy fire as they crossed from the yacht to the beach. And it would also leave her alone with the chef to protect the yacht.

Too many unknowns. And unknowns got people killed.

Besides, her employer's orders couldn't have been clearer.

Find out what Hobb knows. Find the leak, Verena. And plug it. Permanently.

Sending her crew to help Pam would be careless and distract her from her main objective. Her gut told her to play it safe. At least until she knew exactly what the threat was.

"Warn our friends in the engine room that we're about to leave, Justin."

"Now? But . . . what about Pam and Oscar?"

She looked at him, daggers in her eyes.

"Don't make me repeat myself," she hissed.

"Where to?" Burton asked, lowering his eyes. "Back to the marina?"

Verena considered the question. If someone was here for Hobb, it meant they had resources. That meant they might already have people waiting at the marina. The right call was to move out, regroup, and formulate a plan.

"For now, let's head south," she said in a friendlier tone. "We'll be back for Pam and Oscar, I promise."

Burton gave her a sharp nod, then headed toward the helm. A few seconds later, the Azimut's three Volvo Penta IPS 1350s, each delivering one thousand horsepower, rumbled to life beneath her feet.

Verena walked out to the cockpit and gripped the railing, her eyes fixed on the shore.

Whoever this was, they'd just made a powerful enemy.

Verena smiled. Her most dangerous asset was in Palma, awaiting orders. She hadn't activated him for the Hobb job. Instead, she had kept him in reserve, in case there were complications.

It was time for him to earn his keep.

CHAPTER SEVEN

Crouched behind a cluster of rocks, Caspian watched, his grip tight around the gun in his hand, as the Azimut cut through the bay, leaving a foamy wake as it gained speed. The sun, glaring off the ocean's surface, sent a blinding shimmer across the water, forcing Caspian to narrow his eyes as he tracked the yacht's retreat.

Shit. There's no way I'm gonna get to the yacht or to Hobb now.

Someone had seen him. Caspian was sure of it. Why else would the yacht be pulling away with two missing crew members? The timing was too convenient. Now the real question was if they had gotten a good enough look to identify him.

Damn it.

Caspian turned around and scanned the surrounding cliffs and vegetation, looking for movement. The last thing he needed was another surprise. The woman had nearly gotten the best of him. He wasn't about to let that happen again.

Okay. What now?

His initial plan, clearly too ambitious and bordering on reckless, had been to intercept the yacht before it pulled away. He had hoped to force the woman to drive him to the Azimut on the Jet Ski, using her as cover. With luck, the yacht's crew would have assumed he was the woman's colleague. That hope had lasted all of five damn seconds. It had been a poor concept from the get-go—he was aware of that—but it had been the only thing he could come up with at the time. Now, he was stuck on the shore, left with two unconscious crew members and no clear way forward. With the yacht speeding away, his only viable option was to call the authorities. And for that, he had to get closer to town.

Caspian felt his pulse tick higher. Time was running out.

The fastest way back to Port de Sóller was by water. He looked in the direction of the Jet Ski.

That's an option.

Then a low groan pulled his attention to the woman. She stirred, her face contorting briefly in pain before she stilled again. He hadn't searched her yet, so he patted her down and found nothing of interest apart from the waterproof bag she carried across her back. He opened it and pulled out a cell phone, which had a small magnetic leather case attached at the back. Inside was a license to carry and a bank card. Also in the bag were a spare magazine for the pistol, three pairs of flex-cuffs, a bottle of water, and a satellite phone.

Caspian smiled. He could use the sat phone.

He powered it on and waited for the signal. While it booted up, he secured the woman's hands with one set of flex-cuffs, then used a second pair to tie her to her unconscious colleague. It wasn't perfect, but it would hold them long enough for him to get away.

The fact that they were both carrying flex-cuffs hinted they might have been working with the crew who had grabbed Paul Hobb.

Caspian's thoughts drifted to the reporter. He had seen enough to know that Hobb's captors weren't interested in a polite conversation with him. The thought of what Hobb might be enduring at that very moment made Caspian cringe.

The satellite phone beeped. It had acquired a signal.

Caspian bit his lip as he considered his next step. He could call the Mallorcan authorities and report the abduction.

But that's gonna open up a world of complications.

Two incapacitated, tied-up people on a beach and a missing journalist. The police would ask questions. Questions Caspian didn't want to answer. Now that his opportunity to rescue Hobb was gone, he preferred not to get actively involved further, at least until he knew more about the situation.

He knew what he had to do, who he had to reach out to.

Samantha Ranger.

She had told him—very explicitly—to stay out of trouble. And he had fully intended to do just that. Ranger wouldn't be happy about the call, but she'd understand, and she would get the locals moving. Caspian knew that if anyone could get the right people involved, people who wouldn't demand a sit-down with him or Liesel, it was Ranger.

Then he thought about Liesel. She was going to be pissed, no doubt about it. But the truth was, if the roles had been reversed, if *she* had been the one who had witnessed Hobb dive into the water with his hands bound, she wouldn't have turned her back either.

She would have done the exact same thing I did.

Still, a sinking feeling settled over him.

Vacation's officially over.

Caspian shook off the thought and looked at the sat phone. It was an unknown variable. He couldn't be sure who would be listening in, but he had to assume it was being monitored. He couldn't call Ranger's direct line with it. In his mind, he scrolled through several numbers she had had him memorize, trying to remember which one he was supposed to use for this situation.

He dialed a number, not convinced it was the correct one. If he had picked the right number, the call wouldn't go straight to Ranger. Instead, it would bounce through a chain of randomized virtual nodes—an encrypted relay network designed to obfuscate both the origin and the destination of the call. Each hop would strip metadata, encrypt the next leg, and reroute through another anonymized node. Even the most advanced surveillance systems would struggle to trace the call or listen to it. Or at least that's what he'd been told.

The line rang once. Twice. A click. Then it rang again.

"Tell me you're calling from a beachside bar with a drink in your hand," Ranger said, her voice coming through somewhat computerized.

Caspian glanced at the two people he had knocked out, then gazed at the distant white trail of the Azimut.

"No such luck," he said. "I need your help with something."

CHAPTER EIGHT

Palma
Mallorca, Spain

Maximilian Kross turned on his phone, which instantly buzzed with a flood of notifications.

"Someone important?" the woman seated across from him asked, glancing up from the breakfast she was enjoying on the balcony of their luxurious hotel suite.

She spoke in English with a pronounced Spanish accent that Kross had found irresistible the moment he had first heard it the night before.

He raised an eyebrow.

"Jealous already, Mia? We've barely known each other twelve hours."

She laughed softly as she used her fork to cut a delicate bite of her omelet.

"After everything you saw last night and again this morning, twice, do you really think jealousy is something I'd feel?" she asked, her warm eyes brimming with mischief.

Now it was Kross's turn to laugh, genuinely entertained. He liked her. She was confident, bright, and stunningly beautiful. She had thick waves of dark chestnut hair cascading down her back, and her skin had a golden tone that he knew didn't come from a bottle but from a life spent under the Andalusian sun. But it was her eyes that he'd found impossible to ignore. They were a rich hazel green, the kind that seemed to shift in shade depending on the light.

He took a sip of his coffee. It was strong, black, and just a touch bitter. Exactly the way he liked it. As the flavor settled on his tongue, he wondered, not for the first time, why anyone would want to ruin something so honest with milk, or God forbid, honey. Kross winced at the thought.

Coffee should taste like coffee.

As the warm liquid slid down his throat, he took a moment to enjoy the scenery. From the suite's veranda, they had a spectacular view of the Mediterranean Sea and of the turquoise waves that broke gently against the golden sand three stories below. To their left, they had a side view of Palma's skyline, crowned by the majestic Gothic spires of the Cathedral of Santa Maria of Palma. The warm breeze coming from the ocean drifted gently through the balcony, carrying with it the scent of sea salt mingled with hints of the fresh lavender plants he'd seen the day before in one corner of the hotel's lush garden.

"This is lovely, Max," Mia said. "My room is nice, but it isn't facing the sea. This is so much better."

He smiled at her.

Despite her undeniable beauty, it was Mia's performance at the piano the night before at the lobby bar that had truly enchanted him. She hadn't just played; she had commanded the room with every note, her fingers gliding over the keys like she'd been born to do it. Watching her play had felt magical, as if he'd been caught in a spell. But it wasn't just the music that had drawn him in. More than once, Mia had looked up from the keys and found his eyes with hers. Never long enough to be obvious, but just enough to make him wonder if it was intentional. Each glance had felt like an invitation, a dare for him to cross the room and to introduce himself. Something he knew he shouldn't do. Not when he was working, but in the end, it had been an invitation he hadn't been able to resist. He had found her after her last set, near the bar, nursing a glass of white wine. As he watched Mia take another bite of her omelet, he replayed their conversation in his mind.

"You play like you're hiding something," he had said to her in Spanish.

"Maybe I am," she replied in the same language.

"You kept looking at me," he said.

"Did I?" she asked, taking another sip. "Then maybe I wasn't subtle enough."

"You're talented. I mean you no disrespect, but if you ask me, you're too good for hotel lobbies."

"It's a hard business to be in, you know? But I've played bigger venues. Smaller ones too. Touring Europe mostly. I play classical, but I can do the occasional jazz set if the mood's right," she told him with a smile.

"So . . . this is what you do?"

"No. It's who I am."

"Right. Well, you don't seem like the type who stays in one place for too long," Kross said.

"Neither do you. And let me guess, you're not here on vacation."

The silence that had followed had stretched for a minute or two, but not in an awkward way. It was she who had broken it.

"You're not going to tell me your name, are you?" she asked him, her fingers tracing the rim of her wineglass.

"I was wondering the same about you."

She laughed at that. "Mia," she said, offering her hand.

He kissed the top of her hand, and said, "Max."

"Mister Max," she said, testing the sound of it as if it was a note on the piano. "Let me guess . . . you're not a reporter, and your shoes tell me you're not a banker either."

"What's wrong with my shoes?"

"Make my day, Mister Max. Tell me you're a talent agent that will help me fill the biggest auditoriums."

He smirked at that. "Sorry to disappoint. I just drink whiskey and watch beautiful women play piano."

"Oh? And that's a full-time job?"

"Lately, yeah."

She laughed again. "I hope you've enjoyed tonight's assignment?"

"How could I not?"

"Do you always flirt this much with women you've just met?"

"Only the ones who make it impossible not to."

Mia's eyes narrowed slightly. "And what happens when the music stops?"

"Honestly, it's up to you," he replied. "I'm headed up."

She'd held his gaze for a moment, then picked up her wineglass and took the last sip before she'd stepped away from the bar and followed him to the elevator.

———

The elegant dress she'd been wearing the night before, which Kross had removed hurriedly, almost violently, as they had undressed each other, had been replaced by one of his white dress shirts, the sleeves casually rolled up to her elbows and the top three buttons left undone. He could see a gold necklace glisten as it caught the sunlight each time she moved.

Since neither of them had felt like leaving the room, Kross had ordered an impossibly large breakfast, selecting pretty much the entire menu.

Another notification appeared on his phone.

"Seriously, who is it?" Mia asked again, dipping a piece of avocado into Greek yogurt.

Kross looked at his screen, then said, "My parents."

As soon as the words left his mouth, Kross wondered why he had told Mia, a woman he barely knew, the truth. Lying should have come easily to him; it always had before. Yet something about Mia disarmed him and made him want to be truthful. The realization unsettled him.

Mia leaned in and asked, "Then why the death stare at your phone?"

Kross considered the question. The truth was, though he loved his parents very much, he regretted sharing his personal phone number with them. Every time he turned it on—no more than once a week for operational security—there were at least half a dozen messages from them. He had made them promise they would contact him only in case of emergency. But it was now clear to him that his definition of what consisted of a strict emergency wasn't the same as it was for his parents, who had both turned seventy in the last six months.

"How often do you check in with your folks?" he asked, curious but uncomfortable with the idea that he genuinely wanted to know the answer.

"Coffee every other morning, dinner every Sunday," she replied. "When I'm not traveling, of course."

He studied her face, waiting for a playful smirk that never came. *She's serious.*

"Wow. You're like a family-values propaganda poster, aren't you?"

She laughed, then turned serious. "They probably miss you, that's all. You have any siblings?"

Not willing to share any more personal details with Mia, he scrolled through a few messages, then said, "Apparently, my father thinks Monday's meal-kit potatoes were fifty grams short."

"Meal kit? I will never understand Americans," Mia said, shaking her head. "It doesn't make sense to me. Going to the market for fresh produce is half the pleasure of cooking."

Kross didn't disagree with her, but before he could reply, his work phone buzzed twice, signaling the reception of a text message. He reached for the device and checked the screen.

49234. An urgent code that meant he had to call back his employer. Immediately.

Kross got up, a dark pulse of anticipation running through him.

Mia gave him an annoyed look.

"Am I boring you?" she asked.

"Far from it. But this is work, and it pays for all this luxury," he said, gesturing to their breakfast and the ocean view.

"I thought your job was to drink whiskey and watch beautiful women play piano?"

"Just give me a minute," Kross said, shaking his head.

He stepped inside the hotel suite and closed the patio door behind him. The interior was as luxurious as the balcony view. It had hardwood floors, plush furniture in tones of beige and gray, and a massive bed draped in Egyptian cotton sheets. Kross allowed himself a smile as he looked at the bed, which was unmade with its sheets tangled, the sight reminding him of the several passionate lovemaking sessions he had enjoyed with Mia.

He'd been in Palma for almost a week, and it was the first time his employer had tried to contact him, which was fine by him. He had needed the rest. They had put him to good use in Manchester the month before, and he had started to believe they had sent him to Palma as a reward for his performance in England.

Kross recalled the fate of the British forensic accountant who had been a little too diligent in scrutinizing his employer's financial records. The man's frantic pleas—when Kross had secured the electric clamps to the accountant's nipples—were still vivid in his mind.

The accountant had spilled the beans even before Kross had turned on the power. Of course, Kross had to inflict some pain to confirm the man had been telling the truth. The accountant had received an anonymous tip, letting him know exactly what to look for in his employer's financial statements. Though the accountant didn't know the name of the person who had reached out to him, he had provided Kross with the email address from which the tip had originated. Information Kross had then shared with his employer.

Kross was a top performer when it came to making people talk. It was one of his specialties. After serving two tours in Iraq and one in Afghanistan as a Green Beret, he had left the army to start working as a freelance contractor for the CIA, where he'd become an enhanced interrogation expert.

He had enjoyed the work a bit too much, apparently, because he'd been let go after two years.

Thankfully, he'd quickly found another organization that needed his skill set. One that paid a lot more than the United States government. Kross dialed the number he was to call back.

Someone picked up on the first ring. "I'm listening."

He recognized the voice instantly. *Verena Kaine.*

Kross had met her twice and found her to be a bit weird, but she hadn't tried to micromanage him, so she had that going for her.

"What can I do for you?" he asked, looking at Mia who was gazing at the ocean with a cup of coffee in hand.

"Sorry to cut short what I'm sure was starting to feel like a vacation," Verena said, not sounding sorry at all. "I need you to kill someone for me."

"Who's the target?"

"Not sure yet, but I suggest you start making your way to Port de Sóller."

CHAPTER NINE

Port de Sóller
Mallorca, Spain

Caspian entered the hotel room he shared with Liesel, expecting to find it empty. Instead, and to his relief, he found Liesel sitting on the sofa, her arms crossed tightly over her chest. She wore a fitted white tank top and linen shorts; her dark hair, still wet, was loose around her shoulders. The look on her face stopped him cold. Something was wrong.

Her eyes met his. "Where the hell have you been?" she asked.

"I'll tell you everything, but for now, we need to pack our stuff," he replied, locking the door behind him. "I want us out of here in ten minutes."

His words instantly wiped the frustration from her face. Caspian knew this wasn't because of his power of persuasion, but because she was a professional. As an intelligence officer with the BND, Liesel could grasp the seriousness of a situation faster than most.

"I'm already packed, but we can't leave the island," she said. "Not yet."

That caught him off guard. "I wasn't planning to. But why?"

"You first."

Caspian shared with her what had happened, telling her about Hobb's abduction, the yacht, the two armed people he'd been forced to neutralize, and his call to Samantha Ranger.

"Holy shit," Liesel muttered when he was finished. "You think this has anything to do with Florence?"

"Not sure yet. Ranger will send someone to check on her, covertly of course. She'll let me know," he said.

"What else did she say?"

"She wants us ready in case she needs us. But we need to get to Palma. Port de Sóller is too small. We, or I should say I, could be found easily here."

"Someone has already found us," Liesel said.

"What do you mean?"

She handed him a folded note.

"This was inside a pastry box that was left for me," she said.

Caspian read the note, then looked at Liesel.

"You believe Sofie dropped this off?"

Liesel shook her head. "Not personally. I went to the front desk to ask if they were aware that someone had delivered a pastry box to our room."

"And?"

"The box was left for me at the front desk by a local deliveryman they're familiar with. The concierge delivered it to the room."

Caspian's gut tightened.

"You were right," he said, handing the note back to Liesel. "Whoever sent it knows where we're staying. Maybe not our room number, but the hotel."

"Hacking the hotel database isn't complicated," Liesel pointed out. "We have to assume they know everything."

Liesel wasn't the type to scare easily, but the tightness in her jaw and the way her fingers fidgeted against her thigh told Caspian how much the note she'd received had shaken her. He reached out and cupped the side of her face, his thumb brushing lightly against her cheek. She leaned into his touch, closing her eyes.

"Do you think it's her? Do you think it's really Sofie?" he asked.

"I . . . I don't know," she replied. "But what if it is? What if she really needs me?"

"Then we go," he said without hesitation. "You're not doing this alone."

"But what about Ranger's orders?"

"This is your family. Let's deal with that first, okay?" he said. "But we need to do it right. I'll loop in Ranger."

"If it is my sister, she might not show up at the restaurant if she sees you there," Liesel said. "She did ask me to come alone."

"She knows who I am. I'm in the photo too," Caspian reminded her. "But you're right, I shouldn't sit with you at the restaurant."

He moved to the desk and grabbed a map of Port de Sóller, then spread it out on the bed. He tapped the location of the restaurant with his finger.

"You're supposed to meet Sofie here. I'll find a spot from where I can keep an eye on you."

Liesel leaned over the map, studying the layout.

"There aren't a lot of places where you'd have a good vantage point," she said after a moment.

Caspian grunted. He'd come to the same conclusion. The restaurant was separated from the beach only by a pedestrian road and the tram tracks. Adjacent to it was a narrow street, Carrer d'Alaró, and beyond that, another restaurant. On the other side of Ses Oliveres was a private residence with an iron fence.

"I wish I could be on overwatch, but without a rifle, that's not happening," Caspian said, his finger hovering over the end of the large concrete dock that jutted out of the waterfront promenade and cut through the bay. "Even if I had a long gun, the only viable place I could set up to have an overall view would be here. And that's about three hundred meters away."

"What if I make another reservation, this time for one?" Liesel suggested. "That way, you could sit a few tables away from me."

Caspian didn't like that idea. "If we're being watched, and whoever's after us sees me sitting alone a few tables away from you, they'll know something's off. They might realize we're onto them."

"So, we sit together? Just a regular couple having dinner?"

"A regular couple?" Caspian smirked. "More like a great-looking couple having dinner."

Liesel took his hands, lacing her fingers through his. "We'll be sitting ducks," she said.

Caspian smiled, then squeezed her hands and leaned in, kissing her gently. He then set his backpack onto the bed, unzipped it, and took out the two pistols he'd earlier confiscated.

"At least we'll be armed sitting ducks," he said.

Liesel let out a small laugh.

"Let's just hope we won't need them," she muttered.

CHAPTER TEN

Caspian held Liesel's hand as they walked through the crowded streets of Port de Sóller. They didn't speak much, but their eyes were constantly moving. Before leaving their hotel, they had challenged each other about the layout of the town and the different escape routes around the restaurant.

Caspian adjusted their path slightly, leading her through a curved route around the plaza, then down a quieter side street before returning to the main promenade. It wasn't a full SDR—surveillance detection route—but it was enough to potentially flush out an inexperienced watcher.

But even then . . .

With all the tourists lingering in the shops, the couples sipping sangria along the waterfront, and the families enjoying dinner on the many terraces, Caspian knew it would be near impossible to spot a tail, let alone a professional surveillance team.

They arrived at Ses Oliveres fifteen minutes before 7 p.m. The sun was getting low, and it would be dark in less than thirty minutes. A coastal breeze threaded through the air, bringing with it the smell of grilled seafood. The hostess greeted them with a warm smile and led them to a table on the terrace. It was set for four. When she reached to clear the third and fourth wineglasses and the tableware, Liesel stopped her.

"Leave this one," she said, taking off the white sun hat she'd been wearing. "We're waiting for someone else."

Caspian took the chair facing the pedestrian promenade, which gave him a clear view of the bay, the pedestrian road, the tram tracks, and the steady stream of foot traffic. Anyone looking at him would see a relaxed man enjoying the company of a beautiful woman. While this was true, Caspian was clocking everything: the couple holding hands and laughing a little too loudly, the lone man nursing a beer three tables to their right, and the woman pretending to read the menu while glancing at them over her sunglasses.

Caspian knew Liesel was doing the same.

"Anything?" she asked.

"My sixth sense isn't tingling," he replied.

It was a few minutes past seven when the waitress approached their table.

"Should I bring you something to drink while you wait for your friend?" she asked in Spanish.

Liesel ordered a bottle of sparkling water and small plates of Iberian ham and fried anchovies.

"She probably has eyes on us," Liesel said once the waitress had left.

Caspian scanned the crowd again.

"Maybe," he said. "If she's watching, she's doing it from a distance."

As they waited for the appetizers, and for Sofie to show up, Liesel asked, "You think the folks you zip-tied got free?"

"Yeah. I'd be shocked if they didn't. I'm sure they weren't out for long."

"Then we have to assume they've reported back and they're now actively looking for you."

"If they're looking for me, then the window for us staying static here is closing fast."

"If?" Liesel asked.

"Maybe they already got what they came here for," Caspian replied. "Paul Hobb."

"Yep. Why risk coming after me if they've already accomplished their mission? To settle a score? Because I bruised their egos? I don't think so."

The appetizers arrived, and Caspian forced himself to eat. He chewed, but he didn't taste anything.

"She's half an hour late," Liesel said, munching on a fried anchovy. "What do you want to do?"

Caspian looked at her. She smiled, did her best to appear casual, but the tension in her shoulders and the slight crease in her brow told him the truth. Liesel was worried.

Worried about what I'll say. Worried about us leaving before she could see her sister.

"We're here. Let's order mains and wait. If she doesn't show by the time we're done, we'll head back to the hotel, grab our gear, and drive to Palma."

Liesel looked relieved, but before she could reply, two local police officers came into view. They were walking their bikes side by side along the promenade, chatting. Both wore short-sleeved blue uniforms, shirts and shorts. One was in his late forties and seemed to have a permanent squint, as if he was annoyed by the sun. He had a strong build and a calm, seasoned look that suggested a couple of decades of patrol work and regular gym sessions. The other was younger, lean, and had a pair of sunglasses perched on his cap.

Caspian bit the interior of his lower lip as the two officers stopped by the hostess stand. He had a side view of the officers, but Liesel would have had to turn her head to see them.

"The local cops just stopped to talk to the hostess," he said.

Had he been wrong about the two people on the beach? Had they reported the incident and given his description to the police?

Without making it obvious, Caspian watched the exchange. The hostess nodded at something the older cop said, then her eyes swept casually across the terrace and briefly landed on their table. Was she about to point them out?

Caspian forced himself to stay relaxed, but his heart rate climbed anyway.

The young officer laughed and said something Caspian couldn't hear. Then, he leaned in and pressed a quick kiss to the hostess's lips.

"I think the hostess is the younger cop's girlfriend," he said. "They're leaving."

Still, knowing this could have gone very differently, the tension didn't drain from Caspian's neck and shoulders right away.

Movement from inside the restaurant pulled his attention. A woman approached their table. Caspian sat upright. The woman looked like Liesel.

But older, and roughened, somehow.

Her skin was sun worn, and her eyes were shadowed by fatigue. She wore a plain olive green blouse tucked into black pants. Her dark hair was pulled back into a hasty knot. Caspian thought there was something feral about the way she moved.

"Liesel," he murmured. "Your sister's here."

CHAPTER ELEVEN

Port de Sóller
Mallorca, Spain

Maximilian Kross sat at a table on the shaded terrace of a gelateria, a half-eaten cup of frozen yogurt in front of him. He stirred the melting dessert with his plastic spoon as his eyes lingered on the photo glowing on his phone screen. A picture of his target.

No name. No dossier. Just a face.

The only additional intel Verena had shared with him had been that this operation was a continuation of his last mission in Manchester.

Kross leaned back in his chair and glanced at the sky. Bright blue, with a few white clouds, but the sun was dipping lower now, edging toward the horizon. He had been made aware that there were at least three drones circling overhead, their powerful cameras tracking and scanning dozens of faces per minute. Despite the drone's facial recognition algorithms running at full capacity, they hadn't yet located Kross's target. Port de Sóller was small, but it was dense with tourists.

Way too many faces for only three drones.

His phone buzzed.

"Yes."

Verena's voice came in through the wireless earbud in his left ear.

"We're still searching for the primary, but I just got word that someone of interest was identified by the drones," she said.

Kross didn't respond. He kept stirring his frozen yogurt.

"I have a pair of two-man teams on their way to intercept," Verena continued. "I'm sending a pic to your phone."

A notification popped up. Kross tapped the screen. The man in the photo looked to be in his thirties. He wore a pair of white pants and a loose, light blue shirt with the top few buttons undone. He had an average build and brown hair. Clean cut. Bland. Nothing special. Kross used his fingers to zoom in. The picture quality wasn't good enough for Kross to see what color the man's eyes were, but was still sharp enough to have triggered a hit with the recognition software.

The photo, taken from a high angle and slightly distorted by motion, had clearly been taken from one of the drones.

"Why are you sending me this?" Kross asked.

"I want you to support the grab. Don't get involved but keep an eye on things."

"From a distance?"

"Yes. From a distance. If we find the primary, I want you to be able to redeploy in less than five minutes."

Kross wiped a drop of yogurt from the rim of his cup. "That might not be possible," he said.

"Will you at least try?"

He considered his options, then said, "Yeah. I can do that. But if I feel it's too risky, or there's too much heat—"

"I get it," she interrupted. "I can live with that. I just want to make sure the guys I'm sending won't encounter anything they can't handle."

Kross glanced at the photo again. "Don't you think four men are enough? The guy doesn't look like much."

"He neutralized two of my officers earlier today. He left them zip-tied on the beach, one of them with a sock in his mouth."

He zoomed in again on the man. Some of the most dangerous men he'd ever met and served with hadn't looked like much either.

"Where is he now?" he asked.

"He just sat down at Ses Oliveres. It's a restaurant—"

Kross cut her off. "I know where it is."

"He's seated on the terrace with a woman. She's wearing a sun hat, so we haven't been able to identify her."

"Understood. I'll provide overwatch. Let your men know. I'll be in position in about fifteen minutes. I'll let you know when I'm set."

"Do that," Verena said. "I won't send the teams in until you have eyes on the target."

Kross ended the call, looked at his cup, then sighed. The yogurt had completely melted at the bottom of the cup. He shrugged, then raised the cup to his lips, drinking its contents as if it was a milkshake. He stood up, picked up his backpack, and started toward the marina.

As he moved through the crowd, a face flicked in his mind. *Mia.*

It started with a memory of her laugh. She had the kind of laugh that lingered in a man's mind for a long time. Then came the curve of her hips and the warmth of her naked body pressed against him.

His morning with her had been . . . enjoyable. Too enjoyable, maybe? He knew he shouldn't have invited her to his suite, but he had started to feel lonely over the last year or so. He had had a lot of opportunities to be with someone since he had started taking contractual work, but operational security had always taken precedence over his desires.

Until last night.

What was it about Mia that had pulled him in so deeply? It wasn't just her looks and her wild energy in bed. He knew that. It was harder to define than that. Maybe it was the way she seemed so at ease with the world, like nothing bothered her?

Carefree.

Or was it how she'd straddled him without a word that morning, half asleep and warm, like it was the most natural thing in the world. He shivered at the memory. It had been as if she had belonged there, and it had driven him crazy. Then, when they were done, she had traced lazy circles on his chest with her fingers. Kross absentmindedly passed his tongue over his lips as he remembered the taste of cinnamon and espresso on hers when he had kissed her goodbye a few hours ago.

Maybe that's it. With her, things feel simple. And real.

For a few precious hours, she had made him forget the violence, the blood, the lies, and the weight of everything he'd done. She had given him silence in all the noise. And he was starting to need that more than he was ready to admit.

I'm getting too old for this shit. I really am.

Across the marina, a large yacht let out a deep, resonant blast from its horn that startled him and sent a flock of seagulls into the air. Kross's head snapped toward the sound, his instincts overriding the memory of Mia.

What the hell's wrong with me?

Kross forced Mia out of his mind. He hadn't expected to think of her again so soon, and so vividly.

You're slipping, Max. Get your head in the game. Complete this op, then reassess your priorities.

The concrete dock he was now walking on stretched into the bay like a fat finger. It was lined with sailboats and yachts of different sizes. Kross walked its length, his eyes scanning the promenade and Ses Oliveres's terrace in the distance. From the end of the dock, he had a clear view of the restaurant. The position where he stood was perfect, but it was too exposed with too many people moving in and out. He needed somewhere he could work from.

Somewhere quiet, with good concealment. And with a stable shooting platform.

Kross examined the boats docked nearby, his eyes stopping on a sixty-foot sloop-rigged sailboat. It had a white fiberglass hull, teak decking, and a blue canvas dodger. The boat was past its prime, but it had been well kept. The lines were coiled neatly, the fenders hung in the right places, but more importantly, the companionway hatch was of an older design.

Kross knew the type. He was confident he could pick the lock in under ninety seconds. He stepped onto the sailboat as if he owned it. No one nearby paid him much attention. He knelt by the cabin door, slipped a thin pick and tension wrench from a side pocket of his backpack, and inserted them into the lock. He applied light pressure with the wrench, feeling the subtle resistance of the pins. Less than thirty seconds later, the lock clicked open with a satisfying snap. Kross slid the door open and stepped below deck, closing and then locking the door behind him.

The cabin was dark, and a faint scent of varnish and burnt coffee hung in the air. A midsize galley with a double sink and stovetop was on one side, opposite a built-in bench and a large fold-down table. Sunlight filtered through the portholes, casting shafts of light across the floorboards and catching dust particles in the air. Kross quickly cleared the interior of the boat, sneezing once thanks to a swirl of dust motes he had kicked up with his movement. He sniffed, wiped his nose with the back of his hand, then continued to check for cameras or any sort of electronic surveillance. Not finding any, he dropped to one knee by a porthole and looked out. From this position, he had a direct line of sight to the Ses Oliveres terrace and a partial view of the promenade.

Perfect.

Kross unzipped his backpack and began to assemble his rifle, a Remington Defense Concealable Sniper Rifle—or CSR. The rifle was built for operations just like this one. Optimized for subsonic ammunition, it featured a fourteen-inch barrel, a fully adjustable stock, and a suppressor. The entire rifle broke down into three parts, which made it ideal for covert carry in a standard backpack. Once he had assembled the rifle, he retrieved two ten-round magazines from his backpack's side pouch. He inserted one into the magazine well and set the other within easy reach. Kross removed the daytime scope that was already attached and replaced it with one that was optimized for low-light conditions. If he had to make a shot after sunset, he'd be ready.

He pulled out his phone and sent a brief text to Verena to let her know he was in position. He then settled in behind the rifle, its stock tucked tight into his shoulder. He adjusted the magnification, then checked the rooftops, the balconies, and the moored yachts across the bay, looking for any elevated vantage that might conceal a spotter or a second sniper.

The last thing he wanted was for Verena's men to walk into an ambush. Not seeing anything that represented a direct or immediate threat, he began to scan each table with methodical precision, his finger resting along the trigger guard. Kross noted the layout of the terrace as the waitstaff moved around the tables.

And there he is . . .

Seated at a table near the edge of the terrace, the man from the drone photo was leaning forward, elbows resting on the table, listening to a woman talk. There were two women seated with his target, both were almost identical. Dark hair, same facial structure. One was wearing a green blouse, the other a pink one.

Twins?

His phone buzzed. It was Verena. He accepted the call by tapping his earbud.

"Talk to me," she said.

"I have eyes on him. He's at the restaurant," he replied. "But he's not alone."

"I know. He's with a woman."

"Two women," Kross corrected her. "And here's the interesting part. They look alike."

"Like twins?" Verena asked.

"Yeah . . . and there's more," Kross said, zeroing in on the woman seated to the man's right. "They both match the primary's description. What do you want me to do?"

There was a long pause, but when Verena replied, her voice was calm and decisive.

"I just checked in with my men, and they'll be on-site in two minutes. But as far as I'm concerned, the two women and the man with the blue shirt are now fair game. From where you are, do you think you could take out both women?"

Kross adjusted his scope again. The two women were seated close to each other. He'd only have to make a small adjustment between the first and second shot.

"Yes," he said. "Not a guarantee, but close."

"Wait until my teams get there, then you're free to engage the women. If the man becomes trouble before my men can grab him, take him out too."

Kross ended the call, his eyes never leaving the scope. Something told him this wasn't going to be a simple grab. And he couldn't be more thrilled. Maybe he wasn't ready to retire just yet.

He allowed himself a faint smile. This was turning into a fantastic day.

CHAPTER TWELVE

Ses Oliveres Restaurant
Port de Sóller, Mallorca, Spain

Liesel stopped breathing, her lungs refusing to move as her sister, Sofie, sat in the chair next to her. Sofie reached out and squeezed Liesel's forearm as if doing so was the most natural thing in the world. The gesture was simple, familiar, but it gave Liesel the chills.

"Hi, Schnecke," Sofie said softly. "I didn't think you'd come."

Liesel had a hard time swallowing. Her eyes were fixed on her sister's hand on her forearm, like the hand was an alien object.

The nickname. The touch. Sofie's voice. None of it seemed real.

Her baby sister, dead for five years, or so she'd believed, was now sitting beside her.

Alive. Breathing. Touching me.

Liesel was motionless, but in her mind, the memories came crashing in. The funeral, the empty coffin, the years of grief and guilt. She wanted to cry, to laugh, to fucking scream. She wanted to throw her arms around Sofie and never let go, but at the same time, she wanted to grab her little sister by the shoulders and demand to know where the hell she'd been all those years and why she hadn't given her sign of life.

It was Caspian who broke the spell.

"I'm Caspian," he said. "I think we met once. In Kenya."

Sofie looked at him, clearly surprised. "I don't think so."

"You were just outside the Kibera slum, at the back of a motorcycle," Caspian said.

"I honestly have no idea what you're talking about—"

Caspian cut her off. "Don't. I know you were there, and Liesel knows it too," he said.

Sofie's expression darkened. "Is that so?" she asked.

"What were you doing there? Help me understand," Liesel said.

But Sofie didn't reply to her. Instead, she looked at Caspian. "I saw you, too, you know?" she said.

Caspian let out a dry chuckle. "Yeah . . . I figured you had. You took out one of Dolores Araujo's bodyguards."

"What is this? An interrogation?" Sofie asked.

"I just want to make sure we're on the same side," Caspian said. "You came to us, remember? So, no more games. Answer your sister's question."

Sofie pursed her lips, then looked at Liesel.

"I was there to protect you," Sofie said. "That bitch, Araujo, she would have sent killers after you for killing her ex and wrecking her operation in New York. I . . . I couldn't let that happen."

Liesel already knew that—Caspian had told her as much when he had shared with her his reasons for conducting his own unsanctioned operation in Kenya—but she was still taken aback by Sofie's words. "How did you know about Araujo?" she asked. "What's your connection to her?"

"As much as I'd like to chat about me and what happened in Africa, Schnecke, now isn't the—"

"Time?" Liesel finished for her, doing her very best to keep her voice from rising. "Well, make the time, little sis. Because for the last five years, I thought you were dead. Do you have any idea what that's done to me?"

Sofie looked away. Liesel's heart pounded in her chest, and she could feel the rage building inside her. What game was her sister playing?

"I'm sorry, Liesel. I really am," Sofie said a moment later. "But I can't."

Liesel shook her head. "I love you, Sofie. But if you don't tell me what the hell is going on—"

"There's no time for that," Sofie insisted, grabbing Liesel's hand. "My life's in danger. And so are yours."

Liesel shot a glance at Caspian, then back at Sofie. Her sister's tone was different than she remembered. It was edgier, unstable.

And her eyes . . . they don't look the way they used to. Something happened to her. But what?

"Why would our lives be in danger?" Caspian asked.

"I know you both have questions, and I promise, I'll answer all of them. But not here. You need to follow me. Right away."

Sofie let go of Liesel's hand and pushed her chair back, getting ready to leave. But Caspian caught Sofie's wrist.

"No," he said. "You'll have to do better than that."

Sofie stared at him for a moment, then slowly sat back down.

"I'm not a good person, Liesel. I'm not like you," Sofie said.

"What are you talking about? You're not making any sense," Liesel said, exasperated by Sofie's unwillingness to share anything with her and Caspian. Was she suffering from PTSD? Or had she completely lost it?

"In Afghanistan, I was given an opportunity. And I took it. I wish I hadn't, but I did."

Caspian leaned in. "What kind of opportunity?"

"To provide intelligence."

Liesel felt her chest tighten. "To the Taliban?" she asked in a whisper.

Sofie recoiled. "No. Of course not," she snapped back, disgusted. "To Hearts United."

Liesel blinked. "The charitable organization? That Hearts United?"

"You know any other?" Sofie asked, then added, "Yes, that one. But Hearts United isn't what people think it is. It never was."

Caspian scoffed. "Come on. Hearts United is one of the most respected NGOs in the world. The good they've done—"

"Stop. Just stop!" Sofie said. "You know nothing, Caspian. Nothing!"

Liesel raised her hand, coming to Caspian's defense. "No, he's right, Sofie. Hearts United's reputation is beyond reproach. If you're telling us otherwise, you need to give us more than riddles."

Sofie glared at them. "I shouldn't have come. Asking for your help was a mistake."

Then, from the corner of her eye, Liesel noticed two men cutting across the promenade. They were heading straight for the restaurant. There was something about them that stood out. They didn't fit with the crowd of vacationers and sunburned families who were searching for a restaurant to enjoy dinner. The men's clothes were utilitarian and looked nothing like what most tourists wore. Their eyes were scanning as they walked, not lingering on anything for too long. One of them met her eyes briefly but then quickly looked away.

Sofie must have noticed them, too, because she said, "They found me."

"Who found you?" Caspian asked.

"These two were part of the team who grabbed my contact this morning," Sofie said, rising from her chair. "Follow me. There's a rear exit behind the kitchen. Come now, or you'll die."

Liesel froze, her mind spinning.

Part of the team who grabbed my contact this morning . . .

Then something clicked in her brain.

"Paul Hobb. Your contact was Paul Hobb?"

Sofie, who had already taken two steps toward the restaurant, turned to her, eyes wide. "How . . . how did you know?"

Before Liesel could answer, Sofie jerked backward, violently shoved by an unseen force.

And then something hit Liesel, hard, and she was thrown sideways, her world spinning as her shoulder slammed into the tiles of the terrace.

CHAPTER THIRTEEN

Ses Oliveres Restaurant
Port de Sóller, Mallorca, Spain

Sniper!

Caspian, recognizing the moment for what it was before Sofie had even hit the ground, didn't hesitate. He launched himself toward Liesel, tackling her sideways as the sniper's next round zipped past.

The world around him exploded into chaos. Screams cut through the air, tables crashed over, and shards of glass skittered across the tile as wineglasses shattered. Someone behind him yelled in pain.

Caspian landed hard on top of Liesel, his body protecting hers as they slid along the floor. Liesel let out a grunt, and for a moment, fear clutched at Caspian.

"You good?" he asked, quickly patting her down, checking for blood.

His hands came back clean. No blood.

Thank God.

"Where's my sister? Where's Sofie?" Liesel asked, frantically looking around.

Behind them, an older man was down, clutching his face. Blood was gushing through his fingers, staining his white shirt. To the man's right, Sofie was sprawled on the floor, the front of her blouse darkened by blood. She moaned as she tried to sit up.

"Stay down!" Caspian ordered. "Don't move!"

Liesel crawled toward her sister.

Movement toward the front of the restaurant caught Caspian's eye. Two men were elbowing their way through the crowd of screaming diners. One of them had a pistol in his right hand. The gun was low, his muzzle pointed at the ground, but it was still a threat. Caspian reacted on instinct. In less than two seconds, his hand had moved to the small of his back and had drawn the pistol he'd stuck inside his waistband. Aiming at the man's torso, he didn't pull the trigger, hesitating for the briefest moment as he studied the man.

Friend or foe? Could the man and his partner be plainclothes police officers running toward danger? Maybe off-duty cops trying to help? The man with the gun locked his eyes on Caspian, just as a young mother tripped, dragging her crying child into his path. The man swatted them away with a powerful shove. Then he raised his gun in Caspian's direction.

Definitely not a cop.

Caspian waited half a heartbeat longer, just enough for the muzzle of the man's gun to confirm his intent, then fired. The round hit center mass, punching into the man's upper chest and knocking him flat on his back. The second man, who was two steps behind, dove behind a table and rolled out of sight.

Shit!

Caspian stayed low. Getting up now would be suicide. He and Liesel had studied the map earlier and knew the only clear sniper angle came from across the bay.

Somewhere along the cement dock. Maybe a boat.

If he stayed beneath the railing height of the terrace, he'd be out of view. That was the only explanation as to why the sniper hadn't fired at him. But staying low also meant he couldn't maneuver cleanly to get a shot at the second shooter.

The first man wasn't dead, at least not yet. He was writhing, clutching at his chest, one arm reaching out desperately toward his partner.

"What's Sofie's status?" Caspian asked without turning.

No response.

"We need to move, Liesel! Now!" Caspian shouted, his eyes and pistol covering the position where he had last seen the second shooter.

Still no response.

He repositioned, shuffling to his right and angling his body in a way that if the second shooter tried to hit Liesel or Sofie, it would be Caspian in his line of fire, not the two women.

"Talk to me, Liesel," Caspian barked.

That's the moment the second shooter chose to reappear, but this time, he had taken a teenage boy as hostage. The teen, who was tall and thin with blond hair, didn't look a day older than fifteen. The gunman held him tightly, the muzzle of his pistol jammed against his temple.

The moment brought Caspian back to Zermatt, to that evening when Florence Aldrich had nearly been abducted. She'd been about the same age, and he had been the only one in a position to save her. He'd acted on instinct that day, not only going against everything he'd been taught at Onyx but also against the direct instructions of his handler. They'd told him to stay away, that it wasn't the mission, and that to deviate from the mission would lead to consequences that would follow him for the rest of his life.

And they had been right.

His actions in Zermatt had changed everything and exposed truths he hadn't been ready to face. But he didn't regret it. Not for a second. He had saved Florence because it had been the right thing to do.

And now, it was happening all over again.

Caspian briefly looked into the kid's eyes. The young man was trying to be brave, to hold it together, and to project some illusion of courage, but the trembling in his jaw and knees and the tightly clenched fists betrayed how he was really feeling.

Careful, Caspian. One wrong move, and this boy's dead.

"I'll let him go," the man called out. "But only once I'm out of here."

Caspian tracked the shooter with his pistol, finger on the trigger, but he didn't have a clear shot. The terrace was still in chaos with panicked patrons fleeing in every direction, knocking chairs and glasses over. Caspian couldn't afford to miss. One bad shot could mean hitting the young man or a bystander. Still, he hated the situation he found himself in. He was exposed, which made him an easy target for any other shooter out there. Every second felt like a lifetime.

But he couldn't back off. The boy needed his protection, and so did Liesel and Sofie.

Caspian had to cover them the best he could, even if it meant putting himself in the crosshairs. A blur of motion to the side drew Caspian's eye. A broad-shouldered man in his mid-forties with short-cropped hair charged the shooter, holding a steak knife as if it was a bayonet.

"Let my son go!"

The gunman, surprised, shifted his aim, moving the muzzle toward the charging father.

That was the window Caspian had been waiting for. He fired. The bullet struck just below the kidnapper's ear. The man dropped instantly, but so did the father.

Fuck! The sniper.

Any doubts Caspian still held that the sniper and the two men might not be working together evaporated. The father stirred, holding his upper left arm. The teenage boy scrambled to his father, dropping beside him. He gripped his dad's hand and tried to pull him up.

"Stay low!" Caspian shouted. "Keep your heads down!"

The boy and his dad both nodded as they sought cover behind an overturned table.

Caspian scanned the terrace, then turned and sprint-crouched toward Liesel, who was working frantically on Sofie's wound, her hands covered in her sister's blood.

"Let me see," he said, kneeling beside her.

Sofie's chest rose in shallow, jerky movements. Blood bubbled at her lips. She tried to speak.

"You . . . can't trust . . . Westcott . . . you . . ."

"Don't talk," Caspian said, holding her hand. "Keep your strength. Help is coming."

Sofie coughed, choking on blood. Then more shots echoed against the nearby building, followed by panicked shouting and police sirens. The terrace was nearly deserted now. Everyone had fled. Only the dead and the three of them remained.

Sofie's hand clenched his forearm with surprising strength.

"Listen . . . to me . . . they . . . they are . . . everywhere," she managed to say, her voice strained and broken.

Her words stunned Caspian. He knew *they* meant something. But what? He'd heard similar words not long ago.

We. Are. Everywhere.

He'd been in Tanzania then, and now he was hearing them in Mallorca. Both times he'd heard them, they'd come out of the mouth of someone who was dying.

"Who's 'they,' Sofie? Who's 'they'?"

But Sofie's eyes had already rolled back. Her hand gently slipped from his, and her face slackened. He checked her pulse. Nothing.

More gunfire. This time even closer. *Shit.*

He hadn't known Sofie, not really, but in those brief minutes he'd shared with the two sisters, he'd seen enough to understand how much Sofie mattered to Liesel. Caspian closed Sofie's eyes.

"No," Liesel cried out, then pushed Caspian aside and started compressions. "Come on, Sofie! Stay with me!"

After a few seconds, Caspian said, "She's gone, Liesel."

Liesel looked at him, panting, her eyes wild. "No. She can't be."

"We have to go. We don't know who else is coming."

Liesel's hands were trembling, and her face was pale, spattered with blood.

She's shell shocked.

Liesel lowered her head. They didn't have time to mourn, but Caspian gave Liesel the time of one breath, of one second of silence. He owed her that much.

"We can't stay, Liesel. We need to get moving."

Liesel nodded. She wiped her tears with the back of her hand, then said, "Okay."

"There's a sniper. Probably on the dock," Caspian said. "We can't exit from the terrace, and we need to stay low. Understood?"

No reply.

"Liesel! I need you to focus."

"I . . . I can't think," she murmured, looking at her dead sister. "My head's not right, Casp."

Caspian looked around him, then grabbed a tablecloth from a fallen table and laid it over Sofie.

"I've got you, okay?" Caspian said. "Just follow me."

He dragged Liesel low across the terrace, keeping below the sniper's line of fire. He entered the restaurant and headed toward the far side. Behind the bar, he spotted a service door he assumed led to the kitchen. His pistol up, he opened the door and cleared the space. It was indeed the kitchen. It was empty. He guided Liesel through, past the prep stations, and into a corridor stacked with crates of sparkling water bottles. There was a delivery door at the end. Caspian, still with his pistol in his hand, opened it a crack and peeked out.

No one.

"Let's move," he said.

They stepped into the alley, Caspian leading the way. At the T-junction, Caspian paused. He checked left. Two police vehicles were parked less than sixty feet away, their emergency lights casting harsh blue flashes across the facades of the nearby buildings. Two officers were crouched behind the passenger door of the closest car, weapons drawn. Another, clearly injured, was seated next to them, his back resting against the front tire as a fourth officer was applying pressure to his leg.

None of the officers were looking his way.

Caspian tucked his pistol inside his waistband, then turned to Liesel. Her expression was steadier now. The raw shock of her sister's death still lingered in her eyes, but Caspian could see she had pulled herself together and had regained most of her composure.

"Ready?" he asked her.

"Yeah. Let's get out of here."

CHAPTER FOURTEEN

Port de Sóller
Mallorca, Spain

Maximilian Kross stepped off the sailboat. The suppressor on his CSR had done its job. But he couldn't be sure no one had heard the faint thumps of the three subsonic rounds he had fired. Disassembled, his rifle now sat in his backpack, each of the three major components secured in its foam-cut compartment. But he kept his pistol—a Glock 19 holstered under his light jacket—within easy reach.

The firefight that had erupted across the bay between the police and Verena's second two-man team had done him a favor. The chaos had thinned the crowd, and most of the dock had emptied except for a few curious onlookers. Kross kept walking, trying to blend in with what little foot traffic remained. He replayed the engagement in his mind, frame by frame.

His first shot had been perfect. He had dropped the woman in the green blouse with a well-placed shot close to her heart. He'd followed with a second shot, this one aimed at the woman in the pink blouse, a second later.

That was the moment everything had turned to shit.

The man with the blue shirt had moved at lightning speed. He had tackled the woman out of the line of fire just as Kross had pulled the trigger. The bullet meant for her had caught another man in a white shirt instead. Kross wasn't proud of that, but he wouldn't lose sleep over it either. In his line of work, a certain number of collaterals were to be expected.

Still, he couldn't stop thinking about the man in the blue shirt. How had Blue Shirt reacted so damn fast? How had he seen it coming? There had been no muzzle flash to warn him and no sound to tip him off.

He acted on pure instinct.

Kross remembered what Verena had told him about Blue Shirt.

He neutralized two of my officers earlier today. Left them zip-tied on the beach, one of them with a sock in his mouth.

Whoever that man was, and despite his nonchalant demeanor, he was a trained operator. Of that Kross was sure.

Kross had remained in position, waiting, watching. He'd seen one of Verena's two-man teams close in. Then the lead man had dropped, shot through the chest. The second had dived to the side, only to reappear with a hostage. Kross had taken his third shot when a civilian—probably the kid's father—had charged in with a knife. Kross had aimed fast, and it hadn't been a great shot, but at least his round had nicked the man and stopped him in his tracks.

But it hadn't been enough, because at the same moment, the hostage taker had collapsed, picked off by Blue Shirt. Kross hadn't seen him fire his weapon, but who else could have killed Verena's men? That was when the first police vehicle had arrived, and instead of retreating, Verena's second two-man team had panicked and opened fire on the officers.

Bunch of fools!

Kross, who had already fired more rounds than he had wanted to, had no intention of adding cops to his list of targets. That was how you ended up dead.

Or hunted for the rest of your life.

Kross had taken a room at a small hotel in Port de Sóller earlier in the day, just in case. It had been the right call. On his way to the hotel, he ran a mini surveillance detection route, half expecting to be intercepted. Mallorca wasn't a place used to gunfire and dead bodies. The police would be crawling all over town within minutes. There would be roadblocks and plainclothes officers posted everywhere. He had to get to the hotel quickly and find a way to dispose of the rifle.

And the Glock too.

He'd have to stay in Port de Sóller for a few days at least. Until things quieted down a bit. That meant he'd probably never see Mia again.

He sighed.

Despite what he'd felt earlier when he'd taken position inside the sailboat's cabin, maybe it was time for him to call it quits. He'd had a good run. Better than most, to be honest. His numerous contracts with Blackstone Security had paid well, and though he wasn't a rich man, he had more than enough to live comfortably for the rest of his life.

No more risks. No more close calls.

Once he was confident that he hadn't picked up a tail, Kross entered the modest three-star hotel where he had booked a room. Having checked in earlier, he crossed the lobby without stopping by the reception desk. He took the stairs to the fourth floor and walked down the hall, thinking of Mia.

He'd only known her for a day or so, and while he was at least ten years her senior, she hadn't seemed to mind. He could see himself settling down with someone like her somewhere in Europe. For him, it would certainly not be the white-picket-fence version of settling down, but something close enough. He could tell that Mia was clever, intuitive, and that underneath her playful exterior there was . . . something else. And he wanted to discover what it was.

He would text her after he had updated Verena. He'd tell Mia that something had come up and that he'd be back in a few days. In the meantime, she could stay in his room if she wanted, all expenses paid.

How can she say no to an offer like that?

Kross smiled as he slid his key card into the lock, then he stepped inside his room. He shut the door, locked it, then switched on the light. A soft glow spilled from the two bedside lamps.

He froze.

Mia was sitting on the bed, one leg crossed over the other, smiling. She wore a black baseball cap pulled low; every strand of her hair was tucked neatly beneath it. A silky camisole clung to her frame, paired with fitted jeans.

She looked casual. Relaxed. And completely out of place.

"Surprised to see me?" she asked.

It wasn't her words that made his gut twist, but the suppressed pistol in her hand.

He staggered back, stunned. "What—"

But he never finished. Two bright flashes exploded in front of him.

And then nothing. Just blackness.

CHAPTER FIFTEEN

Mia Hernandez stood over the lifeless body of Maximilian Kross, who had landed face down on the floor of the hotel room, and calmly fired a security round into the back of his skull. His head jerked once.

Fifteen.

She lowered the pistol, its suppressor still warm. She relieved Kross of his room key and pocketed it. He had been a fair lover, but she'd had better. Much better, if she was to be honest. But it wasn't only Kross's performance in bed that had been disappointing. His lack of common sense and situational awareness was almost shocking. She was sure there was a time when Kross had probably been a top operator, but time caught up with everyone, didn't it? In her professional opinion, Kross had been running on faded instincts. Why else had he let her get so close to him?

Her orders had been clear. Assess and report.

This morning, after he had left the luxurious suite for what ended up being his final operation, Mia had transmitted her assessment and recommendation to Operations. They hadn't waited long to authorize the kill. She thought it was the right call. Kross was slipping. And that couldn't be allowed.

Contractual or not, Kross knew things. After the great work he'd done in Manchester, he'd become privy to operational details that couldn't be permitted to live in the memory of a man who was no longer sharp. His work had been valuable, but like any tool dulled by time, Kross had become a liability.

At least he went out with a win, she thought, hoping that one day she'd be given the same opportunity.

It was because of Kross's work that they'd finally located and neutralized the mole, hadn't they?

And . . . I let him sleep with me. Three times. How's that not a win?

Mia pulled her encrypted phone from her bag and typed.

It's done.

The response, as usual, arrived seconds later.

Very well.

Now, she needed to make a clean getaway from the crime scene she had orchestrated. She pulled a pair of latex gloves from her purse, then spent the next five minutes methodically wiping down door handles, the nightstand, the light switch, and every other surface she had touched.

When she was done, and with her gloves still on, she unlatched the window and slipped outside, lowering herself cautiously onto the narrow ledge that ran along the fourth floor. She pressed her back flat against the stone wall, holding her small backpack in her left hand. One step at a time, she inched sideways toward the window of the adjacent room, which was already cracked open.

The night was warm, and as it had been for the last few days, the sky was cloudless and the stars sharp. The town had gone mostly quiet after the gunfight at the restaurant, but now it was beginning to stir again, as if trying to convince itself everything would be okay.

Somewhere beyond the rooftops, laughter floated up, along with the occasional rev of a moped engine.

Mia reached the window, and for a moment, she paused.

It would be so easy to fall.

Or jump.

A slight lean forward and gravity would do the rest. She wondered if it would hurt.

It might. But probably not for long.

She didn't want to die; she enjoyed her work too much. The control, the adrenaline rushes, the thrill of being part of something much, much bigger than her; she loved it all.

I'm an instrument of chaos, she told herself.

Still, this urge, this flicker of temptation to let go was stronger than it had been before. It wasn't the first time she'd felt it. She'd fought it before, in Paris, where the Seine had called for her from the edge of a bridge, and in Marrakech, after a difficult performance on the piano at the hotel Oberoi. It had always been fleeting, easy to dismiss. But not tonight.

Tonight, as she stood on the ledge four stories above the street, the impulse roared louder than it ever had, rising like a tide inside her chest. It was daring her to let go, to find out if anything waited beyond the fall.

Enough!

Mia gripped the wall harder, forcing herself to concentrate on everything she still had to accomplish. She had a job to finish, and work steadied her. It always had. She gritted her teeth and refocused her footing.

Move, Mia. You can't stand here much longer. Someone will see you.

She reached for the window and opened it fully. She entered the room, which was almost identical to Kross's room.

The woman was exactly where Mia had left her. She was on her bed and unconscious from the powerful sedative Mia had given her. Mia sat her upright on the bed, then pressed the pistol she'd used to kill Kross into the woman's right hand. Mia positioned the woman's finger on the trigger, guided the suppressor to her temple, then gently squeezed the trigger.

The gun discharged, and the woman slumped sideways.

Sixteen.

Mia went through her mental checklist. Midway through it, she remembered she still had Kross's room key in her pocket. She pulled it out and slipped it into the dead woman's jeans pocket.

Voilà.

Her deception wouldn't fool a thorough police investigation, but it would buy her more than enough time to leave the island.

Mia got up from the bed and made her way to the door. From her bag, she took a snake camera and uncoiled the thin cable before connecting it to the small handheld monitor. Mia lowered herself to one knee beside the door and slid the tiny lens under the gap. The camera was infrared capable, high res, and tuned for low-light conditions. She worked the control dial with her fingers, slowly panning left and right. The hallway was empty.

She retrieved the camera, tucked it back into her bag, and opened the door. She closed it behind her, then, using the room key she'd taken from the dead woman's wallet earlier, she unlocked the door, opened it, threw the room key on the nearby bathroom counter, and closed the door again.

Satisfied that if anyone were to check the log, they'd see that the woman had used her key to enter her room at that specific time. With the hallway still free of guests or staff, Mia made her way to the service staircase, descended four floors, and exited the hotel by the rear service entrance.

Outside, like she'd seen while on the ledge, Port de Sóller was coming back to life. The people were trickling back out, and the terraces were filling again. Two blocks away from the hotel, she reached the bicycle she'd locked to a bike stand hours earlier. She had just undone the chain when her phone vibrated.

Operations.

We know you have a concert in Budapest in three days, but we have an immediate tasking for you. Details are in your inbox. Let us know by 11pm if you can do it. Another asset can be on location in two hours if necessary.

Mia smiled. Operations had given her a new assignment. She swung onto the saddle and started pedaling. The urge to jump she'd felt on the ledge was gone, replaced by something sharper, something familiar. Purpose.

CHAPTER SIXTEEN

One Mile South of Cabrera Island
Mallorca, Spain

Verena Kaine stared at the frozen drone footage, her thumb trembling slightly over the playback control. She rewound the feed for the sixth time. Not because she needed to—she already knew what she'd seen—but because something in her brain demanded it.

Six is a clean number. A safe number. Five isn't.

She hit play again. *There.* Just a blur of movement on the edge of the screen. A figure, balanced on a ledge between two windows on the fourth floor of Kross's hotel, was standing there, perfectly still, as if carved from the night itself. Verena paused the frame. The resolution was poor, distorted from the drone's speed and the low-light condition it operated in, but there was no mistaking it. The figure was a woman.

Verena leaned closer, analyzing the image again. The ledge appeared to be narrow, no larger than six inches.

Who would be crazy enough to just stand there?

She wished she could send one of the drones back for another pass, but that wasn't an option anymore. All three units were on an automated exit trajectory, heading two miles offshore and self-destructing in less than thirty seconds. A miniature explosive charge set next to the battery would ensure the midair disintegration of the drones. Their carbon fiber carcasses would scatter into the ocean like spent ash. As it rushed toward the Mediterranean, one of the drones had briefly flown over Kross's hotel. That's how she'd seen the woman.

Verena dialed Kross's number again, the third time in two minutes. Like the two previous attempts, her call was unanswered.

"Damn it!" she shouted, tossing her phone across the flybridge.

The phone sailed over the dining table and bounced off the stainless-steel barbecue before skidding to a stop near the bar fridge. Verena clenched her jaw, resisting the urge to retrieve the phone right away. She could feel the disarray prickling at her skin. She wiped an invisible smear from the edge of her laptop with her sleeve. She hated mess, hated disorder.

She closed her eyes and thought about Oscar and Pam and the two other officers who'd lost their lives. All had happened in less than sixty minutes. Twenty-five percent of her European team was gone. Evaporated.

And now Kross is off comms.

Damn it! We should have been halfway to Valencia by now.

She stood and walked to the railing, her boots clicking against the teak deck of the flybridge. *Veloce* bobbed gently at anchor, and all around it the sea was dark and glassy, the moonlight catching the faint swell. Verena's gaze drifted to the north, toward Cabrera Island, which loomed about one mile out like a sleeping beast.

The day had started so well, with Hobb being snatched cleanly off the streets of Port de Sóller. Everything had turned to shit when Pam and Oscar had been surprised by a lone operator on the beach. Verena shook her head. Pam and Oscar hadn't been rookies. In the last three years, they'd pulled off some complex operations. But today at the beach, they'd gone down like amateurs, taken out by the same man who'd been seated at the restaurant with Sofie Bergmann, Hobb's contact. And now, that same man had managed to take out two more of her officers on the terrace. Pam and Oscar had been about to engage when the police had arrived. Verena, her eyes glued to the live feed, had seen Pam fire at the police. That had been a fatal mistake. Seconds later, she'd been gunned down along with Oscar, caught in the open between the restaurant and the police cars.

The only good news in all of this was that Sofie Bergmann—the fucking mole they'd been after for months—had been dealt with permanently. Kross had seen to that.

Now what?

You have to call him.

Verena reached for the black phone in her pocket, her fingertips brushing the matte surface. She'd never reported a failure before. She'd had setbacks, yes, but a complete disaster like this? This was a first.

Her stomach turned.

Verena adjusted her ponytail, then straightened the files on the chart table even though they didn't need straightening. Thinking about what she'd say to her employer, she tapped her fingers on the edge of the table once, twice, three times.

You can't lie to him. He'll find out everything anyway. He always does.

Her only path forward was to be honest and hope—not beg—for forgiveness.

She began to dial, her mind going back to the woman standing on the ledge of Kross's hotel. Was she even a player? Was it possible she was simply trying to escape her violent husband or a dangerous lover she'd picked up in a bar?

No . . . she's involved. It's not a coincidence. She's the reason why Kross hasn't picked up my calls.

Then whose team was she on? Was she with the man who'd taken out her officers? Had she been to Kross's hotel to kill him? To interrogate him? If so, who had sent her? And why?

Then a thought crossed her mind, and she froze.

Am I her next target?

CHAPTER SEVENTEEN

Through a narrow gap in the curtains, Caspian stood by the window, watching the quiet street two stories below. The studio apartment he and Liesel had found refuge in was tucked inside a nondescript residential building. With only a small LED night-light near the kitchenette offering illumination, it was mostly dark inside the apartment, but it was enough. Caspian didn't want to silhouette himself.

The apartment was located in a sleepy corner of Palma between rows of aging buildings with wrought-iron balconies. It was the kind of street that didn't see much foot traffic even during the day, and now that night had fallen, the neighborhood was practically deserted. Across the street, a small family restaurant had gone dark thirty minutes ago. Caspian had watched as the last employee had stacked the terrace chairs on the tables and rolled up the awning.

Samantha Ranger had booked the apartment through an offshore shell company run by the Strategic Support Unit. The building had no front desk, no doorman, and access to its minuscule lobby required a key or a five-digit code. There was one tiny elevator, but it was out of service. Caspian had deadbolted the front door of the apartment the moment they'd walked in. Apart from a two-story jump from the Juliet balcony, the apartment had no secondary exit. Still, Caspian believed he and Liesel were under no immediate threat. They were safe. For now.

Behind Caspian, the room was quiet. Liesel sat slouched on a gray couch. Her body was heavy with fatigue, and she looked at him with hollow eyes.

He'd seen that look many times before, and more recently on Florence Aldrich when she'd realized her dad was dead. He knew the emotions Liesel was going through.

Loss. Shock. And heartbreak.

Caspian felt he needed to say something to break the silence.

"Ranger's digging into it, you know? The Azimut yacht, Paul Hobb, Hearts United. All of it."

Liesel shook her head.

"I'm not holding my breath," she said. "Hearts United has been investigated before. Nothing ever sticks."

"Maybe that's because there's nothing to stick," he replied.

"My sister wouldn't lie."

"I'm not saying she did, but Hearts United? I mean . . . Everett Westcott is a highly respected philanthropist. He's—"

"Did you ever meet him? In person?" Liesel interrupted.

"I haven't, but my—"

"You haven't? So, you'll agree with me that it's possible it's all smoke and mirrors, right?"

Caspian didn't think it was. "Sure. It could be, but what I was going to say is that, even though I've never met the guy, Nelson has."

Nelson Anderson, Caspian's brother, was an emergency room physician who had joined Doctors Without Borders more than a decade ago. He was now the organization's medical director in Kenya. The fact that Nelson had met Westcott seemed to take Liesel by surprise, but only for a second. "So what?" she asked.

Clearly, Liesel wasn't ready to let go just yet.

"Nelson spoke highly of Westcott. And as you know, my brother isn't someone to throw around compliments if they aren't warranted."

"What did Westcott do to impress him so damn much?"

"Why don't you ask him yourself at the end of next week?" Caspian said.

"Next week?"

"We're all meeting at my parent's place to celebrate my mom's birthday, remember?"

"Of course," Liesel said quickly, though it was obvious that, with everything going on, it had slipped her mind. "But why don't you tell me now?"

"Hearts United financed Nelson's new project in Kenya," Caspian said. "Entirely."

"Doesn't mean he isn't crooked," Liesel said.

"Right. But I think you need to—"

"What?" she snapped back. "What do you think I need to do? Say it."

Caspian paused, aware that he had to choose his next words carefully. But there was no point in sugarcoating them too much either.

"I think it's possible the Sofie we saw tonight wasn't the same woman you once knew. She let you believe she was dead, for God's sake. Who does that to her sister?"

Liesel blinked at him. "What are you saying?"

"She disappeared for years, only to resurface in Kenya. She admitted to us she took out one of Dolores Araujo's bodyguards."

"Yes. To protect me!"

"I don't disagree," Caspian said gently. "There's no doubt in my mind Sofie loved you very much. What I'm saying is that logistics officers aren't trained to take out bodyguards. And there's the fact that Sofie had access to intel about you very, very few people had."

Though there wasn't much light in the room, Caspian could see that Liesel's eyes were brimming with tears.

"I know," she whispered. "I . . . I just don't know what to think anymore. I feel . . . lost . . . betrayed. And so damn stupid."

Caspian crossed the room, sat next to her, and wrapped his arms around her. For a beat, she resisted, but then she melted into him, clutching his shirt.

"So, what now?" she asked moments later, her voice muffled against his chest.

"Now? Now we sleep. We're safe here. At least for tonight."

Liesel took a long breath, then said, "I need a hot shower first."

Caspian watched her walk toward the bathroom. Once she had closed the door behind her, he returned to the window. He scanned the parked cars, looking for anything remotely suspicious, but none of them had moved since he'd arrived.

His phone chirped. It was Ranger.

"How's Liesel?" she asked.

"Holding together," Caspian said. "She'll be fine."

"We think we found the Azimut," Ranger said.

Caspian cocked his head to one side, his curiosity piqued. "Where?"

"Anchored about a nautical mile south of Cabrera Island."

Cabrera was a small rugged island that was part of a national park roughly twenty-five miles south of Palma. It was known for its steep cliffs and crystal-clear coves. The island was largely undeveloped and uninhabited, which made it the perfect spot to lie low or stash someone you didn't want found. But it was a popular boating destination, so the Azimut wouldn't have gone unnoticed forever, but it had likely bought whoever was on board some time to deal with Hobb.

"Do you want us to go check it out?" Caspian asked.

"It's not that I don't want you to, but I can't get you transportation until morning. Every charter operation in Mallorca is closed."

"If Hobb's still aboard—"

"Then time is of the essence," Ranger said, finishing his thought. "That's why we've sent a discreet back-channel alert to the Policía Nacional. We didn't give them too many details, it would raise too many questions, but the message was urgent enough that I'm confident they'll get eyes on the yacht shortly."

Caspian agreed it was the right move. "If Hobb's alive, the local authorities are indeed his best shot," he said.

"They are."

"So . . . I guess you want us out of here?"

"I do. But I need a bit more time to make sure you and Liesel aren't compromised," Ranger said. "So far, your pictures haven't popped up anywhere, but that doesn't mean the authorities haven't circulated them internally. Getting out of Mallorca on a commercial flight is too dangerous at the moment. It would be a different story if I could get my hands on an air asset, but right now none are available."

"What do you want us to do?"

"Get some rest while we continue to monitor the situation. I'll check in with you again in the morning."

"Understood. What about Westcott?" Caspian asked before Ranger could end the call. "Did you find anything?"

"No, but what did you expect? We just started working on this. The man has powerful friends and a halo around him the size of a solar flare. If we poke too hard, too fast, we'll draw attention."

"We need to get our hands on Hobb. He knows something. Something that may have concerned Westcott," he said.

"Careful, Caspian," Ranger warned him. "Ask anyone in the street what they think of Westcott, and they'll all tell you the same thing. Everett Westcott is a stand-up guy that put his money where his mouth is. Heck, I would have told you that, too, three hours ago."

"Liesel's sister was convinced otherwise."

"Maybe. But the good that man has done is undeniable. Even you have to admit that," Ranger said.

"Well, Hobb could clarify all of it. But someone got to him," Caspian said.

"I'll keep working back channels, of course. And if tonight's operation near Cabrera Island bears fruit, I might get a shot at seeing the reports, but no promises."

"That's not good enough."

"Then give me something better," Ranger snapped. "Because if Sofie was right, and Everett Westcott isn't the demigod people think he is, there could be trouble. You have no idea how much reach Westcott has."

Well, I'm starting to, Caspian thought.

Behind him, Caspian heard the bathroom door open. Liesel stepped out, steam curling around her in the dim light. She wore a white towel wrapped snug around her.

"Did you hear what I said?" Ranger asked.

"Yeah," Caspian said absently.

"Get some sleep. I'll contact you tomorrow morning," Ranger said, then ended the call.

Liesel crossed the room slowly. Her gaze was clearer now. Tired, yes, but steady. There was something raw about her posture, something vulnerable and unguarded, but also unmistakably strong. And it was intoxicating.

My God, she's beautiful.

"Ranger?" Liesel asked.

He nodded.

"Do we need to leave, or do we have until tomorrow?"

"Tomorrow."

She dropped the towel and pressed her body to his.

"I need you right now," she whispered, reaching for his belt.

Once they were both naked, she leaned into him, her forehead resting lightly against his chin. For a moment neither of them moved. Exposed in every sense, Caspian felt his heart pounding in his chest. But this time, it wasn't from the adrenaline but from the sheer weight of the emotions going through him. Here he was, standing skin to skin with the woman he loved, having escaped death once again. How many more times would they have to do that? At some point, their luck would run out.

He felt a slight tremor ripple through Liesel's body, and he lifted her in his arms, carrying her to the bed without a word.

Later, as he lay there with her beside him, her breath warm against his shoulder, Caspian couldn't shake the feeling that death was closing in on them. For once, he hadn't been the instigator of what had happened. This time, trouble had found him. But that didn't bring him any comfort. He knew the risks of the job. So did Liesel. They had both accepted that long ago. But here, in Mallorca? On what was supposed to be a break from it all?

Caspian closed his eyes. *Will it ever stop?*

Of course it wouldn't. Not unless he made some drastic changes. And even then . . . would Ranger ever really let him go? Would she allow someone like him to walk away? With everything he knew, everything he'd done? He doubted it. They didn't let operators like him fade into civilian life.

At least not without strings attached.

He thought of his parents, Elizabeth and Richard. Their love for each other had weathered time, and Caspian had always admired them for it. And now, not for the first time, he realized he truly wanted that too.

With Liesel.

Was that too much to ask? That was a question he didn't have an answer to. And then his phone vibrated. It was Ranger.

"Yeah?"

"Two things. Number one, I just heard back from my team in the field. Florence is fine. But in an abundance of caution, someone will be keeping an eye on her until we know what's going on."

At last, some good news, he thought. "And number two?" he asked.

"You and Liesel need to leave the island. You have two hours to get ready."

"Okay . . . what changed?" he asked.

"An air asset has become available, but I only have a short window to divert it to Palma. It's presently in Madrid. I'm having someone from the Madrid office prepare documents for you and Liesel. I can have the plane at PMI's private terminal in two hours, but it has a schedule to keep. It's on a priority flight to Algiers to pick up a high-value target.

The plane won't stay on the ground for more than fifteen minutes. Understood?"

Caspian looked at Liesel, who was still sleeping soundly.

A high-value target. Well . . . that explains why a plane has suddenly become available.

"Understood," Caspian said. "We'll be there."

CHAPTER EIGHTEEN

Estación Naval de Porto Pí
Palma, Mallorca

Mia Hernandez didn't touch the brakes of her moped as she cruised past the open gate of the Estación Naval de Porto Pí. A single uniformed guard stood near the yellow security booth. Mia was aware there might be more guards inside, but if the earlier shoot-out in Port de Sóller had raised any alarms, it wasn't visible from the street.

The naval station, which sat quietly off Carretera Dic de l'Oest, was delimited by an eight-foot see-through iron fence. From the street, Mia saw several low, functional sand-colored buildings with weatherworn facades. Farther east she could see the Porto Pí lighthouse—one of the oldest operating lighthouses in the world—standing watch over the bay, its forty-one-meter-high tower casting a long silhouette against the clear night sky.

Not many of those lighthouses left. And that's too bad.

She'd always found that there was something noble about lighthouses. They stood firm at the edge of the world, helping others find their way.

Just like the Fisherman once did for me.

She continued south, then veered left onto Castell de Sant Carles, coasting down the slope toward the parking lot outside the Museu Històric Militar. The lot was deserted, and Mia backed the moped into a space near a squat pine. She killed the engine and took off her helmet.

She took her small backpack out of the storage box attached to the back of the scooter, then stashed her helmet in the compartment beneath the seat. She uncapped a bottle of water, swallowed two amphetamine tablets, then chased them down with a long drink.

She powered her encrypted phone, then read through the mission brief Operations had sent her one more time. When she had committed all the information to memory, she deleted the file and made her way back to the main road. Underneath her clothes—which consisted of a pair of black jeans, a black long-sleeved hoodie, and a pair of dark hiking shoes—she wore a thin 3/2 mm wet suit. The night was warm, so the wet suit made her extra sweaty and uncomfortable, but if things went sideways and she ended up in the harbor's black water, she'd be glad for it.

———

Water . . . Mia had been forged in it.

She often thought about the night her family's migrant boat had capsized off the northern coast of Venezuela almost two decades ago. She'd been eight years old, clutching her little brother's hand as a towering wave flipped their overloaded vessel like it was nothing. One moment she was screaming, the next, she was underwater, her arms thrashing in the darkness, her legs kicking blindly as tiny air bubbles raced past her face before disappearing into the void. All she could hear was the distorted roar of the ocean in her ears. She twisted, turning in the water, trying to find the surface.

Trying to find *him*. Her brother.

She tried to call out his name, but every time she did, water rushed into her mouth, choking her. Panic bloomed in her chest, threatening to paralyze her, but she clamped her lips shut and forced herself to push upward. But the ocean didn't want to let her go. Still, she kicked and clawed her way back to the overturned hull of the boat, her fingers slipping twice before finally finding purchase on the slick fiberglass. Coughing and shivering, she pulled herself halfway out of the water.

Her brother never made it back to the boat. And neither did her parents.

Twelve hours later, sunburned, shaking, and barely conscious, she was about to let herself sink beneath the water when she was pulled from the sea by an American fisherman off the coast of Aruba. The Fisherman's boat was white and black and gigantic, larger than anything she'd ever imagined. To Mia, it looked more like a floating city than a vessel. Her rescuer, who was in his forties then, had strong, weathered hands, but he had the kindest eyes she'd ever seen. He wrapped her in thick, impossibly soft towels and carried her below deck to the medical bay, where a nurse tended to her wounds. Later, she was escorted to a small dining room, where she ate a simple but so delicious meal of rice, beans, and fresh-caught fish, and a warm slice of something sweet she couldn't name at the time but later learned was apple pie.

The next morning, she woke up in the most comfortable bed she'd ever slept in. A breakfast tray had been left on a table beside her bed. She devoured the scrambled eggs, the slices of papaya, and the two golden toasts—with real butter—the chef prepared for her. There was a folded napkin with a note tucked beneath it:

Descansa todo lo que necesites. Ya estás a salvo, Sirenita.

Rest as long as you need. You're safe now, little mermaid.

It was then, in the quiet of her spacious stateroom, that she'd truly understood that she owed the Fisherman her life. And she'd made a promise to herself. She wouldn't just survive, she would live, and she would dedicate that life to something greater. She would pledge her life to the man who had saved her, *the Fisherman*, and to the greater good he embodied. So even though she was aware that tonight's operation was risky, she knew she'd pull through.

Because I have to. Because there's still so much to do.

———

Mia turned north onto Carretera Dic de l'Oest. The sidewalk was lined with tall trees planted every sixty feet. Each tree created a pocket of darkness along the fence. Mia slowed her pace as she neared the section of the fence she'd chosen earlier during her drive-by. That section was one of the few stretches without barbed wire at the top. A nearby tree provided the necessary shadow, and a line of thick, overgrown bushes on the other side of the fence would make for great concealment once she got over.

She glanced over her shoulder. There were no pedestrians, no headlights.

As she reached the spot she'd selected, she stepped up to the fence, planted her right foot on the fence's midsection, and with a tight burst of speed, pushed with her left leg. Her hands latched onto the horizontal rung, and she used her legs to push higher. She positioned one foot over the top rung and brought her torso above the fence line. She then swung her left leg over, pivoted sideways, and dropped down, absorbing the impact with bent knees. Staying low, she dashed to the nearest tree and dropped to her stomach.

From there, she could see the patrol boat she'd been ordered to board docked to the north of the base, parallel to Avenida Gabriel Roca. She noticed some lights were on in a few buildings, but she didn't spot any movement. She waited two full minutes to confirm nobody had been alerted by her presence and was trying to sneak up on her, then she moved. She sprinted fifty yards across open space until she pressed her back against the western wall of a yellow two-story building.

She was still catching her breath when the door of the building creaked open and two uniformed Guardia Civil officers stepped out. One was tall and thin, and he had a sharp nose and a buzzed haircut. His uniform hung a little loose on his frame. The other officer was shorter but thicker, with a solid neck and a broad chest. He had a round face and a short beard. The smaller man pulled out a crumpled pack of cigarettes and offered one to his colleague, who nodded his thanks. They lit up.

Mia didn't move. But she did curse her bad luck.

She knew that the average time to smoke a cigarette was five minutes. If the two officers lingered longer than that, she'd have no choice but to strike. She had no doubt she could kill them both, but silently? She wasn't so sure about that.

The two men were speaking Spanish, and Mia picked up fragments of their conversation. Apparently, the men's teammates were prepping for a mission, syncing comms, and heading to the armory to draw weapons.

C'mon guys . . . go back inside.

The two officers had been out for just under five minutes when the tallest finally excused himself and went back inside. The other wished him good night and pulled out his phone. He began scrolling, the glow of his phone lighting up his face. Then, with a muttered sigh, he lit another cigarette.

Mia grimaced. That was it. She couldn't wait any longer.

She reached slowly into the waistband of her jeans and drew her knife. The serrated blade was five inches long and made of blacked-out steel. Mia moved silently while scanning her surroundings, making sure she wasn't about to be surprised by another one of the man's colleagues.

They were alone.

The Guardia Civil officer, totally engrossed by whatever was on his phone, didn't register her presence until she kicked him hard behind his left knee. As he buckled, Mia clamped her left hand over his mouth and drove the tip of her knife deep into his neck. The man dropped his phone, his body twisting in surprise. But despite the knife in his neck and the kick to his knee, he didn't fall. Instead, he backpedaled desperately until he slammed Mia into the wall. The impact knocked the air out of her lungs. Even worse, something hard inside her backpack—most probably her flashlight—jabbed sharply into her spine, momentarily paralyzing her.

Before she could react, the officer swung his right arm back and grabbed her hair with his hand. He then bent forward, and Mia felt herself tumble over his back. She hit the ground on her shoulder but rolled with it, letting the momentum carry her into a crouch. By the time she was on her feet, the man had dropped to his knees, blood gushing from his throat, his eyes distant and confused. Mia approached him, and his mouth opened in a silent gasp.

Mia yanked the knife free and stabbed him in the heart.

Seventeen.

She wiped the blade on the dead officer's shirt, then returned the knife to its sheath.

Now comes the hard part, she thought as she grabbed the man by the wrists and dragged his deadweight behind a parked transport truck. The man was heavy, and her hiking shoes scraped against the gravel as she pulled him with gritted teeth. By the time she had him tucked out of sight between the vehicle and the building, her back and shoulders were burning.

She took a moment to collect her thoughts, then glanced at her watch. She was behind schedule. It was time to move.

She walked alongside the building, making her way toward its easternmost corner. The far side of the building opened into a service yard. Fifty feet to her right, mechanics worked beneath a set of harsh lights. A garage door was wide open, and Mia could hear tools clanging from inside. The start of the quay where the Rodman-55 was docked was twenty feet in front of her. The boat was another twenty feet farther away.

Twenty feet of open ground followed by twenty feet of partial concealment. I can do this.

Now the question was, should she run and risk attracting attention, or should she move slowly, which meant she'd stay in the open for a few seconds more? She looked in the direction of the workers. None of them were looking her way. The high-speed patrol boat was waiting for her, no lights on board and no crew. But that would change soon.

Mia darted from cover and sprinted. She only stopped running once she reached the stern of the Rodman-55. The boat's hull was sleek, painted white and blue with a yellow-and-red stripe. She climbed aboard, ducked into the shadows, and swung her backpack forward.

She grabbed her pistol, attached the suppressor, and inserted a full magazine. She racked the slide, chambering a round. Then she waited, listening for anyone approaching.

Satisfied no one was about to board the vessel, she approached the cabin. She had come prepared with a lockpick gun in her backpack, but the cabin door wasn't locked. She slid the heavy door open and entered the cabin. She was immediately hit by a sharp smell, a combination of diesel fumes, marine-grade oil, and the musty odor of something that had been stowed wet before being fully dried.

The patrol boat's interior was bare bones but functional. There were five forward-facing shock-mitigating seats, a chart table, and a rack of communication equipment. There were also two flat screens next to the helm station. Mia assumed they were for the radar and the FLIR.

She moved forward, opened another door, and descended two steps into the sleeping quarters. There were two low berths with thin mattresses, each with a blanket and a rolled-up sleeping bag at its head. There was a galley on the port side with a microwave, a mini fridge, and a small sink. Opposite the galley was the lone marine head of the boat. It was cramped, with a metal toilet, a sink, and a handheld showerhead mounted on the wall above the toilet. There was no luxury here, just a space built to allow the boat's crew to crash between shifts.

There weren't many hiding places, but she had done her homework. She lifted the starboard berth. Underneath it was a storage compartment where rolled-up tarps and canvas bags were stuffed, their fabric still damp. She pushed them aside, cramming them into a corner. The compartment was hollow, made even more cramped due to the presence of the tarps and bags, but she wasn't a big woman. She'd fit. She climbed into the storage cavity and pulled the lid down over herself. Darkness swallowed her and the air quickly turned heavy and sour, thick with the trapped smell of the wet canvas. There was no light, no air movement, and the only sounds were the steady thumps of her own heartbeat and the faint creak of the hull settling in the water. The space was too small to breathe properly, but she'd suffered through worse.

Mia adjusted the position of her suppressed pistol across her chest and lay still, knees drawn up, one shoulder pressed against the fiberglass hull at the bottom of the compartment. The space was barely long enough for her to stretch out if she turned sideways, but it was okay.

She didn't need to be comfortable.

The life she'd been given after the wreck; that had been comfortable. *More than comfortable,* she corrected herself.

Thanks to the Fisherman, she'd been granted a future, a new identity, and more importantly, a purpose. He had enrolled her in a private school in Florida, where she had learned English. Music lessons had followed.

"You have a gift," he had told her after listening to her first piano recital.

And it was true. She'd gone on to become a world-class pianist before she'd turned twenty-five. There were articles about her, and even radio and TV interviews one could find online if one knew where to look, but she wasn't famous by any stretch of the imagination.

And this was on purpose. With her talent, the spotlight could be hers anytime she wanted it. But she didn't want it. She liked the piano, loved it, even, but the stage never stirred her the way an operation did. A Steinway couldn't make her pulse quicken like a gun could.

She knew she wasn't the only one working for the Fisherman. He had hinted once, and only once, at the breadth of his reach.

"There are more like you, Mia. Some are working in labs, some on trading floors, some sitting on the bench in federal courts. Some are teachers, chefs, professional athletes. Some are spies. We are everywhere, Mia. Everywhere. And together, we will make the world a better place."

There had been only one operation in which Mia had worked with another operator. It had been in Aruba, when she'd killed the two shitbags who'd been stealing from their countrymen. She wondered if their bodies were ever found or if the sharks had gotten to them first.

Mia kept a private tally of her kills. She didn't do it because she carried guilt, as guilt was for the weak and the unfocused, but because her mentor had drilled it into her from the start.

Never deceive yourself with pretty ideas, Mia, he'd once told her. *You must quantify your impact, or it doesn't exist. Count them. Own them. That's how you know you're shaping the world, not just surviving it.*

Each number in her ledger was proof.

Proof that she was still fulfilling the purpose he'd given her.

Proof that she was still worthy of having been saved while so many others had drowned.

A gentle shift in the boat's hull pulled her back to the present. Then she heard heavy steps thudding onto the deck above her. Mia's finger settled gently beside the trigger.

The wait was almost over.

CHAPTER NINETEEN

One Mile South of Cabrera Island
Mallorca, Spain

Verena glanced at her watch. Again. Twenty-four seconds had passed since the last time she'd checked. She resisted the urge to adjust the bezel. She'd already done it twice. Once more would make it three. She didn't like the number three.

She pressed her hands to the sides of her thighs to stop them from fidgeting. How much longer would she have to wait? It had been almost four hours since her call with her employer. Four hours since he'd barked at her to stay put, to stay on the yacht, and to await further instructions. He hadn't given her any clarification. Just to shut up and wait.

That's what he'd told her. *Shut up.*

Never in five years had her employer spoken to her that way, with such venom. But then, she'd never fucked up this bad before, had she? But tonight . . . tonight had unraveled.

She'd lost four officers. That represented a full quarter of her European personnel. And Kross, her most valuable asset, was still in the wind. The best-case scenario was that he'd been compromised. The worst . . . she shook her head, thinking of the woman she'd spotted on the ledge.

Verena paced the flybridge, counting her steps. Twelve paces from the upper helm station to the stern rail. Twelve back.

Twenty-four total.

She repeated the loop, then forced herself to stop on the fourth pass. Four was a clean number, safer than five. Grabbing the rails, she stared north toward the black silhouette of Cabrera Island. The Faro de Punta de n'Ensiola lighthouse blinked in the distance, its pattern perfectly measured. Every five seconds there was a crisp white pulse that Verena found hypnotic.

Same length. Same space between. No variation. Per-fec-tion.

Apart from her, there were only four people left on *Veloce*. The skipper, Justin Burton, was manning the helm and the comms. The chef was asleep in his cabin, and Bernard, the only security officer she had left, was in the engine room guarding a sedated Paul Hobb.

Hobb . . . he's a problem I should have dealt with when I had the chance.

She had kept him alive solely because her employer had rescinded his own directive. This was a contradiction that had shaken her more than she was willing to admit, especially when she added this to the fact that when she'd reported the woman outside Kross's hotel room, her employer hadn't even acknowledged it.

Verena looked at her watch and cursed. *We should have left hours ago.*

If they had done so, they would be in international waters by now, well beyond the reach of the local authorities. Instead, they were exposed and waiting for what felt increasingly like a setup. She'd instructed Burton to disable the AIS—Automatic Identification System—that transmitted the yacht's identity, position, and speed to nearby vessels and coastal authorities. By turning it off, the *Veloce* was invisible to commercial and civilian maritime traffic, but anyone looking for them with intention—like the Guardia Civil or the Spanish Navy—would find them. Turning off the AIS bought them time; it didn't guarantee them immunity.

"Ma'am." Justin Burton's voice came in through her earpiece. "I've got a contact approaching. It just popped up on radar. It's coming around the cape near the lighthouse. It's moving fast. Could be a Rodman-55 from the Guardia Civil."

Verena squeezed the railing harder. "How long until they're on us?" she asked.

"Two minutes. Three tops. What are your orders?"

Running was pointless. She knew that. The *Veloce*, despite its sleek design, would top out at thirty-four knots. If the incoming vessel was indeed a patrol boat, it would overtake the Azimut within minutes, even if she ordered Burton to start the engines and punch the throttles. Worse, fleeing would draw even more scrutiny.

Better to stay and to appear cooperative.

"There's not much we can do," Verena said. "If they want to board, we'll let them. Make sure all the paperwork is in order, Justin. I'll meet you on the main deck."

"Yes, ma'am."

"And Justin, keep your firearm handy."

There was a beat of hesitation, then Burton said, "Verena, I'm not getting into a firefight with the Guardia Civil."

Verena made a face. What was her skipper thinking? Did he expect her to simply surrender to the authorities? With that damn reporter in the engine room?

He's getting cold feet.

She would have to keep an eye on him.

"Neither am I," she lied. "But what if it's not the Guardia Civil?"

There was another pause. "Understood. I'll meet you on the main deck."

Verena reached into her pocket, retrieved her compact encrypted radio, and turned the dial to the frequency she shared with her security team.

"Come in, Bernard," she said.

"I'm here," the security officer replied.

"We've got a contact approaching fast. Could be the Guardia Civil, or something else. I'm not sure. In any case, stay with Hobb. If they come aboard, Justin and I will try to appease them. But if things go sideways . . . we might have to go to plan B."

Bernard grunted. "And . . . what's plan B exactly?"

Verena looked once more at the lighthouse, the beautiful, tireless blinking rhythm soothing her.

"We fight our way out," she replied.

"Understood. I'll be ready," Bernard replied.

She descended to the main deck and thought she could hear the high-pitched whine of marine turbines grow louder. She hesitated. Then pulled out her phone. Though this was the last thing she wanted to do, she had to let her employer know what was about to happen. For the second time that night, she dialed his number.

It didn't even ring. An automated voice answered, "This number is no longer in service."

Her blood ran cold.

"Fuck me," she whispered.

CHAPTER TWENTY

One Mile South of Cabrera Island
Mallorca, Spain

Mia Hernandez had forgotten just how punishing fifty knots on open water could be. The crew of the Rodman-55 had talked casually about the forecast before leaving the naval station in Palma.

"Seas aren't glass tonight, but nothing over two or three feet," one had said. "We won't run wide open, but we'll still be on target in under thirty-five minutes."

Two or three feet. Right.

To Mia, folded up in the cramped, fiberglass-lined storage cavity beneath the starboard berth, it felt like being trapped inside a steel drum rolling down a cliff. Her body had been slammed into the hard corners with every rise and crash of the patrol boat's hull. Now her elbows throbbed, and her shoulders felt like someone had taken a baseball bat to them. Her head had knocked against the ceiling of the storage cavity more than once. She was dehydrated, soaked with sweat, and nauseated from the motion and the stifling heat inside the wet suit. The neoprene clung to her skin like freaking shrink-wrap. She'd drained her water bottle fifteen minutes into the ride, or at least tried to. A third of it had ended up splashed on her face, her chest, and onto the floor. The rest had barely made it into her mouth. The patrol boat's lurching turns and sudden drops had made drinking a test of precision, a test she'd miserably failed.

The entire trip was about control. Control over her discomfort. Control over the creeping claustrophobia. Control over her anxiety of passing out in her hiding place only to be found and shot by a crew member. Control over the fear of failing her mission.

A sudden wave lifted the hull and dropped it hard, the motion sending her head against the bottom of her hiding space. She cursed out loud, then froze, realizing her mistake. After a few seconds, she relaxed, confident the whine of the powerful engines had covered her shout.

Mia closed her eyes, breathing the stale, musky air through her mouth, forcing herself to focus and to forget how uncomfortable she was. She let her mind take her back to Egypt, to the brutal fourteen months she'd spent training under a cadre of former Unit 777 operators.

Unit 777, which was part of the El-Sa'ka Force of the Egyptian army, specialized in irregular warfare, manhunts, and hostage rescue. The curriculum of Mia's all-women class, supposedly tailored to the specific needs of the people paying for their training, had nothing delicate about it. Sixteen women had started, but only nine had finished. Mia had never seen the others again, and she rarely thought about them, to be honest. What had stayed with her wasn't the camaraderie; it was the hardness that the training had instilled in her. That fourteen months of hell had rewired her thinking. She'd learned that pain was information, and that exhaustion was a test. The instructors had shown her no mercy, and they'd taught her to never expect it from anyone. She'd learned to strike without hesitation and to suffer without complaint. But even more valuable, she had come to understand and to believe that she could endure almost anything. And that belief, more than any weapon or tactic, was her most reliable asset.

A drop in pitch coming from the engines brought Mia back to the here and now. She felt the hull level, and a moment later, the forward motion became a crawl rather than a sprint.

Finally.

The crew on the deck was moving with purpose now, and Mia heard the unmistakable sound of a shotgun being racked.

In her mind's eye, Mia pictured the scene above her: the patrol boat drifting into position alongside the *Veloce*. One crew member would stay behind the helm, hand on the throttle, just in case. The others would board the *Veloce*. She wasn't sure how many they were. Four? Five? It didn't really matter. Timing would be everything. She had to time herself perfectly.

Mia felt the jolt of hull meeting hull despite the fenders absorbing some of the impact. There were more voices now, louder too. She closed her eyes again.

Operations counts on you. Do your job.

While it was true Operations handled her, it wasn't for him that Mia killed. No, she was doing it for the Fisherman, Everett Westcott. She wanted to make *him* proud. She didn't give two shits about Operations.

Her hand tightened around the grip of her pistol. It was time.

CHAPTER TWENTY-ONE

One Mile South of Cabrera Island
Mallorca, Spain

Verena's heart was beating so fast she thought it might punch through her sternum. The Rodman-55's powerful spotlight had snapped on a few seconds earlier, and now its beam was pinned on her. She raised an arm to shield her eyes from the cone of blinding white light, but it didn't dull the sting.

A voice barked commands in rapid-fire Spanish through a bullhorn.

"This is the Guardia Civil. We will be boarding your vessel. Keep your hands where we can see them."

Any remaining hope that Verena had that this might have been a regular maritime inspection vanished. Though she spoke Spanish fluently, she decided she wasn't about to reveal that fact to the boarding party.

Twenty seconds later, the hull of the patrol boat nudged against the Azimut's.

Verena scowled and shouted in English over the engine noise. "Careful there! Any damage will come out of your pocket!"

Moments later, four figures stepped aboard—three men and one woman—all in Guardia Civil uniforms. They wore dark green coveralls, black bulletproof vests, ball caps, and bright orange personal flotation devices. The woman carried a shotgun, and one of the men held a compact submachine gun. The other two had holstered sidearms.

No one was pointing a weapon at her yet, so she took that as a small victory.

"Can you turn this away from me?" Verena asked in English, motioning toward the spotlight. "It's blinding me."

An officer with a well-groomed beard stepped forward. "I'm Capitán Molina. You the owner?" he asked in heavily accented English.

Verena gave a dry laugh. "I wish. It's a charter. Captain Burton has all the documentation," she said.

She gestured for Burton, who was standing beside her, to hand over the papers.

"It's a two-week charter, Capitán," Burton said, offering the charter agreement. "We're scheduled to return to Valencia in nine days."

"This vessel was seen near Port de Sóller this morning," Molina said, flipping through the manifest.

As he spoke, Verena noticed that two of the officers were fanning out across the deck.

"That's right," she said. "We anchored about two miles south of there. Gorgeous diving site."

"Are you aware an American journalist was abducted in Port de Sóller earlier today?"

"Today?" she repeated, feigning surprise. "In Port de Sóller?"

Molina gave no reaction. He just stared at her. He was tall, trim, and looked to be in his late twenties. Verena wished she knew what Molina had been told about *Veloce* and what his orders were. She assumed that if the Guardia Civil knew Hobb was aboard the yacht, they would have sent more than one patrol boat and maybe even a chopper for support.

"How many people aboard?" Molina asked.

"Three. Myself, Captain Burton, and the chef. He's asleep in his cabin."

"So . . . you're the only guest? Miss . . . ?"

"Verena Kaine."

"It's a large yacht for just one person."

"Didn't realize that was a crime," she replied.

Molina flipped another page on the manifest. "This shows six guests and two crew members."

Verena shrugged. "Yeah . . . well, they're in Palma. Club-hopping is my guess."

"Are there any weapons on board? Anything me and my team should be made aware of?"

She tilted her head, as if offended. "Of course not!"

"Then you wouldn't object if we search the vessel, would you?"

A bolt of anxiety crawled up Verena's spine. "I mean . . . don't you need a warrant for that?"

Molina smirked, crumpled the manifest, and tossed it overboard.

"Not in this case," he said. "You're missing proper ownership documentation."

The man's action gave her pause. Was this a bribe shakedown? She'd expect that in Mexico, but not in Spain. Still, it was an option worth exploring. If all this could be solved with cash, she was willing to play the game.

"I'm sure we can come to a reasonable arrangement, Capitán Molina," she said, letting a faint smile touch her lips. "I'm sure these nighttime boardings can be stressful—"

The smirk on Molina's mouth vanished. "Are you suggesting a bribe?"

Verena was caught off guard. She'd clearly misjudged the situation.

"I . . . I certainly wouldn't call it that," she replied. "But I understand operations like this aren't cheap—"

"Search it!" Molina snapped, gesturing for the two officers patrolling the deck to get inside the yacht.

Verena scratched her ear, taking the opportunity to subtly tap her earbud once. Bernard would hear what came next and would get ready.

"You want to search it, then search it," she said, then added, "but do you really need four officers to do it?"

Molina studied her for a few seconds, then he smiled, though it was devoid of any warmth.

"Thank you for giving us your consent, Miss Kaine."

"Of course. We've got nothing to hide."

Verena could see that Burton was getting anxious beside her, shifting his weight from one foot to the other.

"While my team sweeps the boat, I'd like to see the ship's log."

"The logbook is in my quarters," Burton said. "You can follow me."

Before anyone could move, the patrol boat's spotlight was suddenly powered off. Verena didn't move right away, her instincts telling her something had just happened. Her pulse spiked, and her pupils contracted, then widened again as her eyes tried to recalibrate.

And then she saw it, movement on the patrol boat. A small silhouette, more like a shadow, really, had appeared on the Rodman-55's deck. Verena blinked. Were her eyes playing tricks on her? No, it was real. The silhouette darted across the deck, moving impossibly fast. The figure was dressed entirely in black, easily blending into the night.

Verena heard two muffled pops.

And then everything turned into chaos.

CHAPTER TWENTY-TWO

One Mile South of Cabrera Island
Mallorca, Spain

Mia quietly climbed out of the storage compartment beneath the berth, then stretched to work the stiffness from her limbs. Her back and shoulders ached the most, and her legs tingled with the familiar pins and needles as her blood started circulating again. She took twenty seconds to regain full control of her body, focusing on her breathing to suppress the disorientation she suffered from lying cramped in the dark for so long.

Once she had regained full control of her extremities, she opened the sleeping quarter's door, and leading with her suppressed pistol, she climbed the two short steps to the cockpit area. She expected to find one of the patrol boat's crew members, but the space was empty. The dim interior offered a clear line of sight forward, though her vision toward the stern was limited due to the Rodman-55's design. Still, she had enough visibility to see that the boat's spotlight was locked onto the *Veloce*, its light flooding the Azimut's main deck and stern.

Since the patrol boat sat lower in the water than the *Veloce*, Mia had a slight tactical disadvantage, and she could only see the Guardia Civil officers who were on the *Veloce* from the waist up. To compensate, she would need to use extreme violence and move fast to maximize her biggest advantage: surprise.

She debated whether to leave the spotlight on. It would blind anyone trying to look toward the Rodman-55, which would make it easier for her to engage targets on the *Veloce*. But it would also silhouette her the moment she stepped onto the Azimut yacht.

Better to kill the light and use the cover of darkness.

Mia flipped the spotlight's switch at the helm station, and the light went off. Not wasting time, Mia moved to the cockpit door and opened it. As she emerged onto the deck, she immediately spotted a short Guardia Civil officer standing near the bow, his eyes on the now extinguished spotlight. He turned toward her and was about to yell a warning to his colleagues when Mia's pistol barked twice. Her two rounds shattered the man's mouth, and he crumpled backward.

Eighteen.

Mia pivoted to her right before the officer even hit the deck. A female officer was on the *Veloce*'s aft deck, holding a shotgun across her chest. Another uniformed figure stood beside her, slightly to her right. Mia's brain registered both as threats and noted their black bulletproof vests.

Mia squeezed the trigger again, sending two rounds at the woman. The first grazed the officer's right temple, but the second hit an inch to the right of her nose. Blood sprayed, and the officer went down.

Nineteen.

Though the suppressor attached to her pistol somewhat quieted her shots, it didn't completely silence them. The other figure, a good-looking man with a closely trimmed beard, must have heard them because he turned around, his hand reaching for the pistol holstered at his right hip. Behind him, stood a tall woman with black hair.

Verena Kaine.

Fearing overpenetration or a miss, Mia hesitated to go for a headshot. She lowered her aim and squeezed the trigger once just as the officer managed to pull his weapon free. Her round struck him high on the chest, just above his light body armor. The officer dropped his pistol and stumbled backward and to his left into one of the cockpit's chairs, disappearing from

Mia's view. She moved forward and jumped onto the swim platform of the Azimut and raced up the four steps leading to the main deck.

The first person she saw was Justin Burton, the *Veloce*'s skipper. She remembered his name and face from the mission brief Operations had sent her. Burton was frozen in place with his hands raised to his side. But Verena Kaine, who had jumped away from Mia's line of fire, was another story.

That woman isn't giving up.

Kaine dove for the pistol the male officer had dropped. Since the gun lay far closer to Mia than to her, it was a reckless, desperate move.

But it certainly shows courage, Mia thought as she stepped forward and kicked the pistol away, sending it sliding across the deck and out of Verena's reach.

Then Mia adjusted her aim and fired one round into her target's forehead.

Twenty.

CHAPTER TWENTY-THREE

One Mile South of Cabrera Island
Mallorca, Spain

Verena's eyes followed the pistol as it skittered across the teak deck.

Shit. I'm dead.

She raised her gaze, bracing for the muzzle of a pistol pointed at her head, but the woman wasn't aiming at her. Her gun was pointed at the wounded Guardia Civil officer slumped into one of the cockpit chairs. The woman pulled the trigger, and the back of the officer's head blew open, spattering the deck with brain, blood, and bones.

"How many more?" the woman asked.

Verena hesitated. Was she a friend or foe? If the woman had meant to kill her, she'd already be dead.

"Two more," she replied. "They're inside, searching the cabin. One has a sidearm and a compact submachine gun, the other only a pistol."

The woman nodded. "Wait here. I shouldn't be long."

———

Mia ejected her partially spent magazine and inserted a fresh one. She then hunched to pick up the pistol she had kicked away and tossed it overboard. She did the same with the female officer's shotgun and pistol. She didn't think Burton would attempt anything, but there was no sense leaving potential threats lying around, was there?

He's a fucking coward, she thought, glancing at the *Veloce's* skipper.

Burton hadn't moved. He stood rooted to the deck, wide-eyed, with his hands still raised. He hadn't gone for a weapon when he had the chance.

Pathetic.

She was about to step past him, then changed her mind, disgusted by his lack of action. She shot him point blank in the side of his head, her round entering through his left ear, and he collapsed without a sound.

Twenty-one.

Mia looked at Verena. She hadn't flinched.

Good.

She didn't look overly concerned either. Maybe she, too, had realized that Burton was a useless tool. Mia stepped over the body and entered the interior of the Azimut S8. The ambient lighting coming from the ceiling gave just enough glow for her to navigate the space without bumping into furniture, allowing her to see that the interior was minimalist and modern, with lots of high-gloss surfaces. She cleared the main salon in seconds.

Pistol raised in front of her, Mia took the companionway down to the galley. The space tightened, and all her senses were on high alert. She paused at the bottom step. She'd heard something coming from the master stateroom.

Mia scanned the hallway. Several closed doors stood between her and the master cabin. *Not great.*

Tactically, it wouldn't be optimal for her to walk past these doors without clearing the rooms first.

Gunfire erupted close by. She flinched, the sound jolting her. She hadn't anticipated it, especially not coming from behind her. Then, an officer—a man of medium height with a thick black mustache—dashed out from the master stateroom just as a man wearing pink pajamas stepped out from another stateroom.

The chef.

Mia locked eyes with the cop for a fraction of a second. It was clear that the man was as surprised as she was. He had a submachine gun—an MP5—in his hands. Mia's pistol was already up, but the chef was in her line of fire.

She fired, squeezing the trigger four times.

The first round hit the chef in the forehead. The second struck the officer in the abdomen just below his bulletproof vest. The third and fourth rounds slammed into his body armor as he ran toward her but weren't enough to fully stop his momentum. He crashed into her before she could fire again, driving her hard against the bulkhead. Even though she had wounded the man, he was still much stronger than she was.

Mia heard one more gunshot, but she had to finish off the threat in front of her before dealing with anything else. She grappled with the man, but somehow the blood oozing from his abdomen had slicked her hands, allowing him to wrestle her pistol away. He tried to drive her to the floor, but Mia twisted out of his clinch. She brought her knee up, connecting with his groin. He grunted, but didn't go down. He swung wildly, got lucky, his fist catching her on the chin. Her vision momentarily spotted, but she managed to keep her footing. Another punch came, but slower this time. She ducked, drove her shoulder into his gut, and heard him gasp in pain as she pushed him against the opposite wall. Her hand found the hilt of her knife, and she drew the blade. She brought the knife up and stabbed her opponent several times under his rib cage, right below his body armor.

The officer let go of her, and stumbled back, dumbfounded. He fell on his ass, his hands clutching his wounds.

Breathing hard, Mia picked up her pistol and fired twice into the man's face.

"Twenty-two," she murmured to herself, making the conscious decision not to count the chef.

She turned around and climbed the stairs back to the main deck. As soon as she reached the main salon, she saw Verena with a pistol in her hands. As Mia got closer, she spotted the last Guardia Civil officer. He lay on his back, blood pooling beneath him on the teak deck. Standing a few feet behind the dead officer was Paul Hobb, his eyes wide and fixed on Verena's gun, which was now pointed at Mia.

"He had a pistol on him," Verena said, nodding toward Burton's corpse.

Mia shrugged. "Then he was an even bigger coward than I thought."

"Are you here for me, or for the journalist?" Verena asked.

"I'm here to clean up your mess, Verena. That's all."

"My mess?"

Mia nodded. "It is what it is."

Verena studied her, then said. "Today could have been better . . . so what now?"

"It's really up to you," Mia replied truthfully. "I won't kill you, if that's what you're asking. Not after what I saw tonight. But then, how can you be sure I'm telling the truth?"

"It's as if you want me to shoot you."

Mia smiled, then shook her head. "I don't. I believe in what I'm doing. And there's still so, so much to do. Besides, I need to be in Budapest in three days. I'm playing at a big-venue concert."

Verena gave her a quizzical look. "What?"

"I'm a professional piano player, Verena. Name's Mia Hernandez."

Her explanation didn't remove the puzzled expression from Verena's face. On the contrary, the woman was now looking at her as if she was batshit crazy.

Mia shrugged, then said, "What I can tell you is that if you kill me, you'll be dead before the end of the week."

"Yeah? How's that?"

"Because there are others like me. We're everywhere, Verena. Everywhere."

———

Verena didn't know what the hell to think anymore. Three minutes ago, she'd been a breath away from being handcuffed and hauled off by the

Guardia Civil. Now four cops were sprawled dead across the deck of the *Veloce*. At least one more had dropped on the patrol boat. And the woman who had executed four of them, and Burton, stood calmly in front of her, a suppressed pistol still in her hand.

A concert pianist, she'd claimed. *Right.*

Verena thought about squeezing the trigger, but her gut told her otherwise. The woman had warned her she'd be dead within a week if she did so. And Verena believed her. There was something terrifyingly competent about Mia Hernandez, but there was something else too. She just couldn't quite put a finger on what it was. Yet.

She looked the woman over. She was much smaller than Verena. Her chestnut hair was slicked to her face with sweat and blood. Still, her golden skin shimmered in the moonlight. But it was her eyes that stopped Verena. Mia's eyes weren't cold. Not dead. In fact, they were surprisingly kind. Too kind for someone who'd just killed five people without blinking.

So why am I not dead?

Could Mia have been sent by Verena's employer to rescue her and her team? Unlikely. The way Mia had offed Burton said otherwise. And there was the fact that her employer's number was no longer in service. No, Mia Hernandez wasn't a rescuer. She was damage control. She'd said as much herself, hadn't she?

"Ticktock, Verena," Mia said. "Whatever you're going to do, decide now. I'm four seconds away from making the call for you."

Four. Not three. Thankfully.

Verena lowered her gun, half expecting the other woman to shoot her. But she didn't.

"Throw that pistol overboard," Mia said.

Verena tossed it over the gunwale on the starboard side. Then, taking Verena by surprise, Mia handed her suppressed pistol to her.

"Now, kill that reporter," Mia said, her eyes flicking toward the stern where Hobb was on his knees.

She followed Mia's gaze. The reporter was tied up, his mouth duct-taped, his eyes wide with panic. He was making noise, garbled pleas behind the tape, and tears were running down his cheeks.

She didn't look at Mia. She didn't need to. *She's testing me.*

It wasn't lost on her that she'd been fired from the LAPD for having killed the two men who had executed her partner. And now, here she was with real blood on her hands. Still, killing the Guardia Civil officer might have been self-defense, depending on how one chose to frame it, but this? What Mia was asking of her was something else entirely. This was cold-blooded murder. She'd already crossed a line when she'd accepted the position to lead Blackstone Security. Since then, she'd done things she never imagined she'd be capable of. Illegal things. Morally gray things. She'd been on a slippery slope for a while now. She knew that. But since the operation in Manchester, it hadn't just been steep, it had become slick with oil. She'd ordered people killed, hadn't she? Was there really such a difference between giving the order and doing it herself?

Maybe. Maybe not. But I'm in too deep now. I passed the last exit ramp a long time ago.

Her finger hovered on the trigger, and she closed her eyes, but only for a second. Then she opened them, leveled the pistol, and fired, sending four rounds into Hobb's chest. The reporter slumped to the side.

Three would have done it, she knew, but three felt careless. Four was safer. Cleaner. Five would have been too much.

"Good," Mia said, as if Verena had just passed a field test. "Give me my pistol back."

Verena did.

"Now, get the *Veloce* ready to move. I'll scuttle the patrol boat, then we go. I want to be out of here in ten."

Verena nodded, her ears still ringing from the shots she'd fired at the Guardia Civil officer. "Where are we headed?" she asked.

"A few miles off of Ibiza. That's where we'll sink *Veloce*. Once that's done, I'd like to pay a visit to someone in Valencia."

Verena almost asked why. But she already knew. They were going after the yacht broker. The one she'd used to charter the Azimut.

"Ten minutes. Understood," Verena said. "I'll be ready."

CHAPTER TWENTY-FOUR

This was going to be their third flight in less than six hours, and Caspian felt every hour of it in his bones as he stepped into the brightly lit cabin of the Boeing 777-300ER. While Caspian wasn't usually a fan of a 2-3-2 configuration in a business class cabin, it would work perfectly fine this time around since he'd be seated in a window seat next to Liesel and didn't mind not having direct access to the aisle.

Thanks to Samantha Ranger, their escape from Mallorca had been a clean one. Ranger had arranged for a private jet to take them to Algiers—which was a short seventy-five-minute hop from Mallorca—just before 11 p.m. Though they were both exhausted, neither he nor Liesel had managed to get any shut-eye on the short leg. In Algiers, they had blended in among regular travelers and switched to commercial air, catching the last direct flight to Istanbul. Caspian had used the freshly SSU-issued passports Ranger's people had left for them in the private jet to book two economy tickets to Turkey's capital. Once in Istanbul, Caspian had bought two business class tickets to JFK. While it was Ranger who was footing the bill, Caspian would have had no issue spending his own money for the business class fare. He needed the rest, and an eleven-hour flight in a cramped economy seat wasn't how he was going to get it. He intended to eat, down a whiskey, and then pass out until final descent.

Caspian slid into 7A. Though he was grateful for the lie-flat seat, row 7 was the final one before the economy section and was adjacent to the galley and lavatories, which meant there would be more foot traffic than he had hoped. He might need a second whiskey to get to sleep. Next to him in 7B, Liesel took her seat, her face as pale as he'd ever seen it. He didn't need to ask her how she was doing. He knew. She was shattered.

Who wouldn't be?

Her sister had died right in front of her, and that made Caspian's stomach twist in knots. Their time in Port de Sóller was supposed to be the perfect Mediterranean vacation, the one they'd both been craving. Instead, it had turned into a nightmare. As Elias, Caspian had been through war zones, pulled off hits in urban centers and back-alley shitholes, but somehow, Port de Sóller, that little seaside paradise he'd chosen for their vacation, had turned into one of the most dangerous places he had visited.

Caspian felt his thoughts spiral, and too tired to force them away, they brought up questions he didn't care to answer. What if it had been Liesel who had caught the bullet in the chest? What if she'd been the one gasping her last breath on the terrace? The mental images made him feel sick.

Onyx had trained him as a singleton operator. As Elias, he'd been a ghost, a scalpel wielded by the most clandestine hand of the US government.

And he had worked alone. For a reason.

It had taken some time for Caspian to admit it, but having Liesel in the field with him distracted him.

"Romantic partners are emotional weights you don't need," one of his Onyx instructors had once told him.

Liesel was capable—brilliant, even—but she hadn't been through the same hellish training pipeline he had. She hadn't spent endless months learning how to kill with a ballpoint pen or how to disappear in a foreign city without a trace and with no logistical support. She was a spy, a damn good one for sure, but she wasn't a killer.

Still, she had saved his life in Bordeaux, hadn't she? Liesel was smart, fearless, and resourceful in ways that constantly surprised him. And yet, no matter how capable she was, Caspian couldn't deny the shift in his mental state when she was with him. Some part of his usually razor-sharp focus diverted to her well-being. Not because he didn't trust her, but because he loved her. And that love came with weight. He knew she loved him, too, but last night, that weight had felt heavier. They had made love the way they always did, as if the world outside their room didn't exist, but this time something in her had felt . . . absent. He couldn't quite put his finger on it, but to him, it had felt as if she had needed the closeness, the escape, but not him. Not fully, anyway. And it had left a hollow space in his chest.

And now, although he didn't know what it was yet, he could feel something bigger, something dangerous, coming their way. It had started in Tanzania. The operative he'd killed had mouthed words that had been haunting him since.

People like me . . . we are . . . everywhere.

He had seen the conviction in her eyes and heard it in her voice. She'd been fighting for something she had truly believed in. But what? And then, in Port de Sóller, he had heard almost the exact same words coming out of Sofie's mouth. In her dying breath, Sofie hadn't told her sister that she loved her; no, she'd used her last few precious words to warn her.

They are everywhere.

Caspian reclined his seat and rubbed his eyes, fatigue pulling at every muscle. He would have to become Elias again. The real one. The one with thirty-four sanctioned kills. The detached, cold, and focused one. But to do that, he needed to be alone.

That was going to be a problem, he knew. Liesel wouldn't step aside easily. Not after watching her sister being murdered.

Should I talk to Ranger about it? Could she help me convince Liesel to take a step back?

Truth was, he had no idea if Ranger would even green-light an operation to suss out who was behind Sofie's killing. The Tanzanian operation had been an SSU job, so if Caspian could link the events that had happened in Mallorca to the ones in Tanzania, there was a chance Ranger would say yes. In his mind, the threads were unmistakably connected. The operative in Tanzania had worked with North Korea, but she'd made it clear her employers had flexible allegiances.

And now, this thing—whatever it was—had swallowed up Sofie and placed targets on his and Liesel's backs.

He sighed, his mind spinning. He didn't even know if he wanted the meal service and the whiskeys anymore. Maybe he should just skip everything and try to sleep.

"Two glasses of white wine, then I think I'll go right to sleep," Liesel said, her eyes red and puffy.

A flight attendant appeared to Liesel's right, balancing a tray of predeparture drinks.

"I have sparkling water, champagne, and orange juice," she said.

"Definitely the champagne for me," Liesel said.

Caspian hesitated, then said, "One of each, please."

The flight attendant raised an eyebrow, then offered a tight smile and placed the drinks on his tray table. "We're taking off soon, so I'll circle back in about ten minutes to pick up the glasses," she said.

Caspian took a sip of water, then his eyes were drawn to a flicker of blue lights coming from outside the window. Three emergency vehicles were moving quickly along the tarmac.

He frowned.

There were dozens of aircraft lined up at various gates. The cars could be headed anywhere. Liesel must have noticed them, too, because she leaned forward to get a better view. As the vehicles closed the distance, two things became apparent. First, the vehicles were police cars.

And second, they were headed directly toward their plane.

CHAPTER TWENTY-FIVE

Istanbul Airport
Arnavutköy District, Turkey

Caspian's pulse picked up as the three Turkish police vehicles screeched to a halt beside the triple seven. From his seat in business class, he had a clear view of the vehicles. He wondered how thorough the SSU analysts had been in stitching together the new legends for him and Liesel. They had had only hours, so Caspian didn't think their aliases would hold up to scrutiny.

He felt Liesel's hand on his forearm.

"If they're here for us, Casp, we stick to the plan," she whispered. "We don't resist. We let it play out, just like we said, right?"

He nodded. They had discussed this eventuality during their layover in Algiers. If they were about to be apprehended by local authorities, they wouldn't engage. There would be no fight, no desperate attempt to break free on a plane full of innocent passengers.

"Even if it means we'll end up in a Turkish holding cell for a few days," Liesel had said.

A few days?

Caspian didn't share Liesel's optimism about the length of their potential all-inclusive stay with the Turkish police. Ranger had helped them escape Mallorca, but Caspian wondered if she would stick her neck out to help them out of a sticky situation in Istanbul. Organizing a private jet and preparing a set of fresh identities was one thing; orchestrating a prison extraction was another. That would require resources she might not be willing—or able—to deploy.

Caspian sighed. The gamble to route through Turkey had been his call. He'd wanted another layer of separation from the chaos in Mallorca. But now, as he watched uniformed officers climb the jet bridge stairs, he wasn't so sure it had been the right move.

At the front of the plane, the cockpit door opened, and the captain and the first officer stepped out. They were met by a police officer seconds later. Caspian tried to read their body language, but the angle from his seat in row 7 made it difficult. Then, coming from the back of the economy cabin, Caspian heard a scream, then several loud crashes. He turned in his seat and craned his neck to see what was going on.

Two men barreled down the aisle, shoving passengers out of their way who were trying to fit their outsize carry-on bags into the overhead bin. Both men were skinny, though they were mismatched in height like a badly paired set of bookends. The taller one, who was leading the way, had a patchy beard that clung to his jaw like moss. A gentleman, whose wife had been violently thrust aside by the first man, tried to intervene but was elbowed in the face by the short one.

They're trying to escape, Caspian thought as he watched the pair cram themselves into the emergency row.

Seconds later, just as the police officers were about to intercept the two men, the tall one yanked the emergency lever. The door exploded outward and fell onto the wing. The shorter man, who'd been waiting for his friend to clear out, was tackled to the ground by one of the officers. The tall one managed to leap onto the wing. Through the window, Caspian watched as the man sprinted toward the edge of the wing and launched himself into the air. The man landed on the roof of a police car parked below. Caspian didn't hear the bone break, but the way the man rolled off the roof of the vehicle and fell onto the tarmac, with his right leg twisted at an impossible angle, told him he wouldn't walk again for quite a while. Seconds later, the injured man was swarmed by several police officers. The entire incident had lasted less than thirty seconds.

All around Caspian and Liesel, passengers had their phones out, filming.

"They weren't here for us," Liesel said. She tried to smile at him, but it faltered halfway.

"We're not out of the woods yet," Caspian reminded her.

He knew what was coming. Every passenger would be asked to leave the plane. Because the emergency exit had been triggered and the door had fallen onto the wing, the aircraft would need to be inspected by the airline and cleared before it could fly again. And given the level of response he'd seen, Caspian suspected the Turkish authorities would use the delay to dig for intel and to search for accomplices among the passengers. The scrutiny wouldn't stop with the two men who were now in custody.

Caspian sent a quick update to Samantha Ranger using the encrypted messaging app, warning her they had been caught in the net of a larger police intervention and requesting that actions be taken to strengthen his and Liesel's aliases. Ranger replied within seconds.

Already working the problem. We're checking the Istanbul police databases now. Stand by for further instructions.

Fifteen minutes later, Caspian was still waiting to hear back from Ranger when a voice over the plane's speakers informed all the passengers that they would be deplaning shortly, row by row, and would then be escorted to a bus. He didn't like that. He had hoped to be sent back to the terminal near the gate area where they would be waiting for a replacement plane. Why the buses? Where were they headed?

Liesel must have come to the same conclusion because he heard her swear under her breath. "They'll investigate everyone who's aboard the plane," she said.

When a flight attendant motioned for Caspian and Liesel that it was their turn, they stood and began to shuffle toward the door. Caspian scanned the other passengers. Everybody seemed compliant. He even saw a few passengers smile as they talked among themselves. He stepped onto the mobile staircase and descended onto the tarmac where the blinking orange lights of a nearby airport tug reflected on the wet concrete.

Though it was still morning, the sky had gone dark with thick storm clouds hiding the sun with a heavy gray canopy. It was hot and damp outside, and there was a thick scent of jet fuel in the air. A low rumble of thunder rolled in the distance as Caspian and Liesel made their way to the bus waiting a short distance away.

The nondescript bus was flanked by two uniformed officers who were checking the boarding passes and passports of each passenger. Caspian and Liesel approached in tandem, smiling at the officers, and presented their forged documents without a hint of hesitation. The officers didn't return their smiles but cross-referenced their names and handed the passports back with a curt nod before motioning them to step aboard.

Once inside the bus, another officer held out a clear plastic bin.

"Phones," he said simply.

The passengers grumbled, but they all complied. Caspian, just like Liesel, had two phones. Caspian didn't see anyone being frisked, so he decided to only hand over his burner. He then walked to the back of the bus and took a seat beside Liesel. He patted his breast pocket to let her know he had kept one phone.

"Same," she said.

The bus left as soon as all the seats were filled. Caspian looked outside and noted that the airport wasn't in lockdown. Planes were being guided to their gates while others were being pushed off. Whatever the authorities suspected, they hadn't felt the need to ground any other flight.

Just ours.

The bus rolled for only five minutes before it drove into a large hangar. The interior was cavernous, but it was well lit. Caspian thought the size of the hangar was big enough to accommodate two wide-body airplanes. Yellow maintenance ladders, tool carts, and canvas-covered equipment had been pushed off to the side, leaving most of the space open for what had clearly been transformed into an improvised detention zone. Rows of molded-plastic chairs had been made available for the passengers, and a bottle of water had been placed on each seat.

Caspian and Liesel, along with the other passengers, were asked to take a seat and wait to be called by an officer. As they waited, Caspian took in his surroundings and started to think of the possible scenarios he was about to face. Best-case scenario: His and Liesel's documents would hold up and they'd be permitted to board the next flight to JFK. Worst case, they would be arrested and brought in for further questioning. He had just taken a sip from his bottle of water when he felt the interior of his jacket vibrate. He leaned toward Liesel.

"Just got a message from Ranger," he told her.

Liesel angled her body to block the view from his right, and Caspian checked his left. An elderly couple he'd seen seated a few rows ahead of him in business class were conversing in Portuguese. Caspian slid his hand beneath his jacket and used the tip of his fingers to ease the phone out of the inside pocket. Once the phone was nestled in his palm, he tilted it slightly behind his jacket, quickly entered his password, then read the message.

We know where you are. We've hacked into the Istanbul Police Special Operations Division database. Liesel's passport has been flagged. We don't know why.

Caspian looked at Liesel and said, "Your passport's flagged."
Liesel pressed her lips together but didn't say anything.

"It could be random," Caspian said.

"Please tell me you don't really believe that," she said.

He shook his head. He didn't.

Another message appeared. Caspian read it and felt a chill wrap around his spine. Liesel stared at him. "What now?" she asked.

"I've been flagged too," he said. "We're both wanted for murder."

CHAPTER TWENTY-SIX

Restaurant Unique
New York City, New York

Everett Westcott had learned years ago that few things encouraged diplomacy quite like a candlelight dinner. Not just one or two candles to accent a table—though even that was better than nothing—but dozens, each one deliberately set in the dining room to bathe the space in a warm, golden light. In Westcott's opinion, candlelight had a way of softening hard lines and melting the otherwise defiant expressions negotiators so often wore on their faces. Candlelight made people feel safe and nostalgic.

And in Everett Westcott's world, that was half the battle won.

The private dining room at Restaurant Unique, which was located just off Park Avenue, radiated the kind of understated elegance that came with money. Nothing was too showy, but everything, from the furniture to the arrangement of candlelight, had been carefully chosen. The stone walls were broken up by deep blue velvet panels and several black-and-white and color photos of French winemakers, though most of the vintners were now long dead.

To the left of the long mahogany table that occupied the center of the room, a floor-to-ceiling window gave a striking view of a curated wine cellar, its racks lined with bottles Westcott had himself selected from his favorite regions. That window had been his idea when he had bought the place seven years ago. None of the men and women seated around the table knew he owned the place, and that was just how he liked it.

Westcott had arrived thirty minutes before his guests, and as it always was before any event he held there, the dining room had been swept for any kind of electronic surveillance. The wine served to his guests was excellent, but short of exquisite, and the food sublime. But for Westcott, total privacy was the real luxury. Phones had been collected at the door, no exception.

In comparison to the big-event dinners he often held at Restaurant Unique, tonight's guest list was tight. Seated at the table were three high-ranking UN representatives, two deputy directors from the World Bank, and the ambassadors of France, Sweden, and the Democratic Republic of the Congo. Westcott had invited these specific people because each of them had a stake in the success of tonight's conversation.

Westcott sat at the head of the table, his sleeves rolled up, revealing strong, tan forearms shaped by years spent hauling sails and casting lines. His tailored navy dress shirt, which hugged his athletic frame without clinging, was crisp and open at the collar, and his charcoal gray trousers were impeccably pressed. On his feet, he wore a pair of butter-soft, Italian-made yachting shoes that were scuffed just enough to suggest they'd seen some real use. He kept his hair, which had turned gray years ago, swept back. All in all, Everett Westcott looked more like a man who'd stepped off his yacht in Monaco than someone who made policy recommendations to world leaders. Though he knew he had a disarming smile, Westcott never let it smother the raw edges that made people—especially the kind who were seated around the table—believe he'd seen things, done things that very few had.

Since the start of the dinner almost three hours ago, Westcott had smiled a lot, drank little, and listened more than he spoke. But that was about to change.

He set his fork down and glanced at the Congolese ambassador seated to his left. Ambassador Amadou Nyambe was in his late fifties, with smooth, dark skin and a shaved head, and he never seemed to be in a hurry. He wore a finely tailored navy blue suit. Westcott offered the ambassador a gracious smile.

"Ambassador," he said, "I trust the meal lived up to your expectations?"

Ambassador Nyambe dabbed the corner of his mouth with his napkin, then smiled at Westcott.

"It was exceptional, Mr. Westcott. It truly was. Many thanks for your invitation."

Westcott chuckled softly. "I do what I can to keep the diplomatic community well fed, Ambassador. Hungry people make rash decisions."

A few around the table laughed quietly, Nyambe included. Westcott leaned in, his tone shifting just enough to signal a turn in the conversation.

"Ambassador, two months ago, you asked me how Hearts United could help your government reach its development targets by the end of the decade."

The ambassador straightened his back. "I did."

"Since then, Hearts United has been working closely with members of your government to make sure the solutions we would be offering truly represented the will of the people."

"I'm aware of that, of course."

"Well, I'm pleased to let you know we now have a final proposal," Westcott said. "I'll be presenting the initiative to your National Assembly shortly, but I thought it would be best to share it with you first. Would you like to hear what it is about?"

The question was a formality. Everyone at the table knew why they'd been invited tonight. Westcott wasn't seeking permission; he was giving the Congolese ambassador the courtesy of asking.

"Of course," Nyambe said. "Please, I'm listening."

Westcott placed his hands on the table, lacing his fingers loosely. "The Congo River is the heartbeat of your nation, Mr. Ambassador. It's the second-largest river in the world by volume. But less than ten percent of its hydroelectric potential has been tapped."

"I'm well aware that—" started the ambassador, but Westcott raised his right hand.

"Please, sir, let me finish," he said, then continued to speak. "What that means for you, for Central Africa, and for the whole continent, really, is untold power. Literal power, Ambassador. The capacity to provide electricity to half of Sub-Saharan Africa."

The French ambassador, a woman with silver hair and red glasses, said in heavily accented English, "But exploiting that potential will require massive infrastructure. As I'm sure you know, Mr. Westcott, Inga III has been stalled for over a decade. The Chinese, the South Africans, and even the Spaniards tried. But ultimately, they all failed."

Westcott nodded in agreement. Inga III was a proposed hydroelectric dam project on the Congo River that was intended to be the first phase of the larger Grand Inga complex. Inga III alone, if done right, could generate up to eleven thousand megawatts of electricity. But political instability in the region and concerns about the project's governance had scared away many of the project's initial backers.

Westcott looked to his right, where the two World Bank representatives were seated. While the World Bank had initially backed a German-led initiative for Inga III, it had pulled out in 2016 following a disagreement over the *strategic direction* of the project. In plainer terms, widespread corruption within the Congolese government had forced the World Bank to cut its losses.

"These consortiums failed because they focused on megaprojects with top-down financing."

"And because there were heavy political strings attached," the Swedish ambassador chimed in, his gaze steady on the Congolese ambassador.

Westcott's face remained neutral, but he was glad the words hadn't come from his own mouth. What the Swedish ambassador had said was true, but the message was far more palatable coming from a neutral and well-respected European than from someone perceived to have an agenda. Westcott knew about the Swedish ambassador's reputation. The man had once been a high-ranking officer with the Swedish police and was known as a corruption fighter. Westcott had counted on him to speak plainly; it was, in fact, the sole reason he'd been invited. And with just these few words, the ambassador had done his job.

Nyambe gave his Swedish colleague a warm smile, but Westcott noticed the smile didn't reach the man's hard eyes. Nyambe might speak with the soft cadence of a seasoned politician, but the eyes belonged to a man who had survived more than one corrupt regime.

"What I'd like to propose, Mr. Ambassador," Westcott said with a disarming smile, "is something more . . . elegant."

"What do you have in mind?" Nyambe asked.

"A hybrid model, some would call it," Westcott said. "Hearts United would like to form strategic partnerships with local ownership and have a community-linked distribution."

From the corner of his eye, Westcott saw the Swedish ambassador nod in approval.

"You see, my friends," Westcott continued, addressing the whole table, "I don't believe any of us, Hearts United included, have the means to electrify a continent overnight. But what we can do is to start where it matters the most. And we do that by empowering the local communities along the Congo River."

"You mentioned a hybrid model," Nyambe said, his eyes lighting up. "Does this mean you would bring private investment?"

"I would bring much more than investment," Westcott replied, making eye contact with his guests around the table. "Hearts United would bring stability. And only once the first stage proves viable would we expand. Think about it: Clean energy from the Congo River could power industries in Kinshasa, Brazzaville, and even into Angola."

Turning to Nyambe, Westcott said, "Ambassador, Hearts United's project would enable your government to export power to the fragile economies of your neighboring countries. The Democratic Republic of Congo could then reclaim its rightful place as the region's stabilizing force."

While Nyambe slowly nodded, Westcott looked at the UN and World Bank representatives. "And even more importantly, my friends, Hearts United's plan would lower Africa's reliance on fossil fuels and build the continent's independence, not deepen its dependence. And I know this is a goal we all share."

As if on cue, a man in a black suit entered the dining room, carrying a stack of dark blue folders embossed with the Hearts United emblem. He moved from guest to guest, placing a folder in front of each. At the same time, five uniformed waiters stepped in to clear the table.

"This isn't a detailed plan," Westcott said, watching the folders make their way around the table, "but it will give you a clear overview of what I have in mind. Read through it, it's only five pages, and let me know what you think."

One of the UN representatives, a distinguished woman in her thirties who Westcott knew was a rising star within the Office of the Special Adviser on Africa and who had the secretary-general's ear, was the first to finish reading. She gently closed the folder and cleared her throat.

"Mr. Westcott," she said, her South African accent unmistakable. "I'm not sure about this. Your plan calls for the relocation of thousands of people. Maybe more. There will be protests and international pushback, and even accusations of neocolonialism."

Westcott had expected the woman's reticence. In fact, he had counted on it.

"I understand the optics," he said calmly. "But history favors those who see beyond the moment, doesn't it? The reality is, to raise a nation, sometimes a village or two must be moved. Mind you, we're not talking about forced displacement here, but about dignified relocations with planned communities, clean water, medical clinics, and schools. It's an upgrade, ladies and gentlemen, not a loss."

Westcott let his words settle. He knew that by responding to her openly and without sounding too defensive, he'd just addressed the concern that at least half of the guests seated at the table were thinking but were hesitant to voice. Her doubt had served its purpose.

"But still a sacrifice," the UN official murmured.

Westcott looked around the table once more, meeting every eye in turn.

"I don't take that lightly. But ask yourselves . . . what's the greater injustice? Delaying meaningful progress for another generation, or offering millions the opportunity to break free from fossil fuel dependence and step into a future powered by clean energy? And, if you look at the bottom of page four, you'll see that the revenue the government will be able to generate from the sale of electricity will be enough to fund nationwide universal health care."

Westcott let that sink in for a few moments, then said, "I won't apologize for Hearts United's ambition, dear friends. The world needs bold leadership, and that's what I'm offering you."

A beat of silence followed, then Ambassador Nyambe leaned back in his chair.

"I'll need additional details, of course," he said, "but I'm prepared to speak to the new minister of land management and support any action plan that has your name on it."

"I have a feeling he'll be much more receptive than his predecessor," Westcott said.

"He will. And I've received word from Kinshasa, no later than yesterday, that our president trusts you. In fact, we all do, Mr. Westcott."

Westcott inclined his head. "And I can assure you that trust isn't misplaced," he said, then added, "Thank you all for coming. Your presence here tonight means a lot to me."

The guests rose, thanking him not only for the fabulous meal but for his vision. It was like a scene from the Vatican. One after another, the UN representatives, the World Bank executives, and the ambassadors offered their gratitude with the subtle reverence of men and women who knew real power when they saw it. Westcott offered them polite nods and calm assurances he'd take care of everything, but still let them feel that they were part of something noble.

Eventually, the room emptied, and with the large double door of the private room now open, the soft jazz coming from Unique's main dining room a floor above filtered through. Westcott remained seated, one hand resting on the rim of his wineglass, then decided, since he'd been so reasonable, that he could indulge in one more sip.

The wine was a Louis Jadot Clos Vougeot Grand Cru 2015. Westcott closed his eyes to really focus on the notes of cooked cherries, dense blackberries, and black pepper on his palate. While the wine had a long finish, the tannins were still a tad high, which he thought muted the flavor complexity of the wine. He knew the 2015 vintage was still a bit young and needed another three to four years to fully bring out the depth it promised, but it hadn't mattered tonight. With the guests he'd hosted, none of them would have noticed the difference anyway.

Still, the wine pulled him back to a morning two decades ago—before the diagnosis, before the speeches, and before Hearts United had become more than an idea—when he and his wife, Nailah, had visited the estate. Clos Vougeot was one of Burgundy's most storied—and most famous—grand cru vineyards and had been producing wine since the twelfth century. His kind—and oh so beautiful—Nailah had laughed that day. And it hadn't been the composed, diplomatic laugh she'd come to offer at galas or donor dinners after the diagnosis, but the real one, full and melodic, with a little hitch at the end that made it sound like she'd surprised herself. He remembered exactly how it sounded, and he could still hear it . . . when he let himself. For a moment—a second, really—the memory caught him off guard. He felt the beginning of something stir in his chest, but he shook it off, as if brushing away a speck of dust from his cuff.

I can't let myself go down this rabbit hole. There's nothing for me in there.

Westcott set the glass down gently in front of him, just as the figure of a man appeared in the doorway. Westcott gestured for him to come in and take a seat.

Charles Mpassi stood well over six feet. He was lean, fit, and built like the sprinter he once was. In 2005, he'd brought home a silver medal in the four hundred meters at the Francophone Games that had taken place in Niamey, Niger. After that, he'd served five years in the Congolese Republican Guard. That was when he'd seen firsthand the brutality, the corruption, and the cowardice of the men in power. It had driven him to leave the country of his birth behind and to start over in France. He was now the director of the Office of Special Projects at Hearts United and had been so since its inception. There wasn't a single file that crossed Everett Westcott's desk without first passing through Mpassi's hands. He was the only man Westcott trusted completely.

Mpassi pulled out the chair Ambassador Nyambe had occupied earlier and sat down.

"What is it?" Westcott asked.

"I have news from Mallorca," Mpassi said. "And it's not good."

CHAPTER TWENTY-SEVEN

Istanbul Airport
Arnavutköy District, Turkey

Caspian read the message again, then looked at Liesel. She had kept her composure, but he could see that she was deep in thought.

"It's them. It must be. It's the same people who killed Sofie," she whispered.

Another encrypted message from Ranger came in, and Caspian's phone hummed again in his hand. But this time, the elderly couple to his left had heard the faint buzz of his phone, and the older man's eyes narrowed at the sight of the glowing screen half shielded beneath Caspian's jacket.

"Work," Caspian said in English, giving the couple a tired, apologetic smile. "I work at the Canadian embassy, and I'm supposed to be on vacation, but . . . you know how this goes, right?"

He offered an exaggerated shrug and tilted the phone so that the couple could see the blurred interface of what looked like a secure diplomatic app. The woman gave a small shake of her head, but there was a sympathetic smirk tugging at her lips. The man just shrugged and resumed his conversation with his wife.

Caspian read the message, then stared at his phone for a moment.

"What did it say?" Liesel asked.

"As far as Ranger can tell, the warrant didn't originate from anywhere in Spain. The request came from inside the Istanbul police and is about to be pushed out to all the divisions."

"That . . . that makes no sense," Liesel said.

They had arrived in Turkey less than two hours ago, and they hadn't even left the airport. The implications of the content of Ranger's message were enormous, because it meant that someone—someone who had somehow managed to track them to Istanbul—had access to Turkish law enforcement or judicial systems.

"You might be right," he said finally. "Could be the same people."

At the opposite side of the hangar, two members of a cleaning crew had just entered the hangar through a side access door, pushing a supply cart toward the rear corridor leading to the bathrooms. They wore matching blue coveralls and baseball caps and orange reflective vests. As the outline of a plan began to form in his mind, Caspian watched two passengers return to their seats, escorted by a police officer. Caspian had seen the pattern repeat itself over the past half hour, with one officer shepherding one or two passengers at a time. But never more than two.

"You saw the cleaners?" Liesel asked.

"Hard not to with their reflective vests," he said. "You think they might be our way out of here?"

Liesel nodded slowly. "We need a pretext to get to them," she said.

"If we do this, we're committing ourselves," he said. "There'll be no going back."

"I know, but if Ranger's right, every officer here is minutes away from learning about our warrants. Heck, maybe they already know."

"They'd be on us if they did," Caspian said, his eyes moving to a cluster of officers hanging together close to a makeshift table on which were several opened laptops. "No one is looking specifically at us. So far."

"I hope Ranger's wrong, but we don't have time to play wait and see, do we?" Liesel asked.

"I love you. You know that, right?" he said, surprising himself. Not that he hadn't told her many times before, but he was confused as to why he had felt the urge to profess his love to her at this very moment. And, from the way Liesel was staring at him, she hadn't expected it either.

"Yeah . . . I do," she replied without the hint of a smile and somewhat cooler than he'd wished. "But we'll need to figure a lot of stuff out, Casp. Once we're out of this mess."

Caspian swallowed hard. "Right. Follow me."

He rose from his seat, and they made their way toward a patrolling officer. The man was stocky, with a thin mustache and a heavy brow.

"Excuse me," Caspian said in Turkish. "My partner and I need to use the bathroom."

The officer gave Caspian a surprised look, as if he hadn't expected him to speak Turkish. Caspian had once worked as a translator for the United Nations, a cover identity during his time as Elias. Prior to joining the Department of Homeland Security, he had completed a bachelor's degree in applied languages. He was fluent in five languages and conversational in several more, including Turkish.

The officer gestured for them to follow him. "This way. And stay close."

They trailed the officer as they walked the length of the hangar toward the bathrooms. As they neared the restrooms, Caspian caught a glimpse of the two-man cleaning crew. To his dismay, the men had already changed out of their blue coveralls and into their regular clothes and were on their way to the side door from which Caspian had seen them enter the hangar.

Damn it. Thinking the janitors had been on their way to clean the restrooms, Caspian's plan had been to subdue the officer and then do the same to the two janitors. From there, he and Liesel would have "borrowed" the men's uniforms and access passes. With the janitors now out of reach, Caspian would have to rethink his escape plan.

Unless . . . the janitors . . . they had stripped out of their uniforms, hadn't they? Maybe he wouldn't have to reconsider his strategy too much after all.

With the bathrooms straight ahead, he could see three doors, one labeled **WOMEN**, the other **MEN**. The third was unmarked but appeared to be a supply locker. Where else could the cleaning crew have stashed their cart and uniforms? He glanced at Liesel, to make sure she was tracking his thoughts.

She gave him an almost imperceptible nod.

The police officer slowed as they neared the bathroom, and he stepped to the side, leaving plenty of space for Caspian and Liesel to walk past him.

Caspian quickly looked behind his shoulder and, after confirming they weren't being followed by another group of passengers, he made his move.

As he walked past the policeman, he pivoted hard to his left and rammed his shoulder into the officer, slamming him against the wall. Before the man could react, Caspian grabbed his wrist, bent it, and forced the officer to spin around. Caspian hooked an arm around the man's throat, dropped his weight, and yanked the cop back while tightening the choke, cutting off the blood to his brain. Caspian applied as much pressure as he could to the carotid artery while shifting his hips to the right to break the officer's balance. The man struggled, elbows flailing, but Caspian kept his stance wide, absorbing the blows. Two seconds later, the policeman went limp in his arms and Caspian began to drag him toward the supply closet. Liesel was already there and opened the door for him.

———

Liesel figured out what Caspian wanted to do the moment he looked at her. When she saw him spin the officer around, she rushed past him and pulled open the supply closet door. She turned on the lights. The space was a small windowless room of roughly ten by twelve feet. The interior was packed with mops, buckets, cleaning products, and a shelf stacked with paper towels and several boxes of rubber gloves. There was also a supply cart, a partial roll of duct tape, and four spare janitor uniforms.

Behind her, Caspian was dragging the unconscious police officer toward the supply closet. Liesel grabbed the duct tape, and as soon as Caspian pulled the officer into the room, she closed the door and covered the officer's mouth with a large piece of tape, pressing it flush against his cheeks. She then taped his ankles and wrists.

"The cleaners must have taken their ID badges with them," Caspian said, already pulling on one of the blue coveralls.

Liesel showed him the downed officer's access badge. "This will have to do," she said, pocketing it.

She pulled the officer's pistol from its holster. It was a Yavuz 16, a Turkish pistol developed from the Beretta 92FS. She checked that there was a round in the chamber, then handed the gun to Caspian along with two spare magazines. She then slipped into one of the coveralls, tucking her hair beneath a faded blue cap, and grabbed a clipboard from the cleaning cart. Caspian wheeled the cart in front of them, and as they were about to leave the closet, the officer stirred. The man blinked twice. Though the tape over his mouth muffled any sound, he groaned faintly and began to twitch.

Liesel leaned over him. "You want me to keep the light on?" she asked. "Is that what you're saying? No problem."

The officer blinked again, his face a mixture of confusion and helpless rage.

Liesel closed the door and, along with Caspian, stepped into the hallway. They exited the hall a few seconds later and entered the open space of the hangar. A uniformed officer who was standing with two passengers midway between Caspian and Liesel and the rows of plastic chairs looked up from a tablet and gave them a quick once-over. Seeing only two cleaners with a cart, he turned his attention back to his device.

"Another minute or so and he'll go investigate what's taking us so long," she said.

Liesel spotted the gray double door the janitors had used to access the hangar. Reaching it, she saw a red light blinking on the keypad. Next to it was an electronic scanner. If the officer they'd left behind in the supply closet was a backup from another division and not permanently assigned to the airport, his badge might not unlock the door, and it might be game over for her and Caspian. She pulled the access badge from her pocket, then swiped it into the reader, aware that the officer holding the tablet was staring at them.

She held her breath.

The red light turned green. Liesel pushed the door and held it as Caspian maneuvered the cart inside. The door led to a softly lit warehouse where the ceiling stretched three stories high. From the look of it, the space was used to temporarily store cargo awaiting transit or inspection. Half a dozen forklifts were parked next to stacks of wrapped pallets close to a shuttered loading dock. A large corner office stood to the left, walled in by plexiglass panels that allowed whoever was inside to see what was happening on the floor. There was nobody inside, and the warehouse looked to be deserted.

"Let's leave the cart here," Liesel said. "Keep watch while I go search for keys."

Caspian replied by giving her a thumbs-up, but she was already jogging toward the corner office.

The office had several desks, all of them cluttered with staples, plastic binders, and maintenance checklists. Liesel yanked open the top drawer of the desk closest to her only to find a bunch of loose pens, a few receipts, and a forgotten sandwich in a wax wrapper. She didn't fare any better with the second or third drawers. Then her eyes caught something. She had missed it at first because of the poor lighting, but a key rack was bolted to the far wall next to an old ticking clock. There were three sets of vehicle keys labeled in smudged black marker.

She snatched the three sets of keys and was about to head back to Caspian when the overhead lights of the warehouse powered on, flooding the entire space in white.

Then, in the open doorway of the office, a uniformed security guard had his eyes locked on her. And he had a radio in his hand, which was already halfway to his mouth.

CHAPTER TWENTY-EIGHT

Caspian spotted the uniformed security guard as soon as the man entered the warehouse through a side door near the loading dock. While the guard's footsteps looked unhurried, Caspian was already on the move, intending to intercept the guard before he could surprise Liesel or switch on the lights.

He'd already traveled five long strides when he heard the click of the double door's electronic lock disengaging. He froze.

Should he cut off the security guard or neutralize whoever was about to enter? His decision, made within half a second, was based on probability. If it was a police officer coming through those doors, odds were high he'd be armed. The guard likely wasn't. Or at least Caspian hoped he wasn't. It was better to gamble on the softer target—a threat he knew Liesel could handle—and keep the most dangerous threat in his line of sight.

Caspian turned sharply and hustled back to his earlier position in the shadows along the wall. He flattened his back against the wall just as the double door swung open and two uniformed police officers stepped inside. Caspian's eyes went straight to their hands.

No weapons.

That alone told him what he needed to know. They hadn't found the bound officer in the supply closet yet. If they had, or if they thought for a second that they were walking into danger, their sidearms would have already been out. Instead, they moved with no urgency whatsoever.

And then the lights came on.

Caspian cursed under his breath. The damn guard had ruined everything. If the warehouse had remained dark, the officers would have likely passed through without noticing him or Liesel at all. Now, the entire dynamic had shifted. Caspian looked toward the office window just in time to see Liesel kick a radio out of the security guard's hand. But the startled movement hadn't just drawn his attention, the two police officers had seen it too.

One of them reached for his holster.

"Stop right there!" Caspian shouted in Turkish, pulling the pistol out of the pocket of his coveralls.

His command struck like a bolt of lightning. Both officers flinched and pivoted sharply toward his voice. The taller of the two officers let out an involuntary yelp—a strange, high-pitched note that sounded odd coming from such a large, broad-shouldered man.

"Hands where I can see them!" Caspian ordered.

He had the drop on them, and they knew it. To complicate even further the tactical position they were in, the officers weren't more than three feet apart. Caspian could take them out with two quick shots if he had to. Of course, he had no intention of killing them, but they didn't know that. What gave Caspian the confidence to take the risk was the obvious bulk beneath their uniform shirts. They were wearing body armor. If they forced his hand, he could put rounds into their chest, taking them down without killing them. Still, that would draw a hell of a lot of attention and totally go against what he and Liesel had agreed on. But when they'd decided not to fight back, they hadn't realized they were wanted for murder either.

"Cuff him," Caspian said, jerking his chin at the shorter officer. "Now."

The officer hesitated, glancing at his partner. Now that the shock had worn off, there was a sparkle in the two officers' eyes Caspian knew he had to extinguish.

"I know what you're thinking. Don't do it," Caspian warned. "Don't be heroes. That's the last thing you'll ever do before I drop you."

"You shoot us, you'll have twenty officers on you in less than a minute," the shorter officer said.

"You're right," conceded Caspian. "And they'll kill me, but not before I drop at least half a dozen of your friends as they come through the door. How many of your colleagues are fathers? How many of them are mothers? Think about the families they'll leave behind. Is that really what you want?"

A heartbeat later, the taller officer looked at his colleague and said, "Just do it."

"Tighter," Caspian said, once the man's partner had complied. "Now, cuff your own left wrist. Then get on your knees and look away from me."

As the second officer knelt, Caspian dropped the pistol deep into the pocket of his coveralls, then secured the man's wrists behind his back. Caspian disarmed both officers, then marched them across the warehouse and into the office, where Liesel had already subdued the security guard and zip-tied him to a metal desk leg. The guard sat on the floor with his back pressed to the desk, eyes wide and terrified, but he was otherwise unharmed.

"You okay?" Caspian asked Liesel.

"He had these in one of his belt pouches," she replied, holding several heavy-duty zip ties.

"Perfect."

One of the officers muttered something under his breath, and Caspian slapped him across the face before he was done.

"Make another sound and you lose a knee," he said.

The officer sneered and spat something crude in Turkish. Before the insult could finish leaving his lips, Caspian shifted his weight and drove the toe of his shoe into the man's knee. The blow didn't break bone, but it was hard enough to rupture a ligament. The officer collapsed with a strangled howl that was muffled by Caspian's hand over his mouth.

"Duct tape," he said to Liesel.

She passed him the roll, and he spent the next minute sealing the mouths of the injured officer, his partner, and the security guard. Then, using the remaining zip ties, he secured the two police officers the same way Liesel had done with the guard.

"Did you find anything?" he asked, looking at Liesel.

"Yeah," she said, holding up three sets of keys. "Let's go."

They stepped out of the office and moved quickly through the warehouse, Caspian leading the way. Using the security guard's badge, Liesel opened the side door the guard had used.

Outside, the rain had stopped, but it was still humid and warm. Looking around to get his bearings, Caspian realized they were on the far edge of the airport. Several vehicles were parked in a gravel lot adjacent to the warehouse. The vehicles were mostly airport utility trucks and ground crew vans, but there were a few private cars too.

Next to him, Liesel pressed the first key fob. Nothing. She tried the second, and a set of hazard lights blinked to life on a dusty gray maintenance van. Seconds later, they were in, with Liesel behind the wheel. The engine started on the first try, and they pulled away from the lot and merged onto the perimeter road that looped around the outer edge of the airport.

In the glove compartment, Caspian found a pocketknife, which he gave to Liesel, and a paper map. He unfolded the map and placed it on his lap. He studied it for a moment, searching for an egress route.

"There are several exits, but I'm sure they are all heavily guarded," Caspian said, reaching for his phone.

He used Google Maps to zoom in on the exits he had located.

"Yeah," he continued. "I don't think we'll be able to bluff our way through one of the checkpoints. Any second now, one of the officers we neutralized will be discovered."

"And when that happens, all the exits will be shut tight until we're found," Liesel said, her eyes on the road. "What's on your mind?"

CHAPTER TWENTY-NINE

Istanbul Airport
Arnavutköy District, Turkey

Caspian looked out the van's side window. The airport was surrounded by a thirteen-foot-tall metal fence topped with razor wire. He checked the map again.

"There's a large fuel farm on the west side of the airport. Keep driving north on this road, you should see it soon," he said. "Let me know when you do."

Caspian moved to the back of the van and opened the cabinets and storage bins as the van continued to bump along the cracked pavement. The bins and cabinets were filled with socket sets, jumper cables, spray cans of lubricant, and several other tools useless to him. But in one of the compartments, he found what he had been looking for. An industrial-size bolt cutter.

"I'm at the south end of the fuel farm," Liesel said.

He returned to the passenger seat, bolt cutter in hand.

"Keep the fuel depot to our right," he said. "There's gonna be a wooded area to our left very soon. That's where we'll make our exit."

"Right there," Caspian said a moment later, pointing a finger to a specific spot along the fence.

Liesel pulled the van to a stop, keeping about four feet between the fence and the vehicle. Caspian grabbed the bolt cutter and climbed out of the van. Using the van as cover, he slid the bolt cutter around the first link at the bottom of the fence and applied pressure. The blades bit into the metal with a crunch. It took him just over two minutes to cut a small access hole large enough for him and Liesel to squeeze through without getting shredded by the sharp ends of the metal.

He looked up at Liesel, who was still behind the wheel of the idling van, and gestured for her to lower the window.

"I'll cross over," he said. "Once I'm there, I want you to park the van real close to the fence. Make sure the side sliding door is aligned with the opening I made. And bring the keys."

She gave him a thumbs-up. Caspian pulled back the cut section of the fence, bending it against itself to widen the opening. He slipped through first as Liesel maneuvered the van into position. Caspian stripped off his coveralls and tucked the pistol into the waistband of his pants. Two minutes later, Liesel, also out of her uniform, climbed out the side door. Caspian held the fence open, and Liesel stepped directly from the van to the other side. Caspian tossed his coveralls inside the van.

"Let's go," he said to Liesel as she slid the door shut.

As he'd seen on Google Maps, there was a strip of dense brush and trees that separated the airport property from the beginning of an agricultural zone. From where he stood, Caspian could make out wide patches of farmland and a few irrigation ditches, but no buildings.

"There are buildings about half a mile west," Caspian said. "With luck, we'll be able to get ourselves a vehicle."

Liesel pointed to a shallow depression in the field.

"Natural cover," she said. "And it's heading west."

The terrain was rough and uneven, but they were making good time. Every few strides, Caspian glanced over his shoulder to make sure they weren't being followed.

"You still have the keys?" he asked.

"You want me to toss them?"

"Yep."

Liesel threw the van's keys into the air, sending them sailing deep into a section of tall grass to their left. With the van blocking the hole and the keys gone, any would-be pursuers would either have to waste time cutting a fresh breach or race back to a gate, both of which would buy him and Liesel precious minutes. They continued to push forward until they reached a low rise where Caspian dropped to one knee. He motioned for Liesel to do the same, then scanned the area carefully. Ahead of them, scattered along a dirt road, were several modest farmhouses. Four of them had a detached garage tucked behind them.

"I see a lot of rusting tractors and battered pickup trucks," Liesel said, "but by the look of them, I'm not sure they'll be of any use to us."

Caspian didn't disagree.

A dog barked in the distance, and Caspian tensed. He watched for movement, his hand going to his pistol. "You see it?" he asked.

"I heard it. Hopefully it's chained up," Liesel replied.

He spent another minute studying the arrangement of the buildings, noting the distance between them and the main road. None of the properties had heavy fencing, just low stone walls or basic wire stretches that were designed more to keep livestock in than people out.

"You think any of these folks keep their daily drivers in their garages?" Liesel asked.

"Hard to tell, but if they do, I'm hoping they left the keys in the ignition," he said.

"Old habits die hard in places like this," Liesel said. "So, we might have a shot."

Caspian gazed toward a slightly more isolated farmhouse near the end of the dirt road. A garage sat detached from the house. It was a small concrete structure, and dark green mold had long ago taken hold on the roof tiles. The garage's main door was closed, and so was its side door, but there were no visible locks. More importantly, Caspian saw no evidence of security cameras. A dirt driveway ran from the road to the garage. Parked outside in the grass, and just off the driveway, was a blue tractor. Its two rear tires were half deflated.

"Should we start with this one?" Caspian asked, pointing to the farmhouse.

"Lead the way," Liesel replied.

Caspian approached the garage first, his pistol in the low-ready position, while Liesel hung back to provide cover. He tested the handle to the side door. It was unlocked. He eased it open, wincing as the hinges groaned.

He stepped inside. The air was heavy with the smell of motor oil and warm metal. The odors brought Caspian back decades, and for a moment, he wasn't breaking into an old, run-down garage in Turkey, looking to steal a car . . . no, he was twelve years old again and stepping into his father's garage after a Sunday afternoon spent playing in the woods with his friends. In front of him, his dad was under the hood of the '65 Stingray he loved so much, humming to the Stones with his sleeves rolled up and grease on his hands.

Caspian blinked and pushed the thought away.

The garage was cluttered but not abandoned. Tools were scattered across a workbench on the back wall, and a red jerry can was in one of the corners next to a stack of firewood. An old Fiat Regata sat lopsided near the center of the space, its front wheels removed and its undercarriage resting on small jack stands. One of the Fiat's side mirrors hung loose by a wire.

He was about to exit the garage when he saw something bulky resting beneath a black, dusty tarp. Caspian pulled the tarp back.

A motorcycle.

He allowed himself a small grin, but it disappeared after he checked the ignition. No keys.

"It's an old Honda dual sport," Liesel said as she entered the garage. "Great bike. And this one looks in decent shape."

"At least it's not missing a tire," he replied, looking at the Fiat. "Can't say the same about this one."

"You found the keys?" Liesel asked.

"No such luck."

"Okay . . . I can hot-wire it," Liesel said, examining the motorcycle.

"Yeah? You sure?" he asked.

Liesel flashed him an annoyed look. Caspian raised his hands in surrender. "I . . . never mind. Sorry."

"We can't start it here. It will be too loud," she said. "Help me push it out of the garage."

After verifying that no one was waiting for them on the other side of the door, Caspian joined Liesel, and together they wheeled the motorbike outside, rolling it as silently as possible down the dirt road. The more distance they put between them and the house, the better.

They were sixty feet down the road when, cutting through the relative silence, Caspian heard a furious bark echoing.

Caspian spun around, only to see a shepherd mix tearing across the field, its eyes locked on them, snarling as it sprinted in their direction.

"Dog," Caspian hissed, pulling his gun. "Start the bike!"

Next to him, Liesel pulled the Honda's seat up, exposing the ignition wires. Caspian didn't dare look at her; his eyes were fixed on the charging dog. The animal was lean, fast, and its muscles rippled as it ran. Caspian raised his gun, willing Liesel to work faster.

Damn it.

Killing a dog hadn't been part of his plan.

———

Liesel cursed as her fingers searched for the ignition wires in the tight space. The bike was older than she thought, and the wiring felt ancient and stiff. She could hear the low, furious growl of the approaching dog, and she felt the pressure tighten around her chest.

Focus. Start the bike. The rest is Caspian's job.

She pulled the small pocketknife Caspian had found earlier in the van and used it to strip the ignition wires. Her hands trembled slightly, not from fear of the dog—though there was a bit of that too—but from the knowledge that she only had seconds.

Seconds to get this right or everything would fall apart.

Another growl. Much closer now. Liesel forced herself to block it out, narrowing her world to the three frayed wires in her hands. Sparks jumped as she twisted two of them together, the acrid smell of burnt plastic stinging her nose.

Five more seconds. That's all she needed.

"C'mon, Liesel," she heard Caspian mutter. "C'mon. It's about to turn ugly."

She connected the final wire, praying the old bike still had enough life left in it. The engine coughed once, then caught with a roar that felt like salvation. Adrenaline flooded through as she swung onto the seat.

"Let's go! Get on!" she shouted to Caspian, looking over her shoulder.

That's when she realized she'd taken too long. Not by much, just a second or two, but still too long. The dog had launched itself into the air, its jaw wide open, aiming straight for Caspian's throat.

———

Caspian held his fire. The dog wasn't attacking out of malice; it was just protecting its territory and owners. He couldn't bring himself to shoot it. Not for doing its job.

Instead, attempting to draw the dog off course and give Liesel a few extra seconds, Caspian stepped away from the bike and raised his arm like a bullfighter offering his cape. The dog was charging even faster than Caspian had estimated. Which was a good thing because it would be harder for the dog to adjust its trajectory. Behind him, the bike's engine roared to life, and he heard Liesel yell something at him, but Caspian didn't dare look back.

Eight feet in front of him, the dog had launched itself, its mouth wide open, its teeth bared.

At the last moment, Caspian ducked. The dog soared over him, and Caspian heard the vicious snap of its jaw as it missed his head by less than two inches. A millisecond later, one of the dog's hind paws clipped his shoulder. Not willing to go for another round, Caspian spun, then leaped onto the bike. To his right, the dog skidded to a stop, its claws scrambling for traction as it prepared to attack again.

"Hold on!" Liesel shouted as she gunned the throttle.

The rear tire sprayed loose gravel in every direction as the bike lunged forward. Caspian glanced over his shoulder. The shepherd mix was looking in their direction, but it wasn't chasing after them. It had done its job: scared away the intruders.

Caspian wrapped his arms around Liesel. Ahead of them, the dirt road curved toward open farmland.

And in the distance, Istanbul.

CHAPTER THIRTY

New York City, New York

Everett Westcott poured himself his first coffee of the day as sunlight spilled through the tall windows of his penthouse dining room. The night before, after all of Westcott's guests had left the restaurant, Charles Mpassi had briefed him on the events that had taken place in Mallorca. While Mpassi's update about Mallorca had carried some not-so-good news, Mpassi had kept his voice composed, as he always did. But now, as Mpassi stood in front of him, Westcott could see his associate was close to losing his temper.

"Coffee?" Westcott asked.

Mpassi shook his head as he sat down in front of him. "I had one my way here," he said. "But thank you."

"More bad news?" Westcott asked.

For the next little while, Mpassi shared with him the numerous situation reports his men had given him from Istanbul.

"Are we in any way exposed?" Westcott asked once Mpassi was done talking.

"Mia handled Mallorca," the man replied. "But there's still more work to be done."

"What do you mean? Where is she now?"

"She's resting in Ibiza with Verena, waiting for my instructions. I wanted to speak with you before issuing her new orders."

"You're considering sending her to Istanbul, aren't you? That's fine. Do it."

Westcott knew Mpassi well enough to recognize when his director of the Office of Special Projects didn't agree with him. "What is it, Charles? You don't think it's a good idea?"

"Maintaining Mia's cover should be our priority here, sir. That's what allows her to move pretty much anywhere she wants. Sending her to Istanbul will make it impossible for her to get to Budapest in time. And honestly, I wouldn't even know where to send her in Istanbul. It's too soon to send Mia."

Westcott thought this over, then said, "Then I'd like her to pay a visit to the yacht broker Verena used to charter *Veloce*."

Mpassi nodded. "I think that's a great idea, one she herself suggested."

Of course she did, Westcott thought.

The Egyptian army officer attached to the El-Sa'ka Force, the unit that had overseen Mia's fourteen-month-long training program, had deemed her the best female student he ever had. Westcott wasn't surprised. From the beginning, since the very day he had rescued her off the northern coast of Venezuela after the seas had capsized the migrant boat she'd been traveling on, he'd known that Mia Hernandez was cut from a different cloth. She was more than a reliable field asset—Westcott had many of those—she was the best operative he had. As talented as she was as a piano player, it was nothing compared to what she could do during an operation. Mia was the kind of operative that could, in the blink of an eye, become emotionally inert when the mission called for it. Pulling the trigger had never been a problem for her. And she'd proven it again in Mallorca.

As long as she believes she's doing it for the right reason. And it's my job to make sure she does.

But, even more important to him than her tactical skills was her loyalty. It was a trait he valued more than anything. If she'd made the decision to keep Verena alive, then Verena had done something to earn it. That alone intrigued him.

Westcott's decision to hire Verena hadn't come from a file or a recruiting pitch. He had known her father, a talented pilot who'd died during a mission Westcott had assigned to him. So, when the opportunity to bring Verena into the fold had presented itself, Westcott hadn't hesitated. He wasn't the kind of man who forgot a debt. Nevertheless, Verena had been a gamble from the start. A former LAPD detective with a tarnished badge and a chip on her shoulder, she'd brought grit and practical instincts to Blackstone Security. She had shown promise, even leadership, but Mallorca had been dangerously close to becoming a disaster, one that could have unraveled more than just a side operation. Had Mia not stepped in, Westcott would have been forced to clean up a much bigger mess. He was looking forward to speaking to Mia directly to hear why she'd decided to give Verena a second chance.

He took a sip of his coffee, then asked, "Getting back to Istanbul, what do we know about the couple who dismantled part of Verena's team in Port de Sóller?"

"Not enough," Mpassi admitted. "We thought they were Canadian operatives at first, but the documents were sophisticated forgeries. Not perfect, but very, very good."

"How did you figure out they were fake?"

"I haven't seen the passports myself, but my contacts told me they checked the stamp entries in their passports and found two that didn't match the database we have access to. One was in New Zealand, the other Egypt. We would have never figured it out if we didn't have a gate into these countries' visa information systems. Whoever these two operatives are, they have a good team backstopping them. And the fact they escaped Turkish authorities confirms they're also well trained."

"Mossad?" Westcott asked, setting his coffee mug down.

Mpassi shook his head. "We're checking, but it doesn't feel like Mossad. They're too preoccupied with Tehran and southern Lebanon. If I had to guess, I'd say they're Americans, or maybe Brits."

Westcott crossed his legs and was silent for a moment.

"That could complicate things," he said.

"It could," Mpassi said. "But I believe we've contained the threat. The mole's dead. And so is Hobb. Mia disposed of Hobb's body offshore, miles away from the location she sunk the *Veloce*."

"Hobb might be dead, but what about his employer?" Westcott asked.

"Hobb was working freelance. We checked his emails, hacked into his phone and his two laptops. We found nothing. He had just begun his investigation. Verena's team acted before he could release any compromising information."

Westcott considered that, drumming his fingers on the table, then said, "I'm worried about Istanbul. I understand sending Mia would be counterproductive at this time, but can't we send someone else after them?"

"We could, but our resources in Turkey are thin. We have several of our top operatives working to soften the leadership in the DRC. Their efforts are bearing fruits, but if we pull them out now, it could jeopardize our plan for the Congo River. We could task Blackstone Security, they've done great work for us, but they're now compromised. And, as we've seen in Mallorca, they aren't the right fit to go after two trained operatives."

Westcott narrowed his eyes at Mpassi. "Maybe your decision to remove Maximilian Kross off the board was a bit premature, don't you think?" he said. "We could have sent him to Istanbul."

"He was getting sloppy, sir," Mpassi replied, shaking his head.

"So you said."

"May I remind you that it was Mia who recommended Kross's termination?"

Westcott slammed his palm on the table. It was so sudden that Mpassi, who was usually stoic, jumped in his seat in surprise.

"Don't you dare put the blame on Mia," Westcott shouted, pointing a finger at the man seated next to him. "Mia is a technician, you're the strategist."

While Mpassi looked repentant, he didn't avert his eyes like Westcott thought he would.

"Mia was right. Kross had become a liability. He knew too much, and he talked too much," Mpassi said with conviction. "Maybe I did drop the ball about the timing of it all, and if I did, I apologize. But, sir, Kross had to go. After Manchester, it was just a matter of time."

Westcott knew that, but that didn't mean he had to like it.

"As I said," Mpassi added, his tone more conciliatory now, "if you really wanted to, I could move an asset or two out of the DRC and send them to Turkey."

"But you think it would be counterproductive," Westcott said.

"I do. Momentum is everything, and we have it now. We can see this through. We're close. I can feel it. We can't take the foot off the pedal now. Last time we decided to veer off course—"

Westcott interrupted him by raising his hand.

"If you were about to mention North Korea, don't," he said. "We knew from the get-go it was a long shot."

Months ago, Westcott had authorized a risky operation to help North Korea acquire a new generation of optical packages for satellites and guided missiles. The operation had failed, and Westcott had lost one of his most precious assets in the process. Furthermore, in prioritizing the North Korea operation instead of the one in Africa, he'd almost lost the momentum he had worked so hard to get in the DRC.

"Nailah would have wanted us to push through, Everett," Mpassi said, his voice low and compassionate.

Westcott knew his friend was right. On both counts. He'd made a promise to Nailah. And he intended to keep it. There was just too much at stake to slow down.

Thirteen percent of the world's global hydropower, to be precise.

Since he had founded Hearts United, he'd watched Africa continue to tear itself apart, thanks to the corrupt governance structure of many African countries. But blaming everything on the unethical regimes that plagued the continent—or even on extremist groups like Boko Haram and

Al-Shabaab, who had no morals and weren't shy about exploiting weak states, poverty, and poor education to recruit and terrorize civilians—would be shortsighted.

Westcott had studied history, and it was obvious to him that Africa had been dealt a bad hand by the colonial powers who had completely disregarded the ethnic, linguistic, and cultural boundaries of the African people when they had drawn the borders during the Berlin Conference of 1884. In dividing the continent the way they had, the fourteen countries that had attended the conference, the United States being one of them, had forced rival groups into the same states and split unified people into different ones. In Westcott's opinion, this had planted the seeds for many of the current internal conflicts.

While he didn't have the power to rewrite history, he did have the influence and the means to do something about the current leadership in the Democratic Republic of the Congo, a country he deeply cared about. Not just because of its mineral wealth and strategic potential, but because his Nailah had been born there. The DRC was where Hearts United was the most needed. The country could still be saved, but only if its future were guided by the right hands.

His hands.

The country's enormous population growth, if not controlled, would lead to an even worse humanitarian crisis. The numbers were terrifying. As of this moment, the population explosion had no infrastructure to support it, and the country's institutions were gutted by corruption and fear. If he didn't intervene, there was a chance the DRC would never recover.

I can't let that happen.

In order for the DRC to rise, he would have to break it first. The old guard needed to be removed, surgically and one by one. Like he'd done in Aruba. There, too, Mia Hernandez had excelled.

But there were many others who needed to be shown the door.

And if he was to trust Mpassi, this part of the plan was coming along nicely. In their place, Westcott would install leaders loyal not to foreign interests or their own clans, but to a vision. His vision. Nailah's vision.

Just like I've done in Senegal and Kenya.

There had been resistance there too. But resistance had a way of vanishing when roads were paved, when lights came on, when fresh water was readily available, and when jobs returned. While there was still a lot of work to do in these two countries, Westcott, through Hearts United, had brought much-needed political stability to these regions. Hearts United had poured a lot of money into Senegal's growing energy sector and had sponsored a multitude of vocational youth programs that had helped thousands of young men and women.

And, of course, Westcott had also backed the right people to run the show. The soft coup hadn't been perfect, but it had wielded positive results.

As for Kenya, Westcott had solicited private equity firms to invest in Nairobi's booming start-up ecosystem. It hadn't been easy, and it had taken a few more years than he had hoped, but ultimately, his plan had worked, and everyone involved had benefited from it. Though he'd always refused to take credit for it, Westcott knew it was because of him that Nairobi had earned the nickname of Silicon Savannah. But he hadn't stopped there; he had teamed up with Doctors Without Borders and funded its intervention in Garissa County, a large-scale operation focused on the communities in and around the Dagahaley refugee camp, a location that had been affected by severe flooding. Hearts United had financed all needed medical care and the distribution of hygiene kits to displaced families. Westcott had also traveled to the Dadaab refugee complex to personally supervise the construction of two hundred communal latrines as well as a medically assisted therapy clinic, which offered methadone and buprenorphine treatments, mental health services, and social-reintegration support to drug addicts. These initiatives had earned him favors not only with Doctors Without Borders but with the Kenyan government too.

Favors he had already called in to appropriate large mineral-rich swaths of land, which would help Hearts United finance its other initiatives, like the one in the DRC.

Now, Westcott's eyes were on the Democratic Republic of the Congo. And the clock was ticking. He would do anything in his power to restore the dignity of the Congolese people. And if that meant silencing critics, bypassing democratic delays, and sending highly skilled operatives like Mia Hernandez to get the job done, then so be it.

"Sir," Mpassi said, pulling Westcott out of his reverie. "What do you want to do about Istanbul?"

"You really don't think these two operatives are a threat?" Westcott asked.

"I'm not worried about them. As I said, I believe we mitigated the fallout. We flushed them out with the arrest warrant. And with what they've done at the airport, I can guarantee you the police will be looking for them."

"But they're still out there," Westcott said.

"They are, yes, but we must think strategically here. If we pursue these two further, we increase our profile. And right now, they have nothing. They may be good, lucky, or both for all I care, but they're in the wind now."

"And what about your contacts outside of law enforcement?" Westcott asked. "Do you know anyone in Istanbul that could help? Discreetly?"

"Not directly, but there's a broker I've done business with in the past who could potentially reach out to his own contacts. Using him would keep Hearts United out of the picture."

"Then do it, Charles," Westcott said. "Now, tell me about the warrant. Can it be traced back to us?"

"My team is scrubbing the origin request from the Turkish systems as we speak."

Westcott studied Mpassi and thought he detected a tell that his man wasn't being totally transparent. "I feel like there's a 'but,'" he said.

Mpassi shifted in his seat. "But . . . if someone with enough juice digs deep enough, they might find fingerprints we missed."

Westcott didn't answer right away. He appreciated the honesty, but didn't care that he had to probe to get it. He reached for his coffee mug, took a sip, and let the silence stretch, his way of showing Mpassi he wasn't pleased. If there was one thing Westcott despised, it was uncertainty. And these two operatives and that arrest warrant represented just that.

"I don't like loose ends, Charles," he said finally.

Mpassi swallowed hard. "And neither do I," he said. "Our two biggest threats are gone. Hobb and that treacherous bitch, Sofie Bergmann, are both dead."

Westcott nodded slowly, absorbing it all. Sofie had shown so much promise. It was too bad she hadn't been able to see past the few unpleasantries Westcott needed to do to bring order to the DRC. Maybe he had brought her into his circle of trust too soon. Mpassi had warned him about that, but he hadn't listened.

He sighed. He wouldn't repeat the same mistake twice.

As for Istanbul, this cloak-and-dagger stuff was Mpassi's area of expertise, not Westcott's. Then he remembered a discussion he once had with Mpassi about an elite group that specialized in tracking and eliminating problems.

"Are you still in touch with your contact in the United States? The one who handled the kind of problem we're facing in Turkey?"

Mpassi shook his head. "Her name was Laura Newman."

"Was? What happened?"

"She's dead. Her husband too," Mpassi replied. "No one really knows what truly happened. The official police report said it was a murder–suicide. They found Laura's body in the Potomac, shot in the neck."

"And her husband's?"

"In the woods, behind the rifle that killed his wife."

"He killed her?" Westcott asked.

"Again, that's what's written in the police report. Apparently, he shot himself after killing his wife. But I don't believe it. Someone took them out."

"A competitor?"

Mpassi shrugged. "Who knows?"

"That's too bad. You told me she was running one of the best freelance assets there was."

Mpassi nodded. "She did. Elias. That was the asset's moniker. Nobody knows who he, or she for that matter, is. And Elias hasn't reappeared since."

"Maybe Elias is the one who killed Laura and her husband," Westcott said, thinking out loud.

"Could be, but it doesn't matter, because I have no way of contacting Elias. Laura was Elias's handler. She controlled everything."

Westcott sighed.

"Fine," he said. "Apart from the broker, let's not spend any more resources actively chasing these two ghosts. But I want you to upload their data and behavior patterns to our systems. If they surface again, I want to know."

"Understood," Mpassi said.

"And make sure to ask your contacts in Turkey to share their passport photos with your broker."

"Of course."

"Is there anything else?" Westcott asked.

"No, sir."

Mpassi stood, offered a short nod of respect, and left the dining room without another word. Westcott didn't watch him go. Instead, he stared at the last dark sip of coffee. He trusted Mpassi. The man was competent, he had good judgment, and he was loyal.

Still, there was something about the two operatives who had disappeared in Istanbul that made Westcott's instincts itch. Loose ends, no matter how quiet, had a habit of unraveling entire empires.

And Westcott had no intention of letting anyone undo what he had built.

CHAPTER THIRTY-ONE

Defense Intelligence Headquarters
Joint Base Anacostia-Bolling
Washington, DC

The migraine was a freight train. She had felt it coming. At first it had been distant, like a rumble on the tracks. And then it had become louder, sharper, and angrier. And now she could feel it drilling into her skull just behind her right eye. Her doctor had warned her.

"Too much coffee. Too little sleep, and too much stress, Samantha," she'd said. "You need a break."

A break. I wish.

It had been a long day. Ranger's stomach growled. She glanced at her watch. It was well past dinnertime and the cafeteria's closing time. Though she hadn't eaten anything since the two reheated pizza slices she had for breakfast, she didn't think her digestive system could handle another packaged burger from the vending machine. She reached into the top drawer of her desk, unscrewed the cap of a white-and-blue bottle with a snap, and swallowed four Advil pills using the dregs of her fifth coffee of the day. She then made her way to the espresso-colored leather armchair that she kept by the window and sat down, propping her legs on the matching ottoman. The number of nights she crashed here every month, a secure tablet still glowing on her chest, was embarrassing.

Her office was as no nonsense as she was. It was utilitarian, somewhat spacious, but definitely not modern. Apart from the armchair she slept in more often than her own bed, everything else in her office was government issue. Even the generic pictures of the Swiss Alps on the walls, though she had selected them herself. Ranger leaned back and stared at the ceiling. Despite the large amount of coffee she had ingested, she was dead tired. She, along with her team, had worked nonstop for the last twenty-four hours trying to figure out what had happened in Mallorca, and then in Turkey.

A knock at the door jolted her, and she looked at her watch again.

Shit. I fell asleep.

Her assistant, a young man with perfectly combed hair and orange-rimmed glasses, poked his head in.

"Nicklas Drescher is here," he said.

"Yeah. Send him in," she replied, getting to her feet.

Drescher stepped in a moment later, walking with a slight limp—the cost of a mission in Venezuela where he had saved Ranger's life and lost his right leg. He was of medium height and build and wore a gray suit that wasn't tailored but seemed to hang perfectly on him. His face was unreadable, almost bored, but Ranger knew better. Behind those eyes was a mind that never stopped turning.

"Nicklas," she welcomed him with a genuine smile. "It's good to see you."

He took her hand and brought it to his lips, but didn't touch the skin. It was a courtly habit she'd once found annoying. Not anymore.

"The pleasure is all mine, Sam," he said.

"Coffee?"

He waved her off and sank into one of the chairs in front of her desk. "Did you hear from them?" he asked.

"As a matter of fact, I did. A colleague in Istanbul confirmed Caspian and Liesel made contact. They're in a CIA safe house waiting for instructions."

Drescher nodded, and she saw the relief on his face.

"If the BND can help in any way . . ."

"I appreciate it. And I'll make sure to ask if we do. But we've got it handled for now," she said.

He gave her a skeptical look. "You do?"

Ranger arched a brow. "Is this your not-so-subtle way of telling me I missed something?"

"Not at all. Just wondering where you stand on Everett Westcott."

Everett Westcott. The name alone made her temples throb harder. Ranger reached for the Advil bottle again, thought better of it, and placed it on the desk instead.

"We've started looking," she said. "Quietly. But like I told Caspian, Westcott isn't just connected to the highest levels of power, the man's revered in many circles."

Drescher nodded. "We feel the same way."

"We? As in the BND?" she asked.

The German spy gave a noncommittal shrug. "And the entire German government."

She looked at the bottle of Advil. Her doctor had warned her to cut back. Apparently sixteen pills a day wasn't sustainable. She sighed and reached into the mini fridge behind her desk. She grabbed two bottles of water and tossed one to Drescher.

"Hearts United has your government's support?" she asked.

"Full support," Drescher confirmed. "And to be honest, I understand why."

Ranger popped four more pills and took a swig from her bottle. Her doctor would throw a fit, but her doctor wasn't trying to hold the world together with chewing gum and half-truths, was she?

"What about Sofie?" she asked.

A shadow flickered behind the German spy's eyes. "Not much more than what you already know," he said.

"You believed she was dead?"

"We all did. Until we didn't."

"Meaning?"

Drescher leaned forward. "She's the reason we recalled Liesel to Berlin a few months back. Facial recognition flagged Sofie in an African airport."

"An African airport? Can you be more specific?"

"I'm afraid not."

Ranger understood. The BND was clearly breaking a few laws in accessing a foreign nation's security system.

"What's the BND doing scanning for long-dead logistics officers in African airports?" Ranger asked.

"That's just it, my friend. We're not."

She set her water down. "Then who submitted her into the system?"

"Not sure, but if you're asking me to guess, I'd say it's probably the same people who green-lit the arrest warrant for Caspian and Liesel in Turkey."

Her pulse ticked upward.

"We're trying to trace it," she said. "But Ankara isn't exactly cooperating. I don't need to tell you how strained our relations are with them at the moment."

Drescher didn't reply. He didn't have to. Every intelligence officer worth their salt knew that the United States' relationship with Turkey had shifted from alliance to uneasy coexistence. The Cold War had bonded them, and NATO had reinforced the link, but now? Turkey was hedging its bets. Buying the S-400 missile systems from Moscow hadn't just sent shock waves through the Pentagon, it had triggered sanctions. Ankara claimed it allowed them a certain strategic autonomy, but Washington had called it a betrayal. Add in the disputes over Syria and the American support for some Kurdish groups, and the whole relationship had turned into a transactional mess.

"It's a different world, I guess," she offered.

"Different times, different rules," Drescher said.

"Okay. Let's assume you're right and that the same person flagged Sofie and framed Caspian and Liesel. That means we're asking the same two questions."

"Who. And why," Drescher said.

"Outside of our respective organizations and a few other agencies allied to us, there aren't many players who could pull off both," Ranger said.

"Hearts United is one," Drescher suggested.

She stared at her friend. "You really think that NGO is pulling the strings?"

"I don't know. I'm not jumping to conclusions here, Sam. I'm just asking questions."

Ranger crossed her arms. "Hearts United has done real work, with real, positive impact. They installed solar grids in Chad, provided access to clean water across the Sahel—"

"And food aid to Ethiopia," Drescher interjected. "I know all that, Sam."

But Ranger wasn't done. "They're planning huge infrastructures projects, and they've already transformed whole regions—"

Drescher cut her off. "There. You just said it."

"Said what? I don't understand."

"They've transformed whole regions," Drescher said.

"Yes. For the better. C'mon, Nicklas, Hearts United is one of the few organizations that's actually helping."

"I'm not saying they aren't."

"For God's sake. Then what are you saying?"

He met her eyes. "Have you looked closely? At the projects themselves?"

"I've read the briefs."

"The briefs. Right," he said, standing.

She rose with him. "Wait a goddamn second, will you? You just planted a bomb in the room, and now you're leaving?"

"I have to go back to the embassy. I'm sorry."

Ranger sighed. "All right. You want me to look closer, I'll look closer. I owe you that much."

"And more," he said, a smile appearing on his lips.

"Yes. And more," Ranger agreed. "But you need to help me out here. What should I look for exactly?"

"Sam, I don't want to skew your judgment," he said.

"You're kidding."

"I'm serious," he insisted. "If we both reach the same conclusion independently, we'll know it's solid. As I said, I'm not jumping to conclusions."

She knew he was right. "A hint, then?"

Drescher paused at the door. "Kenya," he said. "Start there. And again, don't hesitate to reach out if you need our help."

And with that, he walked out of her office, leaving her staring at the bottle of Advil, wondering if she was going to need a hell of a lot more.

CHAPTER THIRTY-TWO

Ibiza, Spain

Mia sat on the edge of the bed, elbows on her knees, reading the message she'd received from Operations.

Your plan is approved. Proceed to Valencia.

She had expected to hear back from Operations sooner. She'd submitted her idea almost twenty-four hours ago. Now, to make it in time for her concert in Budapest, she'd have to hurry. But that was fine. She had an idea how to expedite the mission. She'd put Verena to good use.

The small studio apartment she'd rented for two nights through a house-exchange app was located above a ceramic shop in Santa Eulària, a small town on the southeastern coast of Ibiza. There was no air-conditioning in the unit, only a ceiling fan that was stuck on the lowest setting. A table and two chairs were by the kitchenette, and a drying rack leaned against the wall by the balcony door. For the last two nights, Mia had slept in the folding cot that was wedged in one corner of the room. The cot had barely been wide enough for a child, but Mia didn't care. She had slept like a baby.

Verena stirred under the thin linen sheet. Mia studied her. She thought the other woman looked younger in her sleep, almost innocent. It was hard to believe she'd killed a cop and helped Mia sabotage a multimillion-euro yacht. Mia had seen Verena as deadweight when she'd first boarded the *Veloce*. But, contrary to that useless skipper Justin Burton, Verena had fought back. Mia had seen the shift in her. Verena hadn't just accepted the danger, she'd embraced it. Maybe she'd understood the stakes, or maybe she had simply nothing left to lose. Either way, Mia could work with that.

She stood from the bed and padded across the tile floor, opening drawers in the dresser by the small bathroom. They had spent the previous day shopping around town, and while Mia's primary objective had been to acquire a pistol, they'd also bought several pieces of high-end designer clothes that would fit today's mission. Mia tossed a few pieces onto the bed. She headed for the kitchenette, started the coffee machine, and rummaged through the cabinets. She found a tin of oatmeal that was still sealed. They had eaten out the day before, but today's tight schedule wouldn't allow them to repeat the experience. The oatmeal would have to be good enough. She boiled water and poured it over the oats in two bowls. As steam rose from them, she crossed the room.

"Time to get up," Mia said, placing a hand on Verena's shoulder.

Verena flinched awake, blinking at her. There was a second—just one, though—where Mia saw Verena's fear and confusion. Then Verena relaxed, her gaze steadying on Mia's face. Wordlessly, she pushed herself upright.

Five minutes later, they sat at the dining table, their knees almost touching. Mia took a spoonful of oatmeal and said, "Eat fast. We're going to Valencia."

They ate in silence for a minute. Then Verena set her spoon down.

"How will we get to Valencia?" she asked.

"By helicopter," Mia replied, checking the time on her watch. "And we're leaving in twenty minutes."

"Really?"

"Is that a problem? Don't tell me you're afraid of flying?"

"I'm not."

"Good. Then get ready," Mia said, getting up. "Expensive yachts like the *Veloce* just don't vanish off the face of the earth. So, sometime today, or tomorrow at the latest, someone will start panicking. And I want to deal with the broker before anyone figures out what happened to the yacht."

CHAPTER THIRTY-THREE

Caspian knew the safe house was bugged. It belonged to the CIA, after all. But at the moment, he didn't care. He was grateful for the shelter. The apartment was on the third floor of a four-story, white-colored building along Güneşli Sok, a secondary street in the Cihangir neighborhood of the Beyoğlu district of Istanbul.

They'd ditched the motorcycle about half a mile away, locking the steering but leaving the keys in the ignition. Caspian had no doubt it had already been stolen and, if they were lucky, was either stripped down for parts or already parked in some underground lot waiting to be sold on the black market.

The news had covered the airport incident briefly, thirty seconds at most. Caspian had tried multiple channels, but nothing else had come up. Online, there were no headlines and, even better, no images. That didn't mean they wouldn't have to be careful. Istanbul's surveillance network was dense, with thousands of CCTV cameras located across the city. From where they had left the bike, Ranger had directed them on a route that avoided known cameras, and she'd even sent them a marked-up map of blind zones, but it wouldn't help if they had to leave the safe house in a hurry.

He and Liesel had taken turns sleeping. While one got some shut-eye time, the other kept watch on the grainy video feed streaming from the two miniature cameras mounted discreetly across the street. The interior of the safe house was sparse, but it was functional. The fridge was stocked with sodas and bottled water, and the shower had decent water pressure. In one of the cabinets of the tiny galley-style kitchen, Caspian had found cereal boxes and canned beans. Even better, Liesel had discovered travel-size toothbrushes and toothpaste under the sink and had declared it a minor miracle.

He was about to open the last can of beans when his phone vibrated. It was a message from Ranger.

Call me. I've worked out an egress route for you and Liesel.

He turned toward Liesel, who was sitting cross-legged near the window, sorting through the map on her phone. He held up his phone and gestured for her to follow him to the bathroom. Caspian closed the door and turned on the shower and the faucet.

He dialed Ranger.

"Everything okay?" she asked.

"You ever tried cereal and beans in the same bowl?" he asked.

"Excuse me?"

"Never mind. What've you got?"

"Sending you a location now. It's an underground parking garage beneath the Grand Hyatt. It's not too far from where you are, but it's still a thirty-minute walk or so."

Liesel showed the hotel's location to Caspian on her phone.

"Once you're there, look for a blue van with diplomatic plates in slot G33," continued Ranger. "Someone will be waiting for you. I'll text you the cipher through the encrypted app."

"To drive us where?" Caspian asked.

"To the German consulate. It's right next to the Park Bosphorus Hotel. It's literally a five-minute drive from the Hyatt."

Caspian frowned, but it was Liesel who asked the question. "Why the Germans? Is the BND involved?"

"There's too much heat around the American, Canadian, and British embassies. Turkish counterintelligence flagged them all this morning. They'll be watching everyone who goes in and out. That's why I don't want you two to simply walk into the German consulate. And to answer your other question, Liesel, yes, Nicklas is facilitating everything on the German side."

"And what happens after we get to the consulate?" she asked.

"You'll be taken to Hezarfen Airport," Ranger said. "It's a private airfield about thirty miles west of Istanbul."

"You sure that's a good idea?" Caspian asked. "Last time we were at an airport, we almost got caught."

"This isn't a commercial airport," Ranger said. "You'll be flown out on a private jet Nicklas arranged through the German executive-transport wing. There's no manifest."

"Okay . . . and where are we flying to?" Caspian asked, trying to keep up.

"Valencia."

"Spain?" Liesel asked, stepping closer to the phone. "We're going back? Why? I thought you wanted us back stateside."

Caspian had been about to ask the same question, so he listened to Ranger's reply carefully.

"*Veloce*, the yacht Caspian spotted, was chartered from a brokerage firm in Valencia. It's a small operation, and they don't keep digital records."

"No online records? You mean everything is still on paper?" Liesel asked.

"Either that or they have a server that's not connected to the internet. We couldn't find anything."

"Can't you hack into their bank records?" Caspian asked.

"We did. They do have smaller accounts with local banks, but their main accounts seem to be with a Swiss bank. And, as you both know, the Swiss banks are much harder to break into."

Caspian looked at Liesel, then asked, "Didn't the Guardia Civil already check the boat out? And what about Hobb? What did you learn?"

"Yeah . . . well, that's where it gets a bit murky," Ranger said. "The Guardia Civil sent a patrol boat, but it never came back."

"Wait . . . what?" Caspian asked.

"It has gone silent, and so did the *Veloce*."

Liesel cursed under her breath. Caspian thought this over, then said, "Even if we get our hands on the charter records, it will probably trace back to some shell company."

"Maybe, but if you can find the hard copy of the contract, I bet the banking info, or at least the name of the Swiss bank they're dealing with, will be on it."

"That's not much to go on," Liesel said.

"But it's the only thread we've got. For now," Ranger replied.

Liesel crossed her arms. "You're working on something else?"

Ranger paused. "Kind of. Too early to share anything with you. But I'll keep you in the loop. For now, get to the Hyatt's parking garage. If *Veloce* truly disappeared, you won't be the only ones looking for answers."

Caspian hung up, turned off the shower and the faucet, then met Liesel's gaze.

"Back to Spain," he said.

Liesel shook her head. "You got to be kidding me."

———

They slipped out of the safe house ten minutes later, blending into Istanbul's early morning beat just as the first light of dawn streaked the horizon. The scent of warm, freshly baked sesame bread drifted from a nearby bakery, which made Caspian's stomach growl, making him wish he had eaten something more substantial than a bowl of beans for breakfast.

The steep streets of Cihangir were slowly coming to life. All around them, vendors rolled their carts into place and shop owners got ready for the day ahead. To Caspian's right, a boy zipped past on a scooter.

Caspian had visited Istanbul before, but he'd never set foot in that particular neighborhood. To him, with its cute little streets, squares, and alleys, Cihangir felt like the most European sector of the city, though he couldn't believe how many stray cats there were. In front of him, the Bosphorus was visible in the distance, like a ribbon of steel cutting the city in two.

The Grand Hyatt Istanbul, and its underground parking garage, was just beyond the Gezi Park and the bustle of Taksim Square. But instead of heading directly there, Caspian and Liesel weaved a meandering course through secondary streets and pedestrian alleys, doing their best to stay away from the CCTV cameras Ranger had identified. They hugged the corners and paused before each intersection, and Caspian kept his eyes scanning for anything that felt off.

As they made their next turn, Caspian slowed. A bit farther on, two police officers stood near a tram stop. They weren't talking, they were looking down the street. One held a tablet angled up toward the foot traffic. He grabbed Liesel's arm and pulled her close to him and into the recessed doorway of a closed antiques shop.

"Two cops. They're scanning for faces," he said.

She peered past him, then nodded. "I bet they're looking for a man and a woman," she said.

"Right. And there are probably more of them. Some of them in plain clothes," Caspian said, glancing down the hill toward the Bosphorus.

"We need to split up, Casp. They're looking for a couple. We'll have a better shot at reaching the Hyatt if we separate."

He nodded, knowing she was right. But he didn't like it. And that was a problem too.

Stop being overprotective. She can handle herself.

Caspian pulled his phone out of his pocket. "Okay. Let's link up," he said, sliding a Bluetooth earpiece into his ear.

Liesel did the same.

"I'll take the Taksim route," Caspian said. "I'll head up through the square, past the Cumhuriyet Aniti, then east down Mete Caddesi. I'll cut through the pedestrian path near the Dolapdere lights and circle around to the Hyatt's service entrance."

Liesel looked at her phone, using the map Ranger had sent them. "I'll loop west and cut through the antique district."

"This shouldn't take us more than twenty-five minutes," Caspian said, dialing her number.

Liesel accepted the call, then she looked at him, holding his gaze for a few seconds. Without a word, she leaned in and kissed him. For a moment, and for the first time since they had fled the airport, everything slowed, and the noise in Caspian's mind faded.

Liesel broke the kiss, stepped back, and pressed her hand on his heart. "See you in twenty, okay?"

Then, before he could respond, she turned and walked away. As he watched her turn right at the next intersection, one thought stayed with him, an unshakable whisper at the edge of his mind.

Your luck is about to run out.

CHAPTER THIRTY-FOUR

Istanbul, Turkey

Caspian adjusted the collar of the lightweight jacket he'd borrowed from the safe house and made sure to keep his eyes shaded beneath the brim of the black baseball hat he'd just purchased. Though it was still early and he had only left the safe house less than fifteen minutes ago, morning had now fully arrived in Istanbul, and the closer he got to Taksim Square, the busier it got.

Caspian turned onto Siraselviler Caddesi and slipped into the flow of pedestrian traffic. The air, tinged with diesel fumes, was getting warmer, and Caspian knew he would have to shed his jacket soon. Keeping it on would make him stand out. But he'd have to be careful to leave his shirt fully untucked to conceal the pistol wedged into the waistband at the small of his back.

The earbud in his right ear crackled. "I'm making a quick detour, Casp," Liesel said. "I might have a tail. Not sure yet. I'm heading south toward Tomtom Kaptan."

Caspian pursed his lips, but he didn't slow his pace. In his mind's eye, he visualized the map of the area. "I can be there in six minutes," he said.

"No," Liesel said. "I'm not new at this. I'll see you at the Hyatt."

Caspian didn't like it, but he had to let go. Liesel knew what she was doing. She didn't need him to babysit her.

His lips barely moving, he said, "Copy that. I'm two minutes from Taksim Square."

He passed a shop window and caught his reflection. Nothing about him stood out. His posture, his clothes, even the way he walked. Everything he did was calculated to avoid drawing the eye. His decade of operating solo had drilled it into him.

He turned right onto the southern edge of Taksim Square, merging with a cluster of about thirty tourists gathered near the Cumhuriyet Aniti, the eleven-meter-high Republic Monument that honored the founding of the Turkish Republic in 1923. The tourists were led by a guide holding a laminated paddle labeled with the logo of a popular cruise line. Being this early in the morning, Caspian assumed it was a predeparture tour. Their chatter was cheerful and oblivious, but even better, most of them were Caucasian. He fit right in.

He stayed near the rear of the group, using their collective bulk as a screen while he scanned the plaza. He spotted six police officers scattered across the square. Two stood near a taxi stand. One of them, just like the cop he'd spotted earlier, held a tablet. Two more officers leaned against a police van near the park entrance, scanning the crowd with a relaxed but alert expression. Another pair stood near the edge of the monument, speaking with a city sanitation worker. Caspian, still with the group of tourists, walked past them. They glanced his way, but only briefly, before continuing their conversation with the city employee.

A minute later, he split from the group of tourists, who seemed to be heading back toward a waiting bus. He followed the curve of Mete Caddesi, his eyes constantly moving.

"Liesel, update," he said.

She came back immediately. "I think I'm good," she replied. "I'm about to head north. I'll be there in twenty minutes. I'll let you know if anything changes."

"Understood. Approaching the Hyatt now."

As he neared the Hyatt, he took a hard right into a side alley that ran parallel to the hotel's delivery entrance. Caspian walked toward the entrance, carrying himself like someone on the payroll. He stepped inside, nodded to a hotel employee who was pushing a laundry cart, and moved deeper into the corridor, heading toward the elevator bay.

"I'm at the Hyatt. Give me an update," he said.

No reply. He tried again.

"Liesel? Everything okay?"

Still nothing. Then he heard someone take a sharp breath, and it took him a second to realize the noise had come via his earbud.

Then someone yelled, and Caspian froze in place, his heart pounding. *Liesel.*

Everything around him seemed to mute as he concentrated on the sounds and voices coming through his earbud. He didn't call out her name, didn't ask if she was okay, because he knew that if she could talk, she would.

A faint sound bled through his earbud. A grunt? Then he heard something else. It was the unmistakable thud of something solid striking flesh.

Caspian's gut clenched, and he knew, without the shadow of a doubt, that Liesel had just been taken.

CHAPTER THIRTY-FIVE

Istanbul, Turkey

Liesel Bergmann had spotted the man a few turns ago, about seven minutes after she'd split with Caspian. The man was short and wore a pair of blue jeans, a dark jacket, and a beige ball cap. Both times she'd glanced at him, his hands had been in his pockets and his head was just low enough that she hadn't been able to see his face.

She updated Caspian, letting him know she might have picked up a tail. As expected, he offered to come to her assistance, but she refused. There was no point in him exposing himself further. And to be honest, she wasn't sure she was being followed. Yet.

The man with the beige ball cap hadn't been looking directly at her, but something had seemed familiar about him. Had she first seen him while she was still with Caspian? She didn't know. Istanbul was full of men who looked like him. But something inside her was triggered when she'd noticed the man again. As a deep cover operative who had worked in the United States for years, Liesel had learned a long time ago that the moment you think someone might be following you, that's the moment everyone suddenly starts to look suspicious. Her BND instructors had warned her about this, and they'd taught her to keep her cool and to keep an unflustered, critical eye on the world around her.

Don't get tunnel vision, Liesel, she reminded herself.

Still, right now, everyone *did* look suspicious. Fifty feet in front of her, a woman was talking on her phone, gazing Liesel's way. Across the street, a city worker was sipping his coffee, and Liesel could feel his eyes on her.

Liesel tensed as her mind began working the situation. Had she been compromised? And what about Caspian? Had he picked up a tail too?

She forced herself to calm down and to concentrate on her breathing for a few seconds.

While she didn't take the possibility of being tailed lightly, did it really make sense that someone would be following her? Either the authorities had pegged them, or they hadn't. And if they had, why play cat and mouse? Why not just pounce on her? Subtlety wasn't part of the Istanbul Police tool kit, not when one of their own had been hurt.

She and Caspian had left a trail of unconscious bodies in their wake. Three police officers and one security guard. They hadn't killed anyone, and they had used the least amount of violence possible to neutralize them, but she didn't think their "restraint" would count for much in the eyes of the Turkish authorities. She and Caspian had embarrassed them. Big time.

Liesel knew what the unwritten rules were . . . they were the same across police departments all over the world. Take one officer out, and the entire department will hunt you, looking to get their own kind of justice on the perpetrator. She didn't blame them. She'd do the same. But that didn't mean she was going to let them catch her and drag her into a van.

Liesel moved through the winding streets with calm, her eyes constantly moving. She performed a quick series of turns and double-backs, but without making it obvious that she was running a quick surveillance detection route. As tired as she was—though the few hours of sleep she'd managed to get the previous night had taken the edge off—all her senses were on alert. Her SDR wasn't perfect—it was way too short—but she hoped it would be enough to flush out a poorly trained plainclothes officer.

She'd joined the BND because she wanted to make a difference and do cool, dangerous stuff. When she'd been accepted into the elite unit of the BND tasked with deep cover operations on foreign soil, she was sure she'd hit the jackpot. But when her training ended and she learned that she was going to New York, she'd been less than thrilled. She'd thought that speaking four languages, including Arabic, would have guaranteed her a position in the Middle East where she would have helped break up terror cells. It hadn't.

Apparently, the BND had more than enough intelligence officers with the same language skills she had. What had set Liesel apart was her accounting degree and her two years of experience in forensic accounting. So instead of chasing terrorists, she'd become a corporate espionage specialist—a far cry from the glamorous spy stuff she'd envisioned she'd be doing.

Then Caspian Anderson had entered her life, and everything changed. Her life had become much more dangerous.

She knew something inside her had cracked when she'd been shot in France. And again, when Sofie had died in Port de Sóller. The adrenaline rushes she'd been craving earlier in her career didn't feel like premium fuel anymore; they felt like fucking poison.

While she wasn't certain, she had the impression that Caspian acted differently with her since she'd nearly died in Bordeaux. He was more protective of her, too much sometimes. She appreciated the love, but whatever additional attention he was giving her meant he wasn't focusing on the task at hand.

At the airport the day before, she hadn't lied to him. They really needed to talk.

She loved Caspian, but if the last year had taught her anything, it was that *this* life, as much as she had once wanted it, was no longer for her. She wanted to slow down, not live constantly on edge. She wanted kids. A garden. She wanted the life Caspian's parents—Richard and Elizabeth—had.

But what about Caspian? He loved her, she knew that. But did he love her enough to step back from this crazy life? That was a question she didn't have the answer to. And it scared her.

And even if he wanted out, would Ranger let him?

Liesel made a left onto a pedestrian street and immediately turned into a cluttered antiques shop. She played tourist, browsing through the scarves, rugs, and brass bowls while keeping watch on the street. After two minutes, when the man with the beige ball cap didn't appear, she let herself relax, just a bit, and exited.

She was about to inform Caspian of her status when his voice came in through her earbud.

"Liesel, update," he asked her.

"I think I'm good," she replied. "I'm about to head north. I'll be there in twenty minutes. I'll let you know if anything changes."

"Understood. Approaching the Hyatt now."

Liesel stepped into Muammer Karaca Tiyatro, an alley carved between two aging buildings that led to Istiklal Caddesi, one of the most prolific pedestrian streets in Istanbul. A black cast-iron gate stood under an archway, but it was open. The alley, much narrower than she expected it to be, was lined with overflowing garbage bins and stank of urine. Graffiti covered the outside walls of the buildings in layers of angry, spiked scripts. Homeless men and women huddled in small groups, talking loudly in Turkish as she walked past them. One man offered her a drink from his bottle. She ignored him, but thanked him nonetheless.

Liesel quickened her pace. She was only twenty meters away from Istiklal Caddesi when she sensed movement to her left. She turned, just in time to see a man lunge from the recessed doorway of a long-ago closed shop. His face was covered with large reddish blotches, his eyes were bloodshot, and he was swinging a long, serrated knife at her heart. She pivoted, deflecting the attack with her forearm, but the blade snagged her jacket, slicing through it, and the tip of the blade tugged against her belt.

Pain shot up her side.

Then an elbow slammed into her jaw, snapping her head sideways with such force that her earbud popped free. Before she could recover, thick arms wrapped around her from behind. A second man had locked his forearms around her torso, pinning her arms, his chest pressing against her back.

Her body, honed by countless hours of Krav Maga classes, reacted before her brain fully comprehended what was happening. She thrust the heel of her left foot into the shin of the man behind her. He barked in pain but held on, which turned out to be a good thing because it allowed Liesel to draw both knees up, feet off the ground, and kick forward. She caught the charging knifeman in the gut as he was about to stab her in the abdomen. But the hit wasn't clean, and the man's knife nicked her right leg, slicing through her skin from ankle to mid-shin. She screamed as the energy of the impact sent her and the man holding her crashing into the wall. The man lost his footing, and Liesel twisted out of his grasp as they fell, landing partly on top of him. She drove her right thumb deep into his left eye, and the man yelled in pure agony.

She rolled away from him and scrambled to her feet, her injured leg buckling under her. Her wound was already leaking through her pants, but she had no time to assess its severity, because the knife-man was closing in again. But this time his approach was slower, more cautious. He telegraphed his next strike, and when he lunged, she stepped forward and parried with her left forearm, knocking his knife hand aside. She pivoted to her left and hammered the chop side of her right hand into the inside of the man's forearm with as much power as she could muster. The man's fingers opened, and the knife dropped.

But Liesel wasn't done.

She shifted her weight and drove her left fist into his throat. His eyes opened wide in shock, and his hands shot up to his crushed wind-pipe. It wasn't a killing blow, but it was enough to drop him to his knees, choking. She was confident the man would be forced to eat his meals through a straw for a week or two.

She turned to face the other man, and she saw him coming at her with a steel pipe. The man was huge and very tall. He had the shape of a heavyweight boxer who had fought his last bout years ago, but who could still be dangerous. His left eye was shut and bleeding, but the right one was rage filled. He swung wide. She ducked, and the steel pipe flew over her head. Pain flashed up her bad leg as she dipped low. She came up off balance, half falling into the wall.

She had to end the fight. Now. She was losing blood faster than she thought.

She tried to kick low, go for the man's knee, but her leg gave out and she dropped to one knee. Her eyes locked onto her assailant's remaining eye. The man, who was now madly smiling, reset his swing.

Shit. I'm dead.

In desperation, she brought her forearms up, but the blow never came.

Instead, there was a crash of glass, and she heard the man grunt. One of the homeless men, the one who had offered her a drink, was behind him, wild-eyed and completely drunk, clutching the jagged remains of a broken liquor bottle. Liesel's attacker turned, pipe raised, and began to swing it toward the other man's head when the drunk charged him, plunging the broken liquor bottle into his ribs.

Liesel, wanting to take this new opportunity to get out of the alley, forced herself upright. Everything throbbed, and her leg was soaked in blood. Her coat too. She staggered forward, toward Istiklal Cuddesi.

She could see it. It was right there. Only a few more steps.

Behind her, she heard the steel pipe clang to the ground. She glanced over her shoulder. The homeless man had jumped onto the other man's back and seemed to have his teeth buried deep in his neck.

The hell?

Liesel tried to pick up the pace, but she couldn't. She didn't have the energy. Her hand went to her side. It came back wet and sticky. She looked. Blood. A lot of it.

Had she been stabbed twice? She'd been so focused on fighting the two men, she couldn't remember.

She pulled her phone. Her hands were shaking. Caspian's number glowed on the screen. The call was still active, connected to her now-lost earbud. She moved to switch off Bluetooth, but her vision swam. Then the world tilted, and she slumped against the wall.

Fuck.

Her hand found her side again. The pain was sharp now, definite. Her knees folded, and Liesel felt herself slide down the dirty, graffiti-colored wall in slow motion. She could see the people on Istiklal walking by, but none of them looked her way.

And even if they had, they would have only seen another drunk. Another ghost.

And then her eyes closed.

CHAPTER THIRTY-SIX

Istanbul, Turkey

Caspian didn't want to do it, but he had no choice. He had to sever the connection to Liesel. His thumb hovered over the screen of his phone a beat longer, then he pressed the button to end the call. Whatever had happened in the alley, whatever had silenced her, it wasn't the kind of trouble he could help her with from where he was. Even if he was to sprint to her location, he'd be too late. If she was still alive—and he hoped to God she was—his running blindly through Istanbul wouldn't accomplish anything.

She needs help. Real help.

He called Ranger's emergency line. She picked up immediately, her voice brisk.

"Caspian, I can't talk right—"

"I need your help. Now."

"What's going on?" she asked.

"Liesel's last ping was at the corner of Istiklal Caddesi and Muammer Karaca Tiyatro," he said, walking toward the elevator bank. "Something's happened. I don't know what, but she's not responding. I think she's hurt."

"You're not with her?"

"We had to split."

"Okay. What do you need me to do?" Ranger said.

"The driver who's waiting for us at the Hyatt," he said, watching the elevator numbers descend, "I need you to contact whoever controls that asset and tell them we need to get to Liesel. And I want everyone the German consulate can spare to look for her. I don't care if they're desk jockeys or fucking interns."

"Caspian, I can't just redirect—"

"For God's sake, Samantha, Liesel might be bleeding out in an alley," he said, his hand clenching the phone.

There was a moment of silence, then Ranger said, "I'll do what I can. But this is still a BND operation. I don't control their assets."

"Nicklas does," Caspian said, then ended the call before she could respond.

The elevator doors opened with a shudder, and he stepped inside, punching the underground-level button with his fist. There was no one else in the elevator, so Caspian allowed himself to curse out loud. This wasn't how today was supposed to go.

At this very moment, Liesel might be bleeding out in some piss-soaked alley, and all he had was a damn code phrase and Ranger's word that someone would be waiting for them in the parking garage. The elevator doors slid open again.

The underground parking level smelled like concrete dust. Faded directional arrows were painted on the floor, but most of them were covered by oil stains. Caspian checked his phone. He had one bar. He called Liesel's number. It took a few seconds, but it started to ring.

C'mon, Liesel. Pick up.

She didn't.

Caspian lowered the phone, then scanned the garage. The lot was about three-quarters full, but he saw only a few people. A young couple pushing a stroller was about to exit near the far stairwell, and a man in a suit was walking toward the elevators, talking loudly to someone via Bluetooth.

That's when Caspian spotted him.

A man stood by a support pylon, leaning just enough to look casual. Caspian didn't buy it. The man was in his late thirties, maybe early forties. He had a lean build and a clean-shaven face with short-cropped hair and was wearing a blue tracksuit. His eyes met Caspian's for a full second, then darted away.

Definitely not a tourist, Caspian thought. *But not a pro either.*

Caspian adjusted his angle, walking toward the far side of the F row before dipping behind a silver four-door sedan. He moved quickly, his steps absorbed by his rubber soles and the worn asphalt. He cut between two cars, then another, approaching the man's blind side. Caspian dropped into a crouch behind a red SUV and waited, watching through the passenger-side window as the man scanned the garage, clearly alert.

He's looking for me.

Caspian looked around to make sure no one else was closing in on him, then glanced back toward the watcher. He was coming his way, and his lips were moving. He wasn't alone.

Sliding along the back of the SUV, Caspian circled wide, staying out of the man's line of sight before closing the gap once the man had walked past his position. Caspian came in from the man's blind side and grabbed him by the collar of his tracksuit, yanking him backward, using the man's own momentum to unbalance him. Caspian hooked his heel behind the other man's ankle and swept his legs out from under him, sending the man face first onto the ground. Caspian was on him in an instant, one knee digging into the small of his back, and the tip of his pistol pressing firmly against the base of the man's skull.

"Who are you talking to?" Caspian asked in Turkish as he patted down the man with his free hand. "And keep your voice low."

"I . . . I don't speak Turkish," the man sputtered, his voice cracking in surprise.

Caspian recognized the accent and switched to German. "Fine. Who were you talking to?"

"No one!"

Caspian used two fingers to dig out an earbud from the man's right ear.

"Don't fuck with me," Caspian growled.

"I'm . . . I'm a diplomat. From the German consulate," the man pleaded.

Caspian narrowed his eyes and dropped the first line of Ranger's cipher.

"I'm looking for someone to take me to Silivri," he said.

The man hesitated, then replied, "Too much traffic at this time of day."

"Maybe tonight, then?" Caspian asked.

"Tomorrow would be even better," the man said, finishing the coded exchange.

Caspian muttered under his breath. He'd been ready to kill the man if he had to.

"You alone?" he asked.

"There's a driver."

"Where?"

"Parking slot G33."

Caspian helped the man to his feet. "Lead the way."

They moved quickly, but Caspian kept the man five steps ahead of him. As they turned the corner into the G section, he spotted the vehicle. It was a compact commercial van, a dark blue Mercedes-Benz Citan. It was parked facing out. A woman stood beside it. She had short blond hair and wore a pair of black jeans and a black leather jacket. She was on the phone, but the second she saw them, she hung up and shook her head at the man Caspian had just tackled. No words, just a look that said *you screwed up*.

She clicked the fob in her hand, and the van gave a soft chirp.

"You, get in the back," she said to Caspian. "We're leaving now."

"Not yet," Caspian said. "Has anyone contacted you?"

"Yes. Orders have changed. I was told to expect two passengers, but not anymore."

"We need to pick up someone," Caspian said. "A friend of mine."

"No, we don't. Hop in—" she started to say but stopped when Caspian brought up his pistol.

The woman sighed, but didn't look overly worried. It was clear to Caspian this wasn't the first time someone had pointed a gun at her. She remained composed, contrary to her colleague who looked like he was about to vomit.

"I told him this was going to happen," Caspian heard the woman murmur. Then louder, she asked, "Can I reach for my phone? It's in my pocket."

"Slowly," Caspian warned her.

The woman dialed a number, then put it on speaker.

"What is it, Frieda? Why aren't you on your way?"

Caspian recognized the voice instantly. It belonged to Nicklas Drescher.

"I'm afraid Mr. Anderson isn't cooperating," Frieda said, her eyes boring into Caspian.

"Let me speak to him," Drescher said.

"I can hear you, Nicklas," Caspian said, lowering his gun.

"A team from the consulate is already en route to her last known location," the German spymaster said. "Please follow Frieda's instructions. She'll tell you everything you need to know."

CHAPTER THIRTY-SEVEN

Valencia, Spain

Francisco Morientes thanked the barista with a bright smile and stepped out into the morning sun, a double espresso in hand. The scent of the sea, mixed with the aroma of freshly baked bread from a nearby panadería, drew another smile from him. He loved this town, and he loved his life. He was living the dream.

As he walked along the curved path that followed the marina's edge, he passed a row of sailboats, their freshly polished hulls catching the sunlight. He recognized one of the sailboats, a six-year-old, forty-six-foot Beneteau Oceanis. Its previous owner, a lovely lady who had inherited it from her husband, had given him the listing. The boat hadn't sold, and the lady had ended up gifting it to her son who wasn't using it more than once or twice per month. In Francisco's opinion, the boat was being underutilized, which was a shame.

A bit farther on, he spotted a Riva Virtus, a sixty-three-foot Italian beauty he'd never seen before at the marina. The boat had aggressive lines and a low, muscular profile. Boats like these made his heart beat faster.

It's probably a transit, he thought. But he made a note to come back a bit later and introduce himself to its owner. Who knew, maybe he could convince them to move into an even bigger, newer yacht?

Francisco smiled at a crew hosing down the deck of a Sunseeker, then waved at a harbormaster he'd gotten to know over the last year. Francisco liked people, and they liked him back. He had a quick smile, always made time for a chat, and was good at remembering their names. But under that easygoing charm was a relentless drive. He wasn't in this game to be liked—though in this business it helped that he was—he was in it to win.

His parents had never understood his love for the yachting industry. His father had sold cars for thirty years and still lived in the same two-bedroom apartment on the outskirts of Valencia. His mother, a nurse, had always told him to find something stable.

"Get a government job, Francisco," she'd said. "One with a pension."

Instead, Francisco had followed an attractive yacht broker on Instagram when he was sixteen. That woman's feed had changed his life. Every post of hers had fed Francisco's ambition. It seemed that every week she was on a different superyacht or at a different boat show. And the car she drove, that Maserati convertible she raced along Monaco's streets . . . that's the life he wanted. And he knew it was up to him to build it. It wasn't going to be handed to him.

So, he'd studied hard, got good grades in high school, and got accepted at the IE Business School in Madrid. His parents didn't have the money to support him, so during the summer months, he'd worked fifteen-hour days, six days a week, washing boats to pay for his tuition. And he'd taken his job seriously, always going above and beyond. The owners appreciated his hard work, and he'd befriended many of them. During his last year of college, he had made friends with trust fund kids by starting a yachting club, which had given him the experience he needed—and the connections—to get a job as a junior yacht broker in Valencia. Now, at only twenty-four, he was already closing deals the other junior brokers at the brokerage firm could only dream about. He still lived with his parents, yes, but not for long. Not if he kept closing these lucrative deals.

Francisco arrived at the brokerage's glass-fronted office and opened the door. He stepped into the cool air-conditioned space and made his way to his desk, waving a hand to Esmeralda, the hardworking receptionist and office manager. Francisco's desk was located by a large window with a view of the canal that linked the east and west sides of the marina. He tossed the empty espresso cup in the bin, sat down, and woke up his computer. The screen flickered to life, showing the digital dashboard of the brokerage firm's yacht-management system.

He rubbed his hands together, looking forward to whatever was coming his way that day.

Francisco's last deal, a two-week charter for the Azimut S8 he managed for the owner, had brought in close to 45,000 euros in commission for the firm. He'd only pocketed 30 percent, but that was still over 13,000 euros in his account.

Tonight, he was taking his girlfriend, Jana, out to celebrate. He'd met her in business school. She was brilliant, funny, and gorgeous, especially with the oversize sunglasses that made her look like a movie star. Francisco could already picture the life they'd build together . . . in Monaco. Once he'd gotten his promotion to senior broker, he would pitch his boss the idea to open a branch in the principality. A branch he, Francisco, would manage.

He opened his inbox. No new inquiries for the yachts he had for sale, but there was a new notification. He clicked on it. The app was no longer in contact with the *Veloce*'s onboard systems. It had also lost the GPS signal over the weekend.

Francisco frowned. "Weird," he muttered.

It had happened before. Network issues with the application weren't as rare as the people selling it claimed they were. But Francisco had seen other causes too. A faulty antenna, a skipper disabling the system by mistake, or a failure of the electrical system on a yacht. In theory, the system would reset itself automatically. Still, Francisco was the kind of man who liked to stay ahead of things. If something had gone wrong, he wanted to be the guy who'd already dealt with it when the others walked in.

He glanced at his watch. 9:35. His colleagues would be here shortly.

He pulled up the *Veloce*'s charter contract from the file cabinet and found the skipper's number. He remembered the man. A former US Navy officer named Justin Burton. Francisco had gone out of his way to make a good impression when the man had come to pick up the yacht last week.

"If there's anything, anything at all, just call me, day or night," Francisco had said, handing over his business card like it was a backstage pass to a Taylor Swift concert.

He dialed Burton's number, but it went directly to voicemail.

Probably out of range.

Then, a new notification pinged on his screen.

A lead!

He opened it. Another broker was in town with a client and had stumbled on his boosted Instagram post about the Absolute Navetta 52 he had listed not even forty-eight hours ago. She wanted to know if it was still available.

Francisco grinned. That post had cost him sixty euros to promote. If that post was all it took to sell the yacht, it would be the best sixty euros he'd ever spent. He typed a crisp but professional reply to let her know the yacht was indeed available and that it was in immaculate, show-ready condition. And that he'd be delighted to arrange a visit.

Two minutes later, the broker responded via text.

She had a tour at 12:00, but she was free now.

He typed his reply.

Perfect. I'll meet you at the dock in fifteen minutes. Sending pin.

He checked the asking price of the Absolute Navetta 52 again. *1.35 million euros.* Ten percent commission. Half for the seller's side, which left 67,500 euros for his brokerage. Out of that, Francisco would net 20,000 euros.

He jumped from his seat, grabbed his sunglasses, and practically bounced out of the office. Maybe the Maserati in Monaco wasn't so far away after all.

CHAPTER THIRTY-EIGHT

Valencia, Spain

Mia Hernandez stood just outside the gated pier entrance that led to Dock H, where the Absolute Navetta 52 was berthed. The gate was secured by a small electronic keypad and a simple magnetic lock. Over eight hundred moorings were nestled between the commercial port and the seafront promenade, and even on a weekday, the marina buzzed with activity. On Dock G, Mia could see charter guests rolling suitcases toward a catamaran. On Dock I, crew members were busy hosing down the decks of several yachts.

Mia wore slim white pants paired with a green blouse. Around her waist was a knockoff Louis Vuitton fanny pack. A white scarf was draped loosely around her neck, which she thought looked very glamorous with her pair of oversize sunglasses. She hoped that she looked like a successful yacht broker, the kind who had nothing to prove because the brokerage firm and the clients she represented guaranteed her access and respect.

Mia glanced at her phone, checking the time. By now, Verena was where she was supposed to be, nursing a latte two hundred meters from the broker's office, waiting for the text that would launch the next phase of the operation.

From where Mia stood, she could see the Navetta 52. It was docked halfway down the pier, its freshly polished structure gleaming under the sun. She had studied every inch of its layout on the flight over and knew it as if she was the boat's owner.

She spotted Francisco Morientes a minute later. He was in his mid-twenties, medium height but athletic, with the kind of tan that came from year-round, by-the-sea living. His white pants and pink dress shirt looked to be freshly pressed, though the baby blue jacket slung over his shoulders was a touch much for Mia's taste. Still, she appreciated his confidence. This was his stage after all.

As he neared her, a huge, sincere smile appeared on his lips. "Miss Torres?"

Mia returned it, dialing up the charm. "Pleasure to meet you, Francisco. I really appreciate you making time for this on such short notice. I know last-minute visits aren't the easiest to manage."

He waved the concern away. "Not at all. I'm happy to show it, and proud to do so. The yacht's basically still in showroom condition," he said.

"Then I can't wait to see it. My client's eager to move fast if it fits his needs."

Though she didn't think it would be possible, Francisco's smile widened. She could practically see him calculating his commission. He pulled out a small fob and tapped it against the gate panel. The lock disengaged with a soft beep, and she followed him through the gate and onto the dock. She noted how he instinctively walked to the right, leaving her the side with the view of the boat.

"This way," he said. "It's the best specced Absolute Navetta 52 on the market right now. It's only been on the market for a few days, but I've already had serious interest."

"I'm sure," she replied.

"Several other brokers are scheduled to see it this week."

"Is that so? But I'm the first to see it, right?" Mia asked, as if this had any importance.

"You are," confirmed Francisco, solemnly. Then, with more pep, he added, "And I think you'll be impressed."

They passed a few smaller boats, some sailboats and an RIB, but apart from a couple snapping selfies beneath the sailcloth of a monohull, the dock was clear.

"So . . . where's your office based, if you don't mind me asking?" he asked.

"Monaco," she replied.

He stopped mid-stride.

"Monaco? Really? Which brokerage?" he asked.

"Fraser Yachts," she replied, naming the largest full-service yacht brokerage firm in the world.

Francisco's eyebrows shot up. "No way. I was in Monaco last year and stopped by your offices. I didn't—"

Mia cut him off. "I've only been with them for six weeks," she said, her pulse spiking.

"That explains it," he said, almost to himself. "Well . . . you have my dream job. I'd love to work in Monaco someday. How did you end up there?"

Mia offered him a polite smile as they got closer to the boat. "It's not quite the dream you think it is," she said.

"No? How come?"

"I'd be happy to fill you in later, if you want," she replied, quickly glancing at her watch. "But I've got a noon meeting, and I'd really love to see this one."

Francisco recovered quickly and gestured toward the Navetta, now only two berths away. "Absolutely. It's a gorgeous yacht, and its layout is super efficient. You'll see."

At the base of the passerelle, he slipped off his loafers and set them neatly by a beige mat left there for that specific purpose. Mia mirrored his gesture and followed him onto the boat.

"The swim platform is hydraulic," Francisco said, "and the owner has equipped the transom with a barbecue and a bar."

She nodded. While she couldn't care less about the yacht, she had to admit it was stunning. The aft deck was shaded and staged with a teak table and four chairs, connected with the galley through a pair of large sliding glass doors.

"Francisco," Mia said, touching the man's arm. "Quick question for you."

"I'm listening."

"My client is someone who values his privacy, if you know what I mean," she said, giving him a knowing look. "So, if we were to move ahead with the purchase, and we might, because I really like what I'm seeing, I was wondering how your brokerage handles these sorts of . . . situations."

"I understand. Listen, Miss Torres—"

"Mia, please."

Francisco smiled, then said, "We have plenty of clients who are in the same situation, Mia. This isn't a problem for us. Over the years, we've figured out legal ways to keep the names of our customers buried. It's a bit more expensive, maybe another percent and a half, but for certain people, it's well worth it. And for added privacy, we keep all records of our transactions on a private server that isn't connected to the internet. Nothing, and I truly mean that, gets uploaded to the cloud."

"That's great to hear. And what about the payments?" Mia asked.

"Well . . . there are two options. Our brokerage deals with local banks here in Valencia, but for our clients who prefer a tad more discretion, we've partnered with a Swiss bank that can handle the financial transactions, but only if the money comes from outside Spanish borders."

Now it was her turn to smile. "That's perfect."

"Great. Should we start with the upper deck?" Francisco asked, his hand already on the polished steel handrails.

"Actually," Mia said, "would you mind showing me the twin cabin first? I know it's a strange request, but my client has two grandkids, and that third stateroom is a big factor for him."

Francisco nodded. "Completely understandable," he said. "It's more generous in size than people expect. Let me show you."

They entered through the galley and walked through the salon, which was bright and modern. Francisco led the way down the staircase. Directly ahead was the VIP stateroom. At the bottom of the stairs, Francisco turned and gestured to the right. "The twin's just here. Across from the guest head."

He stepped aside, holding the door open.

"After you," he said.

"Not at all," Mia replied. "Please, you go in first. It will give me a better feel for the space."

Francisco chuckled and stepped inside. That was all the time she needed to pull the garrote out of her fanny pack. A second later, she stepped behind him and looped the garrote over his head.

And then she pulled. Hard.

———

Francisco was about to turn around when something looped around his neck and then bit into his skin with shocking speed. At first, he thought it was a stray fishing line he hadn't seen, but then something slammed into the back of his knee, as if someone had hit him with a hammer, and he buckled forward. The thing around his neck, whatever it was, dug in deeper, tearing his skin. He clawed at it, but there was nothing to grip. It wasn't a rope . . . it felt like a guitar string, but sharper. Much sharper.

He couldn't breathe, and he couldn't speak, but he tried to call out anyway. No sound came out but a single low wheeze of air. Only then did Francisco realize he was no longer standing. He was on his stomach on the floor between the two berths. A knee drove into the small of his back, pinning him, then his head was yanked back, arching his spine unnaturally.

Torres? Was Torres doing this? *Why?*

His thoughts scrambled, and his vision blurred at the edges. He spent every ounce of strength he had left trying to wedge his fingertips underneath the wire cutting through his neck, but he just couldn't get his fingers to grip on anything but flesh and blood.

Jana.

Her face came to him in a rush. She was smiling, and not just with her mouth but with her eyes, too, the way she did when they talked about moving to Monaco or about buying their own boat someday.

She'd said they'd be unstoppable. And he had believed her.

He still did.

———

Twenty-three.

Mia stood still for a moment, listening.

The twin cabin was silent now, save for the subtle hum of the yacht's systems as the air-conditioning kicked in. Francisco lay face down at her feet, one arm curled under his torso, the other stretched toward the edge of one of the berths, as if he was still reaching for help with his bloody hand.

She didn't feel bad for him. Not exactly.

He hadn't deserved to die. But he'd been in the wrong place at the wrong time and had shaken the wrong hand.

Mia crouched over him and rolled the body onto its side, just enough to reach into his front pants pocket. His phone came out easily. She slid it into her bag. His key fob was a bit harder to pull out, but at least he had kept it in the same pocket, so she didn't need to roll the body to the other side.

She took a long look around the cabin. It was a bloody mess, but there was no sign of struggle outside the twin cabin. The garrote had done its job. It had been a while since she'd used one, but it was always great fun. Definitely more so than a gun.

Mia straightened her blouse, then grabbed her phone. She opened the secure messaging app and typed a short message to Verena.

CHAPTER THIRTY-NINE

Valencia, Spain

Caspian pulled the vehicle Samantha Ranger had set up for him—a black Audi Q5—into a curbside slot near the south end of Passeig de Neptú. He kept the engine running as he checked his surroundings through the side mirrors. After a minute, he shut it off and stepped out into the Valencia midday heat. Across the street stood La Pepica, a paella institution that had been open since 1898 and had seen everyone from Hemingway to royalty walk through its doors.

The eleven-mile drive from Manises Airport had taken just over thirty minutes, which wasn't bad considering the traffic along the A-3 and the midday surge along the Avenida del Puerto. Caspian hadn't expected to be here alone, but with Liesel's injuries, that's how it was going to be.

Thanks to Nicklas Drescher's fast coordination, a BND operator stationed in Istanbul who had clearly been ready to intervene had reached Liesel within minutes of Caspian alerting Ranger. The contact had exfiltrated her from the alley and gotten her to a private clinic on the Asian side of the city. The doctor—who Caspian had no doubt had been well compensated for his effort and discretion—had worked quickly. While Liesel's blood loss had been significant, the wounds were noncritical. She would need rest and probably rehab, again, but she was alive.

And out of the fight, he thought.

Caspian wasn't sure whether to feel grateful or cursed.

She'd been shot in Bordeaux and stabbed in Istanbul. Two different cities, two different operations.

And both had nearly killed her.

He sighed. Either someone upstairs had their hand on her shoulder . . . or she was running out of time. Now, it was up to him to figure out who had ordered Sofie Bergmann killed, who had taken Paul Hobb, and why.

And step one was right here in Valencia. He would find out who had chartered *Veloce* and go from there.

Caspian adjusted his shirt as he rounded the rear of the Audi, ensuring it draped cleanly over the concealed Kydex holster at the small of his back where the Wilson Combat SFX9 was secured. Whoever had staged the Q5 for him had done it right. Not just with the pistol but with the extra magazines, the suppressor, the industrial zip ties, and a lockpick kit that had been neatly stowed into the low-profile backpack that now hung over his shoulders. He hadn't taken a spare magazine with him because he hadn't liked the printing through his jeans. The SFX9 held sixteen rounds—fifteen in the magazine and one in the chamber. If he needed more than that today, then this operation had already gone sideways.

Hopefully, he wouldn't need any.

Like it had been in Port de Sóller, the streets were alive with the kind of crowd that masked threats well. There were plenty of families wandering around with strollers, tourists photographing anything and everything, and local cyclists weaving through selfie takers along the boardwalk. Caspian walked at a casual pace. His eyes, hidden behind a pair of polarized lenses, moved constantly but never paused too long on anything.

Just before he reached the Marina Beach Club Restaurant, his peripheral vision tagged a figure.

A lone man was seated on a bench beneath a palm tree that bordered the public footpath, right in front of a children's playground. The man's sunglasses made it impossible for Caspian to determine if the man was observing him or not. Caspian looked around, searching for anything else that would trigger his suspicion. But nothing did. The man had no obvious support, but Caspian had been in the field long enough to know that a good surveillance team was hard to spot.

He filed the man's face, his clothes, and his posture into his mental Rolodex, and kept walking. The brokerage office was housed in a modern ground-floor space between a strip of restaurants and the towering concrete elegance of Veles e Vents, the striking architectural landmark that had been inaugurated in 2006 as the centerpiece for the thirty-second America's Cup. To Caspian, the twenty-five-meter-high building loomed over the marina like a maritime control tower.

He didn't walk straight to the brokerage office. Instead, he ducked into a frozen yogurt stand and ordered a small chocolate cup. He paid cash, left a small tip for the teenager behind the counter, then carried the yogurt to a tall metal table near the sidewalk.

He didn't anticipate a trap, but that didn't mean he was about to walk blindly into the office of the broker who had chartered out *Veloce* either. Caspian gave himself five minutes to observe the restaurant terraces, the office's door, and the decks of nearby yachts.

Satisfied his sixth sense hadn't been tickled, he spooned the last of the yogurt into his mouth and wiped his hands with a napkin. He threw the empty cup into the bin, adjusted the pack on his shoulder, and headed toward the brokerage office.

As he reached for the door, he paused just long enough to scan his surroundings one more time, and that's when he noticed someone he hadn't picked up on earlier.

CHAPTER FORTY

Valencia, Spain

From her table on the mezzanine level of the restaurant, Verena Kaine had a perfect line of sight across the promenade and the yacht brokerage firm's entrance. She stirred a third espresso she didn't need, her eyes hidden behind her round mirrored sunglasses. She wore a flowing linen shirt over a tank top, and a brimmed hat sat low on her forehead, its front tilted down toward her eyes. She didn't particularly like the hat, she thought it made her look older than she was, but Mia had insisted on it. When Verena had first tried it on, she'd worn it a bit higher. Mia had shaken her head.

"You know, Vee, even the cherry on top of the fudge sundae needs to be put there with a certain flair, don't you think?" Mia had said, adjusting the hat. "See? Now it's better," she'd continued. "This way, you're wearing the hat, not the other way around. And it helps cover your face without making it obvious you're doing so."

Verena's phone was on the table beside her coffee, and a fashion magazine was open next to it. To anyone watching, she looked like another tourist killing time while waiting for her overpriced tapas to arrive. The brokerage office had been mostly still for the last thirty minutes. There had been only one visitor, a man in a blue shirt, but he hadn't stayed more than ten minutes.

She set the spoon at the center of the paper napkin, positioning it parallel to the cup. She made a quick adjustment to the napkin, then angled the cup's handle with the edge of the table.

Perfect.

Her phone buzzed. *Finally.*

She read Mia's text. Things were getting interesting, but a bit scary too. She still didn't know what to think of Mia Hernandez. Verena adjusted her sunglasses by the bridge, not because they needed to be, but because she just needed something to do with her hands while she thought.

She was usually good at reading people. It had been one of her strengths as a detective. Whether it was nervous energy behind a fake smile, the twitch of a jaw, or the widening of pupils when one of her questions hit too close to the truth, she'd been great at picking apart a suspect. But Mia Hernandez?

That woman was a goddamn cipher.

Verena couldn't tell if Mia trusted her, liked her, or had already decided she was disposable. And the worst part in all this was that she knew she was in too deep to walk away. Her gaze dropped to the spoon on the napkin. It was still perfectly centered, which was a relief.

Mia had done her job. The broker that Justin Burton had used to handle the charter agreement and the payment was dead. In her last text, Mia had confirmed that the broker, Francisco Morientes, had kept the original charter agreement tied to *Veloce* at his office. It was now up to Verena to get it and to erase all traces of its existence.

Verena got up, careful not to touch the napkin, and froze mid-movement.

A man was headed straight toward the brokerage firm. She only caught a quick glimpse of his face as he had glanced over his shoulder, but she knew him. Not by name, but from the drone footage over Port de Sóller. She remembered rewinding the video feed over and over, studying the way he moved. She was sure of it. This was the man who had taken out her team at the restaurant. This was the man who had bested her two security officers, Pam and Oscar, at the beach.

And now he's here?

Verena snapped a photo with her phone, doing it as discreetly as possible. She opened the encrypted thread and sent the picture to Mia with a single line.

The man from Sóller. He's heading into the office.

She sat back down, hand clamped on her phone, waiting for Mia's reply. The response came quickly.

Stop him. Now! I'll back you up, but I need six minutes to get there.

She stared at the message, her stomach tightening. She was too late to stop the man. He was already crossing the final stretch of the promenade. He was less than ten seconds from the door. She considered texting back to tell Mia the truth, that she'd missed her window. But she didn't. Instead, she slipped her phone into her pocket and stood.

Her hands moved automatically, aligning the chair she'd just vacated so its back was perfectly parallel to the one beside it. She straightened the small table, adjusted the salt-and-pepper set by less than an inch, even though every single fiber in her body screamed that she was wasting precious seconds. She wasn't doing this by choice; her mind simply wouldn't let her leave the table disorderly.

Satisfied, she stepped away, her chest hammering. There was something in the way Mia had worded her message that suggested this wasn't a request, but a directive. One that Verena had no choice but to successfully handle. She had the distinct impression that she was being tested, and that if she didn't act now, decisively, she wouldn't get another chance.

CHAPTER FORTY-ONE

The air-conditioning hit Caspian as soon as he stepped through the door of the brokerage office. Even after finishing the small cup of chocolate frozen yogurt just minutes ago, sweat clung to the base of his neck and along the spine of his shirt. The midday heat outside was climbing toward brutal, and the light breeze off the water hadn't done much more than move the humidity around.

The woman he'd spotted hadn't set off any alarm bells in his head, but while her face was partially hidden behind round sunglasses and a brimmed hat, he thought she looked somewhat familiar. But he wasn't worried, at least not enough to alter his plan.

Caspian let the heavy glass panel swing shut behind him. He kept his sunglasses on, if only to buy him a few seconds to survey the space discreetly.

A woman sat behind a sleek reception desk. She was in her late twenties, sharply dressed in navy and white, and was tapping a stylus against a digital tablet. Two men—who Caspian assumed were brokers—stood farther back near a glass-walled office, reviewing what looked like a set of yacht specs. They were both in their thirties and were dressed as if they were on standby for a regatta shoot. None of them looked up. Caspian stepped forward.

"Good afternoon," the receptionist said in Spanish, then repeated it in English without missing a beat.

Caspian answered in lightly accented Spanish. "Afternoon. I'm hoping you can help me. My client received an invoice from your office. The charge was over five thousand euros, and it was processed through his credit card without his authorization. I was never contacted about this, and now my client thinks I withheld information from him."

The receptionist was alarmed enough to set her tablet down on her desk. "Are you a broker?"

"No. I'm a lawyer."

The receptionist sat straighter in her chair. "Do you have the reservation number?"

"I do, but my phone's dead. It should be easy for you to look it up, though. It's still ongoing."

The receptionist stared at him, dumbfounded. "Are you saying your client got an invoice while his charter is still underway?" she asked.

"Yes. He's not thrilled about that. And I'm not, either, considering I wasn't even informed. Now I have an angry client mid-voyage and no information to work with."

The receptionist hesitated, but only for a moment. "Shit," she murmured, then asked, "What's the name of the yacht?"

"*Veloce*," Caspian said. "It's an Azimut S8."

"Let me check who the broker of record is," she said, pivoting to a different monitor behind her. "I'll need to access the charter log on our secure server. It will just take a moment."

"Of course," Caspian said, feigning mild irritation. "I'd appreciate it."

She began navigating through the internal system. Caspian shifted his backpack to his other shoulder as he scanned the office. The two men he'd seen earlier had now moved deeper inside the office. They weren't interested in him.

"Here it is," she said. "The broker of record is Francisco Morientes."

"That's right. He's the one who handled the booking for us."

"And just to confirm, your client is Blackstone Security, right?"

Caspian had to make an effort to keep a straight face. The receptionist had just given him what he'd come looking for. He could leave now, but what if he could get more intel out of the helpful receptionist? It was worth a shot.

"Also correct," he replied.

"I'll call Francisco," she said, reaching for the desk phone next to her. "He'll help you out."

Caspian's mind was racing, trying to figure out what he'd say to the broker. From where he stood, he could hear the phone ringing. It rang five times before Francisco's voicemail picked up. The receptionist hung up with a frown.

"He's not picking up," she said, clearly annoyed. "Now that I'm thinking about it, I believe he's out with a client."

"I can't come back later," Caspian said, letting a touch of irritation bleed into his voice. "My client's furious, and he's threatening to pull any future bookings. I'm not leaving without something I can show him."

Again, the receptionist hesitated, caught between protocol and practicality. An instant later, she gave in with a sigh.

"That's just the thing," she said. "I'm sorry, but I don't have anything to show you. I didn't see any damage listed in the file. There's no incident report, and no invoice logged in our system. I really don't understand how your client could have been billed."

Caspian didn't say anything. He let the silence sit just long enough to make her uncomfortable. After a few seconds, she offered a strained smile.

"Let me print the charter agreement for you," she said. "I'm not supposed to, only the broker of record is, but this is silly. Normally, any damages would be reviewed after the charter ends."

Caspian felt it was now the time to give the woman some slack.

"Maybe my client jumped the gun," Caspian said. "He can be overly dramatic."

She gave a half laugh and tapped a key. The printer behind her desk came to life, spitting out a three-page agreement.

"Here," she said, handing it to him. "This should clear things up. If you want, I can have Francisco call you as soon as he's back."

He looked at the agreement, skimming over it. There it was.

Blackstone Security—Client

Justin Burton—Registered Skipper

Francisco Morientes—Broker of Record

He folded the sheets in half and looked at the receptionist.

"Okay," he said. "Thanks for your help. You've been very professional."

"Can I take your number in case Francisco needs to reach you?"

Caspian rattled off a bogus number, two digits off a real diplomatic number he'd once used in Geneva. She wrote it down without question.

"Thanks again," he said, then turned and walked out of the office, the cool air giving way once again to the heat.

He unfolded the printout and stared at the names.

Justin Burton. He'd never heard the name.

Blackstone Security. That didn't ring a bell, either, but he knew Samantha Ranger would find something. He'd call her once he was back in the Audi, with the air-conditioning at full blast. He folded the agreement again and slid it into a side pocket of his pack.

CHAPTER FORTY-TWO

Verena waited twenty seconds after the man exited the brokerage office before following. Tailing someone solo wasn't easy, but she'd done it before. She was experienced at this kind of thing. Still, the man she was following had dismantled her team with chilling efficiency, so she wasn't going to underestimate him.

But right now, she had the upper hand. She had studied him, not the other way around. He didn't know she was behind him; she was sure of it. She could tell by the way he walked. The crowd helped, because despite the heat, the promenade was packed. It was filled with locals out for their lunch break and with families returning from the beach. Somewhere behind her, jazz music drifted from one of the beachside cafés.

Then, overhead, flying over the canal, a cheap plastic drone flew past, its high-pitched whine almost lost in the ambient noise. Verena looked up, trying to pinpoint the drone's exact location, and almost bumped into a pair of American tourists who were blocking the walkway while licking at their melting ice cream cones.

When she looked back toward the man, he had stopped at a juice bar and seemed to be ordering a lemonade. She stopped beside a vendor's cart and looked at the display of handmade jewelry. She turned a pair of earrings in her hands.

When she glanced up again, the man was gone.

Shit. Her heart rate skyrocketed. *Where the hell did he go?*

Verena turned slowly, pretending to examine another set of earrings. He couldn't have gone far. There were too many people for him to sprint without drawing attention. He had to be somewhere close. She stepped away from the vendor's cart, searching for the man with her eyes.

Someone grabbed her arm, and Verena spun to the right, ready to strike.

It was the vendor, a small woman with a surprisingly strong grip.

"You need to pay for those," the woman loudly said in Spanish.

Verena was about to reply, when she realized that the woman was right. She'd walked away from the vendor's cart with a pair of earrings still in her hands. She cursed herself and gave back the earrings with an apology.

Her phone vibrated in her pocket. She knew it was Mia. She didn't answer. She couldn't. She had to fix things first. She needed to know what the man had learned at the brokerage firm and if he'd shared his findings with anyone. Then she'd kill him with the knife Mia had given her.

Just then, she spotted him. He was fifty feet away, walking away from her.

She followed him as he stepped past the shaded plaza by the Veles e Vents building. Then he turned right, and she lost sight of him. She regained visual contact thirty seconds later as he headed toward the city.

The promenade soon gave way to narrower streets lined with low-rise residential buildings. Since the foot traffic had dropped significantly, Verena slowed her pace to widen the gap between her and the man. She removed her hat to alter her looks.

There was something about the way he moved that rubbed her the wrong way. Something that unsettled her. It had taken a while for her brain to register something was wrong, but now that it had, it wouldn't let go. She'd felt the same way a few times when she'd walked a beat in

Los Angeles as a young LAPD officer. Her instructor had drilled into her to trust her instincts.

And right now, her instincts were screaming at her. She just didn't know what they were saying. What she did know was that she had to end this soon because her phone was vibrating again. Mia would have to wait.

She let her hand brush against her waistband, where her knife was clipped. She would need it soon. She counted the distance between her and the man in her head.

Thirty meters.

Twenty.

She was ten meters away when the man made a left into an alley. She reached the mouth of the alley a few seconds later and stepped in without hesitation, her hand drifting toward the knife. This could be the perfect place.

She made the left turn, then froze, a flash of heat rushing through her spine.

He was there. Right fucking there, standing five feet away from her.

He had drawn her in. She'd never had the upper hand. Not even for a second. But it didn't matter.

She lunged at him with the knife.

Twenty seconds.

That's how long he had before she made the turn. Caspian had pushed his countersurveillance run for as long as he could, trying to figure out if the woman following him had backup. He hadn't spotted any, but it didn't mean she had none or that drones weren't flying overhead. Still, whatever backup she might have, it wasn't close enough to matter. Not yet.

Caspian had given her just enough room so that she felt confident, but not so much that she'd lose him. He had let her believe that she was getting closer, that she had him.

She was good, like a police officer would be, but not trained the way he was.

The first clean look he'd gotten of the woman—after only catching a glimpse of her right before entering the brokerage office—had come when he'd stopped at the lemonade stand, where he had pretended to glance at the chalkboard menu while actually catching her reflection in the glass behind the counter. From that new angle, he'd recognized her immediately.

The woman from the *Veloce*.

And now she was there, following him. She'd taken off her hat in what seemed like a weak attempt at blending in, but the move had only confirmed Caspian's conviction that the woman didn't want him to realize she was tailing him.

Caspian waited in the shade of the alley, his back against the stone wall. He thought about pulling his Wilson Combat SFX9 out of its holster, but there were too many people. And he wasn't about to shoot the woman anyway. He needed answers, and she might be the key, the one who could unravel the entire thing. Having a gun in his hand would only complicate things.

Five seconds. Then he heard her footsteps. Light and quick.

She came around the corner fast, too fast in his professional opinion, her eyes still hunting forward. Until they locked on his.

He saw the flicker of surprise as her brain caught up to what was in front of her, but then it vanished, replaced by something colder. The knife appeared so quickly it caught him off guard. She moved fast, faster than he'd expected, holding the knife in a reverse grip and stepping in tight, cutting the distance and his reaction time.

Caspian pivoted his hips and sidestepped, his left forearm snapped across her knife wrist, deflecting her strike. She turned, tried to spin with him, but he stepped in, broke her posture with a powerful open-palm strike to her chest with his right hand, and kicked her back leg out from under her. As she fell, he caught her wrist and twisted it in a controlled lock.

"Drop it, or I break your wrist," he warned her, adding a bit more torque.

She let the knife go. He forced her up, almost lifting her clean off the ground, and slammed her, stomach first, into the wall. He heard her breath rush out of her lungs. He pinned her there, twisting her right arm behind her back with enough force to make her knees buckle. But the woman wasn't a quitter. She stomped on his feet, hard. But he didn't let go. Instead, he angled her wrist one inch higher.

"Don't try this again or you'll lose the use of your shoulder for the next couple months," he warned her in English. "Scream, and the same thing happens."

He wasn't bluffing. Another half inch and her shoulder would go.

To anyone walking past the mouth of the alley, they would look like a couple caught in a heated embrace. A little rough, maybe, but nothing alarming.

Caspian lowered his mouth to her ear.

"I'm gonna ask you a series of questions," he said. "Answer them truthfully and you'll walk away from this. If you don't, the first thing that will happen is I'll dislocate your shoulder. There won't be a second warning. I'll snap your neck here and there. Understood?"

She nodded, but he could see she was pissed off and probably surprised to find herself at a disadvantage.

"Who else is coming after me?"

"No one. I'm alone—"

Caspian didn't wait for her to finish her sentence. He cranked her wrist up by at least three inches and drove his weight forward. There was a sharp, wet pop as her shoulder dislocated. Before she could scream, he let go of her arm and clamped one hand over her mouth. She twisted in agony, but he held her still.

He counted to five, then said, "I don't have time for games," he whispered. "You know what happens next time you lie. There's no need for me to repeat it."

Her head, which was turned to the right, was against the wall. He could see tears running down her right cheek. Her breath came in sharp, desperate bursts through her nose.

"Who else is coming after me?" he asked, knowing that this time, she'd tell the truth. He removed his hand to let her talk.

"One more. I swear. Only one more," she said. "Shit!"

"How much time do we have before they show up?"

She started to tremble, but not from pain. From fear. She didn't know the answer to his question, and she was afraid he wouldn't believe her.

"I . . . I really don't know," she said. "It's the truth. You have to—"

"Shut up!" he hissed, not wanting her to think he'd show her even an ounce of mercy.

"You were on *Veloce* in Port de Sóller. I saw you," he said, then added, taking a chance, "And I know you work for Blackstone Security. Now, tell me your name."

If the woman was surprised that he knew the company she was working for, she didn't show it.

Unless she's not working for them and she has no idea what I'm talking about . . .

"Verena Kaine," she said.

The name didn't ring a bell. "Where's Paul Hobb?"

Caspian felt Verena's knees go soft again. He knew what it meant. Hobb was dead.

"He's dead, isn't he?"

She nodded. While Ranger had told him Florence was safe, they still didn't know if this had anything to do with her or not.

"Why were you after Hobb?"

"He . . . knew too much," she said.

"About what?" he growled.

She hesitated, but he didn't. He wrapped his arm around her neck, his forearm pressing up into her jaw, his other hand cupped against the back of her head. One hard twist. One hard pull. And it would all be over.

"About what?" he repeated.

Her whole body shook. Then, breathless, she said, "Hearts United."

CHAPTER FORTY-THREE

Valencia, Spain

Mia lowered the phone. She'd tried to call Verena twice now, and there had been no response. She tapped open the tracking app. A red dot pulsed a quarter mile off from the brokerage office, moving slowly.

She's on foot.

Mia had asked Verena to intercept the man before he entered the brokerage. It was imperative to stop him from getting the records tied to *Veloce*. Had Verena failed? Was she now following him? Mia walked past the brokerage firm, forcing herself to think things through. It was possible that Verena had simply been incapable of acting in time.

If that was the case, and Mia had been in Verena's shoes, what would she have done?

Wait. I would have waited outside.

Then she would have tailed him, and hopefully she would have been able to spring a trap before he could communicate his findings to whoever he was working with. That's what she would have done, and that's probably what Verena had done too. That also meant that Verena was now tailing solo a man who had proven to be dangerous.

She tapped her phone again. The dot was still moving. Mia's options were narrowing. She could double back and talk to the receptionist at the brokerage firm to try to find out what intel the man had managed to access. Or she could go after Verena.

The brokerage could wait. It would still be there in an hour. She couldn't say the same about Verena.

Mia scanned the streets. She needed a way to catch up to Verena. She could hot-wire a car, but that wouldn't help her if she had to access the narrow streets Verena seemed to be headed toward. No, she needed something smaller, something she could park anywhere.

There was a bus idling near the traffic circle at the intersection of Calle del Dr. Marcos Sopena and Calle d'Eugènia Viñes, but that wouldn't do either. A cyclist with a dog in a backpack rolled past her, then her eyes locked onto a young woman pulling to the curb on a turquoise moped. The woman climbed off her scooter and pulled the keys from the ignition with one hand while her other reached to unclip the helmet strap.

Mia crossed the street in a light jog. The woman looked up just as Mia closed the final few feet. Mia snatched the keys from the woman's hand and slid onto the seat before she could even register what was happening. Mia started the engine, kicked the stand free, and veered into traffic, accelerating hard as she checked her phone with one hand.

Behind her, the young woman shouted something, but she was already too far away for Mia to hear what she said.

———

The dot had stopped moving a minute ago. Mia checked the screen again as the moped bounced over a manhole cover, and she almost dropped her phone. Verena's phone was still live, still feeding a location. Not like Francisco's phone, which Mia had thrown into the canal.

If the dot stayed put, she'd be there in less than two minutes.

Mia leaned harder into the throttle, speeding past a delivery van, then a silver hatchback, nearly clipping the driver's side mirror. Traffic had been difficult to navigate near the water, but now, as she moved inland and past the last row of beach restaurants and into the residential grid, the congestion thinned. The buildings got tighter and the streets narrower, but there were also a lot fewer pedestrians.

She slowed as she approached the street that Verena's signal was coming from. Mia knew better than to go blind into what seemed to be a backstreet, so she drove past it, looking left as she did so.

She had eyes on them for only a second, but she saw all she needed to see to establish what was going on. Verena was pinned against the wall of a building twenty or twenty-five feet into the alley. A man stood in front of her, his body blocking Verena from stepping away. Mia hadn't seen his face, as his head had been slightly turned, as if listening for something Verena was saying.

Damn it.

Mia pushed past the alley by half a block, coasting to a stop beside a bus stop bench. Despite the urgency, she let the moped idle for a few more seconds as she scanned her surroundings.

The side street she was on wasn't empty, but it was manageable. A couple strolled along the opposite sidewalk, their eyes on their phones, and an elderly woman tugged a rolling grocery cart behind her. Closer to Mia, a pair of pigeons pecked at something near a storm drain, unbothered by the occasional vehicle passing less than two feet from them.

Didn't they know how close to death they were? They had to, right? So why didn't they care? Mia was about to shake her head at the birds' stupidity but stopped herself. Wouldn't they do the same about her if they knew what she was doing for a living?

She parked the moped near a white sedan and climbed off. In her fanny pack, in addition to her garrote, she carried the SIG Sauer P365 she'd acquired on the black market on Ibiza. It was a small weapon, but it carried thirteen rounds. She wished it had red dot optics for faster target acquisition, but it didn't. She'd have to rely on the gun's iron sights. Mia unzipped the fanny pack and slipped her hand around the grip of the pistol, but she didn't draw.

The old woman was gone, and the couple had turned a corner. Only the two fearless pigeons remained. Mia moved fast, crossing behind a parked van and circling wide. The angle wasn't perfect, but from forty feet out, she had a partial line of sight on Verena and the man.

Verena's mouth was moving, and her right shoulder hung limp by her side, as if it had been popped loose. Mia winced. Not because Verena was clearly in pain, but because she was talking to the man. Mia wondered if she shouldn't have dealt with Verena the same way she had with Maximilian Kross.

It's not too late, she thought, pulling the pistol out but keeping it low against her thigh.

She was thirty feet out when the man turned his head slightly, as if he'd sensed something.

Mia raised her pistol.

CHAPTER FORTY-FOUR

Caspian knew he should have left minutes ago, but he hadn't expected Verena Kaine to fold like this. She was unraveling, and she wasn't faking it. He'd seen enough people in real fear to know the difference. Just as he had thought, she wasn't a hardcore operative. She was a former LAPD detective.

"I'm telling you," she said, her voice trembling, "she's a psychopath. She'll kill us both."

Caspian said nothing, he just stared at her, watching her twitch and glance toward the street as he made up his mind about what to do next.

"Help me, and I'll tell you everything," she pleaded.

"What do you know about the woman who was killed at Ses Oliveres?" he asked.

Verena looked away, averting her eyes.

"Please—"

"Liar! You don't even know her!" he snapped.

"I do!" she blurted. "Her name's Sofie Bergmann."

Caspian's heart slammed once in his chest, but he didn't let it show.

"I know about her. I know why she was killed," Verena continued. "But you need to take me with you."

Caspian's mind was racing now. Every second they lingered in the alley, his odds of making a clean exit dropped. But Verena Kaine was a vault he hadn't finished cracking. He had to find out everything she knew about Sofie. He had patted her down and he hadn't found another weapon. That, combined with the fact he had rendered her right arm useless, meant she was no longer a priority threat to him. He didn't trust her, not by a long shot, but he had to keep moving.

What did he have to lose by bringing her with him? At least as far as the Audi. There, he could continue to pick her brain and make his final decision about what to do with her. If she could help him understand who he was up against, it was worth a shot.

But something felt off.

Before he could decide, Verena once again glanced toward the street, and her eyes widened. Caspian's instincts kicked in. He turned his head just slightly and caught movement at the edge of the sidewalk. A woman wearing a green blouse and white pants was raising a pistol.

Caspian grabbed Verena with one arm and hurled her sideways while drawing his pistol with the other hand. The woman fired just as he launched himself to the left and out of her line of fire. The shot was unsuppressed and loud. The bullet ricocheted off the brick wall where he'd been standing a split second before. Caspian hit the ground and fired as he rolled to his left. His round missed, going wide. The woman darted to her left and vanished behind the corner of the building.

Caspian shifted into a low firing stance.

"Get behind me!" he barked at Verena.

She groaned but pushed herself up from the concrete where he'd thrown her. He hadn't been gentle, but he couldn't care less. Minutes ago, she had tried to kill him, hadn't she?

She stumbled behind him. In the distance, he could hear sirens. Someone had heard the gunshots and called the police.

The shooter peeked out from cover, just for a split second, not long enough for Caspian to aim properly, but he fired anyway, aiming slightly wide. His round hit the wall inches to the right of the edge of the building. He hoped it would be enough to scare her away. The last thing Caspian wanted was to get into a big firefight and hit a bystander or some poor bastard in a parked car.

Caspian crouched low and began shuffling backward, shielding Verena with his body as he moved. Then his sixth sense began to sparkle like a live wire.

———

Verena had never been so scared. Not in her LAPD career, and not even when she'd realized what Hearts United was truly capable of. But now, pinned in a small alley behind a man she didn't know, one who moved like a predator, her nerves were stretched to their breaking point.

Who the hell was he? And how had he known Mia was coming?

Verena hadn't warned him. She hadn't signaled anything, at least not intentionally. But she had looked. It had been a reflex, a split-second glance toward the street when she'd seen Mia walking up. She'd been desperate to get someone's attention. Had this been enough to tip him off?

And then he'd moved so damn fast.

Just raw efficiency.

And not only when he'd thrown her out of the way and drew his weapon, but also when he'd disarmed her earlier like it was second nature.

As if he'd done that a hundred times before.

Verena crouched low, her ribs aching from when she'd hit the ground hard. She risked a peep past the man's shoulder. Mia was still behind the cover of the stone edge of the building, likely calculating her next move.

The man, whoever he was, was protecting her. That much was clear. But why? He could have left her behind. Hell, he should have. But he hadn't. He'd placed himself between her and Mia's line of fire. Which meant one thing.

He needs me.

That realization sent Verena's mind into high gear.

I have leverage.

She didn't know who he was, but she knew leverage when she saw it. The question was whether it meant anything. If she decided to help the man escape, Mia would come after her.

She's gonna hunt me down. And that bitch's relentless.

Verena had a decision to make. And it came down to one simple but very important question: Who terrified her more?

She didn't even have to think.

Mia. And Hearts United.

With her decision made, Verena's muscles tensed. The man was four feet in front of her, walking backward, his eyes scanning the alley's mouth. She could see the corded muscles in his arms, the tension in his neck. He wasn't focused on her, but on Mia.

Move, Verena. Now!

She waited half a beat, then moved.

Twisting her hips, she kicked out with her right foot, targeting the back of his rear leg.

It should have worked. It should have tripped him as he stepped back. But the man turned at the last second, as if he'd read her mind. He raised his leg, and her feet swung into nothing just as the man pivoted and pistol-whipped her on the side of her head.

White exploded across her vision, but somehow, she stayed upright.

And that's when she saw Mia, stepping out from the corner, pistol raised.

———

Caspian moved without thought, pure instinct taking over the second Verena tried to trip him. As she kicked out, he raised his leg and pivoted toward her, his pistol already arcing downward. The steel of the barrel connected with the side of her head. Before he could reassess, movement drew his eye as Mia stepped out from behind the building, gun already raised.

Caspian grabbed a fistful of Verena's collar and hauled her upright, rotating behind her as he brought his weapon up in one hand. It wasn't elegant, but it was fast, and it put something—well, someone—between him and the barrel pointed in his direction.

The woman with the green blouse was the first to get off a shot. Caspian felt the impact slam into Verena's body, a brutal transfer of force that jerked her back into him. A second round followed an instant later, thudding lower, somewhere in the vicinity of Verena's abdomen. Her body jolted again, and a shallow gasp escaped her lips.

Still holding his pistol with only one hand, and with Verena sagging in his grip, Caspian squeezed the trigger twice. His shots went wide, once again impacting the wall near the edge of the building, chipping stones. By the time he realigned, the woman was gone.

In front of him, Verena's body slipped from his grip, crumpling to the pavement. Heart hammering in his chest, Caspian scanned the alley. It was clear.

Well . . . that turned to shit fast.

The sirens were growing louder by the second. The cops were getting close. It was time for him to cut his losses and get out of there.

———

Verena couldn't breathe. Every inhalation sent a bolt of agony through her chest. It was like someone was carving her open from the inside. The pavement beneath her felt slick. She was bleeding out; she knew that. She needed help. She tried to sit up, but the pain was instant and overwhelming. Her vision blurred, and she collapsed again.

Fuck.

She curled into herself, seeking relief from the flame inside her, but it only made things worse. The pain didn't ease; it multiplied.

She coughed, and something wet bubbled up from her throat.

Mia shot me.

Verena had known it the moment the second round had hit. She'd seen Mia do it. Cold and unflinching. Verena let her head fall to the side, her cheek pressing against the warm concrete as her already labored breathing drew even shallower. She'd had a choice; she knew that now. That man, whoever he was, had given her a way out. He had shielded her. Protected her. He'd put himself in Mia's crosshairs, and all she had to do was to stay down and shut up.

But she hadn't. She'd made a play. She'd gambled her leverage. And lost.

Just a few days ago, she'd been on the deck of a luxury yacht under the Mediterranean sun, running what she'd believed to be a simple operation. Now she was lying in an alley, blood pooling beneath her, lungs filling with liquid, and questions screamed in her head.

How did this happen? What did I miss?

She should have killed Mia when she had the opportunity. But then she would have had to run for her life. No, it wasn't this specific operation. It wasn't anything she'd done this week. None of it was the root of her current predicament.

No. The reason she was bleeding out in an alley was Everett Westcott. That's where she'd made the mistake. Saying yes to him. Believing his promises. Buying into the illusion that she could help him achieve his vision. She'd taken his offer because she thought it was a ladder to better things. But now, it was apparent to her the offer had been a noose. A noose she'd willingly put around her own neck.

A coldness started to creep inward from her extremities, and with it, the sickening understanding that she was about to die. She wanted to close her eyes, hoping to find peace, but she couldn't even do that. Her gaze was trapped on the ground beside her. Three uneven pools of her blood spread across dirty stones, each one misshapen and irregular. The number punched through her like a sharp blade.

Three.

Please . . . not three.

The number three always left her uneasy, a wrongness she could never quite ignore. Even now, with her heart slowing, a desperate, absurd wish flared deep inside her. Couldn't there have been two or even four pools of blood? Anything but three?

And then there was nothing.

CHAPTER FORTY-FIVE

Thirty-Eighth Floor, Secretariat Building
United Nations Headquarters
New York City, New York

Everett Westcott stood motionless by the massive window, one hand in his pocket, the other resting on the frame as he surveyed the city. From this height, he had a panoramic view of the East River and the boroughs of Queens and Brooklyn. It was an impressive view, even to him. Views like this had a way of elevating a man's sense of self, of positioning him above everyone else, of making him feel . . . untouchable. And Westcott had no doubt that this very illusion had played a role in Julius Zuma's decision to seek a second term as secretary-general of the United Nations. Apart from the view, the office was sleek and modern and clearly designed to project dignity, resolve, and power.

And Westcott was all too aware that power did strange things to men.

Three men occupied the office now. Zuma sat behind his desk, his hands folded tightly together, while President Leonard Mutombo of the Democratic Republic of the Congo occupied one of the two leather chairs across from him.

Westcott hadn't said a word in almost two minutes. In that very moment, he was close to throwing Mutombo through the glass and letting him fall thirty-eight stories. Another minute passed before he turned from the view and faced the room. He stared at Mutombo and noticed for the first time that the man's suit collar was at least a size too tight.

Mutombo cleared his throat.

"I know this isn't what you wanted to hear, but as I just explained to you, the proposition brought to me by Ambassador Nyambe won't make it through the National Assembly. Again, the proposition is more than satisfactory for me and my party, but—"

"Have you really come all this way to tell me you're too weak to lead? That you aren't willing to move forward?" Westcott asked, cutting him off. "After everything Hearts United has done for your country?"

Mutombo shifted in his seat, his palms pressing against his knees. "Please understand, Mr. Westcott. It's . . . it's not that I'm unwilling. It's just that . . . I can't."

"You're the fucking president. Of course you can!"

Mutombo's eyes flicked toward Zuma, searching for a lifeline. Westcott knew he wouldn't find any. He'd made sure of that months ago. Just as he thought he would, the secretary-general remained silent, his lips pressed together in a neutral line.

There had been a time, early in Zuma's tenure, when Westcott had high hopes for the secretary-general. Born and raised in South Africa, educated in international law, and fluent in the unique pressures and challenges of the African continent, Zuma could have been an effective leader. Westcott had seen in him the ideal candidate to advance Hearts United's pragmatic vision for the DRC and, later, for the rest of the continent. But Westcott's optimism had slowly given way to contempt. Zuma had proven to be indecisive, overly cautious, and frustratingly committed to multilateral process and a true bureaucrat's obsession with consensus. After two years, Westcott had grown tired of waiting and had taken matters into his own hands.

Digging into Zuma's past had been a waste of time. The man was faithful, honest, and didn't live beyond his means. His record was annoyingly clean. All in all, Zuma was a decent man.

But his son? Well, that was another story. He had secrets. And Westcott had found them all.

The drugs and gambling could have been enough but then had come the late-night accident in the Dominican Republic where he'd hit a young woman while driving intoxicated. Somehow, he'd managed to bribe his way out of the situation, and without the help of his father. It had taken Westcott's assets a week to verify the footage and even longer to secure the original files. But in the end, it had been worth it. Zuma had folded like a cheap beach chair once Westcott had shown him the evidence.

"You have to be reasonable, Mr. Westcott," Mutombo said. "What you're asking . . . it's not something the National Assembly is ready to accept."

Westcott took a step forward and lowered his voice. "You're a coward."

"Everett, please—" Zuma began, but Westcott turned and leveled him with a threatening look. The secretary-general closed his mouth and looked down at his hands.

Mutombo rose abruptly from his chair, clearly outraged. "I will not be talked to in this fashion."

"Sit down," Westcott ordered.

Mutombo hesitated.

"I said sit down."

"Or what?" Mutombo snapped. "I'm the president of—"

"You're the president because I fucking put you there," Westcott shouted, stepping closer now, his voice booming. "Don't you forget that, you dimwit. You didn't win that office, I handed it to you. I paid for your television ads, your staff, and even your goddamn suits. You wouldn't have made it out of the provincial governorship without my backing."

"I—"

"Enough!" Westcott shouted. "You serve because I allow it. Don't mistake proximity to power for having any of your own."

Mutombo, stunned, dropped back into the leather seat like a man returning to prison. Westcott let the silence stretch. The stick had done its work. He would now offer the carrot.

"Three months ago, you told me your minister of land management, Dr. Hervé Tchangana, and Destin Mpanga, who if I recall correctly, was the number two inside the Congo River Alliance, were the two final obstacles standing in the way of the hydroelectric initiative I'm proposing. You said, and I quote, 'As long as those two are around, the Assembly will never pass the deal.' Well, those two are no longer around."

Westcott moved closer to Mutombo, making sure the man couldn't look away.

"So, tell me, Mr. President, what changed?"

Mutombo glanced again at Zuma, who this time gave a shallow nod, which told Westcott the two men had conferred about this very subject prior to his arrival.

"It's Florent Bongonda, the prime minister," Mutombo said finally. "As you know, he belongs to the opposition. While I still command the loyalty of my party, Bongonda controls the legislative schedule. And right now, he's undermining every single piece of legislation we bring forward. He's consolidated his influence, and now, even my own members are starting to waver."

Westcott digested this. Bongonda was indeed a problem, but until now, a manageable one. But in the power vacuum left by the deaths of Tchangana and Mpanga in Aruba, Bongonda had stepped forward with alarming effectiveness. He was cunning, media savvy, and he had the moral credibility Mutombo lacked. Still, Westcott had expected Mutombo to outmaneuver him. Clearly, he'd overestimated the man.

I bet on the wrong man. Should I give him one more chance, or cut my losses?

"My patience with you is wearing thin," Westcott said a moment later. "But I'm prepared to give you one more shot at greatness, Leonard.

What do you need to make Hearts United's proposition acceptable to your colleagues in the Assembly?"

Mutombo hesitated, clearly uncomfortable. His eyes shifted toward Zuma. Westcott decided to make it easier for him.

"Mr. Secretary-General," he said, not bothering to glance over. "I believe now might be a good time for you to step out."

Despite being in his own office, Zuma stood without objection. "I'll let you gentlemen speak privately. But, Mr. President, please know that I fully support Everett's proposition. Whatever it is."

Westcott offered Zuma a polite smile, and the secretary-general exited without another word. When the door clicked shut, Westcott turned his attention back to Mutombo and let the silence hang for a beat before he spoke.

"Now," he said, folding his arms, "tell me what you need. And don't insult me by asking for Bongonda's disappearance. That's off the table. Another political assassination, especially on your own soil, could unravel everything I built."

Mutombo shook his head quickly. "No, I don't want him dead. I want him arrested. Publicly. The bigger the scandal, the better. If we can somehow suggest financial impropriety tied to the hydroelectric contracts . . . the Assembly will turn. I guarantee it."

———

Fifteen minutes later, Everett Westcott sat in one of the captain's chairs in the second row of his armored black Cadillac Escalade. He looked through the bulletproof glass as the large SUV surged through midtown traffic toward his office where the chair of the Senate Appropriations Committee had been waiting for him for over an hour.

This wasn't about power games or empty posturing. There was no need for that. They both understood the reality of their relationship. The senator might command the budget lines and the televised hearings, but it was Westcott who shaped the outcomes. There was no doubt who sat at the top of the food chain, and it wasn't the elected official. Still, Westcott needed the senator. Hearts United was well financed, but its wealth did have a ceiling. If the US government signed on as a funding partner for Hearts United's initiative in the DRC, it would allow Westcott to accelerate the timelines and even expand the scope of the project.

And it would also add an additional layer of legitimacy.

The money mattered, yes, but only if the terms were right. Westcott wasn't going to leave the government in charge of his project.

Beside him, Charles Mpassi sat upright, phone in hand, and Westcott could hear the man's thumbs darting angrily across the screen as he replied to several encrypted messages. Westcott gave him a quick glance. Mpassi was clearly agitated. Westcott had first assumed Mpassi's tension came from the delays. Westcott got it. Mpassi was punctual by nature, and today's timetable had already been derailed, thanks to the overlong meeting they'd left only minutes ago. But now, as the minutes ticked by, he began to suspect something else was bothering his associate.

"Something wrong?" Westcott asked, not looking up from the legal memorandum in his lap.

"Nothing I can't handle, sir," Mpassi replied, still tapping.

Westcott looked at the man, studying him. Mpassi didn't rattle easily. He'd served in hostile territories and often negotiated with tribal leaders without breaking stride. If something had him worked up, it deserved attention.

"Charles," Westcott said, "what is it?"

"With respect, sir, I'm handling it. I'll bring you up to speed after your meeting with the senator."

"No," Westcott said, setting the memorandum aside. "Tell me now."

Mpassi paused, then lowered his phone with a sigh.

"Verena Kaine's dead. And Mia's hurt—"

Westcott heard the rest, but the words didn't land. His mind had stopped processing new information the moment Mpassi had mentioned Mia. The girl—well, a woman now—wasn't just an asset, she was something more. She was the daughter he never had. He loved her. Not the way he'd loved his wife, Nailah, of course, but it was still love.

Mia did dangerous work. He knew that. Every assignment came with a risk. But she was brilliant, disciplined, and he had given her the tools to succeed, hadn't he? She'd never failed him. She'd walked through hell more times than he could count and emerged without a scratch. Somewhere along the way, he'd begun to believe Mia was invincible.

"Everett," Mpassi said gently, "did you hear what I said?"

"What?" he asked, realizing he had been holding his breath.

"She'll be okay," Mpassi said. "She's being patched up now. One of our people is with her."

"She's going to be fine?"

"That's what I said. A bullet fragment clipped her ear. It bled a lot, but that's all. She'll recover. Though we might have to pull her from the performance in Budapest, and the one next week in Dubrovnik."

"And Verena?"

"Mia killed her."

Westcott closed his eyes, feeling like he was missing part of the story. In Mallorca, Mia had made the decision not to kill Verena on the *Veloce*. What had triggered Mia's change of heart in Valencia?

Shit. Can it get any worse? he thought.

Apparently, it could.

"Mia believes Blackstone Security has been identified as the entity who chartered *Veloce*."

"How? By whom?"

Mpassi winced, as if whatever he was going to say next hurt him.

"Mia confirmed it's the same man," he said. "The one from Port de Sóller."

Westcott shot his Office of Special Projects director an angry look.

"What you meant to say is that he's the same man who killed Verena's crew. One of the two operatives who escaped your trap in Turkey, and the same man you'd promised me was no longer a threat."

"I'm aware, sir," Mpassi said, meeting his gaze. "I . . . misjudged them."

"No," Westcott said, shaking his head. "You underestimated him and the woman who he's with."

This time, Mpassi didn't reply, knowing better than to argue.

But Westcott wasn't just worried about the operative; Blackstone Security was now a concern too. Their leader was dead, and their structure was compromised, which meant their deniability was obliterated. He had known this reckoning would come and that, eventually, he would have to sever all ties between Hearts United and Blackstone. But he'd hoped to be further along in the DRC initiative before doing so.

Westcott's hands curled into fists. Since losing one of his key assets in Tanzania, he'd been reluctant to deploy them without backup. Even in Aruba, he'd insisted Mpassi send Henry to support Mia. Valencia, however, had been pitched as a simple reconnaissance mission, a quick in-and-out intel-gathering operation. And it had turned into a goddamned firefight.

"Scrub everything," Westcott said. "All ties to Blackstone. I don't want a single thread left behind."

"What about the employees?" Mpassi asked. "What kind of severance are we offering?"

It wasn't really a question about benefits. They both knew that. What Mpassi was asking was if they were going to silence them permanently. Truth was, with most of his operational assets already committed in Africa, Westcott didn't have the manpower for that. And even if he did have the manpower, hunting each Blackstone Security employee would be logistically impossible without raising flags.

"Have legal prepare NDAs. Let's do six months' salary," Westcott said. "For all of them."

Mpassi nodded. "Understood."

"Where's Mia now?"

"Still in Spain. She's recuperating. She'll be fit to travel tomorrow. You need her somewhere?"

Westcott shook his head. "She's done enough, don't you think? Cancel Budapest and Dubrovnik. Let her go home. Tell her to take a week to herself."

"A week?" Mpassi asked, raising an eyebrow. "You really think she'll sit still that long?"

"If she ends up doing it or not is up to her," Westcott said. "But I want her to know it's fine if she wants some time to herself."

They sat in silence for a moment, the hum of the Escalade and the horns coming from angry drivers filling the void. After a while, and while still ten minutes from his office, Westcott began to walk Mpassi through his conversation with President Mutombo and the UN secretary-general.

"And now you're wondering how to take down Prime Minister Bongonda," Mpassi said when Westcott was finished.

"I am," he admitted. "But we can't eliminate him. We need a scandal, one big enough to fracture the Assembly. One juicy enough that Mutombo could regain the ground he lost among the Assembly members."

"How fast do you need this to be done?"

"As soon as possible. Every day Bongonda gains more influence."

"Budget limitation?" Mpassi asked.

Westcott frowned at the question. "Why do you ask?"

"Because getting to him physically inside the DRC would be complicated. But—"

Westcott snapped. "Aren't you listening to a word I said? I specifically told you I don't want him killed. I know how difficult it is to get to these assholes inside the DRC. That's why we waited until Tchangana and Mpanga were abroad. For God's sake, what's wrong with you?"

"Sir, I wasn't about to suggest we take him out," Mpassi said. "What I was going to say is that we've gained access to the DRC's internal network infrastructure. We can plant whatever we need, including emails and financial records."

That was news to Westcott. He didn't know they had this kind of access. He'd given Mpassi a lot of latitude on how to manage the DRC operation, but Westcott was starting to feel that he might have given the man a bit too much autonomy. Still, he considered what he had just learned.

"Okay . . . what do you have in mind?" he asked.

"You want him embroiled in a scandal? No problem. I can make it happen. But it needs to be big enough for people to notice. And care."

"I get what you're saying. The good people of the DRC expect their leaders to be corrupt," Westcott said. "A small scandal wouldn't do the trick. People would just assume it's business as usual." Now thinking out loud, he continued, "We need diverted aid funds, preferably to an offshore account and laundered through a shell foundation linked to the Congo River Alliance."

Mpassi was all smiles now. "Exactly."

The Congo River Alliance, which among its members included the brutal, Rwanda-backed M23 rebels, was quickly gaining territory in the eastern part of the DRC and had recently captured Goma, a city of two million people and the capital of the North Kivu province. Since the Alliance had taken over, hundreds of thousands of people had been displaced, with several hundred—held on accusations of supporting the Congolese army during the fighting—being sent to overcrowded, unhygienic cells. Westcott had read reports about prisoners being tortured with electric cables and engine belts.

If he could somehow manufacture a direct link between Prime Minister Bongonda and the Alliance, it would shatter the National Assembly's trust in the man.

"What would 'big enough' look like to you, Charles?" Westcott asked.

"Twenty million dollars," Mpassi replied.

"And you could do this with no blowback?" Westcott asked.

"I guarantee it. In fact, we'd be the one to tip off the ANR," Mpassi said. "I still have plenty of contacts within the agency."

The ANR, or Agence Nationale de Renseignements, was the intelligence agency of the DRC.

Westcott nodded once. "Do it."

CHAPTER FORTY-SIX

Defense Intelligence Headquarters
Washington, DC
Seventy-Two Hours Later

Caspian Anderson sat in a leather chair facing Samantha Ranger's desk. A look through the window showed him a low sky, as if the dark gray clouds were holding their breath.

Two days earlier, Caspian had spent three tense hours with a DIA sketch artist, working to capture the face of the woman who had fired at him and killed Verena Kaine back in Valencia. The resulting image was surprisingly accurate, but so far, it hadn't turned up a single lead. They still didn't know her name.

Another thing that troubled him was that he hadn't heard from Liesel in three days. He had messaged her repeatedly and tried to call her. He'd asked her questions, anything to get a response from her beyond the cold, detached confirmation that she was fine.

I'm safe, Casp. Stop worrying about me.

He hadn't gotten any other explanation from Liesel. Just distance.

Only this morning he had learned from Ranger that Liesel was in Germany with Nicklas Drescher. That hadn't sat well with him. Not because she was with Drescher—the man was, after all, her superior. No, what troubled Caspian was that she was keeping him at arm's length. After everything they'd been through together, he had expected more than radio silence. But right now, there wasn't much he could do about it. She was thousands of miles away, and she wasn't responding to his texts or to his calls.

Ranger handed him a cup of coffee, which broke his train of thought. He thanked her and noticed her tired eyes. She hadn't slept much either; that much was clear. Ranger moved behind her desk, popped a few Advils in her mouth, and washed them down with a sip of coffee.

"Is she still in Berlin?" he asked.

Ranger nodded.

"She's working directly with Drescher on the same operation we are. The BND has given them some maneuvering room, so they're running their own angle. In fact, it was Liesel who flagged most of the discrepancies in there," she said, tapping a finger on a yellow file folder in front of her.

Ranger opened the file and flipped to a stapled packet midway through.

"She's been digging into the financials surrounding Hearts United's medical operations. She picked up anomalies our people missed. She cross-checked patient-intake reports, pharmaceutical shipments, and donor supply chains. What she found led us to ask for NSA's support in accessing satellite imageries and transactional records."

Ranger handed him a summary page, clearly printed with DIA and NSA joint headers at the top.

"You asked me to take a deep look into Blackstone Security," she said. "So I did."

"And?"

"Well . . . here's what we can confirm. Someone's doing a hell of a job removing every trace that Blackstone ever existed. I mean, they disconnected domains, erased registry data, and the analysts are telling me that the effort is still ongoing."

"But you found something," Caspian said.

"The NSA did, yes," Ranger said. "They were able to trace the revenue stream. It seems that every field operation Blackstone mounted over the last five years was funded by Hearts United or one of its known entities. Blackstone Security had no other clients."

Caspian scanned the document quickly. The pattern Blackstone and Hearts United had established was clear. It was a closed loop. A single command structure behind the facade of two separate organizations.

He looked up from the document and asked, "Do you think it's time to bring in the FBI?"

"I talked about it with Director Maples, and he doesn't think we're there yet," Ranger replied. "In fact, he fears the FBI and the attorney general wouldn't even get past a grand jury."

"So, the only thing we'd accomplish by working with the FBI is to tip our hand," Caspian said.

"Seems like it. And it gets more interesting," she added, handing him a second document.

"SSU analysts retrieved this," she continued. "Hearts United partnered with Doctors Without Borders in Kenya. The public narrative focused on mobile clinics, vaccination drives, and basic surgical access. To be fair, all of that happened."

"I feel like there's a 'but' coming," Caspian said, reading through the single sheet of paper.

"But around those medical operations, something else occurred."

Ranger unfolded a satellite-overlay map across her desk. Several swaths of countryside were circled in red.

"What am I looking at?" he asked, very much aware that his brother, as the medical director of Doctors Without Borders in Kenya, was actively involved in some of these regions.

"Entire villages were relocated. At first, we thought it was driven by health concerns, you know? To get people closer to the care they need. But when we cross-referenced the GPS coordinates of the vacated sites, we found this."

She tapped the red zones.

"These areas sit directly on top of rare earth minerals deposits. Niobium, nickel, lithium, you name it."

Caspian nodded slowly. "These are the kinds of strategic metals that help to power everything from smartphones to missiles," he said.

"Correct. And we estimate that the value of the minerals in the ground in the zones colored in red at over twenty-five billion dollars."

"Right," Caspian said. "But this isn't news. The public and the Kenyan government knew these deposits were there."

"They did," Ranger admitted. "But what the public didn't know was that two months after the relocations, mining licenses were quietly issued to firms with financial ties to Hearts United."

Caspian sank deeper into his chair. The weight of what Ranger had just shared with him settled over him like concrete. "They used aid to clear the land," he said. "And somehow, Nelson's involved."

"They used trust, humanitarian trust, Caspian," Ranger said. "Hearts United and Doctors Without Borders presented the relocations as a health initiative, not as a resource grab. But the outcome is the same. Mining companies are now in full operation, and with the full blessing of the government."

"Shit," Caspian muttered. "Nelson is right in the middle of this."

"He is," Ranger said. "But we don't think he did any of this in a malicious way. He supported the relocation efforts, and he played an important role in coordinating the whole thing with tribal leaders, but from everything we've seen, he acted in good faith."

Caspian sighed. He stared at the sheet of paper in his hand. A photo in the top right corner showed Nelson in a field vest, smiling, flanked by several Kenyan health workers.

"Knowing my brother, he was focused on the medical metrics. Saving lives, you know?"

"To be clear," Ranger said, "I think your brother was misled. At this stage, he's not under investigation."

"So, what's the next step?" he asked.

"We keep going," Ranger said. "We peel this back, layer by layer, but we need to hurry."

"Why's that? This seems to me like the kind of op we need to be very careful about how we move forward, no? You said so yourself, Samantha. Everett Westcott is a powerful figure who wields a lot of influence. Poking too hard might blow up in our faces."

Ranger reached for the Advil bottle again but seemed to change her mind. Instead, she took a long sip of her coffee.

"You're right. I did say that," she conceded, setting her cup down. "But I believe Westcott is about to make a similar move in the Democratic Republic of Congo."

"How come?" he asked.

"An hour ago, Prime Minister Bongonda was arrested in Kinshasa on embezzlement charges," Ranger said. "Twenty million dollars were seized from one of his offshore accounts. The account in question is linked to the Congo River Alliance. The scandal has already splashed across four major media outlets. You see where this is going, right?"

"I'm assuming the National Assembly is in chaos," he said.

"You got that right," Ranger said. "President Mutombo is calling for unity, saying the arrest proves his administration's commitment to transparency."

"Of course he'd say that," Caspian said. "You think Westcott did this?"

"He's made it clear that his focus is now on the DRC with his Congo River initiative. Westcott used humanitarian aid to justify displacing populations in Kenya. And now, he's using a political scandal to destabilize the National Assembly, the last serious obstacle to his vision."

"And you believe that if we don't act soon, we'll be watching another land grab," Caspian said.

"I do. One with the full weight of the United States government behind it."

"What do you mean?"

"While I'm not privy to what was said behind closed doors, three days ago Everett Westcott met with the chair of the Senate Appropriations

Committee to discuss the possible financial participation of the United States government in Hearts United's venture in the DRC."

Caspian thought about this for a few seconds, then said, "You think the members of the committee know it's a land grab?"

Ranger sighed loudly. "Honestly, I don't know. But if they do, and this ever comes out, it will erase all the progress we've made in Africa in the last decade."

"The US government would be portrayed as an invader who doesn't give a shit about the local population," Caspian said, thinking out loud. "And that would open the door even wider for Chinese and Russian involvement on the continent."

They remained silent for a moment, then Caspian asked, "You want me to find out what was said between Westcott and the chair of the committee?"

"No," Ranger said. "I'll take care of that."

"Okay. What then?"

"When was the last time you spoke to your brother?" Ranger asked.

"Liesel and I had a half-hour-long FaceTime with him last month. Why?"

"Could you reach out to him again?" Ranger asked. "See if he can make his way here?"

"Here? Like DC?" Caspian asked.

Ranger nodded.

"I don't think that's gonna be possible, but if you want to go to Boston tomorrow, you can see him there."

"Boston?"

"Logan is the closest international airport to Portland, where our parents live," Caspian explained. "It's our mom's birthday next week, and Nelson's supposed to spend the next week or so with our folks."

"Okay, then. Let's go to Boston."

CHAPTER FORTY-SEVEN

Caspian stood by the double-panel glass window, looking at the Boston skyline from the eighth-floor hotel room he and Ranger had booked for the meeting with Nelson. Below, near the hotel's main entrance, guests and conference attendees filtered in and out of rideshares and taxis, and a group of well-dressed Asian men smoked cigarettes, each with a matching conference lanyard around their neck.

"We're one minute out," a voice came in through Caspian's earbud. "Black Dodge Caravan. No signs of mobile surveillance en route from the airport."

"Good copy," Caspian replied.

He'd received a similar report twenty minutes earlier when two of Ranger's men had followed Nelson through the airport after he had landed. They hadn't seen anyone shadowing him through the baggage claim or the taxi stand. Caspian hadn't expected any trouble, but appreciated the fact that Ranger was being cautious. She wasn't taking anything for granted and even had an SSU technician check for electronic surveillance inside the room.

A black Dodge Caravan soon turned into the circular driveway of the hotel and came to a stop in front of the entrance. Caspian smiled as his brother stepped out of the vehicle, a beige duffel bag slung over one shoulder. Nelson glanced up, as if he knew Caspian was watching him.

"He's here," he said to Ranger, who was seated at the desk working on her laptop.

Caspian stepped away from the window and crossed the room. He opened the door, leaned against it so that it would remain open, and crossed his arms, his eyes toward the bank of elevators down the carpeted corridor. Moments later, he heard a soft ding, and Nelson stepped into view. He was taller than Caspian by about two inches, and he had dark green eyes and black hair and a bushy, untrimmed beard. He was dressed in jeans, a polo shirt, and worn hiking shoes. He looked tired from the long flight, but when he saw Caspian, his face broke into a grin.

"Jesus," Nelson said as he got closer. "It's great to see you, man."

"You look good," Caspian said.

"You're full of it, but thanks," his brother replied.

The two men embraced without hesitation, and for a few seconds, Caspian didn't think about the operation, the risks he was about to ask Nelson to take on, or Liesel's not being there with him.

"Still not shaving, I see," Caspian said when they finally pulled apart.

"Still pretending that half smirk of yours counts as a real smile," his brother shot back.

Caspian smiled for real this time, then stepped aside to let Nelson in. "Come on in, I'll introduce you."

"Where's Liesel?" Nelson asked as he stepped through the doorway.

"She's on a personal trip," Caspian replied.

Nelson held his gaze a second longer than necessary but didn't press, for which Caspian was grateful. Nelson gave Ranger a polite nod as he dropped his duffel bag to the floor next to the bed.

"I'm Nelson," he said, extending his hand.

"Dr. Anderson," Ranger said, getting to her feet and shaking the man's hand, "thanks so much for coming."

"Of course," Nelson replied. "But I must admit that Caspian didn't say much on the phone. Just that it was important that we meet, and that there'd be someone else."

"Right . . . well, I'm Samantha Ranger. I work for the US government."

Nelson eyed her for a beat, then asked, "Any particular part of the government? Or is that question verboten?"

Ranger smiled politely. "I don't think it's necessary for me to specify. Can we leave it at that?"

Nelson turned to Caspian. "She's CIA?"

Caspian shrugged. "Let's just say she's someone I trust."

That seemed to give Nelson pause. "Okay. Fair enough. Mom said something like this might happen."

That piqued Caspian's curiosity. "Really? What did she say to you?"

"She said you weren't exactly clerking speeches at the UN anymore, then added something about you helping her and Dad out of a jam they found themselves in . . . with the ATF?"

Caspian chuckled. "Yeah . . . that sounds about right," he said, but didn't elaborate further.

It wasn't that he didn't trust his brother. He did. But Caspian didn't think it was his story to tell. In accepting to assist the ATF with one of their investigations, Elizabeth and Richard Anderson had unknowingly placed themselves in the crosshairs of several Mexican drug cartels, as well as a North Korean sleeper cell. In the end, it was Caspian and Liesel, with the help of Samantha Ranger, who had managed to untangle the whole mess.

"Should we sit?" Caspian asked.

They settled into a loose triangle with Nelson on the couch, Caspian in an armchair, and Ranger perched on the edge of the desk.

"So. You two mind telling me what this is really about and why I'm here?" Nelson asked, once everybody was comfortable.

"Caspian told me you were considering leaving Doctors Without Borders? Is that true?" Ranger asked.

"I'm thinking about it. I haven't made my decision yet."

"Because of Clara?" Ranger asked.

Caspian's head snapped in Ranger's direction. He'd never heard of a Clara. But before he could say anything, Nelson said, "You're definitely CIA."

"Who the hell's Clara?" Caspian asked.

"Should I tell him, or would you prefer to do it?" Nelson said. "'Cause you seem to know a whole lot about me."

Caspian noted that his brother didn't sound pissed off. In fact, he seemed to find this conversation amusing.

"No, you do it," Ranger said.

"Clara's my girlfriend," Nelson said. "She's with the State Department. Legal division. She's in Nairobi for another six months, then she's coming back to DC."

"You have a girlfriend?" Caspian asked, stunned. He'd always thought his brother was going to remain a bachelor his entire life.

"Don't look so surprised, brother," Nelson said. "You don't think I'm worthy of being loved?"

"I didn't—" Caspian started, but Nelson cut him off.

"Relax, bro, I'm kidding. Anyhow, Clara's smart, funny, and she drinks the green smoothies I make for her, even though I know she hates them."

"That's pure love," Ranger said.

"Right?"

"And this Clara, she's the reason you're thinking about coming back?" Caspian asked.

"She's the main one. She's only the second person in years who listens when I talk about what's broken out there. She doesn't roll her eyes, doesn't pat me on the back to say I'm doing a great, honorable job, and that I should just shut my mouth and keep doing what I'm doing. She actually listens."

"And . . . who's the first person, if you don't mind me asking?" Ranger inquired.

"Everett Westcott."

Caspian winced at his brother's answer. "Okay, so, in your opinion, professional and personal, what do you think is broken in Kenya?"

Nelson sighed heavily.

"More than you want to hear," he said. "Look, I love the people in Kenya. That's why I've been there for so long. These people, they're some of the most resilient and kind human beings I've ever met. But their government? I mean, half the ministers would sell their grandmothers' lungs for a payout. The other half already has."

Caspian exchanged a look with Ranger. There was a quiet moment, then Nelson said, "When you're caught between trying to treat patients and navigating which regional official expects a bribe to tell you where they hid the oxygen tanks, it kind of wears you down, you know?"

"Yeah, I get it," Caspian said sympathetically. "You once told me you'd met Westcott a few times, remember that?"

"Of course. I met him a dozen times or so. The man is a force of nature, and he really cares about Africa. He's one of the good guys, that's for sure. I have a good working relationship with him, and with everyone at Hearts United for that matter. They talk a lot, but they do carry through. Unlike so many other NGOs, when Hearts United say they'll fund a project, they do."

"Did Westcott ever talk to you about his project for the DRC?" Ranger asked.

"As a matter of fact, he did. He has a big one for the Congo River. He loved the DRC and its people. Honestly, it's as if the DRC is his spiritual homeland."

"Really? Do you know why?" Caspian asked, intrigued.

"Could be because his late wife was from there," Nelson said. "Nailah was her name, I think. She passed a while back, but man, he spoke like she was still in the room with him."

Ranger leaned forward. "Nelson, would you be willing to help us get close to him?"

Nelson shot Caspian a *what the hell is she talking about* look, then turned his attention back to Ranger. "And why would I do that?"

"Show him, Samantha," Caspian said. "He'll get it."

There was a quiet moment, then Ranger placed her tablet on the desk and tapped a finger on an electronic folder. A map of Kenya appeared, along with a photo of Everett Westcott.

"What am I looking at?" Nelson asked.

Caspian could tell his brother was tired and jet lagged, and he wondered if they should let him rest for a few hours before going through with the briefing. But when Ranger started to speak, she got Nelson's full attention. Keeping her briefing methodical, she talked about the rare earth deposits, the population displacements and the mining operations that followed, and the shell companies linked to Hearts United. Nelson didn't interrupt, but by the end his expression had hardened in a way Caspian had never seen.

"So, you're telling me Hearts United financed our clinics so that they could convince the population to clear the land?" Nelson asked, his face red. "And that Hearts United, with my help, convinced tribal leaders to move? That they funded our projects to make people trust them?"

"I'm afraid so," Caspian said. "Hearts United partnered with you so that Doctors Without Borders' credibility, and yours, would shield them from any suspicion."

Nelson shook his head. "No . . . I don't believe this. Your intel is wrong. Has to be."

"I'm sorry, brother," Caspian said.

Nelson stared at him, his eyes wide. "Do you think I was complicit in this?"

"Absolutely not," Caspian said quickly. "But you were used."

Nelson pushed up from the couch and headed toward the window, where he stood silent for a long time. Caspian sensed that Ranger wanted to say something, but he shook his head, gesturing her to give Nelson some time to think.

"I've given everything to that job," Nelson said two minutes later. "I . . . I bled for that work. But I believed in it, you know? I still do. Despite all the corruption, we do manage to help people every day."

"I know that," Caspian said. "We all do."

"We think Westcott is about to do the same in the DRC," Ranger said.

"What? No. I'm telling you, you're wrong about him," Nelson said, running a hand through his hair.

Caspian looked at Nelson, and a hollow ache settled in his chest. His brother wasn't just angry, he was hurt, betrayed by Westcott and Hearts United.

Torn open from the inside . . . just like Laura Newman and Onyx did to me.

"Nelson, my intel isn't—" Ranger started.

"Enough!" Nelson shouted. "I don't believe it. I don't want to. Because that would mean I helped him do this. That I helped him move people I love, people who trusted me, off their land."

Caspian could feel the conflict tearing at his brother. It hurt to watch Nelson, who was such a good, kind man, struggle like that.

"Maybe we're wrong, then," Caspian said, ignoring the angry look he got from Ranger.

Nelson spun toward him. "What?"

"I said maybe we're wrong. But we need your help to get to the bottom of this."

It took a few seconds, but then Nelson said, "Okay. If I agree to meet with Westcott, it's not because you've convinced me. It's because you didn't, and I want to prove you wrong. You get that, right?"

Caspian nodded, not arguing. He knew better than to push. "Then let's do that," he said. "Let's prove it together."

"How? I'm a doctor, not a spook. I wouldn't know where to start."

Ranger raised a hand. "I can help with that."

CHAPTER FORTY-EIGHT

Restaurant Unique
New York City, New York

Everett Westcott sipped his wine slowly as he watched Dr. Nelson Anderson cut into his last piece of venison. Nelson didn't act like most guests Westcott usually invited. Nelson was relaxed, didn't seem threatened by his presence, which was rare, and everything he'd said during dinner had been thoughtful and earnest.

Still, something about him was off.

"I've been with MSF for a long time," Nelson said, using the French initials for Médecins Sans Frontières. "It's rewarding work, challenging, too, but . . . I think I'm ready for a change."

"Really?" Westcott asked. "You'd like to go back to practicing medicine?"

Westcott had been wondering why Nelson had reached out to him. He had a feeling he was about to find out.

"Maybe," Nelson said, reaching for his own wineglass. "Or . . . if the right opportunity came up, I'd consider something with Hearts United."

There it is . . .

While the statement didn't shock Westcott, it did come somewhat as a surprise. In theory, someone with Dr. Nelson Anderson's reputation and pedigree would be a prestigious acquisition for Hearts United. Nelson not only had a stellar reputation on the world stage, he'd also been doing important, high-profile work for Doctors Without Borders for more than a decade. But while he'd also been a staunch ally to Westcott and Hearts United in Kenya, the last time the two men spoke, Nelson had clearly indicated he wasn't going to leave the NGO.

So, what had changed?

"You're serious?" Westcott asked.

Nelson nodded and offered him a warm, modest smile. "You once said I should reach out if I was ever looking for new opportunities. So, I thought I'd take you up on that."

"I remember. And I meant it," Westcott replied. "We've done good work together."

He let the silence stretch a moment.

"There might be something opening soon in the DRC," he said carefully. "It's a high-level position that requires the kind of expertise you have, Nelson. And now that I think about it, you'd be the perfect fit."

"The DRC? Really? I . . . I appreciate that. I really do," a rattled Nelson said.

From Nelson's dazed expression, it was obvious to Westcott that the man hadn't expected to receive a job offer on the spot. And then Nelson smiled again, but this time it felt forced, as if he had forgotten to smile and had realized his mistake.

"I can't tell if you're happy about the offer or not, my friend," Westcott said.

"I know how much you care about the DRC and its people, but the country is going through some very complex changes at the moment," Nelson said. "The National Assembly is in disarray, since the arrest of Prime Minister Bongonda, and you know, with allegations that he was an operative of the River Congo Alliance . . . I'm . . . I'm just not sure I understand the region well enough to be of service. I mean, Bongonda? With twenty million dollars in an offshore account? I didn't see that one coming."

"Not many people did, so don't get too worked up about it," Westcott said with a smile. "Honestly, I was taken by surprise too. But you know what? As shocking as Bongonda's arrest is, I trust the Congolese people will sort it out. And who knows, with Bongonda's removal, this might clear the way for President Mutombo's agenda, which I support."

Westcott studied Nelson carefully, looking for any clues the man didn't agree with him . . . or that he was too eager to go. If he was to place Nelson in an important leadership and operational position in the DRC, they had to see eye to eye. But on the other end, no sane man, especially not one with Nelson's real-world experience, would accept a high-profile job in the DRC without reticence.

Unless someone asked him to seek me out.

Westcott didn't think it was the case, but since the Sofie Bergmann incident, he was going to be much more careful about who he brought into his inner circle. After dinner was done, he was going to have a long talk with Mpassi about Nelson Anderson.

"The truth is," Nelson said, "depending on what it is you have in mind for me in the DRC, I may or may not be the best suited candidate for the position. I'd have to know a lot more about what would be expected of me before I even considered it."

The man's answer quieted some of Westcott's doubts. If Nelson had been tasked with infiltrating Hearts United, wouldn't he have jumped at the opportunity Westcott had just offered him on a silver platter? But he hadn't. Nelson Anderson was well versed in the complexity of the region Westcott wanted to send him to, and he was intelligent enough to know he might not have all the answers. Which was something Westcott appreciated.

So why do I feel there's something else?

They finished the meal with light talk, mostly discussing what was going on in Eastern Africa and a potential pharmaceutical partnership between Doctors Without Borders and an American company.

"Thank you again for dinner, Everett," Nelson said, shaking his hand.

"My pleasure. I'll be in touch very soon," Westcott said. "How long are you in town for?"

"Tomorrow morning. I'm headed to Portland, Maine, to see my folks."

"All right, then. Enjoy your time in Maine."

Westcott watched the man leave. He didn't like questions without answers. And Dr. Nelson Anderson had just raised a few.

———

Westcott sank into his seat at the back of the armored Escalade. The powerful engine purred as they pulled away from the curb. To his left, Mpassi tapped through an interface on a secured tablet.

"Well?" Westcott asked.

Mpassi looked up. "We may have a problem with the good doctor," he said.

"Go on."

"You asked me to monitor your dinner. We captured the entire conversation and ran it through our analysis software in real time. The AI picked up several inconsistencies with Dr. Anderson's answers."

Westcott tilted his head. "Such as?"

"He told you he flew into Newark."

"He did."

"Well, he didn't. Not really."

"What do you mean?"

"Dr. Anderson did land in Newark earlier today, but he did so because he took a flight from Boston, not Nairobi."

Westcott raised an eyebrow. "When did he get back from Africa?" he asked.

"Two days ago. He landed at Logan Airport in Boston."

"He told me he has family in Maine, so that makes sense, doesn't it?"

"Then why did he tell you he was still jet lagged?" Mpassi asked.

"What's your point, Charles?"

"What I'm saying is that he made it sound like he had just flown in from Nairobi, when in fact he didn't."

Westcott looked out the window, his mind going through the reasons that could have pushed Nelson Anderson to make him believe he had just flown in from overseas. Could it be a simple misunderstanding?

"And there's more," Mpassi continued. "His parents own a trucking company near Portland, Maine. And FYI, the ATF has a file on them. It's unclear why."

"These companies attract federal attention all the time," Westcott said. "Could be tax evasion, interstate-cargo irregularities, drug trafficking—"

"I get it," Mpassi said. "Could be anything. But I'm looking into it."

"Anything else?"

"Yeah. He has a brother."

"I remember him mentioning having a sibling," Westcott said. "Works at the United Nations, right?"

"Name's Caspian Anderson. He was a translator at the UN."

"Was?" Westcott asked.

"My contact said Caspian Anderson is no longer listed as an employee," Mpassi explained. "But what's truly interesting is that there's no photos of him online. Nelson's parents, Richard and Elizabeth Anderson, are well known in their community. Their pictures were easy to find. Local newspapers, chamber of commerce stuff, but Caspian? Nothing."

"You think he's been deliberately scrubbed?" Westcott asked.

"Too soon to say for sure, but that's what I'm starting to believe."

"All right. Keep digging."

CHAPTER FORTY-NINE

Miami, Florida

Mia was sprawled on a white leather sectional in her two-bedroom condo, trying to catch her breath. She glanced at Henry, who had an arm draped across her naked stomach. His chest was rising and falling slowly, his eyes were half closed with a smug but certainly well-earned grin. He was, she had to admit, a hell of a lot better than Maximilian Kross. Not that the bar had been high.

Her condo was located on the twenty-eighth floor of a tower over-looking Biscayne Bay. The unit was hers, and fully paid for. The large patio doors were open, letting in the warm, humid air of the late afternoon. She didn't mind the heat.

To Mia, Miami was home. Spanish was spoken everywhere, the city's energy was contagious, and the summer heat reminded her that she was alive. She loved everything about Miami. Its pastel buildings, its pulsing nightlife, and even its chaotic traffic. There were also a few bars and hotels in South Beach where she'd gotten regular piano gigs over the years, which she'd found was a good way to stay grounded between assignments. She looked at her sleek black baby grand, which sat in one corner of her living room. The piano was polished to a mirrored sheen with its lid propped open. It was too bad Operations had canceled her events in Budapest and Dubrovnik, but there wasn't much she could do about it.

Because she'd turned off the air-conditioning, she could hear the whine of a pair of Jet Skis as they raced across the bay. The faint noise seemed to jolt Henry back from his reverie. He got up, muttered something about making smoothies, then padded off toward the kitchen. She watched him go, her eyes following the sway of his bare, muscular backside as he moved through the apartment.

Damn . . . he's hot.

She stayed where she was, naked, with one leg flung over the back of the couch, her phone balanced on her chest. Her encrypted line buzzed softly in her earbud. She tapped it.

"How are you?" came the voice of Charles Mpassi, or Operations to the assets who dealt with him regularly. "Hope you're enjoying your vacation."

"Not complaining. Sun, sex, and apparently, smoothies will make anyone happy, but I'm a bit bored, to be honest," Mia said as she swung her legs off the couch.

She reached for the silk robe hanging from the armrest.

"Good, good," Mpassi replied absently. "How's your injury?"

She stood and crossed the living room toward a full-length mirror that hung on the wall. She pulled her hair back and angled her head so she could inspect the bottom of her left ear. The bullet fragment had taken a clean bite out of the cartilage. Only the tip was gone, but she wouldn't be wearing earrings anytime soon. Miami being Miami, her plastic surgeon was booked solid for the next six weeks. So, until then, there was nothing more she could do but apply twice a day the special cream her doctor had prescribed.

"It's healing," she said as she tied her robe.

"Glad to hear it. Because I need you back in the game. We've got a surveillance package that can't wait. The dossier's already in your secure folder."

Mia walked out onto the balcony.

"Where do you need me?" she asked, squinting into the glare off the bay.

"Everything you need to know about the target is in the file I sent you, but since you asked, the target is in Portland, Maine."

"Got it," she replied.

"I want to know who he meets and who he talks to. Don't engage. Just watch and report," Mpassi said, ending the call.

Mia dropped the phone into her robe's pocket and stretched her arms overhead.

"Are you, or we, going somewhere?" Henry asked, stepping onto the balcony with two green smoothies in his hands.

"We're going to Portland."

"Cool," Henry replied. "I love Oregon, they make great wines. Their pinot noir is exquisite."

"Portland, Maine, you idiot," Mia said, taking a sip of her smoothie.

"Shit," Henry said under his breath, deflated. "I don't think they make wine in Maine."

CHAPTER FIFTY

I-95 North, Maine
Between Boston and Portland

Caspian kept the Jeep Cherokee steady in the middle lane, his fingers drumming on the wheel to the rhythm of the country song that was playing on the local FM station. Clara, Nelson's girlfriend, was seated in the front passenger seat, her Ray-Bans pushed up into her auburn hair. In her hands, she cradled what looked less like a water bottle and more like a hydration silo.

"To be honest," Clara said, "I never thought I'd see so much action in Kenya. I figured I'd be stuck filling out immigration paperwork and answering the occasional legal question for the ambassador, you know? But I ended up working side by side with the legat. It was fun."

"Legat?" Caspian asked, as if he had no idea what it meant.

"Oh, I'm sorry," Clara said. "It's the term we use for the legal attachés. They're FBI."

"Wow, okay. Very cool," Caspian said, doing his best to sound impressed. "But Nelson told me you were ready for a change? I mean, I don't think I'd ever want to leave an exciting job like yours."

"I wouldn't mind staying another year, but my time's up. It's not really my call, to be completely honest. I'll be in DC for the next three or four years."

"And after that?" Caspian asked.

Clara glanced over her shoulder at Nelson, whose head was against the window, his mouth slightly ajar, snoring like a man who hadn't slept in a week.

"Then we'll see," she said. "Another overseas posting, maybe, or I could move to private practice here in the US. I guess a lot depends on where Nelson is and if I still like him."

Caspian chuckled. "Fair enough."

Clara looked at him. "What about you? Nelson said you used to work for the United Nations?"

"Yeah," Caspian said. "I did. But nothing as exhilarating as what you're doing in Kenya, that's for damn sure."

"So . . . what are you doing now?" she asked, taking a long sip from her water bottle.

"Freelance consulting mostly. Most of my contracts come from the federal government. Like right now, I'm working on translating a nine-hundred-page document for the Animal and Plant Health Inspection Service."

"The what now?" Clara asked.

"APHIS. It's part of the Department of Agriculture," Caspian said. "They regulate the importation of plants, you know? Think cut flowers, seeds, bonsai trees, that sort of thing."

Clara leaned her head back against the seat. "Thrilling."

"Oh, you have no idea," Caspian said. "They even sent me on a weeklong assignment with Fish and Wildlife. That was so intense."

"I bet," Clara muttered, looking out her window.

Caspian decided to push the envelope a bit further. "They're the ones who enforce compliance with international treaties on endangered species. Do you know how much contraband aloe vera is smuggled into the country every year?"

"I . . . I don't know, Caspian. You got me there," Clara said, then she shifted in her seat and asked, "Were you always that into federal regulations, or is this a new thing?"

Caspian smirked. "Only since I realized how hard it is to ship citrus across state lines. Did you know oranges can't legally be shipped into California without inspection?"

Clara stared at him. "You are . . . alarmingly full of fun facts, aren't you?"

Caspian shrugged, but he was still smiling.

"Nelson said he'd always thought you were dangerous, somehow," Clara said.

"Did he?"

"Yeah, but I thought he meant in a Jason Bourne kind of way. Turns out you're more like a particularly diligent park ranger, right?"

Caspian gave her a sidelong look. "Park rangers are armed, so not my bag really. And I'll have you know park rangers have one of the highest rates of on-duty bear encounters."

"Are you saying you fought a bear during your one-week assignment with Fish and Wildlife?"

"What I'm saying is that I've translated documents from people who have," he said, deadpan.

They passed a green highway sign announcing that Portland was thirty miles away. To their right, the coastline came back into view between the trees. From the back seat, Nelson stirred.

"What are you guys talking about?" he asked.

"Your brother's undercover gig at the Department of Agriculture," Clara said. "Apparently, he's become the Indiana Jones of houseplants and aloe vera."

"Your words, not mine," Caspian said. "Anyhow, you've been out for about ninety minutes, brother. We'll be in Portland in half an hour, unless you two want to stop for a lobster roll? Because if you do, I know just the place."

Clara's eyes lit up at the idea. "That would be nice. I haven't had one of those in forever."

An hour later, Caspian guided the Jeep into one of the long, straight driveways on Eastern Promenade. His parents' house was a stately, sea-facing property with clapboard siding and navy blue shutters. It was the kind of house that screamed old money, but the truth was, it hadn't always looked like this. Richard and Elizabeth Anderson had renovated it themselves, slowly, bit by bit, by scraping together the necessary funds.

As he rolled to a stop, his eyes landed on a dark gray sedan already parked near his father's GMC Sierra 1500 Denali. The car's windows were tinted, and the license plate was from New Hampshire. It looked like a rental car, but it could also belong to a federal law enforcement agency.

Like the ATF.

"Hey, Nelson, did Mom and Dad tell you there would be someone else here?" he asked.

"No. Why?"

"Just wondering who owns that gray car," he said.

Caspian's father hated surprises. If the feds had shown up uninvited, Richard or Elizabeth would have reached out. While he didn't completely rule out the sedan and whoever had driven it to his parents' house as potential threats, Caspian didn't think someone who meant them harm would have parked their ride in the driveway. He turned off the engine and resisted his urge to adjust the pistol holstered at the small of his back.

Moments later, his parents appeared on the front porch. Both were beaming and waving at them, clearly happy to see their two sons. Before he could exit the Jeep, his phone buzzed. It was Ranger.

"You guys go ahead," Caspian told Clara and Nelson. "I really need to take this."

"More aloe vera coming across the border?" Clara asked, raising an eyebrow.

"Either that or someone is trying to import illegal citrus fruits into California," he replied.

Clara shook her head, then climbed out of the Jeep as Nelson grabbed the suitcases from the back. Caspian took the call.

"Yeah?"

"Can you talk?" Ranger asked.

"I'm alone, and you're off speaker."

"We ID'd the woman who shot at you in Valencia," she said. "Name's Mia Hernandez. Ring a bell?"

"Afraid not."

"Believe it or not, she has a website. Professional pianist, apparently."

"A pianist," Caspian repeated. "More like a professional assassin, if you ask me."

"She was supposed to perform in Budapest and Dubrovnik this week—"

"But let me guess," Caspian interrupted. "Both events were canceled."

"You got it," Ranger confirmed. "Unfortunately, we don't have much else for now except that she lives in Miami. We also think she's single, but that's not confirmed. But we're digging."

"Okay," Caspian said, opening the door. "Thanks for the update, and let me know when you find more."

"Sure thing. I'll call you tomorrow. Just . . . watch yourself, Caspian. This Mia is a capable lady."

The screen door of his parents' house creaked, and Caspian's gaze drifted back in that direction. His parents, Nelson, and Clara were inside now, but another figure stepped into view.

Caspian's heart skipped a beat.

Liesel leaned against the railing, her arms crossed casually. She wore dark jeans and a red, baggy sweatshirt. Her dark hair was tousled from the breeze coming from the bay. Her eyes were fixed on him, unreadable. But her expression wasn't hard, just cautious.

And maybe a little hopeful?

For a long moment, Caspian didn't move, happy to only stare at her. Then, all the tension in his body subsided, like a muscle unclenching. Just seeing Liesel smoothed the hard edge he'd felt since the last time he'd seen her. Somehow, he felt lighter on his feet. The way she hadn't replied to his emails or to his calls, and how she'd pulled back after Istanbul and let the distance, and silence, grow between them, had bothered him. But he hadn't realized how much weight it had added on his shoulders until now.

But damn was he happy to see her.

"Caspian?" Ranger's voice crackled. "You still there?"

"Yes," he murmured. "I gotta go, Sam."

He ended the call and fully stepped out of the Jeep. The sea breeze hit him, and cool air filled his lungs. Liesel was the one thing in his life he hadn't been able to file into a compartment. She was the risk, and the exception to every rule he'd set for himself.

"Hey, Casp," Liesel said, her soft, familiar voice anchoring him.

He shoved his phone into his pocket and found himself grinning.

"Hey," he said, then started toward the steps.

CHAPTER FIFTY-ONE

Portland, Maine

The sunroom's tall windows caught the last stretch of light as the sun slanted low across the Casco Bay. Inside, the air carried the salty tang of low tide from the breeze that snuck in through the cracked-open window. The room, which was in a quiet corner of the house, had always been Caspian's mother's favorite. From the kitchen at the far end of the hall, Caspian could hear laughter and the clink of cutlery being set on plates.

Dinner was imminent, but he wasn't hungry. Far from it.

He sat in a love seat, elbows on his knees, shoulders hunched. Across from him, Liesel leaned into the cushions of the settee, a throw blanket covering her legs.

"My wounds are healing fast," she said, answering his question. "The stitches are out. Still a little sore, though, but every day is better than the last."

"You look good," he said.

"Thanks."

The laughter coming from the kitchen rose again. Someone had told a joke, probably his father, and it only deepened the contrast with the silence in the sunroom.

"I thought about staying in Germany," Liesel said.

Caspian's throat turned dry. "Because of work?"

"No." She shook her head. "You know it has nothing to do with that. I love my job as a liaison officer with SSU. It's a good challenge."

His chest tightened. "Then what is it?"

She exhaled loudly, folding her arms. "It's about us. About me, really."

Caspian sat forward, uncertain where this conversation was going. He drew in a breath, and doing his best to keep his voice even, he said, "I called you. I emailed and texted, too, but you didn't reply. For days."

"I know."

"That's not like you."

He let his words hang there for a moment, then asked, "Why?"

Liesel looked down at her hands, then out the window. "Because I needed time to think. Really think. And I knew that if I heard your voice, even once, I'd stop thinking and start feeling."

"I don't understand, Liesel," he said, confused. "What's wrong with feeling something?"

"I'm afraid, Caspian," she said.

"Of what?"

"Of believing something just because I want it to be true," she said, her eyes finally meeting his. "I love you, but I don't know if we make sense in the long run. You're always half here, half somewhere else."

"That's not fair," he said quietly.

"That's just the thing. It's not about being fair. It's about being honest with each other."

Caspian sighed, leaning back into the love seat, his hand curling around the armrest. "You think I want this life? You think I wake up excited to lie to people? You think I like getting shot at? You think I like . . . killing people? I don't, Liesel."

"Maybe, but you're good at it, and I think a part of you needs it."

He didn't reply, and he studied her for a long moment, unsure how to respond.

"Again, I love you," she said, "but I'm not sure you're right for me. Or that I'm right for you."

He opened his mouth to protest, but she raised her hand.

"Don't say anything. Not yet, okay? Just . . . think about what I said. Be honest with yourself. I've had time to do that. You didn't. I figured out what I want. You need to do the same."

Caspian's gaze dropped to the floor. His heart hammered in his chest. There was so much he wanted to say to Liesel. There was a knock, then the sunroom door cracked open, and Elizabeth Anderson poked her head in, her bright green eyes flicking from Caspian to Liesel.

"The appetizers are out," she said, cheerful as always. "And we need Liesel to select the wine, because if we let Richard do it . . ."

Liesel smiled, stood, then crossed the room. She hugged Elizabeth tightly, then made her way to the kitchen.

Elizabeth turned to him and said, "She had puffy eyes earlier. Everything okay between you two?"

"We're figuring things out," he replied.

His mother stepped farther in, then sat next to him. "Please do, Caspian. Because that woman is special. Treat her well. Don't mess this up."

That made him smile, just a little. "I'm trying not to."

His mother tilted her head, studying him. "I can see you're conflicted. A mom knows when her child isn't at peace. And you're not. And Nelson isn't either."

Caspian didn't argue. She was right. He wasn't in a good place right now.

"You're good men, both of you," she said. "But you live very different lives. Yours is . . . so dark, love. So freaking dark. Nelson's life isn't easy, either, but he's always been . . . light. Even when things were hard. But today, he's different. I feel like you brought your brother into your world. And he's not built for that."

"Nelson's strong," he said.

"I didn't say he wasn't," Elizabeth said. "But Nelson is . . . he's softer inside. He laughs more, and he believes people are good until they prove otherwise."

"But I don't," he said. "I'm aware."

His mother reached for his hand. "I don't want this to be who you are forever," she said. "I'm not exactly sure what it is that you do, but I'm not stupid. I think I have an idea."

Caspian looked down at her hand wrapped around his. But he said nothing.

"Listen, I'm not saying you're looking for an exit ramp, but if you are, I know Liesel will be there waiting for you."

Caspian wasn't so sure.

CHAPTER FIFTY-TWO

Teterboro Airport
Bergen County, New Jersey

Everett Westcott didn't like being blindsided, and he certainly didn't appreciate being told minutes before boarding that the man he trusted most wasn't getting on the plane with him.

"What do you mean you aren't coming?" he asked.

"I apologize, sir," Mpassi replied. "I really need to get to the bottom of this. Give me a couple of days, and I'll catch up with you in Geneva."

Westcott stared at him, trying to process what Mpassi had told him.

"Are you absolutely sure about this?" he asked, incredulous. "There must be at least two hundred women named Mia Hernandez in the country. Chances are it's not even our Mia."

"It's her. My contact at the FBI confirmed the name's been run in several federal databases. Same from my guy at the IRS. And the date of birth attached to the query is Mia's. There's no doubt."

Westcott slammed his palm against the driver's seat in front of him.

"Fuck," he hissed. Then louder. "Fuck!"

They were still in the armored Escalade, which was parked fifty feet from the waiting Gulfstream G550. The plane's engines hadn't started yet, but the pilots were on board, and the flight attendant was ready. Westcott and Mpassi were scheduled to fly to Paris for several high-level meetings before continuing to Geneva, where they would meet with a delegation from the Democratic Republic of the Congo.

But now it seemed like he'd fly solo.

Westcott had been in regular contact with President Mutombo, who had not only regained control of the National Assembly but had also secured the necessary votes to pass Westcott's initiative. The stakes had never been higher. If things stayed on track, his hydroelectric initiative would begin funneling money into the DRC's government coffers within five years. It would be slow at first—an infrastructure of this scale always was—but the outcome would be transformative. He would live to see the people of the DRC receive the universal health care his wife Nailah had fought so hard for. A rare, near-impossible feat in any developing nation.

But here we are . . . on the cusp of greatness.

The health care system he had envisioned with Nailah, one that was professionally administered and publicly funded with the funds coming from Hearts United's project, would lift an entire nation out of generational neglect. The DRC would go from having 0.2 doctors per thousand habitants to one. Far from the European Union average of four, but still a big step forward, and hopefully enough to drop the maternal mortality rate from 345 deaths per one hundred thousand live births to under 150.

Westcott wasn't doing this for vanity or for accolades. He was doing this for women like Nailah's mother, whose life might have been spared had there been even the most basic medical care within reach.

Nothing was more important than that. *Not even Mia.*

"How exposed are we?" Westcott asked, forcing himself to stay focused.

"We're not, for now," Mpassi said without hesitation. "And that's true across all our operations. But if Mia gets captured—"

"She'd never talk," Westcott said instantly, knowing he sounded desperate.

Mpassi met his gaze. The man's eyes were steady, and there was a weight behind them. One Westcott didn't appreciate.

"Not willingly, I know," Mpassi said. "But people break, sir. Even the best."

Before Westcott could respond, Mpassi's phone buzzed. He answered it quickly and said almost nothing. When the call ended, he slowly brought the phone down to his lap and stared ahead, as if the world had just tilted beneath him.

"Who was that?" Westcott asked.

"Director Cortés. CNI."

Westcott knew Lucía Cortés well. She was the head of the Centro Nacional de Inteligencia, Spain's foreign and domestic intelligence agency. She was more than just a contact; she was one of his most reliable special assets.

"What did she say?"

"It took some time, but they were able to identify the man from Port de Sóller. He used his real passport when he first flew in. Name's Caspian Anderson."

Westcott inhaled sharply, but Mpassi wasn't finished.

"The woman with him was Liesel Bergmann. Sofie's twin."

As if frozen, Westcott's brain simply refused to accept what he'd heard. His face flushed hot, and he felt his gut twist. He'd suspected Sofie might have said something to someone before she'd been shot dead, but her sister? He hadn't seen this one coming.

But I should have . . . what I shouldn't have done was to bring her in.

Liesel and Sofie Bergmann, Caspian and Nelson Anderson? Had they been working together from the beginning? And who were they working for? When he'd recruited Sofie Bergmann, she'd been a German army officer. A logistics specialist who had a lot of contacts in Afghanistan. The Andersons were Americans. Could Nelson or his brother—*or both*—be CIA officers? It wouldn't be the first time an intelligence service embedded one of their operatives with Doctors Without Borders now, would it? But could the Germans and Americans be working together this closely? Was this a rogue operation or a sanctioned one?

But even if they were backed by an agency, what did they know? Could they prove anything? Surely, if there was an active investigation, someone within his deep network inside the US government would have sounded the alarm, right?

"Do we have the influence to shut down any federal investigation into Mia?" Westcott asked, already thinking ahead.

"I can arrange to get regular updates, which would give us ample time to warn her," Mpassi replied. "But shutting it down outright? I don't think it's possible. Not without raising alarms."

"What about Blackstone? Were you able to cut all ties? Do you know if anyone has been digging?"

"There were some inquiries," Mpassi conceded, "but there's no legal link between Blackstone and Hearts United. Nothing admissible. At worst, there might be breadcrumbs, enough to raise suspicions, but not enough to prosecute."

"But they could find out we used them."

"It'd be hard, but not impossible. Again, nothing anyone could drag into court."

Westcott shook his head. What was it that Mpassi didn't understand? Did he not see that even a suspicion by the wrong people could be enough to derail everything? It was as if he didn't care.

"So right now," Westcott said slowly, "you think the only threats are the Anderson brothers and that Bergmann woman?"

Mpassi pursed his lips. "I know you don't want to think this way," he said, "but if Mia's caught and decides to save herself—"

"I told you," Westcott snapped. "She wouldn't. Never."

Mpassi sighed. "We're so close to achieving Nailah's dream . . . do you really want to jeopardize that?"

Westcott pressed his fingers against his temples. A pulse had begun to throb behind his eyes. Mpassi kept mentioning Mia, but he hadn't raised any question about Henry's loyalty. Why was that? Was it because Henry was Mpassi's man? Because Mpassi had handpicked him? Not for the first time, Westcott wondered if he hadn't given Mpassi too much leeway.

"If you'd like to hear it, sir, I have an idea on how we could take care of everything at once," Mpassi offered.

"No! I don't want to hear it. The only thing you'll do while I'm gone is to give Mia and Henry the green light to take care of the Andersons and Liesel Bergmann. That's it. Is that clear?"

"Crystal," Mpassi replied.

Westcott stared at Mpassi, and he didn't like the way the man was looking back at him. He didn't like the faint gleam of calculation in Mpassi's eyes. Trust was a fickle thing. It was slow to build and quick to collapse.

Without another word, Westcott stepped out of the SUV and climbed aboard the Gulfstream where he sank into one of the beige leather seats. He would speak to Mpassi when he returned from Europe. And if his instincts were right, and if Mpassi had started to think of himself as more than just Westcott's number two, then maybe it was time to find someone else to replace him.

And he couldn't think of anyone better than Mia Hernandez to do so.

CHAPTER FIFTY-THREE

Mia's flight out of Miami had been as dull and unremarkable as she had hoped. She and Henry had booked different airlines, checked in for their flights at different terminals, and never saw each other during their journey to Portland. In fact, their itineraries hadn't intersected until Maine, and even then, they had exited the airport hours apart and had headed to separate car-rental counters.

Each of them had checked one bag. Inside those bags, under neatly folded clothing and locked in hard-sided containers, were their firearms. Each had brought along a suppressor and spare magazines. Mia also carried a knife and the last of the antibiotic cream for the wound on her ear, though it was healing nicely, and the scar was mostly hidden beneath her hair.

The sun was low behind a thick bank of clouds, casting a gray pallor over Casco Bay. She had checked, and no rain was expected, but the air had that sticky, weedy scent that was often present during low tide.

Cutter Street's lot wasn't busy at this hour, but she'd seen a few joggers running along the Midslope Trail since she'd parked her rental car an hour ago. To her left and down the slope, anchored sailboats rocked gently in the harbor. The Cleeves and Tucker Memorial stood in the distance.

Two conquerors, probably, she thought, but didn't care enough to check.

From her vantage point, Mia could see the Anderson house through the thinning trees above the promenade. Her angle wasn't the best, but the feed coming in from the drone Henry was piloting from somewhere north of the target told her everything she needed to know.

She glanced down at her phone, where the live feed displayed a stabilized bird's-eye view of the Anderson's three-story colonial home. The porch lights were on, and while the curtains were drawn in some of the windows, they were open in many others. There were three vehicles parked in the long driveway: a Jeep Cherokee, a luxury pickup truck, and a dark sedan.

Henry flew the drone lower, and she saw a figure pass behind a window. It was a man, but she couldn't tell who it was from this distance. Since Henry had launched the drone twenty minutes ago, she'd spotted five different people inside the house. While it was possible there were more people than that, she knew there were at least two women and three men present at the property.

Thanks to the photos Mpassi had forwarded to her and Henry, Mia had been able to identify the three men. While she would recognize Caspian Anderson anywhere, she'd never set eyes on his brother, Nelson, or their father, Richard, before tonight.

Henry's voice came in through her earbud. "What do you think?" he asked.

"Looks like a family reunion to me," she replied. "Exactly what we were hoping for."

She studied the video feed. The lights were on in almost every room. It didn't feel like a trap. But she wasn't about to underestimate Caspian Anderson. She'd seen him in action. In Valencia, he'd almost taken her head off. She'd been lucky. She wasn't planning on giving him a second chance.

She'd gotten off the phone with Mpassi half an hour ago. He'd given her and Henry the final green light, and his orders couldn't have been clearer. The Anderson brothers and Liesel Bergmann had to be dealt with.

Tonight.

Mpassi had been adamant about it. Mia had asked to speak to Westcott, although apparently he wasn't available. But Mpassi had promised her she'd be able to reach him tomorrow.

To complete tonight's mission, there wasn't time for clever cover stories or drawn-out surveillance. She and Henry weren't about to pose as cable-company techs or go knocking on the Anderson's door with phony clipboards pretending to be sales reps. No, they would go in hard and quick, using surprise and violence of action.

She would have preferred to pick her own timing for the operation, but if Mpassi needed these three people gone by the end of the day, she knew he had a good reason. This was the final stitch in closing the wound Verena Kaine had opened, and it was up to Mia to end things now.

Caspian Anderson had been the wild card in all of it, and now he was at the center of what was left. She didn't know how exactly the operation would go down, but she hoped she'd be the one to finish him off.

For this op to work, though, Henry would have to take the lead. Caspian had already seen her. If he spotted her again, they'd lose their biggest advantage—surprise. And if that happened, it could turn to shit real fast.

But she hadn't trained with Henry. She knew he was competent, but there was always a risk when two operators who had never moved side by side joined forces for an operation like this one. Apart from their time together in Aruba and their lovemaking sessions in Miami, they didn't know each other's rhythms, and breaching a house with an unknown layout was a recipe for chaos.

She was about to take a sip of water when a flicker on the screen caught her attention.

"Zoom in on the backyard," she said.

The drone's camera adjusted, zooming in as the rear sliding door of the house eased open. A man stepped out on the back balcony, wearing a red apron and holding a pair of tongs in one hand. His build was heavier than Caspian's, and he was older.

"It's Richard Anderson," Mia said.

She watched as Anderson set the tongs down on the grill, lifted the lid, and checked the burners. He then turned back toward the house. Mia's mind clicked through the implications. An opportunity had just presented itself. She now knew that the back door was unlocked, which meant they had a second point of entry.

Henry must have come to the same conclusion, because he asked, "How do you want to do this?"

"We have our access," she said. "You take the front and ring the bell. They'll answer, someone always does."

"And you?"

"I'll move from the rear. Once you're in, I'll follow. We hit them from both sides, but for God's sake, check your fire, okay?"

Henry didn't reply directly, but he said, "I'm ready to move whenever you are. I need three minutes to get to the house."

"Fly the drone over the side of the house for me and zoom in," she said. "I need to figure out how to reach the backyard without being seen."

She scanned the terrain and noticed a tree line to the east of the Anderson house. There seemed to be a slight dip in elevation between the adjacent property and the fence. If she moved fast and kept low, she could reach the backyard in less than twenty seconds from the street. She shared her plan with Henry.

"I'll go on your mark," he said.

"Not yet, H," she said. "I want to see if anyone else steps outside. I'd rather pick them off outside than get stuck inside with at least five unknowns."

"Five minutes?" Henry asked.

"Give it ten," she replied.

There was a pause, then Henry's voice came back quieter, but she could tell there was a smile behind it. "You're still giving the orders, huh?"

She allowed a small laugh to escape her lips. "That was always the arrangement," she said.

"I didn't mind back in Miami," he said. "I kind of like it."

"Yeah . . . I know," she said.

CHAPTER FIFTY-FOUR

Defense Intelligence Headquarters
Joint Base Anacostia-Bolling
Washington, DC

Samantha Ranger had just reached for her coat when a quiet knock sounded at her office door. Before she could answer, the door opened, and her assistant stepped inside with an apologetic look on his face, holding a manila folder in his hand. Clipped neatly to the two bottom corners were black colored tabs, which meant that whatever was in the folder was urgent.

"It's from your friend at the NSA," her assistant said, placing the folder on her desk with deliberate care. "It just came in. I'm sorry."

Ranger didn't move for a moment. She was already halfway into the mental transition between work and home, where dinner with her sister and a glass of wine were waiting for her. But now, with the folder resting like a loaded weapon on her desk, she shook her head. Her sister would have to wait.

She sighed, slipped out of her coat, and sank slowly back into the chair behind her desk.

"Thank you," Ranger said to her assistant. "I'll let you know if I need anything else."

Her assistant nodded and backed out of the office, then closed the door behind him without another word.

Ranger opened the folder, and her eyes immediately caught on the subject line.

Hernandez, Mia.

Her breath stilled as she flipped through the pages. The file was filled with passenger manifests, flagged metadata, boarding time stamps, and airport-security photos. The weight of what she was seeing settled deep in her chest.

Shit.

Mia Hernandez had flown out of Miami that morning, connected through LaGuardia, and arrived in Portland, Maine, late this afternoon. TSA hadn't flagged her, but the NSA, at Ranger's request, had.

For a long moment, Ranger didn't move.

Mia's in Portland. Caspian is in Portland. And so is his brother, Nelson.

Ranger didn't believe in coincidence. She believed in timing, pattern recognition, and her gut. Caspian had debriefed her about Nelson's meeting with Everett Westcott. They would talk again about it the next day, but tonight Caspian was at his parents' house to celebrate Elizabeth Anderson's birthday.

Had Westcott figured out Nelson wasn't working alone? If he had, it meant that Nelson was now a target. Ranger ran a hand down her face, trying to stay calm, but her pulse continued to climb.

Damn it.

It was possible she was wrong, that Mia Hernandez was in Portland for something that was unrelated to Nelson or Caspian. But it wasn't likely.

Ranger picked up her desk phone and dialed Caspian's number.

CHAPTER FIFTY-FIVE

The Anderson Family Home
Portland, Maine

From his spot in the kitchen, Caspian watched his father step out through the back door and onto the deck—where his beloved grill was already warming—with a glass of Upper Terrace pinot noir from Ribbon Ridge, Oregon, in his hand. Caspian was surprised to see his father drink such an elegant, stately wine since Richard Anderson had long dismissed wine as "overpriced grape juice." Clearly, he had found something redeeming in this one, because it was obvious to Caspian that his dad wasn't drinking the wine to be polite; he was drinking it because he truly enjoyed it. And so did Caspian. In his opinion, the Upper Terrace from the Beaux Frères Vineyard was the best pinot noir in Oregon. Caspian smiled as he saw his dad distractedly swirl his wine as he studied the arrangement of the six rib eye steaks he had lined up on the wooden butcher block.

Caspian leaned on the counter, one hand resting beside a bowl of sliced lemons, the other around the stem of his wineglass. The kitchen smelled of rosemary, cracked pepper, and the faint citrus of his mother's vinaigrette. It had been too long since they'd all been here under one roof, and never, as far as he could remember, had both he and Nelson brought someone with them at the same time. That fact alone made the evening feel strange, not in a bad way, but in a way that emphasized just how far his life had drifted from anything resembling what most people would call normalcy.

Clara had slipped into the tempo of the Anderson household with grace, but Caspian wasn't surprised in the least. One of Elizabeth's many gifts was the ease with which she made people feel not only welcome but wanted, as if every visitor had been expected all along. She had the kind of warmth that made even strangers want to stay a little longer, though Caspian knew her cooking helped too. Tonight's salad for example, with its toasted hazelnuts, blood oranges, and goat cheese, looked like it had been lifted from a food and wine magazine's feature spread.

Through the open door that led to the deck, Caspian could hear his father and Nelson, who had now joined him outside, debating the sacred art of letting rib eye steaks rest after grilling, as if slicing the meat too soon was a crime against humanity.

Caspian turned slightly, glancing across the room to where Liesel stood with Clara. She was laughing at something Clara had just said, her shoulders loose and her smile unguarded. God, he'd forgotten how good it sounded. For months now—since Bordeaux, really—that part of her had gone quiet. Port de Sóller had helped for a while, then things had once again spiraled out of control, and he'd watched her retreat into herself.

Seeing her laugh like this again unlocked something inside him, something that made him want to freeze the room exactly as it was . . . forever.

Caspian exhaled, not in a dramatic way, but apparently loudly enough that his father, who had just stepped into the kitchen to refill his wineglass, looked at him and asked, "You all right, son?"

Caspian forced a smile and said, "I see you like the wine."

He expected a comeback, something dry or teasing, but his father surprised him.

"I think it's glorious," he said. "It's full bodied, for sure, but somehow light on its feet, if you know what I mean? And what about those cherry and raspberry flavors? I don't know, but to me, they kind of open to notes of baking spices. What do you think?"

Caspian stared at his father. "I . . . I didn't expect a tasting note from you, Dad."

His father shrugged. "Well, I didn't expect to enjoy it that much," he said, pouring himself another glass before returning outside to Nelson and the steaks.

Caspian felt Liesel's eyes on him, and he turned toward her. While he was relieved to see warmth in her gaze, there was something else too. Her lips didn't move, but it seemed like her eyes were asking him a question he wasn't sure how to answer. Caspian looked away, having a hard time holding her eyes.

Liesel had told him she knew what she wanted in life. And the way she'd looked at him when she'd said it had made it clear he wasn't necessarily part of the plan. And how could he blame her? She had been shot, and stabbed, because of him. Yes, Liesel was an intelligence officer, but she'd been dragged into his world, a world she hadn't chosen. One she was trying to escape.

And then there was Sofie.

Liesel had watched her sister die. Not from a distance, but up close. Inches away. And even though Caspian knew what kind of trauma this could do to a person, he hadn't let himself really think about it until just now, when he saw Liesel laugh like she hadn't in months.

I've taken so much from her.

Was he doing the same with Nelson? Caspian had convinced himself that his brother would be fine, that it was a calculated risk, that the reward justified it. But Nelson wasn't a piece on a game board. He was a good man, someone who truly helped people.

He's nothing like me. And now I've put him in Westcott's crosshairs.

I should have never agreed to bring him into this operation.

Caspian hated himself for agreeing to Ranger's plan.

What have I done?

He thought about what Liesel had told him earlier.

Be honest with yourself. I've had time to do that. You didn't. I figured out what I want. You need to do the same.

Caspian once again took in his surroundings, his eyes moving from person to person. They *are what I want*. They *are who I want to be with*. They *make me happy*.

He shook his head at the realization. *I'm done.*

As the thought solidified, something inside him shifted. He didn't want this life anymore. He was done with the lies, with the killing. His family deserved better.

Liesel deserves better.

And maybe, just maybe, and despite everything he had done, so did he.

When this thing with Westcott was over, he'd talk to Samantha Ranger. It wouldn't be easy, and she'd fight back, probably even threaten him with the weight of what he'd done with Onyx, but she wouldn't have him killed. And he didn't think she'd bury him either. Ranger wasn't a monster. He was ready to bet his life on it.

He took another sip of wine. Liesel was now listening to Clara describe something about French vintages. Clara's voice was animated, confident, and to his surprise, she seemed to know her stuff. Caspian walked over.

He stood next to Liesel for a few seconds, nodding at whatever Clara was saying, but all he could think about was touching Liesel. With his heart hammering in his chest, he slipped his arm gently around her waist, half expecting her to deflect or subtly lean away, some sort of signal that it was too soon, or too much.

But Liesel didn't move. And when she did, it was to turn toward him to press a kiss to his cheek. She then looped her arm around his back and gave him a gentle squeeze.

Caspian's breath caught in his throat.

He was about to say something when he felt his phone buzz in his pocket. He pulled it out and looked at the screen.

Ranger.

They weren't scheduled to talk until the next day. Liesel noticed the name, too, because she looked at him, raising an eyebrow. He stared at the screen for a second longer, then declined the call and returned the phone to his pocket.

"So, Caspian," Clara said. "Are you a Bordeaux or Burgundy man?"

CHAPTER FIFTY-SIX

The Anderson Family Home
Portland, Maine

Mia moved low through the tree line, doing her best not to snap a loose branch. The incline between the Anderson house and the next property was a bit steeper than she'd expected, but it helped her to stay out of sight. Above her, the overcast sky had deepened in color. In a few minutes, it would be dark, which would make it tougher for her to judge the distance of what she was looking at. Already the outlines were harder to track.

She crept forward, using the dense hedgerow as cover as she moved along the property line. The scent of grilled meat was unmistakable now, and she could even hear the crackle of fat hitting flame. She climbed up the incline, using one hand against the soft soil to stabilize herself. The backyard came into view. First came the grass, which was thick and evenly cut, then the flagstone path, which curved in a lazy arc from the decorative gate at the side of the house to the base of the large, raised wooden deck. And finally, she saw the deck itself, where two men were standing next to a large grill, drinking wine and laughing. Because of the deck's elevation, she could only see the top half of the two men.

Mia dropped to one knee and pulled out her pistol. She attached the suppressor and scanned her surroundings. From her position, she had a clear view of the deck, which she could now see was accessible from the yard and also from the kitchen. Mia recognized the younger of the two men as being Nelson Anderson. She watched Nelson reach for the lid of the grill, but the older man pushed his hand away, shaking his head.

Then, a woman with dark hair and olive skin stopped in front of one of the kitchen's windows, laughing at something.

Liesel Bergmann.

Mia was about to let Henry know that at least two of their targets were confirmed to be on-site, when the scent of grilled meat, perfectly seasoned, hit her again. Before she could stop herself—not that there was anything she could have done to prevent it from happening—from her stomach came a low, traitorous rumble that sounded, at least to her ears, like the cold start of a V-8 engine.

She froze. Had the men heard it? They were still talking, but she couldn't shake the feeling that the sound had carried. She slowly raised her pistol, its red dot optics settling cleanly on Nelson's upper chest. At this distance, she couldn't miss. And for a moment, she considered taking the shot. Well, two shots. She could take both men out in less than two seconds. The suppressor would muffle the cracks.

Two squeezes and both men would go down.

To her horror, her stomach growled again, even louder this time.

Nelson shifted his feet, but he didn't turn, then Richard Anderson said something she couldn't hear.

If I can't hear them, they sure as hell can't hear me.

She held her aim for another beat, but her finger had moved outside the trigger guard. She brought the red dot off Nelson's chest a second later.

"I've got eyes on Nelson," she whispered, knowing the mic on her lapel would amplify her voice. "I had the shot, but I'm holding. Liesel Bergmann is also confirmed to be on-site."

Henry's reply was immediate. "I'll be at the front door in thirty seconds."

"Good copy. Let me know when you ring the bell. I'll breach on the distraction."

As Mia waited, she continued to study the two men on the deck. They looked relaxed. A father and son enjoying good wine together.

They didn't know what was about to hit them.

CHAPTER FIFTY-SEVEN

The Anderson Family Home
Portland, Maine

Caspian felt his phone buzz again and immediately regretted not powering it off when he'd had the chance. It was Ranger. Again. Across from him, Liesel was looking at him, annoyed.

"Please, take it," she said.

Caspian offered Liesel and Clara a tight nod, mouthed an apology, and stepped away from the kitchen table. He brought the phone to his ear as the doorbell rang.

"What is it, Samantha?" he said.

"About damn time you picked up," Ranger said. "Where are you?"

There was an urgency in Ranger's voice that told Caspian this wasn't just a social call. "My parents' house. Why?"

As he spoke, his mother walked past him, already heading for the front door.

"Mia Hernandez traveled from Miami to Portland this afternoon," Ranger said. "I think she's on her way to your parents' house, if she's not already there."

Caspian's body locked as every single muscle in him seemed to coil.

"Mom!" he shouted, spinning around. "Don't open the door!"

But he was too late. Elizabeth had already turned the lock and cracked the door open.

CHAPTER FIFTY-EIGHT

The Anderson Family Home
Portland, Maine

Henry's voice came through Mia's earbud. "Five seconds before the bell."

Then, "Three, two, one, execute!"

Mia heard the doorbell ring. This was her cue to move. She emerged from the tree line and advanced toward the narrow ten-step staircase leading to the deck, her red dot optics steady on the back of Nelson Anderson's neck. She had just begun to apply pressure on the trigger when a loud, panicked shout coming from inside the house sliced through her focus.

Nelson and his father both turned toward the sound, just as Mia pulled the trigger. The round struck Nelson, slamming into his upper back but a good four inches to the right of his neck. Not thinking she'd need a second shot, Mia had already started to switch targets when her brain caught up to what had just happened.

Shit.

She tried to swing the muzzle back toward Nelson, but he had already fallen to the deck. Richard Anderson, who was much faster than she'd expected, had also disappeared, having found cover behind the large grill.

Mia sidestepped to her right, looking for a better angle, but she quickly realized she still had no shot. The deck was too high. Knowing she couldn't stay in the open any longer, she sprinted toward the stairs.

And that's when Richard Anderson reappeared, five feet from where she had last seen him, a pistol in hand. And it was aimed straight at her.

She reacted on instinct and threw herself left, a millisecond before she saw the first muzzle flash. The round zipped past her right ear. She landed on her shoulder and rolled to absorb the fall as two more shots tore into the grass beside her. An instant later, she was on her knees squeezing the trigger.

Richard Anderson staggered and went down hard, collapsing next to his son.

CHAPTER FIFTY-NINE

The Anderson Family Home
Portland, Maine

Caspian dropped his phone and drew his pistol just as the front door exploded inward; a tall man wearing a gray hoodie had rammed it with his shoulder. Caspian watched in horror as his mother was hurled backward, and her head hit the marble floor with a sickening crack.

If there was one positive thing coming out of the mortifying sight in front of him, it was that his mother was now out of his line of fire.

Caspian had a clear shot at Hoodie. And he took it just as Hoodie dove to his right and into the hallway leading toward the living room. Caspian heard the man yell in pain, but he couldn't tell if it was from a bullet wound or if Hoodie had broken a wrist during his hard landing.

Caspian hoped it was both.

In his peripheral vision, he saw Liesel push Clara behind the kitchen island. And then from behind him came the booming, distinctive bark of his father's Colt .45. The first bark was followed by two more a second later. But Caspian couldn't turn, couldn't allow his focus to break, not when his mother lay stunned on the floor with a killer only a few feet away. He had to trust that his dad could hold the line for a few seconds longer.

Caspian advanced toward his mother in a combat crouch, sending rounds into the hallway drywall, aiming low, where he guessed the intruder might be crawling or crouching. Caspian's goal was to keep Hoodie pinned down and to keep him from firing at him or his mother.

Elizabeth was on her knees now, trembling. Her hands shook as she tried to steady herself, her eyes wide with shock.

From the kitchen, someone yelled something, adding to the chaos.

"Get behind me!" Caspian barked, reaching down with one arm to haul his mother upright. His other hand kept the pistol trained forward, toward the threat.

Caspian shielded his mother with his body as they began to retreat toward the kitchen. He kept one arm back to guide her and make sure she stayed behind him and didn't stray too much to the left or to the right.

And that's when—as if he was a predator breaking cover—Hoodie exploded out from the hallway, rolling across the floor as he opened fire. Holding his pistol with only one hand, Caspian returned fire, squeezing the trigger repeatedly as he tracked Hoodie across the marble floor. But Caspian's priority, born out of his instinct to protect his mother, was to make himself as tall and as large as possible, so that he would be the most obvious target—even if it meant he couldn't shoot with optimal accuracy.

If someone was going to get hit, it would be him, not his mother.

And that's exactly what happened. It couldn't have been more than a second or two since Hoodie had rolled out of cover when a burning lance of pain tore through Caspian's leg, just above his left knee. Another round hit him high on the chest, punching the breath from his lungs. He staggered, but he kept squeezing the trigger, and an instant later, one of his rounds struck Hoodie in the forehead, half an inch above his right eye. Hoodie's head snapped backward, and the back of his skull exploded in a red mist.

Caspian could tell his blood had already soaked his shirt and his jeans, which wasn't a good sign.

He turned and used the last of his strength to shove his mother behind the buffet—a thick piece of furniture made of solid oak. Only then, once he knew his mother was out of immediate danger, did he glance out toward the deck and see Liesel rush to his father, who was lying motionless right next to a bloodied Nelson.

Caspian took a step toward the sliding doors leading to the deck, but his left leg collapsed from under him. A heartbeat later, he found himself staring at the ceiling, barely able to breathe.

CHAPTER SIXTY

The Anderson Family Home
Portland, Maine

Liesel crouched behind the island, one arm wrapped tightly around Clara, the other cradling the back of the woman's head, shielding her from what was unfolding just feet away. Liesel wasn't armed, and she cursed herself for it. She scanned the counter and spotted a butcher knife.

She heard Caspian shout, and she craned her neck to look. He had reached Elizabeth.

On the deck, Nelson was down, but he was alive and dragging himself toward the open door leading to the kitchen. Clara must have seen him, too, because she screamed.

Beyond Nelson, Liesel saw Richard Anderson. He had a pistol in his hands, and for one moment, Richard's eyes locked with hers. In them, Liesel saw no panic, only iron resolve. The will to protect. The will to do whatever was necessary to protect his family. The will to die, if that's what it came to.

She watched Richard as he surged up and fired his gun.

Then, Liesel heard Caspian groan, and she snapped her head toward him. For a heartbeat she'd thought he'd gone down, but no, he was still standing.

But Richard wasn't. He was now splayed across the deck, next to Nelson, who was on his knees.

Liesel didn't hesitate. She knew what she had to do.

"Stay there!" she shouted to Clara.

And without waiting for a reply, she rose from cover and ran toward the deck. She didn't think. She just acted. She charged through the open doors, her eyes locked on the Colt .45 near Richard's motionless hand. She dove forward and snatched the pistol just as three sharp cracks echoed through the yard.

Liesel didn't know the exact position of the shooter, but she knew that if she stayed low, the height of the deck would block the shooter's angle of attack.

Unless they're already climbing the stairs . . .

Liesel fired blindly toward the stairs several times. It wasn't about hitting anything; it was about buying Nelson enough time to get inside.

"Stay low! Go! Go! Go!" she screamed at him as he moved forward on elbows and knees.

CHAPTER SIXTY-ONE

The Anderson Family Home
Portland, Maine

Mia Hernandez was pissed off. Nothing had gone according to plan. She was certain Nelson was still alive. Maybe he was already bleeding out, but maybe not. She knew her shot hadn't been lethal. Richard Anderson had gone down, too, but whether he was dead or just waiting to shoot again, she didn't know. At least he'd stopped firing at her. For now.

I have to retake the initiative.

But that was easier said than done because Henry was off comms. She'd heard unsuppressed gunfire coming from inside the house. That meant it wasn't Henry who'd fired those shots. Still, none of it changed the mission. She had to push forward, no matter the cost.

That's what Operations wanted, right?

But what about the Fisherman? Would *he* want her to go in alone?

Stop questioning everything. Move, Mia! Move!

Time wasn't on her side. The neighbors would have heard the shots too. Police were surely already on their way. Her ears were ringing like crazy because of the shots fired by Anderson, so it was possible she simply couldn't hear the sirens.

I've got to end this. Fast.

She rose to her feet, ignoring the throb in her shoulder, and ran toward the stairs. She started up, climbing the steps one by one, her arms extended in front of her, her pistol steady in her hands. Halfway up, her sixth sense flared, screaming at her to retreat. She ignored it.

Then she saw movement in front of her, but because she was still midway up the stairs, she only saw Liesel Bergmann's upper half as she hurled herself across the deck. Mia fired three times in quick succession, and the glass of the patio doors shattered. But Bergmann had already vanished from view.

Shit. She's going for the weapon. Move!

Mia took another step, then a volley of gunfire erupted above her. Mia had nowhere to go, so she did the only thing she could. She ducked and flattened herself against the steps, but the shots weren't aimed at her, and the rounds passed harmlessly over her head.

They're meant to keep me pinned down.

The shooting stopped. And then silence.

Either Bergmann's magazine had run dry or her business on the deck—retrieving a weapon, or a body—was done. She raised herself slightly until she was in a crouch, her breath coming in long, deliberate draws to ensure her brain was fully oxygenated. Only her eyes and the barrel of her suppressed pistol crept above the lip of the deck. She wasn't about to give Bergmann a clean shot in case she was waiting for her.

Richard Anderson was still there. He was flat on his back, his eyes closed. Unmoving. But Bergmann and Nelson were gone. She tried to raise Henry on the comms again, but she got no answer. Either Henry had lost his earbud . . . or he was dead.

And that possibility settled like ice in her lungs. Not because she cared about him, but because assaulting a house on her own without the element of surprise was pure suicide.

Fuck Mpassi. Fuck Henry. I'm out of here. The Fisherman will understand, and he's the only one I really care about.

Before she started down the steps, though, she brought her pistol in line with Richard Anderson's head. He was going to be her consolation prize. She was about to put a security round through his left eye when she saw it.

A glint of metal in his right hand. A small silver revolver with a concealed hammer.

Her brain registered the gun as a Smith & Wesson 640, a five-shot snub-nosed revolver. Before she could do anything else, let alone finish the trigger pull she had started, a burst of light exploded in front of her.

A crushing, hammering force punched through her teeth, driving her backward and down the stairs.

CHAPTER SIXTY-TWO

Teterboro Airport
Bergen County, New Jersey

Charles Mpassi stepped out of the Cadillac Escalade. The wind had picked up in the last ten minutes. It was now whipping across the runway in erratic bursts that lifted the edge of his raincoat and sent it snapping behind him. It had taken longer than expected for the Gulfstream to get its takeoff clearance. Apparently, the controllers who oversaw one of the nearby airport's approach and departure airspace had abruptly lost contact with several airplanes for more than ninety seconds, which had thrown a wrench into all the scheduled flights coming into or out of all the airports around the city.

Mpassi watched as the Gulfstream G550 finally accelerated down the runway, its engines roaring as it lifted into the gray sky.

Westcott was gone, and so was Mpassi's patience with the man.

Everett Westcott, for all his intelligence and influence, was still a man shackled by romantic ideals. He spoke of universal health care as if it was a birthright. He believed, truly believed, that his wife's dream for the Democratic Republic of the Congo could be achieved through diplomacy, infrastructure, and the displacement of tens of thousands of people.

And the curated death of a few hundred.

Mpassi shook his head in disgust. As if by pouring enough clean water and electricity into the veins of the DRC, his nation's heart would start beating in rhythm like it was a Western country. It was noble. It was commendable.

But it was utterly naive.

Mpassi knew better. He had seen his country gutted from the inside. First by warlords, then by the generals, and finally by the glossy foreign aid apparatus, which gave the country just enough to ease the world's conscience. Westcott didn't understand how power truly worked in the DRC. He thought leverage came from policy and partnerships and maybe a little blackmail. But in Kinshasa, power came from fear.

Yes, Westcott had married a Congolese woman, but that didn't make him Congolese.

Mpassi pulled out his encrypted phone and dialed. The line clicked once before it connected.

"Is it done?" asked President Mutombo, his voice laced with anticipation.

"Not yet," Mpassi said, glancing at the Gulfstream's receding silhouette. "Soon. How are things on your end?"

"Everything is ready. We will see this through," Mutombo said. "Just as I promised you a year ago."

Mpassi smiled. He'd always liked Mutombo. Not for his charisma, which was lacking, or for his intellect, which was average at best, but because the man had learned to listen. He understood that true progress in the DRC didn't require idealism, but required pragmatism.

And pragmatism required sacrifice.

"Are you sure you don't need more time?" Mpassi asked more out of caution than doubt.

"I don't need more time," Mutombo said. "We're ready to vote Hearts United's initiative down."

"Good," he said, then ended the call.

It had taken him years of patient maneuvering to position himself as the éminence grise behind every decision. Now, with a single vote, Westcott's humanitarian pipeline in the DRC would collapse. And in the chaos that would follow, the contracts would shift to consulting firms and local logistics companies owned primarily by Chinese interests, while others were shell entities under Mpassi's control. Westcott didn't know it, but he had already built the infrastructure of Mpassi's future fortune. The hydroelectric project would still happen—part of it, anyway—but the spoils wouldn't go toward hospitals; they'd be routed through state-run procurement firms and siphoned into the hands of Mpassi's loyalists.

He had no shame in admitting it. He wanted it all. The money, and the power. He'd finally get the respect he'd never been given by the Europeans, the Americans, and even by his own generals back in the days when he wore a uniform and ran protection for war criminals. He'd played the part of the quiet operator long enough.

Now it was his turn. But first, he had to take care of one important detail.

He dialed another number, and without even a hint of hesitation, he pressed the call button.

———

Everett Westcott drank the last of his first single malt as the Gulfstream continued its climb through the congested airspace over New York. He looked out the window. The city lights of Manhattan were still visible, and from this altitude, Westcott thought they looked like a circuit board. He had always liked the view from above, because from up in the sky, the world never looked angry or broken. It looked composed. Manageable.

He pondered if he should have another drink or not. He knew he should try to sleep, and like his wife had told him many times, he slept better when he had nothing to drink.

Westcott smiled. He knew Nailah only said that because she couldn't sleep when he snored. But this was his jet, and apart from the two pilots and the lone flight attendant, there was no one else on the plane. So, who cared if he snored? He'd have another drink.

Westcott stood and walked to the flight attendant, who was still strapped into her jump seat.

"What was it you gave me? Macallan?"

"Yes, sir. Eighteen year."

He nodded. It wasn't his favorite, but close enough.

"I'll have another," he said, handing her his crystal tumbler.

A few moments later, the flight attendant returned the tumbler to him. He thanked her, took a small sip, and headed toward the aft lavatory.

It was one of the small indulgences of owning his own plane. Nobody told him when to sit down, when to buckle up, or how many drinks were too many.

My plane. My rules.

He entered the large lavatory, set his tumbler on the counter, and unfastened his pants before lowering himself onto the cushioned seat. He had just started his business when the plane jolted hard. His tumbler flew from the vanity and shattered, spraying single malt across the mirror and his bare legs.

"What the hell?"

The first shake had been hard, like hitting a speed bump at one hundred miles an hour, but the second was even more violent. The plane banked sharply to the right, tossing Westcott sideways and then slamming him into the wall. The third shudder was harder than the first two combined and sent him to the floor, his pants still tangled around his ankles. His right shoulder took the brunt of the fall, and he heard—and felt—something pop. The pain was immediate, but his scream was muffled by the high-pitched alarm that was blaring from somewhere beyond the lavatory door.

His left arm was no longer cooperating. It was either broken or dislocated. Still, Westcott tried to push himself up with his one good arm, but the angle of the plane had changed, and the floor was too slanted now, maybe thirty or forty degrees and increasing.

"Help!" he shouted. "Help me!"

A metallic groan rippled through the fuselage, followed by another series of violent shakes. Westcott heard the sound again, as if the Gulfstream was being torn in half. He reached for the counter, his fingers scrabbling at the sink as he tried again to haul himself up in a desperate attempt to yank his pants up. But he couldn't do it. He could feel the nose of the plane dip further. The Gulfstream was no longer flying; it was falling.

Westcott let his head fall back to the floor.

I tried, love. I really did. Maybe too hard. I'm sorry if I failed you.

He closed his eyes, and he saw her. His Nailah. She stood barefoot in the sand, her white dress catching the wind. But she wasn't smiling; she was screaming at him, and her eyes were wild with rage.

Westcott gasped at the sight.

And then his vision stopped as the Gulfstream disintegrated upon impact fifteen miles east of Atlantic Beach.

CHAPTER SIXTY-THREE

Maine Medical Center
Portland, Maine

The first thing Caspian felt was the weight in his chest. It wasn't pain exactly, but heaviness, as if his ribs had been wrapped in lead. Then came the low, dull burn pulsing from his left leg.

He opened his eyes slowly. The light inside the room was dimmed, and there was a recurring beep coming from a monitor to his right. Caspian realized he was connected to machines, but at least he was breathing on his own.

He turned his head, but it required more out of him than it should have. To his left, Liesel sat curled in an armchair. Her arms were folded across her chest, and her head rested on her shoulder.

I'm alive.

A moment passed before he noticed the call button clipped to his bed railing. He raised his hand, but his muscles protested. His fingers were stiff, but he managed to press the button.

A soft chime sounded.

Liesel stirred, and she opened her eyes. When she saw him watching her, she shot to her feet so fast the armchair skidded back, almost toppling. She was beside him in a second, her knees bumping the edge of the bed as she leaned over the railing. She brushed the edge of his arm with her hand.

"You . . . you're awake," she said.

Caspian wanted to say something, but his throat was raw. He winced, and Liesel reached for the cup of water on the nightstand. She guided the straw to his lips.

"Slowly, Casp," she said as he drank.

"Are you hurt?" he asked.

Liesel shook her head, her eyes not leaving his.

"No," she said. "I'm not. But you . . . you almost didn't make it."

"What about—" he started, but Liesel cut him off.

"They're all alive. All of them."

Caspian closed his eyes as a huge wave of relief swelled in his chest. *Thank God.*

Liesel lowered the railing and sat on the edge of the bed, careful not to disturb the lines to the monitors.

"Your father's in recovery," she said. "He was shot, but they stabilized him quickly. He's strong, your dad, Casp. Real strong. Your mother is with him now. She hasn't left his side."

"And . . . Nelson?" he asked.

"He was shot in the back, but he's gonna be okay. He's in a room down the hall with Clara."

A wave of relief passed through Caspian.

"And the attackers?" he asked after a beat. "How many were there?"

"Two," Liesel replied. "Only two. The woman was Mia Hernandez. Your dad shot her."

"He . . . shot her?" he asked.

"He did it with his backup revolver," Liesel said. "Richard's badass."

Caspian managed a small chuckle. "Yeah. He is."

"And . . . what about the man I shot?" he asked a moment later. "Who was he?"

"Henry Harriel," Liesel said. "We don't know much else about him. DIA and FBI are digging, but there's not much yet."

The name meant nothing to Caspian.

"Ranger," he said. "I was on the phone with her when it all started. She must have heard everything."

"She did," Liesel confirmed. "She stayed on the line until the end. She's the one who called the cops. They arrived three minutes after you passed out. If she hadn't acted that fast . . ."

Liesel let the words trail off. She didn't need to finish for Caspian to know he owed one to Ranger. He looked at Liesel's face. She was tired and paler than usual, but her eyes were sharp. He was happy she was there. She smiled at him and placed her hand in his. He squeezed gently.

"How long have I been here?" he asked.

"You've been in and out of surgery for the last two days. They had to remove a bullet from your chest as well as several fragments," Liesel said, her voice cracking. "One of them . . . one of them was real close to your heart.

"And . . . you also got shot in your left leg. The bullet broke your femur. Missed the artery. You're lucky."

He gave her a wry look. "Doesn't feel like it."

"You're alive, Casp. A-live."

"You talked to Ranger?" he asked.

"She came. She was here most of yesterday and this morning," Liesel said. "But she had to return to DC. She said she'd get back as soon as she could. But she did leave a security team behind. 'In an abundance of caution.' Her words, not mine. Anyway, there are two officers outside your door, two more stationed along the corridor, and a few more downstairs."

Caspian processed that as he sipped some more water.

"So . . . this isn't over? There's more coming, isn't there?" he asked.

Liesel's eyes darkened, but she didn't reply.

"What happened? Liesel?"

She sighed. "Ranger wanted to be the one to tell you, but what the hell? She isn't here, and if you turn on the television or browse the news on your phone, you'll see it. That's all they're talking about."

"O-kay. So . . . what's up?"

"Everett Westcott's plane crashed into the ocean shortly after taking off from Teterboro," Liesel said. "The official reports won't be available for months, but Ranger confirmed a bomb exploded in the cargo compartment."

"Holy shit," Caspian said, immediately thinking about the crew members. "How many victims?"

"The two pilots, the flight attendant, and Westcott," Liesel replied.

"Are they sure it was him? Are they sure Westcott's dead?"

"They haven't retrieved his body yet," Liesel said. "But several witnesses saw him climb aboard the aircraft."

"So . . . what happens now?" he asked after a moment.

Liesel shrugged. "Honestly, I have no idea."

CHAPTER SIXTY-FOUR

Defense Intelligence Headquarters
Joint Base Anacostia-Bolling
Washington, DC
Three Months Later

Caspian exited the elevator. He moved slower than he used to, not because he wanted to but because his body forced him to. The surgeries had gone well, but the process of regaining his strength had been slower and more frustrating than he expected. Physical therapy helped, but he wasn't back to his old self just yet. Though he'd started exercising again, his chest still tightened when he exerted himself, and there were some mornings when the ache was such that it reminded him that a bullet had come within inches of ending it all.

But at least he was upright, and he was moving. That had to count for something, right?

Liesel, who'd been his anchor since he'd left the hospital, walked beside him. For the last three months, they'd been staying with his parents in Portland. At first, Caspian had been worried that Richard and Elizabeth might carry the trauma of what had happened the night of the shooting, but to his relief, they'd moved forward with surprising ease. His father had returned to his routines, including his weekly outing to the shooting range. Even his mother had taken up weekly sessions at the range. Caspian was glad his parents weren't consumed by fear. If anything, they seemed more grounded and more present than they had ever been.

His brother, Nelson, had recently accepted a position at the Maine Medical Center. Caspian suspected Nelson's relationship with Clara was getting serious because the last time Caspian had spoken to his brother, Nelson had told him that he and Clara were considering buying a property a fifteen-minute drive from the family house.

As for him and Liesel, they walked the Old Port most mornings. They'd also signed up for cooking lessons, and somewhere along the way, Caspian had developed a deep love for coffee. Liesel called it an obsession. He called it peace. He'd even invested a significant amount of money in an expensive Italian espresso machine. The machine had so many levers and knobs that Caspian had to read the instruction manual several times to learn how to operate it. And even then, it took him at least twenty minutes each morning to calibrate it just right, to grind the beans by hand, and to test the water temperature. Liesel teased him endlessly about it, but he didn't care.

A month ago, at his request, Ranger had withdrawn the last of his security detail. Caspian had told her he didn't want to live under a dome anymore. And Liesel had agreed. There hadn't been any threats since. At least none that he could see.

But then, two days ago, Ranger had called him to request an in-person meeting with him and Liesel at the DIA headquarters. They both knew they would eventually have to return to the DIA.

Ranger's assistant opened the door for them. When Caspian stepped inside Ranger's office, he was surprised to see Nicklas Drescher. The BND officer stood near the window.

"Nicklas?" Liesel said, smiling. "I didn't know you'd be here."

"Neither did I," added Caspian, shaking his hand.

"Apparently, our friend Nicklas has something he'd like to share with us," Ranger said, gesturing for them to sit.

Caspian could tell Ranger was a tad annoyed with Drescher.

"The BND has decided not to renew the liaison officer position with the SSU," he said.

Ranger frowned, her eyes narrowing. "That's ridiculous, Nicklas. Liesel is vital to our coordination efforts with our European partners. You know this." Then, looking at Liesel, she said, "I'll fight this, Liesel. Don't worry."

"I don't want you to fight this, Samantha," Liesel said. "I'm not staying."

Ranger reacted as if she'd been slapped in the face. "What?"

"I'm done," Liesel said.

Ranger turned sharply to Caspian, the heat rising behind her eyes. "And you're okay with this?" she asked.

Caspian met her gaze. "More than okay. We've both given enough. I'm done too."

Ranger's face turned bright red. "You . . . you can't just walk away, Caspian. Not now."

"I've made my decision," he said. "I've been thinking about this for a while, to be honest. I'm not asking for your permission. I'm telling you. I know what I want now."

"Oh, really? And what's that?" Ranger asked.

Caspian leaned back in his chair and let Ranger's thick sarcasm fly by without reacting to it. He said, "I once said this to someone, but she didn't believe me. I hope you will."

"What are you talking about?" Ranger asked, clearly irritated.

"I'm looking into becoming a part-time bush pilot. There's a lodge on Nahmakanta Lake my dad used to bring me to when I was a kid. I'd fly anglers in and out for four to five months a year. I'll spend the rest of the time sailing the coast. I'm about to make an offer on a catamaran."

Ranger stared at him for a few seconds, as if unsure if he was pulling her leg or not, then she let out a dry, cheerless laugh. "You? A bush pilot? You'll lose your mind."

"I don't think so," he replied. "But I guess time will tell."

"You owe me, Caspian," Ranger said. "After everything I've done for you, you still want to walk away? From me? No. That's not how this works. And you sure as hell know it."

Caspian sighed. "I don't owe you anything, Samantha."

A heavy silence hung in the air for a long moment, only to be broken by Drescher.

"Maybe he does owe you, Sam. But you owe me," he said, tapping his fingers on his prosthetic leg. "Remember?"

Ranger looked at Drescher, her face faltering for the first time. Caspian thought he saw her anger morph into something heavier. She closed her eyes, then opened them again.

"Fine," she finally said. "But I need Caspian to do one more job for me."

"I'm not interested—" Caspian started to say, but Ranger raised her hand.

"Hear me out, okay? That's all I'm asking."

Caspian shrugged, then gestured for her to go ahead.

"It's about Charles Mpassi," Ranger said. "Everett Westcott's number two."

For some reason, Caspian's left leg began to throb. "What about him?"

"He was as involved as Westcott in the decision to target your family. Maybe more. And he's not hiding either. He's been seen working with Chinese intelligence operatives in the DRC. He's consolidating power, but not just in his country of origin, but also in Rwanda, Uganda, Burundi, and even South Sudan. That shitbag is destabilizing the entire region. He needs to die."

"But how? I thought Hearts United was done?" Caspian asked.

"Hearts United is done. It imploded after Westcott's death, and we think Mpassi, or someone who's loyal to him, planted the bomb in Westcott's plane."

Caspian stared at the floor. Something Ranger had said stirred something inside of him. Part of him wanted to finish what he had started. Mpassi had come after his family. He couldn't let him get away with it.

"If I go . . . if I go after him," he said slowly, looking at Liesel. "If I do that . . . what happens to the life we've been building?"

Liesel grabbed his hand with hers. "If you need to do this, if you really need to, I'll . . . I'll support you," she said.

Caspian was looking at Ranger now. "I'll ask you one question, Samantha. Only one. And I want you to tell me the truth."

Ranger nodded. "Of course."

"Is Charles Mpassi still a threat to my family?"

Ranger sighed, then she slowly shook her head. "No," she said. "We think that door is closed now. This operation, you'd be doing it for the greater good."

Caspian looked at Liesel, who was still holding his hand. "I don't need to do this," he said. And then, to Ranger, "I'm done, Samantha. Find someone else."

Ranger's eyes narrowed again, but there was no anger left in them. Just exhaustion.

"If you ever change your mind . . ."

"Yeah," Caspian said, getting up and then offering his hand. "I know where to find you."

"Okay, Caspian," she said, shaking his hand. "Go live your life."

Caspian offered his hand to Drescher, who took it. "See you soon."

"I don't think so," Caspian replied.

At the door, Liesel paused and turned back.

"Oh, and by the way, Nicklas, I'm resigning. Effective today."

Drescher gave her a big, almost fatherly smile. "If you hadn't, I would have fired you."

EPILOGUE

Former Onyx Facility
Montana, United States
Several Months Later

Mia Hernandez sat in silence, her hands resting flat on the steel table in front of her. The room was small and cold, its walls painted in white that caught the fluorescent light above. There was nothing on the table. Nothing on the walls either. There was just the buzz of the overhead lighting fixture and the sound of her own breathing.

She touched the scar on her cheek. She didn't do it out of habit, but she did it to remind herself how close she'd come to dying that night. What was left of her original face had been taken apart and rebuilt, bone by bone and nerve by nerve. She thought the surgeons had done good work.

No. They did excellent work, she corrected herself.

Although the mirror showed her someone new and still unfamiliar, it was still the real her underneath.

She remembered the sound of the bullet, the flash, the world going black. She remembered the smell of blood and smoke. And she remembered Richard Anderson's eyes right before he pulled the trigger. He had bested her, so she respected him. She meant him no harm. She wouldn't seek revenge. He'd only protected his family. Like any good man would do.

She should have died that night. But she didn't. She remembered waking up in darkness, unable to speak. There had been tubes in her throat and pain coming from everywhere. Weeks had passed in fragments, until finally, Samantha Ranger had appeared.

"You're very lucky," she'd said to Mia. "But luck will only get you so far now."

Ranger had paid the hospital bills. All of them. And then she'd shown Mia the file about the Fisherman's death. Mia had trusted Mpassi. She had killed for him. But he had used her, lied to her.

Lied to us!

Because the Fisherman had also trusted Mpassi, and it had cost him his life. It had almost cost her hers.

In the end, Mpassi had left her to die.

Ranger hadn't.

For the last several months, Mia had been training, sometimes day and night. Her instructors—men and women who didn't ask questions and who didn't care about her past—taught her everything she needed to know to succeed in her new position. At first, she'd believed it would be a repeat of the training she'd been through with Unit 777 in Egypt, but that thought didn't last long. The training regimen she'd just gone through ended up being exponentially more difficult than anything she'd ever done.

Still, she'd aced everything. When the instructors told her it was finally over, she didn't smile. She didn't feel triumphant. She wasn't trying to prove anything. She just wanted purpose.

And now, it seemed it had arrived.

The door to the room opened, and Samantha Ranger stepped in. She held a small folder in her hand. She didn't sit. "I heard you passed. Congratulations."

Mia said nothing.

Ranger placed the folder on the table and slid it across. "Details of your first mission."

Mia opened the file. Her eyes moved across the photo clipped at the top of the dossier. It was an older picture, but she recognized the man.

Charles Mpassi.

"He's in Kinshasa," Ranger said. "He's under protection, but he's not unreachable."

Mia nodded once. "Thank you," she said.

"Don't thank me," Ranger replied. "I told you that if you made it through my program, I'd give you your shot at redemption. So, I'm only fulfilling my end of the deal."

Ranger started to turn, then stopped and looked back. "One more thing."

Mia met her eyes.

"Your new call sign," Ranger said. "From this moment on . . . you're Elias."

ACKNOWLEDGMENTS

Writing a novel is often described as a solitary endeavor, but in truth, no book is ever written alone. I am deeply grateful to everyone who helped bring *The Elias Conspiracy* to life.

As always, the first thank-you goes to my readers. Your enthusiasm, your reviews, your messages, and your constant support are the reason I get to do what I love. Every time you pick up one of my books, you make this journey possible, and I can't thank you enough for taking these adventures with me.

To Liz Pearsons, Gracie Doyle, Megha Parekh, Jessica Tribble Wells, and the rest of my incredible team at Thomas & Mercer, thank you for your dedication, expertise, and belief in my work. Your passion for my books continues to inspire me. I couldn't be prouder to be part of this publishing family.

To my writer friends—Don Bentley, David McCloskey, Taylor Moore, Jack Stewart, Ryan Steck, Mark Greaney, Brad Thor, Brad Taylor, Marc Cameron, KJ Howe, Jeff Wilson, Brian Andrews, Ward Larsen, Ethan Cross, Steve Urszenyi, Jack Carr, Ryan Pote, and James Hankins—thank you for the camaraderie and the encouragement. You've reminded me time and again that our community is one of the most generous in publishing.

To my agent, Eric Myers, thank you for your guidance, your patience, and your tireless advocacy for my career. A big thank-you goes to Kevin Smith. You're the best at what you do, my friend.

Thank you, too, to my film agents, Debbie Deuble Hill and Alec Frankel, and the rest of my team at IAG, for championing my work in Hollywood. You've done astonishing work! I'd like to thank my good friend and exceptional showrunner, Paul Zbyszewski, for all his hard work. You're a talented writer and a force to be reckoned with!

To Sherry Marsh, producer extraordinaire, thank you for your insight, vision, and unwavering support for the *Elias* universe. It means the world to me. I'm excited for all that lies ahead.

And finally, to my wife, Lisane, and our children, Florence and Gabriel—thank you for your love, patience, and understanding when I disappear into my fictional worlds. You are my greatest joy.

ABOUT THE AUTHOR

Photo © 2024 Lisane Paquette

Simon Gervais was born in Montreal, Quebec. He joined the Canadian military as an infantry officer and in 2001 was recruited by the Royal Canadian Mounted Police to work as a drug investigator. He was later assigned to antiterrorism, which took him to several European countries and the Middle East. In 2009, Gervais became a close-protection specialist tasked with guarding foreign heads of state visiting Canada. He served on the protection details for Queen Elizabeth II, US President Barack Obama, and Chinese President Hu Jintao, among others. The author lives in Ottawa with his wife and two children. He's an avid boater, scuba diver, and skier.

For more about Gervais and his work, visit his website at https:// SimonGervaisBooks.com. You can also connect with the author on Facebook (@SimonGervaisAuthor), Instagram (@SimonGervaisBooks), and X (@GervaisBooks).